SILENCE

IS BROKEN

Yvonne Mikell

Published by Ink to Press Publishing, Philadelphia, PA

Cover Design by http://amygdaladesign.net/

Author websites: http://www.yvonnemikell.com and http://www.intrigueandsuspense.blogspot.com

---

Summary

Business executive Khloe Spencer is surrounded by secrets that are revealed with surprising results.

Acknowledgments

Many thanks to my God and his son, my Lord and Savior Jesus Christ, for the many blessings they have bestowed upon me, for showing me the path that I must take, all the while protecting me from harm. Amen.

To my parents, Edward and Lizzie Mikell, thank you for standing by me these last trying years. I could not have done it without you.

Special thanks to my son Jelani, for being extremely patient during the writing and editing of this book. I didn't think you could do it, but you showed me you are maturing.

Contents

Prelude

Captured by the game

I cannot see. I have been straining my eyes, trying to dissect the darkness in the hopes of discovering a slither of light. I have not found any. I cannot move, not even shift my posterior in this hard rock chair. I am covered in rope from my neck down to my feet. I am not simply tied down, I am hog-tied! My neck and feet seem to be connected by a single rope. Every time I move the line tightens and digs into my skin, burning like the dickens. My neck feels as if it is going to snap. My knees feel as if they are about to pop out of their sockets. Screaming for help only brings about more pain, my tongue lies against the driest of cloths.

I guess I should be thankful for what I do get, two meals and two glasses of water a day. Let me stop lying to myself, I am not thankful. I am in this chair all day long. I am forced to relieve myself right where I sit, downright embarrassing. They have not told me what this is about. They don't say anything. They just shove spoonful after spoonful of food in my mouth. I have no idea of the time or the day, the last day I remember was October 10th.

The door opens. With it comes the coolest of breezes, the temperature must be in the 40s. Winter will be here soon. I am cold because they have taken all of my clothes. They have stripped me bare including my shoes and socks. I do not smell any food, what I do smell is cologne, very loud and pungent cologne. Do not know anyone who wears that fragrance. Not sure of who they are, they are not one of the regulars. It is someone new. New can be a good thing, maybe I can get some answers. Who am I kidding, new is not good at all. New means a change has arrived or is on the way real soon.

"What do you want with me?"

"Personally I don't want anything from you. The people who hired me, they want something."

"They want what? Why am I here?"

"You are here because they want to remind you of all the dirty deeds you have done."

"This does not sound good at all."

"No it does not."

The story begins with…

Khloe Spencer

Mother and Daughter

"It's 6:45 Philly, time to get up and get going. Go on and make that money, then swing by later and spend some of it at Sensations. Tonight's guest is Smokey Robinson, come and hear him croon his greatest hits."

"I am up Patty, I am up!"

I don't feel like working today. I feel like staying home and lounging in my pajamas, similar to Regis who is flat on his back at my feet. Unfortunately duty calls, I kick the covers off of me and he springs into action. He slinks closer to the head of my bed and curls up underneath my arm. I know what he wants, he wants to be stroked and petted. I reciprocate and quickly run my fingers thru his champagne coat.

"Today's weather is brought to you by Paragon, the city's number one source for gas and heating. Today is expected to have plenty of sun, but don't be fooled, the temperature is expected to reach a high of only 55 degrees. We told all of our listeners in the tri-state area that last night was going to be colder than usual. And it was, Philadelphia had an overnight temperature of 33 degrees, our suburbs were below freezing. Overall the region was ten degrees colder than normal."

Well that explains why it's chilly in here. I will grin and bear it, not ready to start the rapid accumulation of a Paragon heating bill. The bathroom, the bathroom, I hope I make it.

"OW! Damn it Regis!"

We both groan. He groans because he knows he is in trouble with me. I damn near break my foot on shoes that I know I put away earlier.

9

I have been told that all puppies like chewing on 'things' like shoes, furniture, newspaper, doesn't soothe my anger. Damn it! I don't make it, waited too late, it's okay, I have to take a shower anyway. It is going to be a quick shower. Mother wants me at her annual mother daughter symposium. Xavier is supposed to be back today, I wonder how his trip went. He never discusses his trips. He doesn't talk much about anything. He is absolutely quiet for a number of days, and then all of a sudden the Xavier I know steps back into the room. The intensity is still there, but not as prevalent.

I turn off the water and wrap up in a towel to hurry back to my bedroom. Since the weather is quite cool I think I will wear a cashmere sweater with some slacks. The office is still running the air conditioning so I know I won't be overly hot. Besides, if Philadelphia is cool I know New York will be cooler. I wonder if Xavier remembers we are supposed to be going to there. I better hurry up, Regis' pacing back and forth can only mean one thing. He needs to go outside immediately.

It is indeed October weather, beguiling sunny skies and chilly breezes. I guess my neighbors have already been here or we are the first to arrive, there are no fresh piles of poop. I release Regis from his leash and watch him run like a gazelle on the African Plains. My peripheral vision detects a shadow. I turn to see who is creeping up on me, and I am not surprised, its Mystery. I call him Mystery because I do not know his name. He's always here when I am here. I never hear him walk up on me, I just turn around and he is there, like now.

Most people who come here have a dog or a cat, but not him. He sits on the park bench and pretends to read the newspaper, intermittently drinking coffee, tea or whatever he has in that cup. He calls himself blending in with the crowd. The plan isn't working, it has never worked. Today I see him as plain as day. His eyes are barely visible in their sockets, almost swallowed by chubby cheeks. He and I are the only two out here. I shouldn't jump to conclusions. The poor sap could very well enjoy the outdoors in the early morning hours.

"Welcome Mothers and Daughters. In honor of Breast Cancer Awareness Month, this year we decided to extend our invitation to not only the survivors, but to their daughters in the hopes of educating them on the importance of early detection, and having the courage to face their fears with the ones they love. I'm Sharon Spencer and I'm here with my daughter Khloe."

I'm lucky Mom's tumor was benign. Most of the women here aren't as fortunate, they're either victims of lumpectomy, mastectomy or double mastectomy. You can point out the woman who has undergone a mastectomy. Their prosthesis sits higher than the surviving breast. Mom is one of the organizers for this event. Although she never had cancer, that time when she suspected she did was agonizing, especially knowing the odds of inheriting it from her mother. She bonded with the women of her church, joining the women's committee and the choir. I'm glad she has them.

I helped her write the opening speech. It's the first time she has asked me to collaborate on a pet project of hers. She asked me to accompany her, taking the opportunity for quality mother daughter time and to discuss something she deemed serious. The podium is empty due to the break. Everyone is sampling the continental breakfast. Mother has returned just in time, the waiter is here.

The tall slender waiter stands next to mother, I can't tell if it is really a man or a woman. Flat-chest and a straight up and down figure suggest male. The face, soft and quite beautiful suggest woman as does the red hair pulled back neatly in a ponytail and centered down by the neck. Ah the neck, thin with no traces of facial hair or a prominent Adam's apple doesn't help me discern either. Then it spoke.

"Morning ladies," he said in a southern voice, "Welcome to the Betsy Ross Hotel, our continental breakfast consists of fresh orange juice, seasonal fruit which happens to be sliced oranges, honey dew melon, and cantaloupe. From the Chef's Bakery we have an assortment of mini-muffins, croissants, sweet butter, preserves and marmalades. Beverages include Columbian coffee and a selection of Earl Grey teas. What would you like?"

Mother orders first, "I think I'm speaking for both of us when I say bring us two of everything."

"I think that is the best choice, sample everything," I said.

"Very well then, I shall return soon with your order," he said.

A quick glance around the room gives me an estimate of at least 300 families here. Mothers are laughing and talking with their daughters.

"Khloe..."

"Huh!"

"Sorry to startle you."

"Oh I was just looking around the room."

"We did have a very good turnout, thank you for your help on the speech, it was well received."

"You are quite welcome. If you ever need help don't hesitate to ask."

"A mother asking her daughter for help, I suppose there is nothing wrong with that, except it makes me feel like the child and you...never mind, Khloe while we are here I have some things to discuss with you."

Suddenly crestfallen, Mother's mood is no longer festive, she is in distress. Her eyes are closed, her hands massage her temples. "Do you have a headache?"

"As a matter of fact I do."

"Do you need aspirin?"

"No I have already taken something though it does not help. The only thing that will help is to talk about why I asked you here. I need to tell you a few things."

"What kind of things?"

Her usual straightforwardness dodges me as does her famous direct eye contact. She is the one looking down at the plate. She is the one with the pitchy voice. Grudgingly she speaks, "Things you need to know about love, marriage, and friendships."

I can't believe she's rehashing this conversation, "Mom, remember telling me all of this the morning of my 16th birthday?"

Mom's eyes lift off the table and make contact. They are red, and moist. Her lips quiver ever so briefly, and then they muster courage.

"That was 12 long years ago and I want to talk about it now! It's important that I say this. It is important that you hear me."

"Sorry to interrupt."

"First you must maintain your weight, exercise…try to keep your figure the way it was when you first met him. Men don't like overweight, shapeless women. Don't let him come home to a woman walking around in a house coat, hair rollers in her hair and a cigarette dangling out of the mouth. When his key turns in the lock, you should be in position, standing at the door looking as glamorous as Naomi Campbell."

"Mom I don't do hair rollers, I don't smoke, and Naomi Campbell is a fantasy, why on earth would you suggest her?"

"Yes Naomi is a fantasy, but that girl got it going on. She makes her own money…"

"I make my own money!"

"Yes you do and I am proud of you, don't ever stop making your own money..."

Her lips are quivering again. Something is wrong, very wrong. She is on the verge of breaking down. She composes herself and continues.

"A man will have more than one woman in his life, e…even, even though he chose you there will always be other lovelies. It is something you will have to deal with."

The waiter is here with his serving cart. He places the small basket of breads in the center of the table. Next to it he sits a small boat of butters, jellies and marmalades. The fruit platters are placed opposite the basket. The coffee is on the left of the plate, the orange juice is to the right. "This looks positively scrumptious."

"I hope everything is to your satisfaction, I will be back a little bit later to see how you're doing," he said.

"Thanks," I said.

"You're quite welcome," he said.

He walks away and Mother's face comes into focus. She is staring at the empty plate. I want to console her but mother is not one for public displays. The last time I did she pushed me away as if I were a complete stranger, contrary to my affectionate godmother Saki. Mother will be fine, like always, I on the other hand am starving. "Can't wait to sample these golden brown pop-ups, I think I'll take a cranberry muffin and a croissant."

I split them open and spread on a thin layer of butter. I look up and see mother still sitting there staring at the empty plate. "Mom, the food is here, aren't you hungry?"

"Not really, my appetite has been poor the last couple of days."

I dropped my croissant, "You're not sick again are you?"

"Physically I've never been better, maybe I should eat something, neglecting myself is not going to change the situation."

"Change what situation?"

She does not give me an answer. Instead, she is adding two teaspoons of sugar, something she never does, and two creams to her coffee. The spoon knocks the inside of the cup as she stirs. I don't think she knows what she is doing. Mother is elegant and refine. She normally would use the butter knife to apply marmalade to her muffin, not a fork. She is stirring the coffee again, irritatingly knocking the spoon against the inside of the cup. She lifts the cup to her mouth, takes a small sip, and slams it down onto the saucer, spilling some of its contents on the table. She is not hungry, she is angry. "Mother why are you angry?"

"Where was I? Oh yeah, I was saying your future husband will always have other women. It is something you will have to deal with. I don't want you to get a divorce either; all it does is let the other woman get more control. When he remarries he'll forget about you and your children."

"You're predicting that my future husband will have an affair."

"Not *an* affair, several affairs."

"Why? Why would he? How can you be so sure about a man I haven't even met yet?"

"Because I know men, at some point during the marriage they will. They all do I'm just trying to prepare you for it."

I cannot believe what I am hearing. My own mother predicting the demise of my marriage before it even happens. Why is she jinxing me? Of course that's it, "Mom…did Daddy have an affair?"

"Yes, he has had several."

"Who? When? Where?"

"Someday I promise to tell you all the details, but for now I want you to listen. Listen to me and remember all that I'm telling you."

"Of course I'll remember, I've remembered everything you ever told me."

"Good. Another point I want to make to you is that wealth sometimes attracts undesirables. Honey carefully choose your friends, you want them to like you for you, not for your money and status. Khloe you cannot tell your friends every little detail about yourself. You will unintentionally reveal your weak spots. You must keep some things to yourself, even when you're hurting."

"I knew it! That's what this is all really all about, you hate Kiera, the only real friend I have. What have you got against her?"

15

"I am not talking about Kiera, *you* brought her into our conversation. I don't want to talk about her, what I have to say pertains to you, for your ears only. Now I am here to give you the heads up, where was I? Oh yeah, if you should get married and your father and I aren't a part of the wedding, please…please get a pre-nup. Don't get married without one, even if he has equal status or money than you."

My engagement is a secret. No one knows except the two of us, the bride and the groom. If I left it up to him he would have it announced in the newspaper. I haven't told anyone because I am not sure. Why is she talking about marriage, did she somehow find out? "Mom why are worrying like this? You'll be there when I get married."

"I have to make sure you know how to protect yourself. Your father and I will not always be with you."

All I can do is look at her. Now it all made sense, the red eyes, the somber mood, the trembling lips, the motherly advice. She is scared. "Oh my God, you are sick! Why didn't you tell me? Does Daddy know?"

"Khloe! Khloe sweetie, lower your voice, everyone is looking at us."

"I don't care who's looking, you can't be sick again!"

"Stop! I'm not sick! I'm hurting! Your father has broken my heart yet again, and this time it's bad…really bad…I always wanted you to have a brother or sister, and now you have them!"

"I don't need siblings, I'm fine."

"Well you have them, courtesy of your father."

"What!?"

"That was a fantastic continental breakfast! I want to thank the staff here at the Double Tree Hotel."

Dr. Stanislaus has returned to the podium. Everyone applauds except me, I feel like crying. For myself, and for my family, how could he? How could he betray her? Who is this woman that he loves so much? Did he purposely give her a child?

16

"Mom let's go."

"We can't leave yet."

"Yes we can, tell them you have a family emergency."

"That would be lying."

"No, it's not! This is a family emergency, I can't stay here another minute. I want to see Dad."

"You can't, he's gone."

"Gone! Gone where?"

"Somewhere, I told him to pack his bags and get out."

Wait! Did she say she threw him out? She just gave me a whole sermon about not getting a divorce, and she threw her husband out. My mind cannot absorb the information just relayed. I can't, I can't get our conversation out of my mind, I have a brother or sister...look at her, she is struggling to hold herself together. This has made her weak. It would make any woman weak. The man you love sleeps around and creates another family. Maybe it is better that I don't see you Dad.

"This concludes our annual symposium on Breast Cancer Awareness. I hope we provided each of you with valuable information. I also hope that many of you have joined one of our support groups. We want you to know you do not have to endure it alone, let us help."

Dr. Stanislaus interrupted my thoughts with the announcement that the symposium is over. I can't take it anymore. I have to get out of here. I turn to her and ask, "What time is it?"

"10:45, we'll be leaving in a minute or so."

I push my way through the crowd, I don't want to talk to anyone but my Dad, the door is up ahead.

"Khloe!"

Who's that calling me? I look in the direction of the guttural voice and find a familiar face, its Mrs. Wilson and I guess her granddaughter. I love her, but Mrs. Wilson is a talker, I am not in the mood to socialize. My getting out of here is not meant to be.

"Khloe? My goodness you have really turned into a fine looking young woman, how you been? Sharon's been gloating about you running your Daddy's company. Think you can give my granddaughter Chandra here a job?"

I lean in to give her a kiss on the cheek, "How are you? You're looking all young! I see you lost some weight. You've been on the treadmill?"

"Forever the flatter, just like your Daddy, I have been in the gym. My knees have been giving me the devil so I decided to take off some of the load."

"I need to lose some weight too."

"Child please, you look like a Barbie doll, you don't need to lose no weight! I bet that man of yours like you just the way you are."

"As a matter of fact he does, I have to get going, I'm late. I'm sure I can find something for her, it'll probably be part-time though." I opened my purse and whipped out a business card, "here this is my business card. Call me sometime tomorrow and we'll set up an appointment."

"Oh shucks now! Ms. Thang has her own business cards, ooh she's a vice president, go on girl which your bad self! That's what I'm talking about Chandra, you gotta have drive and be ambitious to make it in this world!"

Cute little Chandra, most likely a recent high school graduate, just gave me the dirtiest of looks. I don't think she'll be coming to work for me. "I'd love to stay and chat Mrs. Wilson, Chandra, but I'm late for a meeting. Please excuse me."

"You're quite alright."

"Chandra give me a call."

I walk away in search of mother. I see her at the door, saying goodbye to the attendees. She is so graceful. How can she after having a bomb drop in on her life? Graceful or not, she should be leaving like the rest of us, but then again if she did leave where will she go, back to the office to work alongside Dad? I must tell her I am leaving.

"Mom, I want to discuss this further, we will continue our conversation later."

She nods in agreement and pushes me along so she can extend her hand to the next person in line.

At work...

Finally I arrive, it's a little after one o'clock, still lunch time. A Flora's Flowers van has been in front of me the last hour or so, making the exact same turns as me. He or she has been driving at their leisure. Maybe they have all afternoon, but I don't. I want to see dad as soon as possible. I want to hear his side. What mother said cannot be true, it simply can't be. But then again she was pretty torn up at breakfast. She said she threw him out of the house. Did he go willingly?

The van is going where I am going, it turns into the driveway of Spencer Foods. Maybe Dad sent Mother some flowers. Mother, an excellent speaker and company spokes-person, serves as our public relations person. Flowers can go a long way in soothing a woman's heart but I don't know if it can fix this. An outside child is a slap in the face, the type of news that would be a public relations nightmare not mention utterly embarrassing. They are both wrapped up in presenting a picture of the perfect couple who has it all and works together to keep it all. One thing I know about both of my parents is that they will fight to keep this under wraps.

The driver pulls the van up to the curb of the delivery lane. I drive around it to get to my designated parking spot a few feet away and across from him. I get out of my car and close the door, but don't go anywhere. I want to know what is being delivered. I walk around to the passenger side and get my briefcase. I lay it atop the hood of my car, all the while peering at the van. The driver has gotten out and is adjusting his cap, he's rather cute. The majority of his hair is tucked underneath the cap he sports backwards. A few free shoulder length strands fly about in the wind, resisting his attempts to restrict them so he readjusts his cap again.

He glances at me as he walks to the back of the van. I look away and pretend to be rummaging thru my briefcase. I look up. He's standing at the back of the van. He opens the door and tucks the clipboard under an arm. I close my briefcase and walk along the sidewalk, towards him. Just as he pulls on the door latch I cross the driveway and peek inside the van. He is delivering flowers just like I thought. He reaches inside and grabs hold of two bouquets. He's delivering flowers to whom? I hurry to the entrance of the building and wait for him, the perfect opportunity to find out where they are going. Here he comes. "Let me get the door for you."

He smiled. Some people have the perfect smile, the kind of smile that shows all 32 teeth. He does not have a single cavity.

"Jake," he said.

"Well Jake you have a beautiful smile. Follow me and I take you to the front desk. Here, why don't I take your clipboard, wouldn't want you to ruin your delivery."

I eased the clipboard from his slightly opened armpit.

"Thanks," he said, stepping inside the vestibule.

I escort him to the front desk. Lazy Phaedra, one of our security guards, is on the phone as always. I should give her the benefit of the doubt. She could be talking to one of our employees.

"Larry why can't you do your fair share? I can't send kids to school and work too?" she complained.

Totally self-absorbed, we have been standing here five minutes now and she has yet to acknowledge me or the deliveryman. I have been meaning to have her replaced. She is a lovely person plagued with personal problems, most of them caused by her selfish man. Too bad she didn't discover this before her children were born. At last, she ends her call.

"I apologize Ms. Spencer for not greeting you…family emergency…sheez! Some girls have all the luck, red roses in crystal vases. Me, I got stuck with a man from the Stone Age. Sir, what can I do for you?"

"I have a delivery for Ms. Khloe Spencer."

"Wait a minute, that's me, two dozen of roses for me?! Wow! Who are they from?"

"Apparently you are the love of some lucky guy's life, there's a note card, I'll be back," he said.

They are for me, not mother, me! Someone is completely smitten with me. I wonder which one, Xavier or Danny? I pluck the note card hidden amongst the bloom. My name is not on the envelope, there's only a number, the number one is written. What is meant by "1?" I flip the envelope over. It's not sealed very tight. My finger works along the crease rather easily. I remove the note card and read.

"Will you hurry up? Got me sitting here in complete suspense while you take forever to read the card," she griped.

"Okay, okay, okay, they are from…" I look up Jake has returned. He has two more dozen of roses, these are pink. I gasp, "What the?"

"See, we are not all cave men, where do I put these?" he asked.

"I can leave one here with Phaedra," I said.

"You are going to need more room than that, there's more," he said.

"More!" I gasped.

"Yes, more," he said.

"How many more?" I asked.

"Six more," he said.

"Six!" I blurted, "You mean someone sent me ten dozen of roses?"

"Yes," he said.

"Your man sure loves you," she said.

"I guess he does. I am going to share my gifts. One of the pinks can stay here with you the rest can come with me. I need Bailey, have you seen him today?"

"He's here."

She picked up the phone, turned the handset down, push a button on the console and spoke, "Bailey delivery at front desk, Bailey delivery at front desk!"

"I'll take this one, he can bring the others."

I pick up the two note cards and the bouquet and make my way to my office. Co-workers stop what they are doing to glance at me, commenting on their beauty and their fragrance. No one has ever sent me roses. I am not sure which one sent them, but I am willing to bet they came from Xavier. Ten dozen of roses is chump change for him, costly for Danny. Besides Danny and I are friends having fun, nothing serious in the feelings department. Xavier is the one I am serious about, guess these flowers prove the feelings are mutual.

I open the office door. No one has been in here today, the drapes are drawn. My hand brush across the light plate and immediately the lights flicker on. I survey the room, where will I put them all? For starters the one I am holding can sit in the center of the conference table, two can stay on my desk, the others can sit on the window sill. Oh my, their fragrance already wafts in the air.

"Where do you want these?"

It's Bailey, soft-spoken and a bit of a featherweight for a man. His size is not to be underestimated, he is extremely strong. I once saw him reposition one of the boilers in the basement. I think he did it to impress me, I still think he has a crush but has wisely buried it. He knows that I think of him as a brother, "In the window sill."

Bailey talks while I rummaged through my handbag.

"Somebody sure loves you. That's good though, you deserve it. If he does not treat you right let me know, I'll smack'em upside the head."

"I'll be sure to call you."

"What are you looking for in there, the kitchen sink?"

I pulled out a $20 bill and held it between my fingers.

He stepped forward and raised his hand, ready to accept, "For me?"

Jake is here with another bouquet. I promptly pulled back, "It's for him."

"What about me? Don't I get something?" he complained.

"Yes, you can get my Dad," I said.

"Oh so it's like that huh? Okay I'll go find him and send him your way."

"Please close the door behind you."

Note cards stick up out of the orange, yellow, and white bouquets, "What could he possibly have to say on so many cards?"

I arrange them in numerical order and open them one by one. "It's a poem:"

> Red is for the lover in you,
> Yellow is because your warm and affectionate,
> Pink for your elegance and refinement,
> Orange because of my desire,
> White because you are pure and worthy.
> There is more to come, beginning at five,
> Are you sure you're ready to take the next step?

After this morning I'm not so sure...the door opens. It's Tamara the ever prompt secretary that I share with Dad. She is all business, all the time. She has worked here for two years now and I have never seen her wear makeup, change her hairstyle or take off her glasses. Her clothes always scream ultra conservative, the very top button on all her blouses are always fastened, her skirts and dresses are never above her ankles. Her shoes are always flat, she never wears heels. Not good for a young woman in search of a man, assuming she wants a man. I should not jump to conclusions. She may very well be content with her lifestyle.

"How was the symposium?"

"It was a bit of an eye opener."

"Oh."

"What are your plans for the weekend?"

"I don't know probably take in a movie or something. How about you, what are your plans?"

"I haven't made any. How are things around here?"

"Busy as always, Bill Kessler called, he said the coffee shipment would be delayed by two days. Leighton Manufacturing claims their shipment of containers arrived just today."

"The weather out west is horrendous. What affects them affects the rest of the country, anything else?"

"Yeah Philadelphia Liberty Stars' Mark Clothier has agreed to be our spokesman."

"Yayy! I scored my first major contract without Dad. Speaking of Dad have you seen him today?"

"No I haven't seen or heard from him. Someone is trying to get in contact with him. They have been calling him all morning."

"Oh yeah, who?"

"Some lady, she won't leave her name or number. She says it's personal."

"I have an idea who it may be. The next time they call, transfer it to me."

"Sure will. Also Scott Warner wants to speak with you about the advertising campaign involving Mark Clothier. He's put together a few ideas and wants to get your approval."

"Where's Scott now?"

"He's at lunch."

"When he gets here tell him to come see me. Tamara I am starving can you order lunch for me?

"Sure."

"I'd like a grill chicken salad with two servings of Thousand Island dressings. I also want garlic bread and a large ice tea."

"Sure Khloe."

"Any other messages?"

"Remember you have a three o'clock meeting with the Regional Managers."

"You better add a slice of chocolate cake, that'll help me stay awake."

"Sure, that's all that is happening around here unless you need something else."

"No that's more than enough on my plate. Oh wait a minute! I need the folders for the meeting."

"I had them transported up, they are over here."

She turns and walks toward the table. Her hand rests on the back of a chair that she lifts up and pulls out. I see the folders stacked on the seat of the chair she is holding. She pushes the chair aside and stands closer to the table, gingerly she touches the petals.

"They are captivating aren't they?"

She doesn't reply, suddenly she exhales as if she had been standing there holding her breath.

"Tamara is everything okay?"

"Never been better, I heard thru the grapevine that you had gotten flowers today. Didn't realize there was so many, who's the secret admirer?"

"He's no secret to you, Xavier sent them."

"Oh."

She has a frown on her face, "Is something wrong?"

"Nothing, I was thinking, wondering, that's all."

"Would you like to take a bouquet back to your desk?"

"They would not have the same effect. They are for you, not me. I should be getting back to work, enjoy your flowers."

"Thank you, I will, could you close the door behind you."

I pick up the handset and call Bill who answers on the first ring, "Bill this is Khloe, I understand the shipment is going to be late, do we have enough coffee cups in stock?

"No, we have only five thousand cases."

"Is that five thousand cases of cups of each size or the sum total of all cups on our shelves?"

"Total sum of cups, the shipment was to bring in 20,000 cases-- five thousand cases of small, regular, large, and extra large cups, in which we would in turn distribute to the stores."

"Leighton should have a minimum of three thousand cases of our cups already made."

"Jim Leighton sent us what he had in stock last week, which was our emergency supply of 10,000 cases. He said he always has on hand 10,000 products for each of his customers, that's a lot of storage space considering he has a huge customer base. He is asking that we remain patient and give him the extra days to prepare the cups, he's got his staff working overtime…this extreme weather is affecting all of us Khloe."

"Take what we have and divide it evenly among the stores. Wait, that won't work, supply the stores with the most demand, the rest will have to purchase basic styrofoam cups until the shipment come in. Tamara said something about a back order for coffee…"

"The coffee is also going to be delayed. They are having a hard time getting the coffee to the airport due to flooding of the roads."

"How long of a delay?"

"Two days maximum, the roads leading directly to and from the warehouses are clear. It's the low-lying roads on the way to the airport that are flooded."

"Call me back and let me know how things are going."

I hang up the phone, satisfied that our contingency plan works. Now onto problem two-Mark Clothier and the marketing campaign. Our sketch should be similar to his style of playing, fast and smooth. Scott, very blonde and very blue-eyed, stands in my doorway with his portfolio carry all. The man is always prepared.

"Hi Scott, I heard the good news."

"Yeah we got Mark Clothier!"

"I also heard you have a marketing campaign in the works."

"Yeah I do, care to take a look at it?"

"Certainly."

Scott unzips his portfolio carry all and lays his presentation boards on the conference table.

"Beautiful flowers, and so many, what's he apologizing for?"

"Who's apologizing Scott?"

"The man who sent them…never mind, let's stay on task 'cause we don't have much time. I want the commercial up and running before the Stars' first playoff game…anyway I was thinking, *Come to Spencer's, where the food is good, the service is smooth and fast like my fastball.*"

I examine his work, "Here's what I was thinking, of *"Come to Spencer's, where the atmosphere is surreal, the food is excellent, and the service is as genuine and memorable as my fast ball."*

"We can incorporate both ideas. I took the liberty of surveying local advertising companies and Kent and Brown came highly recommended. I met with them and I'm confident they will provide us with exactly what we need."

"Good, can things get underway first thing Monday morning?"

"They said yes."

The button on the phone blinks, its Tamara calling on the speakerphone, "Yes?"

"The regional managers are here, I seated them in Conference Room 2."

"Thanks, have you seen my Dad yet?"

"Not yet."

"Tell them I'm on the way."

I gather the folders while Scott packs up his presentation. He accompanies me down the hall since he is going back to his office, which happens to be right next door to Conference Room 2.

"Is Greg in today?"

"He's not in yet."

"We was supposed to have lunch together to talk about a deal he was working on, he never showed or answered his phone."

"He's probably caught up somewhere."

"I was thinking that too, it's unusual for him not to be in touch though, I hope he's alright."

"I'm sure he is, when I track him down I'll remind him to call you."

"Thanks Khloe, see you later."

I step inside of the room. Four of the six regional managers are here, which is a good thing, this meeting can wrap up a lot sooner than expected and I can be on my merry way to New York. In attendance is: Bob Cummings representing our stores in Delaware, Zachary Buspry representing our stores in New Jersey, Stephen Spiel representing our stores on the Main Line/Western Suburbs of Philadelphia and Central Pennsylvania up to and including State College. Anthony Lipton represents our stores in the Northern Suburbs of Philadelphia up to and including Scranton, Pennsylvania.

Absent are the regional managers representing New York and Maryland. The clock on the wall says four o'clock. I intend to wrap this up in 45 minutes. "Good afternoon Gentlemen, I hope I didn't keep you waiting too long, I know you all have very busy agendas so let's get to it. Let's start with Bob, how are things in Delaware?"

Bob Cummings, a transplant from Oklahoma is a man in his mid-30s with the beadiest of eyes. He is of average height and weight, not bad looking, a few crows' feet has set up shop in his temples. His Stetson pulls your eyes away from those details. Bob loves his western wear. Every time I see him he's wearing some shade of green and brown. Those clothes define him, complimenting his fair skin and curly sandy brown hair. Today he's wearing a sage green western shirt underneath a chocolate suede vest. I have no doubt he's wearing cowboy boots. I bet his Stetson occupies the seat next to him. Boisterous like most mid-westerners, I can say that he takes the time to listen attentively before attempting to hog the spotlight. Now only if he can get rid of that drawl…

"Overall things in Delaware are not bad, the restaurants are making us money, steadily increasing in profits," he reports. "The stores under me have taken the reins so to speak and prepare cuisine unique to Delaware, and even added a few unheard of international dishes. They prefer to use fruits and vegetable from local farmers as much as possible. Customers are not only buying goods off the shelf and taking them home, but they are stopping to have a meal before heading back to the corral."

"I know my restaurants have chosen Loretta Wineries as their source of wine," said Zachary.

Zachary Buspry is the youngest of the four and the handsomest. He's our flamboyant dresser who loves the non-traditional colors. However he makes every effort to wear business attire. I once asked him why he wore such bold colors and he said, '*they make me unforgettable.*' Boy was he right, his presence is quite unforgettable.

Zachary continues, "Loretta Wineries is unique to New Jersey. One would think this region would be too harsh to grow grapes, but the soil is ideal for them. Swedesboro was chosen as our promo site because of its lack of restaurants, this has proven to be a wise decision. Business is booming simply because the people can stay in their own town."

"Well that's two good reports. I wish I can say the same," barreled Stephen.

Stephen Spiel is a middle-aged man quite tall and very noticeable. His voice is the product of years and years of chain smoking. I look at the clock, half an hour has already passed and here he comes with bad news.

"There are too many specialty boutiques, Mom and Pop stores, and restaurants owned by the local rich and famous. Not to mention hot and heavy competition from Hawa's."

"That damn Hawa is everywhere!" thundered Anthony.

Anthony Lipton, the oldest of them all, is chose to sit rather than stand. Bald and significantly overweight, he speaks with his enormous hands, "I was always taught if you can't beat 'em, join 'em!"

Time for me to intercept, "Gentlemen we are, you may have heard we had been pursuing Phillies first baseman Mark Clothier. Well he just signed to be our spokesman."

"What's he going to sell?" asked Bob.

"The Spencer brand," I said.

"Which is?" Zachary asked.

"Genuine," I look at the clock. It is five o'clock, perfect timing, "genuine and memorable like Clothier's fast ball. Further details will be forthcoming as soon as the ad campaign is complete. If you gentlemen will excuse me, I must be going. I have another meeting to attend."

I gather up my folders.

"Where is Greg?" Anthony asked.

"Dad will probably be in later this afternoon."

I try to walk out of the room fast, but the folders are quite heavy and uncomfortable in my arms. I shift them to my hands, instantly feeling relief. Thankfully I don't have too far to walk, next time I will definitely bring a cart. I wonder where Dad is, it is unusual for him to stay away and not phone anyone. He and Mother had marital problems before and it never stopped him from being at work. Unless he is with his girlfriend, but who is the mysterious woman calling him? Here comes Tamara, maybe she's heard something new. "Hey Tamara, have you seen Dad?"

Her eyes shift to the floor. The floor is not talking to you, I am! What's on the floor that is so interesting? Oh no she didn't, she just walked pass me without saying a word. How can a secretary walk pass her boss without speaking? Maybe she did not hear me. "Has Dad called Tamara?"

She pauses where she stands, and at a snail's pace turn towards me, "No he hasn't."

She sounds like she swallowed a frog, maybe she isn't feeling well, "Has anyone called him?"

She slowly lifts her head up to look at me. Bulging eyes appear in her bifocals, "You mean the person I told you about earlier?"

Her voice is back to normal. I don't remember her clearing her throat. Maybe she did, but if she did and I did not hear her, it would not immediately fade back to normal, "Yeah."

She is really irritating me. Her eyes shift up at the ceiling, down to the floor, to the adjacent wall, everywhere but at me, "No they haven't called, neither has your mother."

"Tamara is something wrong?"

"I have a lot on my mind, nothing to do with you."

She is lying. "For a minute I thought I was making you uncomfortable."

"It's not you…I just received some bad news."

"Can I be of help?"

"There's nothing anybody can do. I just have to wait and let it work itself out."

"Okay, well I won't hold you up."

"You're not holding me up. In case I don't see you again I want you to know you've been a great boss."

"Are you leaving?"

"No, I'm not leaving, I don't want to, but I might have to take a leave of absence."

"Listen, take the afternoon off. Don't worry about these folders. I'll hide them in my file cabinet in my office."

"Okay."

She is running towards the exit. Something is wrong, I shouldn't have let her leave, clearly she's upset about something. I sit the folders on the floor against the wall and enter the stairwell. The onslaught of the sun streaming through the glass block momentarily blinds me. I can't see her, but I hear her, her shoes scrape against the steps. I put my hand on my brow like a visor and peer over the railing. She is already on the second floor. "Tamara!"

She ignores me and keeps going, she is running full steam down the stairs, her heels scuffing even louder than before. "Tamara!"

A door opens and closes with a deafening force, there is only one door that opens and closes like that and it's the exit door on the ground floor, it leads to the parking lot. She can't drive in that state. "Tamara, stop!"

I jet downstairs as fast as I can, trying not to wrench my ankles. I finally arrive on the ground floor, but I am too late. She is already in the car and has started the engine. The wheels spin on the asphalt, kicking up so much smoke that I can't see her. Abruptly the car jets out of the parking lot.

"What's wrong with her?"

Phaedra and Bailey have joined me.

"I don't know," I said.

"Probably some man missing with her head," he said.

"What makes you say that?" I asked.

"I'm a man and I know men. Sometimes were the nastiest sacks of shits…" his voice trailed off.

Phaedra replied, "Hear ye! Hear ye!"

"I'll call her later, make sure she's okay," I said.

"Good thinking, by the way Roseman is waiting in your office," she said.

"Who is Roseman?" I asked.

"Mister dozens and dozens of roses!" she blurted.

"He is!! Let me get going," I said.

"Yeah you better get going before I take him from you," she cackled.

I run back to the third floor, to the place where I left the folders and pick them up. I hurry on to my office and find my door shut. They said he was here, where is he? I sit the folders on Tamara's desk and turn the doorknob. I find him, the love of my life sits at my desk with his feet propped up. He stares at me with those big eyes. Sometimes

34

they are gray, other times green or hazel. Regardless of their color, they are eerie, like now, dark and penetrating, burning a hole in my soul. I counter with my own stare.

"Glad you made yourself at home."

His hand glides across his right breast and finds its way inside his jacket. I can see the bulge and I know what it was looking for, cigarettes. He is the first to blink. He lights one and inhale, his square jaw momentarily sinks in.

"It's that good huh?" I asked as I move over to the file cabinet to lay the files in an empty drawer.

"Not as good as you. Enjoying the flowers?"

"Yes I am. I knew you sent them, tell me why so many?"

"Did your mother ever explain that you are supposed to be grateful for the gifts you receive?"

"Yes she did."

"Are you ready?"

"Ready for what?"

"What is this? Answering a question with a question, you know what I'm talking about. Are you ready to take the next step?"

I thought about today, the conversation with mother, seeing Tamara, and Bailey's unforgettable comments. I'm not sure if now is the best time. I won't completely blow him off though. "Sure I am ready to go to New York, first I want to touch base with Tamara, make sure she's okay."

"What's wrong with her?"

"Something happened. She tore out of here like a jet going up in space."

"I just saw her and everything was fine."

"How long ago was that?"

"About ten minutes ago, she let me in here."

"How was she?"

"She was fine. How about you stop worrying about her and worry about me, find out if I am okay."

Xavier stands up and my lips part, I can't help but relish his presence. He is impeccably dressed as always, another characteristic that pulled my attention. His charcoal grey suit, tailored just for him, is very becoming. The skinny tie-black, grey, and white stripe lies against a crisp white shirt. The whole ensemble moves with his chiseled body. Within seconds his eyes close in on mine. His soft moist lips rest on my lips. His sharp teeth sting, forcing my mouth open, his unopposed tongue worm its way in. Hot and cool all at once, I don't dare move, I don't want to move, but he will. I feel his cell phone vibrating in his jacket pocket. I have no doubt he will answer it.

"Hello…oh we'll be right down." He closed the phone and said, "That was the limo driver, we have to get going. You can call Tamara from there."

"Limo! You said limo!"

"Yes I said limo. I want to ride in style. C'mon we gotta get going, get our show on the road. It's only two days, but I promise when we clear our calendars we will sail the world for a month."

"Sail!?"

"Yes sail, okay, fly, whatever method of travel you prefer. We can discuss that in the limo too."

Getting to know your mate

The drive to New York is anything but quiet. Maroon 5 plays loudly while we sing along. Xavier is in a good mood, pouring glass after glass of champagne. I don't have the heart to disappoint him.

"Drink up sweets! This is the last day you will be known as Khloe Spencer. After tomorrow, you'll be Khloe Davidson."

I shouldn't do this. I can't do this, not now...we are entering Lincoln Tunnel. I hate tunnels, too narrow and too closed in. This one has wall to wall traffic. God get me out of here.

"What's wrong babe?"

"I hate tunnels."

He places his arm around me and I settle back into his nest, permitting him to pull me close so that I can fight off a chill that has abruptly entered the cabin. A kiss lands on my head, "Shouldn't be too much longer."

He turns out to be right. The cars are beginning to move. Now is as good as a time to tell him, "Xavier I want to talk about this weekend."

"I'm not telling you my plans for this weekend. You will experience them one by one as they unfold."

He is always full of surprises. Surprises are what I wanted, to break the monotony of my life. The saying goes be careful for what you ask for...unfortunately I have a surprise for him. "Where will we stay?"

"That's definitely a surprise," he said refilling my glass with more champagne, "drink up my bride to be."

"I really can't drink another drop."

"It's a celebration, the beginning of our life as Mr. and Mrs. Xavier Davidson!"

"That's what I want to ta—

"We're almost there."

"Almost where?"

"Our vacation home."

The limo stops in front of a gold plated building. He promptly jumps out and is already on the sidewalk by the time the doorman arrives. He is shaking the doorman's hand. I lower the window so I can hear what is being said.

"Good evening Kurt."

"Nice to see you again Mr. Davidson, welcome to Monument House. I'll get your things up to you."

The doorman knocks on the hood of the limo and signals the driver to pop the trunk.

"Kurt I didn't bring any clothes, what I brought was my lady."

They both laugh like two kids still in high school. The doorman opens the car door and extends his hand. I swing my legs out before taking hold of him and graciously exit the limo. He escorts me to the sidewalk where Xavier awaits.

"Welcome to Monument House," he said.

He walks ahead of us to hold the door open. I step inside the vestibule, ahead of Xavier who he has stopped to search his pocket. He pulls out a roll, not very thick, and gives it to the doorman. He takes the lead and show me the way inside. I cannot help but gasp at the interior. The lobby, dramatically unveiled by recessed lighting, is paved with brown marble floors and supported with brown marble columns. Soft light projects off the marble, onto the metal laminate walls and onto the concierge sitting at the desks. She is a young brunette busy writing in her book. Hastily she rises from the desk and scurries around to hug him.

"Xavier, you made it! How was the drive up?" she asked.

Her hands have moved from his neck to his chest.

"Not bad at all," he said.

"We've made all of the arrangements you requested," she said.

Okay you getting a little too comfy, you can get off of him now...why is she still holding on to him? Why aren't you pushing her away? Finally he returns her hands to her side.

"Thanks Anne Marie, this is my fiancée Khloe. Khloe this is Anne Marie Palacio, the events coordinator."

With a raised eyebrow, she gawks at me from my head to my feet, and then flashes a weird kind of sly grin.

"So you're the object of this man's desire. I hope you find our arrangements satisfactory," she said.

"What arrangements?" I asked.

"I already told you, you have to wait and see," he said.

"Curiosity is getting to you isn't it?" she asked.

"Yes it is," I said.

"Well I hope it is everything you ever dreamed of. If you will please excuse I have some arrangements to make for another couple," she said.

"Thanks again Anne Marie," he said.

"You're quite welcome," she said.

My eyes cut away from her silhouette and focus on Xavier who takes me to the elevator. Nervous with anticipation is my stomach as the doors open upon our approach. Inside he pushes number eleven.

"We're on the 11th floor."

"Yes we are."

"They all know you."

"They should, I've had this place a little over two years."

"Did you say you had this place for two years?"

"Yes, why are you asking?"

"When did you get it?"

"About a year after we began seeing each other. I got it for business purposes."

"Oh really, I didn't know you liked New York."

"Who doesn't like new York?"

"You…I always thought you hated crowds."

He gave me a hard look, "I never told you that, where did you get that assumption?"

"You have never taken me to any event with a large gathering."

"That's because I wanted to focus on you with no outside interference."

"Will you be able to focus on me, solely me, this weekend in this big city?"

"Of course, but the question is will *I* have *your* attention."

"Why wouldn't I give you my undivided attention?"

"Only you can answer that."

"I am baffled, I thought I knew you."

"After three years, if you don't…there's probably a lot I don't know about you. Just like there's a lot you don't know about me," his eyes softened, and he broke out a little smile, "The beauty of it all is that you will spend your married life discovering me."

The doors slide open and we get off. Xavier chooses the left corridor. There is a door all the way at the very end, facing us. Something tells me that is our destination. We walk in silence, the carpet absorbs our footprints, giving the impression that no one is out and about in the hall. I hear the voices of people inside their places and smell their stoves giving off varying scents. I am hungry, but it is too late to eat. I should have eaten when I was drinking all that champagne, to eat now would cause me to vomit. Finally we arrive at the door. He sticks the key in the lock and turns. The bolt, retracting into its sleeve, echoes. Xavier turns the doorknob and pushes inward. His hand swipes the switch plate just on the inside.

"Oh wow!"

"Is that your only response tonight, oh wow?"

The door opens to a huge apartment, much bigger than my own. The décor is quite attractive and manly, black leather and chocolate suede. A woman's touch is not evident, but still, the thought boggles my mind. I manage to maintain my composure and step inside, hurrying over to the sofa. I lean against its back. All I can do is stand in awe, and take stock.

I don't know what to make of this. He has had this apartment for two whole years and kept it a secret, his secret. I rush to the window, instantly drawn to it. It's the only place I want to look. I turn the hand crank around and around, breathing the fresh air that comes in. Down below are lights, headlights, tail lights, streetlights, marquees, and people. Plenty of people of all shades, shapes, and sizes, walking, exploring, I feel like I am going to faint. Fighting back tears, I clear my throat and muffle, "The view is breathtaking."

"Yeah it is. It's what drew me to the place. I could've gotten an apartment on one of the upper floors, but I chose to stay close to the ground, 9-11."

I hear him and I don't hear him. The action down below, probably more truthful than he, has my undivided attention.

"Care to see the rest of the place?"

I turn around and see him standing there, next to the table with an expression that lets me know he is a little incensed. I can only guess it's because of what I said, but what about what I am seeing? I take off

41

my jacket and lay it with my purse on the sofa. "You can begin your tour."

"As you can see the table is here. The galley kitchen is around the corner," he said pulling my hand, "see it's quite small. Just a cooktop, fridge and sink. All I can do in there is cook and wash dishes."

"Nice," is all I can manage to say. He just unloaded another surprise, he cooks and cleans. We travel up the short hall and stop at the first opened door.

"This is a bedroom. It's not the master bedroom as you can tell by the twin beds."

It is nice and gray, very masculine, black leather headboards and gray plaid comforters drape the beds. "Nice."

"Over here are the bathrooms, there are two rooms, one room has a bathtub, the other has the toilet, and here in front of us is the sink.

"Wonderful idea to create three areas for one bathroom."

"I think it's hilarious too, and now onto the final frontier, the room where will be spending a lot of time, the master bedroom."

"Oh wow!"

He opened the door to a gorgeous room with a gracious king sized bed, draped with a burgundy comforter.

"The wow factor again!"

"I have no other words to describe it. I mean this room has two gorgeous views."

"This means we will see the sun rise and set."

He sneaks up behind me and nibbles on my ear. I turn my head his way, and he pulls away his warmth.

"We'll have plenty of time to savor each other. We should go to bed now. Tomorrow is going to be a long day."

"What is on our agenda?"

He walks over to the closet and began to undress, "You must wait and see."

"I don't have a change of clothes."

"Well you have to hang those up in the closet."

I climb into bed wearing only my underwear, and snuggle one of two pillows for warmth. I adjust the other, soft and comfortable, under my head, the lights are off and my eyes are closing…

Go this way! I walk the gnarly path nearly covered by overgrown bushes. Dry bushes with prickly limbs. Keep going! I keep walking. The path grows darker and darker with more twists and turns. Jump back! A giant anaconda lunges at me. He is wrapped around the thick trunk of a tree. Look up! The huge tree is covered with snakes, all kinds, all sizes and all colors. Do you see him? A man sits high up in the tree, playing with the snakes. He lets them crawl around his neck, his arms, his legs. He looks at me, it's Xavier. Jump back! The anaconda lunges at me again. Xavier get down! Xavier! Xavier! "Xavier!"

I struggle to open my eyes, I can't get them open. Why can't I open them, why can't I see? My head is pounding. The blood not only pulses forcefully, but loudly at my temples. I can hear my heart beating. It's beating fast, too fast.

"Xavier! Xavier! Xavier!" I call him but the words are not coming out, my voice is gone. What is happening to me? I rub my eyes, crusted mucous falls on my cheeks. The room comes into focus, "I can see! I can see!"

I look at the window, its daybreak. The sun rises behind overcast clouds, subtlety lighting the room. Wait a minute, I am all alone, where is he? I glimpse at my watch, it's six o'clock in the morning. "Xavier? Xavier!"

He does not answer me. Maybe he's in the kitchen. I sit upright, the room spins, perhaps I am drunk, I must get to the bathroom, my bladder is more than full. Standing up is a bit frightening, the room seems to spins even more. Too much champagne, way too much, gotta get to the bathroom. A surge of strength allows me to make a mad dash, thank goodness I only have to go next door. The seat is down, he thought of me.

"Xavier!"

Still no answer, ewww! I smell like a falling down drunk. Boy do I stink, sweaty too. I need to bathe before he comes back. I turn on the bathtub's faucets. Damn! I don't have my own toiletries. There is nothing in here except these itty bitty soaps in the cognac glass. They will have to do. I take a few of the same color and smell them, they are quite fragrant, hopefully enough to mask the odor. The warm water is so relaxing. I use the soaps to stroke my skin, over and over, every inch. Finally I feel clean, I rinse under the shower and wrap up in a towel from the towel stand. I pick up my underwear.

"Why would I be wearing this, I did not have this on! I had on a white bra and white panties, not a green bustier and thong!"

I only wear green when I am with Danny. It's his favorite color and style, bustier, thongs and garter belts. Something is not right. I would never wear this when I am with Xavier, he likes the color red and baby dolls or no clothes at all…Oh snap! Danny and I had a date last night!

"Khloe!"

Oh my God Xavier is here! What do I do with this?

"Khloe! Are you out of bed yet?"

"Yes I am, I'll be right out."

"I bought you some things, women's underwear. I think I got the right size."

How would he know what size I wear? "Xavier can you bring me a plastic bag? I need to throw something away."

"Sure!"

I stick my hand out the door, but he forces it open.

"What are you throwing away?"

"It's personal."

"Keeping secrets?"

"No, I'm throwing something personal away, where have you been?"

"I told you I was buying you some things, not sure if I got the right size but it's the thought that counts."

"Thank you for being so thoughtful, we didn't do anything last night did we?"

"What do you mean?"

"Did we make love?"

He glares at me with those piercing eyes again. I feel uneasy when he stares at me like that, I'm not afraid of him. I just wish he didn't make me feel intimidated.

"We went to sleep...don't be in here forever, I'm starting breakfast."

His feet tread heavily against the wooden floors. I suppose he's angry because I do not recall last night. He is full of surprises, we've been together for three years and I cannot recall him ever placing a plate in the sink let along lift a pan. Why hide something as petty as cooking? Why hide this beautiful apartment?

"Yo Khloe, c'mon!"

The smell of breakfast has made its way in here, it smells good. Question is will it taste good? I walk into the living room and stop. More roses, there is not an empty space anywhere in the room. I look at the table, it is set as if it's serving the royal family. Everything is absolutely beautiful. He loves me. I had no idea just how much. I love him too, I loved him from the moment I saw him, but love cannot remove the doubt I am feeling.

Being with Danny is different, not so intense. He makes me feel so comfortable and stress-free that I often tell him too much about myself. Maybe I am leaning towards the wrong one, maybe I belong with Xavier. It could very well be that my apprehensiveness is nothing more than a case of bad nerves caused by guilt. I'm curious. I want to see if he is really cooking or if he is heating up delivery from a local restaurant.

I stand in the doorway and watch him, he really is cooking. Eggshells litter the counter, a milk carton stands next to the orange juice, a package of bacon leans on a loaf of bread. "Smells good Xavier didn't know you could cook. Who taught you Ms. Gladys?"

"I learned some things from her, some things from my dad, and a few things from you," he said.

"Me?! What did you learn from me?"

"How to make an awesome omelet."

"So you were paying attention to me."

"I always pay attention to the people in my life. You had no clue I was observing you."

"No I did not, what else did you learn from me?"

"To be more open with my feelings."

"You used to be so wound up and were never one for words either. Then slowly, you started to relax…

"I'm afraid not enough for you. I am an introspective person, others see me as brooding. I have to confess I usually don't let people get too close to me…you are the first in a very long time."

"Why?"

"Because I'm afraid they will disappoint me."

"Have I disappointed you?"

He took awhile to answer, as if he was unsure of what to say. My gut says he is going to say yes. '*Yes, you have disappointed me by cheating with Danny.*'

"No, not yet."

He slid the omelets onto two plates and pick up a plate of toast.

"Here, give me one of them."

"I can handle this. You have a seat at the table."

Look at him juggling platters on the span of his weathered hands. I can feel them touching me, kneading oil into my skin after I've had a bath. He's playing the role of a servant, catering to my every need, and he just bared his soul. I don't have the heart to break his heart. He enters the room. "The table is beautifully set."

"Yes it is. Anne Marie did a good job of picking out the china."

"She did all of this?"

"Yes, she did."

"When?"

"This morning while you were sleeping, its part of the services she provides."

"Ah yes, *I have to make arrangement for another couple.*"

"Why are you mimicking her?"

I won't respond because I think you know already know the answer. Instead I will focus on what's in front of me, "You did a good job on this nice fluffy omelet. I see you added bits of bacon."

"Take a bite and let me know what you think."

I cut into the omelet, "It's nice and fluffy, mile high, just like mine."

I take a bite, it's a little greasy, but that's because he added more bacon. He left out the cheese, he doesn't like cheese. Can stand a little more salt, "Tastes fantastic Xavier, will you be cooking me breakfast every morning?"

"Sometimes, we can take turns cooking the meals. Just know that you will be doing the majority of the cooking as part of your wifely duties, and speaking of wifely duties, I expect you to dress respectful at all times."

"I do dress respectful at all times."

"Oh really, you call what you had on respectful? I had no idea you wore those types of garments to work."

"What types of garments?"

"That hideous green costume you call underwear."

"See that's what I'm confused about, I don't wear stuff like that to work."

"What are you trying to say, someone dressed you?"

"Certainly not! I would know if someone was touching me. I don't know what the hell happened."

"I hope you are not insinuating that I put them on you!"

"I'm not…"

"Hurry up and get dressed I don't want to be late for our appointment."

I have to make him understand as well as myself. "There has to be some explanation for all of this. I did not have those garments on when I went to bed."

"Khloe you did, you did have them on."

"They are not the underwear I wore to work yesterday morning!"

"Could you please do what I asked of you? This conversation is…okay, fine, I believe you, now please go and get dressed…I bought you fresh clothing, they're in the closet, please put them on."

I shove the table away from my chair and head to the bedroom. A Macy's shopping bag sits on the bed. I forage through the items, traditional bra and panties in white, the type I wear to work. Okay Xavier you have made your point. I change into them, wow they actually fit. How did he know what size to get? He said there were clothes on the closet. I see a suit bag, I unzip it and remove the contents, "Oh a suit."

I take the navy blue slacks and slide them over my hips. In the mirror I look, they fit perfectly. Maybe he got lucky in guessing my size. He chose an ivory knit top, obviously he is in tune with the weather, it fits just right too. Lastly, the jacket, the whole ensemble is impressive for someone who has been quietly watching me. Guess he has noticed my style of clothing, could he also know about Danny?

I need to do something about my hair. Static cling is in the air. I borrow some of his hair cream and smooth it on my head, it works, my mane is behaving. I open the bedroom door and look down the hall. The black carpet resembles a runway, in which a lone audience of one sits at the end, gawking at me as if I were Tyra Banks. I am unnerved.

"You look nice."

"Thank you, I'm ready. By the way, how did you know what size to get?"

"I guessed."

He rises to his feet and moves to the door as I grab my handbag. He allows me to sail by him. Out into the hall I begin the long trek to the elevator. Danny is probably pissed, I have to call him first chance I get and explain. Sweet Danny, I'll never forget how we met. It was two months ago, I was out on the town alone. Xavier was on a business trip and Kiera was with Bryce. I didn't feel like being alone so I went into the city. I stumbled on a sports bar called McGuiness. I hadn't been there 15 minutes when he introduced himself.

Tall and handsome with the bluest of eyes and blackest of hair, he pronounced his name with a faint Irish accent, Daniel McGuiness, all of 30 years of age. He then went on to ask me if I was alone. I told him no, but he didn't believe me. He was so sure I had a man in the bathroom taking a piss. He tried to walk away. I didn't want him to leave. At that moment I needed a friend, someone with a different perspective. He complimented me on my good looks then just as quickly offended me by asking if I was deranged. His justification for the insult was own love life. Old loves he considered to be sound eventually verified to be otherwise. It took some convincing, soon after he realized I had all my faculties.

At the elevator I glance back, he is jogging up the hall. I am going to tell him, I have to tell him. The elevator doors open, I board and stand in its doorway waiting for him. He steps inside and let the door close. "Where are we going?"

"You shall see."

"I don't want any more surprises."

"Neither do I."

"Well we are you taking me?"

"You shall see."

The lobby, brightly lit by the dome skylight, is sparsely populated except for staff. Nimbly we move although we hear their greetings. Xavier ignores them, solely focused on leaving the building and getting to that all important appointment. I acknowledge them by giving a quick wave. Once outside we hop into a waiting taxi.

The driver, Middle Eastern, was about to speak, but Xavier spoke louder and in a commanding voice. "We're going to the Meatpacking District."

"Exactly where in the Meatpacking district?" the driver asked.

"Over on 14th Street and 9th Avenue," he said.

"I will take you there," he said.

The car pulls away from the curb and merges with the traffic. Instantly he interrogates the taxi driver as if he is a police officer.

"What is your name?"

"The name is Sayeed."

"What country are you from?"

"Chicago."

"That's an American city, I said what COUNTRY?"

"Egypt."

"How long have you been here?"

"Several years now, why do you ask?"

"Do you always work my neighborhood?"

"Yes.

"How come I never seen you before?"

"I work here all the time, is there a problem?"

"I know all the cab drivers who service my building, I never seen you before."

"I have been working this area for two years now, I never seen you either."

I look at the streets again. People are window shopping while others walk into restaurants. This is too many people in such a tight space. Eight million people living in 303 square miles compared to our one and a half million living in 142 square miles. At least Philadelphia sleeps. I want to know where I am going. "What's at 14th and 9th?"

"Clothing…clothes from the hottest new designers."

"Oh good, I've been wanting some new threads for a long time now. Can you give me a hint about some of the designers?"

"And spoil the surprise, naw!"

The taxi pulls up to the curb in front of Avalon's, "That'll be seven dollars."

Xavier speaks rather gruffly, "Aren't you suppose to let the lady out!"

The driver grudgingly gets out and walks around the car. He opens the door for me, and I step out. Looking down the block I see all the storefronts are converted old warehouses. I step away from them and wait in front of the store. Xavier is paying the driver. The driver gazes at the bill and gives him a dirty look. I take it the run was not very profitable. We leave him standing there alone.

"I want to see Avalon's."

"As if you don't already have enough technology."

"I just want to see what it looks like inside."

I ignore his sarcasm and lead the way into the white loft style building. It's very open, very machine like. Laptops are set upon white tables with stools and cushioned benches, "Let's go up the stairs."

We walk up the winding acrylic stairs only to find more tables and more computers. "Come on let's leave, they don't have anything different here than they do in Philly."

"I tried to tell you."

We walk a little ways down 14th Street, a store named Lola peaks my attention. Stylish and casual clothing in this season's brilliant colors, perfect weekend wear, adorn the storefront mannequins. I select several pairs of jeans, blouses and sweaters and hand him the bill. I thought the price tag would get a rise out of him, it's well over $1000, but he doesn't care. He forks over his credit card.

We walk a few more doors down. Across the street I notice a place called the Retreat. The Retreat must be the local version of Victoria's Secret. I want to go in but he is adamant. He does not want me wearing such garments, even garments in his favorite color—red. Not sure what has put a damper on the thought of sex, usually he's all for role playing.

We keep going, briefly stopping to look and then moving on. Almost at the end, near the corner, is a shoe store called Xapata. The traffic jam at the door catches my attention. To have as many people entering as leaving can only mean one thing, the place is a hot spot. Inside I learn why, the layout is quite attractive, pulsing music vibrates throughout while sales personnel hustle in and out of the storage room. The shoes are irresistible, very attractive and top quality, versatile for casual, professional or nightlife. I buy at least ten pairs and make sure they have a matching handbag. We walked into the store with four bags and leave with five. "We should take these home."

"We could, but our appointment is right down the street."

"Where are we going now?"

"Butterfly McNeil, I want you to take a look at her bridal collection."

"Xavier I have been meaning to tell you."

"Tell me what?"

"I do want to marry you, just *not* right now."

"What do you mean not right now!"

"Because when I marry you, I want my family and friends to be there, and they are not here. I feel like we are hiding something dirty."

"Khloe the family is here."

"Where?"

"Our family-my parents and your parents, and our friends are all staying at The Gardens. I told them about our plans and asked them not to say anything. I wanted to surprise you."

"My Mom and Dad are here?"

"Yes, Sharon and Greg are here, they are staying at The Gardens."

"I want to see them."

"You will see them, just before the ceremony, your Mom has to help you get dressed and your Dad will give you away."

"Xavier, it is bad luck for the groom to see the bride's dress. Why do you want to help me pick out a dress?"

"I want to take you to someone who knows a thing or two about society weddings."

"Xavier we agreed to have a small wedding."

"It is going to be a small wedding."

"But you just mentioned a society wedding, society weddings are anything but small."

"Khloe weddings are not only about the bride, they are about the groom too…I'm not going to look at the dress. I'm just making sure you pick one, the right one."

"Don't you trust me, don't you trust my choices?"

"Of course I trust your choices."

"Then you don't need to help me choose."

"Yes I do, you need help choosing the right one."

Finishing touches

We stop to catch our breath. The bags are not heavy, but our dragging them around feels as if we are lugging around suitcases. Shockingly Butterfly McNeil is an actual storefront, not some conversion, and way better than Maria Roma. Her windows are more than a display, they tell the story of an open field with one or two butterflies feasting on wild flowers. Obviously a play on her name, assuming that it is a woman, Butterfly McNeil could very well be a man, as is the case of the world's best designers.

Xavier holds the door for me and instantaneously a mob of store clerks rush to him. The frontrunner of the group is a young woman inherently tall with platform shoes that give her additional stature. Shame she has below average looks, they are the only thing standing in the way of fame. I wonder if anybody ever recommended a plastic surgeon.

"Welcome to Butterfly McNeil's Mr. Davidson, remember me, Amy McCormick?"

"Of course I do, you are a valued employee. I hope they appreciate you around here."

"They do, feel free to look around, and if you need assistance I'll be at the cash register."

"Amy I do need your assistance, could you let Madame Marie Colette know we are here for our appointment."

"Everyone here knows you," I said.

"They should, I spend a pretty penny in this place," he said.

"Who were you shopping for?" I asked.

"For me," he said.

"This is a boutique for women's clothing, I don't see any men's clothing in here," I said.

"We have men's clothing upstairs," she said.

Amazon is hanging around, I know she is eavesdropping. I am not talking to her, I'm talking to him. She looks at my face and takes the hint.

"Mr. Davidson she is waiting for you, I'll go get her."

"Thanks Amy," he said.

Amy finally leaves us. I see her quickly walking to the office, frantically tapping on the door. A middle-aged woman pokes her head out. Attentively she is listening to Amy, occasionally her eyes dart over at us. She closes her door and together they come towards us. I assume she is Madame Marie Colette, I'd say she is in her late 40's, mid 50's the latest, she is aging quite gracefully.

Very attractively styled blond hair with streaks of platinum, smooth tanned skin with only a few laugh lines, no big deal, even I have laugh lines. Its smart of her to keep makeup to a minimum makeup--pink lipstick and neutral eyeliner highlight her olive eyes. In her heyday I bet she was stunning, heck she is stunning now. She has some height, about 5'8", not exactly short but standing next to Amy she looks diminutive.

"I'll take it from here Amy."

"Nice seeing you again Mr. Davidson."

Amy leaves us to work on a half-dressed mannequin.

"I know you are not the father of the bride, you're much too young. Are you her brother?"

"Actually I am the groom. My fiancée here wants to have a look at your famous bridal collection."

"The groom should not be here."

56

"I'm here to make sure she gets a gown."

"It is bad luck for the groom to see the dress before the ceremony"

"I don't believe in that old wives tale."

"Well I believe in it! I intend to see you get married so do not jinx it."

"We are not getting married anytime soon. I only came because he made this appointment. I have decided that since we are in the area, I can see some of your designs," I said.

"I suppose there is no harm in his being here. By the way how is the Congressman?" she asked.

"Julius has never been better," he said.

Have I missed something, some dialog? They act like they know each other.

"Please excuse my ignorance, I am talking all *around* you instead of *to* you. My name is Madame Marie Colette and I am Xavier's godmother."

"Oh wow! You guys had me going there for a minute," I said.

"That's our little game we like to play with each other," she said.

"I see, well my name is Khloe Spencer, and I am his fiancée. Has he ever mentioned me?"

"No, but that is no surprised. Xavier is a bit of a mystery to all of us. I told Julius Xavier would make a wonderful politician, maybe one better than himself."

"I'm not sure if I want to be married to a politician. Those guys…never mind. I would like to see your latest designs in bridal fashion," I said.

"Khloe do you have a particular style in mind?"

"I like several styles. I like the strapless top with the sweetheart neckline. I like gowns with rows and rows of pretty frilly ruffles. I like gowns with plenty of vavoom. I like glitz, tastefully done glitz, and that fabric the movie stars are getting, I think it's called tool—

"Tulle?"

"Yes that's it, I like it. It's very feminine, and soft, do you have any gowns with that particular fabric. I want a cathedral train and a veil to match the length of the train."

"So you are the bride of plentiful, no specific style, and willing to try anything new. I hope you are prepared to be here awhile because those styles you mentioned—they are plentiful. Our house beauties will model our floor samples for you to see."

"Thank you," I said.

We tag along behind her through an arch doorway to the actual bridal salon. White walls, pristine against dark floors, are a stark contrast to the celery green and gold etageres in the entrance, somehow they get me excited. The dresses, lined up against the wall, twinkle under the sunlight exuding through the windows. We stroll down the white runners covering the dark floors, past pillars with full length mirrors attached onto them. Every two feet I catch a glimpse of myself and see something I had not been aware of, "I am fat!"

"Yes I know."

Playfully I slap him on his shoulder, not appreciative of his honesty. We arrive at a sitting area, four white French chairs with a dark slender coffee table in between. I chose to sit in the chairs facing the stage, naturally bumping my knee against the edge of the table. Carefully I push it closer to the unoccupied chairs. I do not want to risk upsetting the vase holding white tulips the next time I get up. He sits next to me and begins to stare, at me, there's softness in his eyes, a softness that favors Marie Colette, "Why are you staring at me?"

"Because you are gleaming," he said, yanking me close.

He plants a kiss on my neck and whispers in my ear, "Everything is out of place, when I cannot see your face, it'll never be more right than with you by my side. Tonight my dear tonight, you will be my bride."

"Remember we agreed to postpone the wedding."

"I agreed to no such thing! I told you our families are already here so you cannot use them as an excuse not to marry me this weekend."

He is persistent as always. I should be equally persistent in saying no, but I don't want him to go away. Marie Colette comes and sits across from us in one of the chairs.

"Fair warning, our gowns begin at $5,000 and can run upwards of $25,000. Are you comfortable with this price range?"

"Why ask such a ridiculous question?" he asked.

"I know you are set for life. The bride's family is giving her away. They are the ones who bear the costs, in fact they should be here instead of you," she said.

"Whether or not she can afford the gown is none of your business!" he thundered.

And here I thought she was a woman of class and integrity, so much for first impressions, "My family can afford the gown of my choosing. In fact, they can afford every gown in here. Now can I see the collection?"

"Very well then, I will prepare the models. Oh before I forget, do you plan to wear white of ivory?" she asked.

She insults me again, "White, but if I see a gown I like and it comes in ivory, can I have it made in white?"

"Some of the styles are in ivory because Ms. McNeil felt that particular style was more appealing in ivory than in white. If the bride wants white she will make accommodations."

"I always felt ivory was for women who have already been married, older brides, and single mothers."

There it is again, she flashes another one of Xavier's expressions. The one he gives when you have gotten under his skin. She will learn that I can be sarcastic too.

"Give me a few minutes to gather the sample dresses and the models."

I can't believe I actually feel nervous and excited, "Calm down girl you're just trying on dresses."

"You sitting here all giddy like a school girl, talking to yourself, biting your nails, trying to calm down and *you just can't!*"

I crack a smile at him, "No I can't contain myself, every girl dreams of being a bride, of a handsome Prince Charming from a far distant land, coming to whisk her away to his castle."

"Khloe I am your Prince Charming and I'm willing to whisk you away to my magical kingdom, just jump the broom."

Marie Colette is back at our side, I see a procession of models waiting for her cue. Girl number one begins her trek down the runner.

"This is Genevieve. Genevieve is styled in the fashion of an a-line wedding gown. She comes in eggshell white and is strapless, the fabric is silk taffeta. If you look closer at the bodice you will see tiny embroidered butterflies with crystal wings. Organza hovers over a silk taffeta skirt. The organza veil flows from a tiara of crystals and can be short at your elbows or the same length as the dress. Incidentally, Genevieve has a cathedral train."

"She is very pretty," I said.

"She really looks like Cinderella, who's next?" he asked.

"Next is Rosanna, Rosanna comes in eggshell white and has a sweetheart neckline. The bodice is embroidered with pearls and sequins. The skirt has rows and rows of flowing ruffles made from chiffon leading to a chapel train. The veil is also chiffon and is attached to a tiara of pearls and crystals, and can be any length you want."

"This one is pretty too," I said.

"Who's next?" he asked.

"Next is Kara, Kara comes in white satin and has an invisible bustier, perfect for the sensual bride. This one has plenty of sequins and crystals on the bustier, covering up the bones and *important* spaces.

The skirt has a balloon effect, each layer is held in place by a crystal pendant. In the back a big bow is strategically placed just below the butt," she said.

"Very sexy," I said.

"Too sexy for a wedding, next," he said.

"Next is Marilyn, Marilyn is a slinky halter dress made with white lace. The halter is beaded and has a under slip of tulle. It comes with a short, neck length veil attached to a comb or a tiara."

"Not my style," I said.

"Not very attractive at all, totally inappropriate for a society wedding," he said.

"A small wedding," I correct him.

"Moving along, who is the next model?" he asked.

"Next is Sophia. Sophia comes in a heavy ivory silk. Double spaghetti straps and a dropped waist bodice covered in crystals, sets off this elegant yet simple ball gown skirt. Perfect for a woman who loves bling!

"She is very pretty," I said.

"I like her too, how many more do you have to show us?" he asked.

"Just three," she said, "I told you you would be here awhile."

"Yes you did, I want to see what she has next," I said.

"Maria is next. Maria is reminiscent of a flamenco dancer, she comes in eggshell white and has a thigh high split on the right side. You can't really see the split because the roses hide it pretty well. Maria is in the mermaid style, form fitting with roses tumbling at her feet. Oh yeah her back is quite low cut, actually down to her waist, sweetheart turn around so they can see the back view."

"Too sexy, I like it though," I said.

"My exact thoughts, next," he said.

"Mary is full of grace, quite virginal. The fabric is pure white chiffon. The design is simple, not very decorative at all except for the lace trimming on the edge of the bodice which smartly covers the woman's bosom. The veil also has the same lace trimming and is a chapel train."

"I like it very much, simple but chic," I said.

"It sends a very powerful message, one that I don't want sent out. Next…" he said.

"Lastly—

"We are finally at the end," he quipped.

"Don't pout! You arranged all of this!" she said.

"That is why men don't shop with their wives, you all take entirely too long to pick out one outfit," he complained.

"Did I not tell you you were not supposed to be here? Anyway, lastly is Luisa. Luisa is exquisite if I must say so, she is one of our most requested ball gowns. She was made famous by celebrity Maura Hopewell. Luisa is pure white tulle. The strapless bodice has a damask pattern. The skirt has cathedral train with an overlay of embroidered butterflies flying up to the waist. The veil is attached to a crystal tiara and comes in cathedral length."

"Now that is what I call a society wedding dress!" he barked.

"I like it. I want to try on…can you have all the models come back out?" I asked.

"Sure, ladies come back out on the runway please," she said.

All the models returned, positioning themselves arms length from each other. They are all beautiful and I know which one I want. "I want to try on Luisa, Rosanna, Sophia and Genevieve."

"Very well, follow me," she said.

To the dressing room we go, spacious with mirrors covering every wall. I focus on the circular platform in the center of the floor. The platform itself is covered with plush white carpet. Madame advises me to undress prior to standing on it. The dress maids arrive with the first gown, Genevieve, prompting me to lift my arms over my head and tuck in my tummy. I see myself in the mirror, I have been transformed. To wear a dress like this I need to make sure I am marrying the right man.

"You look absolutely beautiful," she said, "Do you love him? Are you sure you want to marry him? Will you take care of him in sickness and in health?"

"Of course I love him, and I will take care of him."

"I hope so…I hope you truly love him. He deserves the best. I am going to make sure he gets the best. Come, let's show him, get his opinion."

Neither of us spoke on the way to the waiting area. Xavier looks at me in amazement, murmuring something. He clears his throat, enabling me to understand.

"You are absolutely breathtaking."

"Do you like the dress?"

"Yes I do, your breasts are about to pop out. I'm sure they can adjust the dress to your measurements," he said.

"This dress has to be adjusted to her cup size. It has a more modest bust line, perfect for the busty woman. By the way, this style of dress is popular year round," she said.

"I like it, but I want to try on Rosanna."

Back to the dressing I go, walking ahead of her. A dress maid comes up from behind and unzips the gown. Gingerly I step out and hand it to her. As she takes it away another comes forward.

"This is Rosanna," she said.

We go through the process again. Madame explains as I am zipped up. "The ruffles make Rosanna stand out…tell me how long have the two of you been dating?"

"Three years."

"He never mentioned you."

"He never told me about you either. I guess he wanted to keep both of us a mystery, not sure why though."

"Maybe he wanted to make sure you were the *one* before he introduced you to the family."

"That's not exactly true I met his mother, Ms. Gladys."

"I see he hasn't told you about his mother."

"What about his mother?"

"Ms. Gladys is not his real mother, she is his stepmother."

"That explains why he doesn't look anything like her, what happened to his real mother?"

She stands behind me and picks the back of the dress off the floor, "Come let's see what he thinks about this one."

I can't help but feel uneasy, the feeling of I am about to be told something I don't want to hear is in the pit of my stomach. What could she possible say that would upset me so? Out in the waiting area, Xavier breaks the silence.

"I like this one too! It's more youthful, maybe a bit too youthful, looks like a prom dress."

"I like it, it's feminine, very girly girly, love the sweetheart neckline and the embroidery on the bodice."

"You are too busty for this, let me see the next one."

Back in the dressing room where the dress maids await, I asked, "Who is up next?"

"Sophia, please be careful, she's a little more delicate than the others," she said.

Two dress maids help me this time. One holds the skirt in her hands the other adjusts the straps on my arms. Once again I had to hold my breath as the zipper squeezed me tighter and tighter.

"I've been carrying him for a long time now. Hoping that one day he would find someone who would love him as he is, someone strong enough to stand by his side, strong enough to stand firm…in his family."

"He has found *that* someone, he found me."

"Don't go into the dark unless you like the dark."

What a cryptic thing to say. When I was a child, I always felt that someone was standing in the dark looking at me. I mustered the courage to scream and would scream as loud as I could from under my pillow. Mom and dad would come running, the lights would come on and it would be just the three of us, no one else. I made dad check under the bed and in the closets. He knew no one was there, but checked to satisfy me. Dad always said my imagination was running away with me. If he were here in this instance, he would say my imagination was running away with me except I know what I heard her say. Nevertheless I need clarity. "What do you mean?"

"Things…bad things…happen in the dark. My son lives in the dark, he actually likes it. Be sure that you can stand next to him…in the dark."

"I've been to his apartment, the electricity works fine. He's not sitting in the dark."

"Maybe you are the light sent to guide him out of the dark. Are you going to try on Luisa?"

She keeps talking about the dark. She is right, bad things do happen in the dark—is she saying Xavier is capable of doing bad things? She is wrong. People who do bad things are monsters, evil monsters. Xavier is not a monster, not capable of hoarding evil. I won't let her lead my imagination. I know what she is trying to do. She is trying to stop the wedding. She is the evil one, not Xavier. "Wait! Please explain what you mean. What are you trying to tell me?"

"I want you to come into his family with your eyes open, wide open."

"They are open, wide open. My vision has never been clearer."

"Then you can expect no surprises…come let's put on Luisa so we can get his opinion.

In the mirror I stand, looking at myself, Luisa is the dress for me. This is how I always envisioned myself on my wedding day.

"I think this is the best dress for you," she said, "the bodice is elegant with the damask pattern, and that tulle fabric makes you look like a princess, perfect for a society wedding. I am going to keep tradition and tell him you chose one of the other dresses, I won't say which one. I think you have seen enough dresses for the day. You're starving aren't you?"

"Yes I am. Tell me what happened to Xavier's mother?"

"She was not there because she was not strong enough to stand her ground. I let Julius force me out…I let him force me to leave my son behind. I've regretted it ever since."

"You are his mother?"

"Yes I am."

"But you told me you were his godmother."

"Because that is what he has been told."

"By who?"

"By his father."

"So he doesn't know the truth."

"No he does not."

"When will you tell him?"

"Soon, you should go, don't want to starve the bride."

I put on my pantsuit and walk with her to the sitting area.

Xavier asked, "Did you pick one?"

"Yes as a matter of fact she did," she said.

"Which one?" he asked.

"I'm not telling you which one, you'll have to wait until I walk down the aisle."

"I know which one it is, I think, come on, let's go get something to eat," he said.

The room is swirling again, "I think I should go home and get some sleep."

"Uh oh," she said.

"It's not what you think mother. We were drinking non-stop on the way up here. We went to bed very late and were up at the crack of dawn."

"You called me mother," she said.

"Yes I did…thanks Marie Colette, Mom, for all your help," he said.

A tear rolled down her cheek, "How long have you known?"

"I've known since I was ten years old, the year Gladys came to live with us. The year you were introduced as my godmother…I was angry with you for a long time. Then I grew up…I saw Dad, Julius, for the man he is…I'm not angry with you anymore."

How touching! Now this is the Xavier that I know, the very understanding patient man. He is definitely a man who can keep a secret, no matter how grave the consequences.

Marie Colette continued, "Your family—

"Don't talk about my family!"

"Very well, Khloe I will call when the dress is ready."

"I am your son! Xavier Charles Davidson, remember giving birth to me?"

"Of course I remember that day," she said.

"Will you call me? For once will you call me! Acknowledge me as your flesh and blood, not your godchild!"

67

We look at each other, unable to speak. Xavier is hurt. He's been carrying an unspoken hurt for a very long time. Only now do I see him, really see him, he needs love. His mother stands before him. I can tell she wants to embrace him. He is waiting to be embraced, why won't she? Suddenly he kicks the table over, and storms out. I run after him, there is no trace of him, he is gone. The entrance door swings forcefully back into position. He went outside. I look up and down the street, he is gone. I return to the bridal salon, she is still in the place we left here. She stands there with her head down. I quietly gather my bags.

She breaks her silence, "I will help you to the front of the store. You must be ready when he returns. He will be back, I know my son, he will not leave you alone in this big city."

A cab pulls up in front of the store, its door opens. Seems like she knows her son, he is back. He comes inside the store, seething with anger but does not speak, he just grabs my bags. Instinctively I follow him. Back in the apartment we both bypass the kitchen and head straight for the bedroom. We sit the bags inside the closet and get undress, throwing aside the clothes we are wearing. In bed we snuggle under each other. Sex is very much an after though, he is already asleep.

A stroke before midnight

The sounds of traffic blaring down below awakens me, the window is open. My pillow, Xavier's body, is still in place, warm and firm. Pleasant to my nose is he, due to his unique combination of sweat and cologne. I stare into his face, those piercing brown eyes are closed, his mouth slightly opened let's out stale air. The thrill of him, here with me is sending chills up and down my spine. I had forgotten how persistent he could be when he wants something. It's partly my fault, I told him I was ready to take the next step, ready to be married. In reality, I hadn't thought it thru. I really do want my family and friends at my wedding. Hey wait a minute! He said they are here, I wonder if mom and dad patched things up. I'm going to call them again, I need to talk.

I ease off the bed, not wanting to wake him, and quietly creep into the living room. My handbag is still on the sofa, inside is my phone. I turn on the small table lamp and curl up on the chair. I push speed dial and wait for mother's voice, she is not answering. I whisper a message, "Hello Mom how are you? Xavier says you guys are here, when you get this message call me, I love you."

I end the call and look at the time, it's eight o'clock. I'm taking my shower now so when he gets up I will be ready for whatever else he has planned.

Twenty minutes later…

"Are you done?"

"Partly, I need to brush my teeth."

"Mind if I get into the shower? We have dinner reservations tonight."

"Go ahead."

I step aside to allow him the room to squeeze pass. He has other plans. He clutches me at the waist, restricting my movements. I know what he wants, I can feel him. "Remember we decided to wait…"

"And exactly how long will I have to wait?"

"I don't know, about a month or two."

"Get the fuck out of here! You must be out of your rabbit ass mind if you think I am going to wait that long!"

"Xavier you promised."

"I'm not waiting that long! All right, I'm getting into the shower. See the water is going."

I laugh at him, he never admits defeat. Steam covers the mirror, blocking my view. I move into the bedroom there's a mirror in there. I can decide what to do about my hair. I want something simple and elegant like a chignon, but if we are going somewhere informal…I wish had more time I could braid it in sections and apply some mousse, which would give me a loose curl, maybe next time. He just turned off the shower. Through the doorway he comes with his impressive chest. He stands next to me and brushes his hair in the mirror. He doesn't have a whole lot of hair to brush, not like he used to. He's just as attractive with dread's as he is with a close cut.

"We have to get going, I don't want to be late they might give our table away. In the closet is a cocktail dress."

"I can't decide what to do with my hair."

"I like it the way it is, just brush it."

He leaves me at the mirror and walks out of the room. I hear him next door. The closet doors are opening and closing. I take his advice and brush it in its usual style, applying a little of his crème to tame the frizzes. I separate the short hairs from the long by brushing them onto my forehead. For the rest I give myself a side part and twirl the ends with the hairbrush. I remove the dress off the hangar and slip it over my head, smoothing it along my hips. Oh yeah definitely my type of dress, I guess he has been paying attention to me all along. He emerges in a brown suit and paisley tie, complimenting my sequined taupe dress. Wherever we are going tonight we will definitely be turning heads. People will think we are fashion icons.

"Ready? It's time."

The cab takes us a few short blocks, resting in front of The Seafood House, not a surprise, he loves seafood. Inside the décor is quite elegant, love the mural--plaster simulating the sea. I can see the staircase encased in glass. I guess they take you to the second floor. Not in the mood to climb all those stairs he chose a table near the mural. He dines on lobsters and oysters while I settle for the swordfish and a little steak. He persuades me to try sushi, a dish not for those who prefer thoroughly cooked food. I stick to what I know.

We hop into another cab and go a short distance, this time to a night club called the Red Cavern. It must be quite the hot spot, there is a long line waiting to get in. We have no problem getting in, the bouncer immediately recognizes him and let us in amid the jeers. Inside we walk up a flight of steps only to be met by a landing with another set of stairs. I look back at the first section of steps and count them, twelve in all. The set before us has twelve, and the next set has twelve. It must be a rooftop night club.

Turns out I was right, the night sky is visible. The club, with its decorative red walls highlighted with strobe lights, is unlike any I had seen. The place is crowded, packed like sardines actually. We push our way thru and make our way to the bar where every seat is occupied.

We decide to stay close by in case someone gets up. I look around for signs, the bathrooms are in close proximity, not an ideal place to sit, but a seat is a seat. Fifteen minutes into our arrival, a couple leaves. I claim their stools by putting my hands on the backs. Another couple is right on our heels so Xavier graciously gives up his seat. I scoot my rear onto the extra tall stool and listen to her partner thank us in a faint accent. I look up at them. Her partner is Danny, my Danny.

Xavier startles me with his question, "What would you like to drink babe?"

Here I was, moaning and groaning, missing you, worrying about disappointing you. And you are here, in my presence, with another woman, what a small world, "I guess a Long Island Tea."

The bartender comes over, Xavier place the order, "One Long Island Tea and a Heineken with a shot of rum."

The bartender leaves. Xavier turns to me, "Do you think you'll be okay while I take a leak?"

"Of course I'll be okay."

I study him as he moves across the room. When he disappears behind a door, I turn around to speak to Danny, but he speaks first.

"Khloe what are you doing here, who is that?"

"I'm here with Xavier."

"Is that him?"

"Yes."

"Is he the man you are marrying?"

"I'm not getting married, who told you I was getting married?"

He reach inside his blazer and pulls out an envelope, "This!"

He hands it to me and I open it, there are two invitations. One has a champagne glass and the other is for a wedding. I read the one for the party first:

You are cordially invited
to attend the pre-wedding festivities for

Xavier and Khloe
On Saturday, October 22, 2012 9PM
At the Red Cavern, Times Square, New York

The second invitation:

Mr. and Mrs. Gregory Spencer

invite you

to observe the midnight nuptials of their daughter

Khloe Alyssa Spencer

to

Xavier Charles Davidson

Saturday, 12 Midnight, October 22, 2012

at the

The Gardens Hotel, New York

"Where did you get these?"

"Your wedding planner sent them."

"I don't have a wedding planner."

"Well your wedding planner called me early yesterday morning and told me she was sending me these by courier."

"She, it was a woman?"

"Yes, she said her name was Xena Davidson."

"I have no idea who she is."

"Someone who knew you were going to be here."

"No one knew we were coming here."

"Oh yes they did."

I look at the woman who is with him, a gorgeous blonde laying her head on his shoulder. She is letting me know they are together, as in couple.

"Who is she?"

"Her name is Megan and she is a friend, like you are a friend."

"A friend…"

A knot forms in my stomach. I never meant anything to him. I am probably one of hundreds of *friends*.

"I am surprised you are with him—

"Why are you surprised, do you know each other?"

Xavier, the wedding planner is back, glaring at Danny. Danny does not respond to the question. Xavier is in close proximity, the men stand toe to toe. Suddenly Xavier is the first to move, he takes a step back from the bar and out into the open. He stands with his feet apart and his fist clenched, oh my god he wants to fight. Wait, he has already been in a fight, there is blood on his shirt. His face is a little swollen.

"Problem?!...You puffin up at me like you want to do something, we can do something! Right here, right now."

Danny stays put, yelling out, "Naw man, I'm just trippin that's all. Your girl, woman, wife whomever she is to you, we don't know each other. We just met tonight. I met her the same time I met you."

It is wise of him to offer an apology and then focus on Megan. Unfortunately Xavier is not buying it, he is glued on his target, I have to divert his attention, "Xavier come on, the drinks are here."

I pull him to the bar and gulp down my drink. I look at my glass, it is practically empty. A hand with swollen knuckles reach out for the shot glass, he sits the drink back on the counter and motions for the bartender. "Take these away and bring me a fresh round."

The bartender returns and he swallows the rum, ordering two more. He down those too, and chase them with the Heineken. He pulls me close and begin making out with me. "We are here for a special occasion."

"What's the occasion?" she asked.

Oh my god, this gorgeous woman has the voice of a five year old.

"Our wedding…babe didn't you tell them?" he asked.

He is back to his fun-loving self. "No I didn't. I doubt they would be interested in our lives."

I glance at Danny whose his face is red. He looks directly at us and sees Xavier hands wrapped around my waist, his mouth nibbling on my ear.

Danny downs his drink and asks, "When is the wedding?"

Do I answer him, do I dare answer him? Can I answer without an ounce of care for his feelings without revealing my own? "Tomorrow."

Xavier looks at me, totally surprised by my answer. A sly smile cracks on his face and his eyes light up.

"Actually we are getting married tonight…at midnight, we should get going, we have to get dressed. Don't want our guests wondering what happened to the bride and groom."

With smirks on our faces, we leave Danny and Megan behind and head for the stairwell.

"It feels good to have the last laugh. We must hurry, everyone is waiting for us at the hotel," he said.

"Whoa! Wait, we are *not* getting married. I just said that to annoy them."

He grips my arm and pulls me along, pushing me into a corner of the stairwell. His eyes narrow, all I can see is his pupils. In a hush tone he utters, "Annoy them? Why are you worried about annoying them? You said you didn't know them."

"I don't know them!"

"Lower your voice."

"I'll say what I want and use what tone I want when I say it!"

He let go of me and step back. He turns and walks toward the club. I rushed out of the corner, into the open. I hurried down the stairs and reach the first landing. "I guess this is the end, it should be the end, I don't know you. After all this time I don't know you, I'll flag down a cab, go back to your place, get my stuff, and catch the train home."

He spun around, en route for me. I lose my balance and fall haphazardly down the stairs, landing at the bottom. My face aches, blood oozes from my mouth. He calmly marches down the steps and stand in front of me. The tips of his shoes are inches from my face. I hear him breathing rather hard. He doesn't offer to help me nor does he ask if I am hurt. He just stands there burning holes in my head.

"ANNOY THEM! How about you *annoying* me? You have been jerking me around all day. First you want to get married then you don't. You claim to love me, but your actions are saying something else."

"You don't love me either, you just slapped me down the stairs."

"I didn't mean to make you fall. I'm sorry Khloe, I really am sorry."

"Get away from me!"

"Why so you can run to him?"

"I'm not going after him."

"You're right you are not! You are not embarrassing me in front of my family and friends. They are waiting at the hotel for a midnight wedding, and we are going to give them one."

He jerks me to my feet and pulls me forward. "Stop! My ankle, my ankle!"

"What about your ankle?"

"It hurts, it really hurts."

"Khloe we have to get going. After the wedding the doctor can have a look at your ankle."

Impatient, he drags me down the next flight accusing me of intentionally walking slow. I have to stop this, stop him, I cannot marry him. "I don't have a dress! Marie Colette said the dress will not be ready until next month."

"The dress is at the hotel. A hairstylist and a make-up artist are also there, as is your mother and father. We need to hurry up."

I didn't heed Marie Colette's warning. She kept going on and on about the darkness that dwells within her son. I should have listened to her, now he has me in a death grip. I'll play along and go through the motions until I see Mom and Dad. Why hasn't mother called me back? She usually calls me back right away. If they are here then they can stop this wedding. A cab arrives. He opens the door and shoves me inside, forcing me over. He yells the address at the driver and tells him to hurry. At the hotel he pulls me in the lobby, all the way to the concierge desks where a group of people are gathered.

"Oh Mr. Davidson, you made it. What happened to her face?"

"Gwyneth she fell down the stairs as we were leaving the Red Cavern, make her beautiful for me," he said.

"It's eleven o'clock, that gives us one hour to take her from average June to Cinderella," she said.

"Do what you can, just get her to the altar on time. I greatly appreciate it, see you in 45 minutes," he said.

Gwyneth rushes me to the bridal suite. We are greeted by applauses.

"I'm Herme and I'm taking you first, the hair takes the longest."

"Has anyone seen my mother and father?"

"No, who are they?" someone asked.

"The parents of the bride," I said.

"Oh no, we haven't seen any parental figures this evening," Hermes said, "Can you sit back in the chair please?"

"What kind of hairstyle are you giving me?"

77

"I was thinking something quick and simple, yet elegant like a chignon."

"I prefer to have my hair down with plenty of curls. You have a curling iron?"

"Sure do, don't go anywhere without them, sit in this chair."

I sat in the pink hydraulic chair and reclined back.

"Hi Khloe, I'm Sue, the make-up artist, I want to work on your face while he works on your hair. You got an ugly bruise here."

"Yes I know, I was pushed down the stairs."

"Oh, are you alright?"

"No, but I'll be alright when my Mom and Dad get here. Have you seen them?"

"Afraid not, what colors do you favor?"

"What do you recommend?"

"Brides should go with minimum makeup. You don't want to come off looking like a clown. I'll give you a smooth matte, a little eyeshadow, mascara, eyeliner and lipstick. What's your shade of lipstick?"

"Something in the bronze family, I don't wear much makeup."

"Can you tilt your head this way please?" he asked.

I let him shift my head away from her.

"If you hand me my handbag, I can show you my makeup kit."

I search inside my bag, fumbling around till I find it. I give it to her.

"Can you please tilt your head this way," he asked.

"Oh pretty shade, I have colors that will enhance this."

From the corner of my eye I see her opening her kit. The first thing she takes out is cotton balls and a white bottle.

Can you tilt your head back a little bit?" she asked.

She holds the cotton balls against the mouth of a bottle and tilt. The pungent smell is unmistakable witch hazel. Its coolness is refreshing on my face. I cannot believe he hit me. He did it before I could react. It was deliberate. His hitting me was not about annoyances, it was about me and Danny. He knows. He knows I've been seeing Danny, but how? I had been very careful, only seeing Danny when he was out of town.

"I'm done!" he said in a sing-song way.

"You finished curling my hair, that was quick," I said.

He combs the hair off my face, "The curls will hang on your shoulders. I took it off your face so the veil will fall forward over the tiara. When your man goes to kiss you he will flip the veil off your face."

"Very pretty," she said.

Marie Colette came into the room, "Yes she is very pretty. Sue are you almost done, its 11:45."

"Almost," she said.

I butted in, "Madame, have you seen my Mom and Dad?"

"No I haven't," she said.

"I'm done with make-up," she said.

"Good, it's 11:50. We have five minutes to get this dress on you and another five minutes to get you downstairs," she said.

"Wait a minute! I want to call my Mom," I said.

I open my phone and tap her number, "Mom? Mom? God where are you? I'm not leaving you another message, Xavier said you were here at the hotel, where are you?"

"The party you are trying to reach is unavailable. Please leave a message after the beep."

I slam the phone against the table and close my eyes.

"Khloe it is time to get dressed," she said.

On a day like today, my wedding day, I feel like crying and they are not tears of joy. God what have I gotten myself into? The dress falls around my shoulders. Hands pull it down around my waist.

"Can you please lift your arms," someone asked.

A pair of hands working in the back of me holds the dress together while another pair affixes the buttons. The seamstress asks me to curtsy so she can place the tiara on my head, the veil falls over my face. I open my eyes and look into the mirror. I am Cinderella on the verge of marrying Darth Vader, "We can't have a wedding without my father, someone has to give me away."

"Maybe your father is in the grand room waiting," she said.

We proceed down the marble hall. I feel like a princess being escorted to the royal palace. My entourage in front holds the doors. The ones in back carry my train. We turn the corner and walk down the grand staircase, stopping outside double white doors. I get a glimpse inside when the door man slightly opens them. It is a magnificent room, elegantly decorated and crowded with hundred of guests. I don't see my Mom or Dad. A horn blares and everyone rises to their feet. A man in a captain's uniform comes from behind and stands next to me. He places his arm around mine.

"I'm Captain Russell, I'm standing in for Greg, your Dad."

"Have you seen or heard from him?"

"Yes I did, he's not here. When Xavier called and left a message, your father asked me to stand in for him."

"Why did he not come himself?"

"You're father is in trouble, emotionally in trouble. When he gets himself together he will come and explain everything to you. I am here to give you away to an impatient groom."

The wedding march begins, something is not right, my father would never tell someone else to do his job. A woman in a blue gown stands next to me, its Tamara!

"Hi Khloe, I heard you didn't have a maid of honor so I'm here to take the position."

"How did you know I was getting married?"

"Xavier gave me an invitation."

"I want my Dad, he should be here. My Mom and Dad should be here."

"Dad couldn't be here, but he's here in spirit."

I should leave. Become the runaway bride running down Times Square. I take my arm from under his, Captain Russell repositions it, reaffirming his grip on me. It is not meant for me to get away, I am landlocked. I guess I have to accept the inevitable. I can always get a divorce later. "Tamara you should take your glasses off."

She does, and I had no idea she was very attractive, "You are beautiful Tamara, did you …what a minute, Stephanie?!"

"So are you sis."

"Sis? Stephanie, what…who…why?"

"Yes, we are sisters. Didn't Dad tell you about me?"

Stephanie walks the aisle first. Captain Russell flexes his upper arm again, forcing me to follow him. Unfamiliar guests stare at me, one of them speaks loudly, "Smile Khloe, you are supposed to be happy."

I take a second look, its Ms. Gladys. How did she get here? Who told her we were getting married in New York? My own mother and father don't come, but both of his mothers and my secretary slash friend are here. I will smile when I see Mom and Dad. We arrive at the altar, the musicians have stop playing. Xavier as handsome as ever glares at me. I guess the man next to him is his best man.

"Her father could not be here tonight and has asked me to give her away. I am giving her to you to love and cherish."

"Who are you?"

"My name is Captain Russell and I am a friend of her father."

"I don't believe you, any self respecting father would not let another man stand in for him at his daughter's wedding. I asked who are you?"

"Son, don't ruin your wedding. I will explain everything to the both of you at a later date."

Tonight is a night of many surprises, cheer up Khloe! Xavier is not a bad man, besides you are in the wrong. You made him a promise and he is making you stick to it. The Justice of Peace begins the ceremony.

"We come together this evening to join this couple in Holy Matrimony. Xavier repeat after me, with this ring—

I look at my hand, he is slipping a humongous diamond on my hand.

"…I Xavier Charles Davidson take you, Khloe Alyssa Spencer, to be my wife from this day forward, for better or worse, for richer or poorer, in sickness and in health, to love and cherish from this day forward until death do we part."

This is embarrassing I didn't buy him a ring. I don't have a wedding ring for him. The best man steps forward and hands me a diamond wedding band. He has thought of everything.

"Khloe repeat after me, With this ring I Khloe Alyssa Spencer take you, Xavier Charles Davidson, to be my husband from this day forward, for better or worse, for richer or poorer, in sickness and in health, to love and cherish from this day forward until death do we part."

"If there is anyone is against this marriage, let them speak now or forever hold their peace," said the judge.

The room is silent, except for the humming of central air. Stephanie starts coughing like crazy.

"I am not trying to stop this wedding, my throat tickles."

The guests erupt in laughter.

"I now pronounce you man and wife. You may kiss your bride," said the Judge.

"Khloe bring those luscious lips to me!"

The guests heard him and let out a roar as he flips my veil and kisses me like he had just met me, a simple peck.

The judge announces, "Introducing Mr. and Mrs. Xavier Davidson."

People rush us with their camera bulbs flashing non-stop. Mom and Dad are not here. Where are they?

It's the wee hours of Sunday morning and the reception is still going strong. Earlier the band played a little rock, rhythm and blues, and pop music covering the top hits from the last five years. Every so often they would play a couple of ballads and then the crowd would holler for dance. Xavier seems to be on cloud nine as I *should* be, but I am not. I will be on cloud nine when Mom and Dad arrive.

I don't know what kind of game Tamara or should I say Stephanie is playing, but I don't like it. She came to our company looking for a job and Dad hired her. For two years she's been pretending to be Ms. Tamara Brown, Executive Secretary, when she really was Stephanie Smith, my best friend's little sister. Why the pretense? If she needed a job I would have given her one, why pretend to be someone you are not? I should have realized that her ridiculous get up was nothing more than a disguise. And how did she get here when I did not tell her sister Kiera? What does she mean when she said, *"Did Dad tell you about me?"*

Of all the people here I only recognize Stephanie and Ms. Gladys. Everyone else is a complete stranger. Xavier has been grinning from ear to ear with his best man Reggie. We dated for three long years and I never knew he had a best friend. He never talked about him or communicated with him in my presence. As far as I know, they never visited each other. Reggie has been ogling Stephanie all night long, bad idea. Stephanie is very attractive but something is definitely wrong upstairs, Kiera said so herself. I should warn him. Then again, I should let sleeping dogs lie.

"Listen Reggie, it's obvious you want to talk to her so go do it," I said.

"I don't know about her. My man here has been saying she is inexperienced—

"How would you know she is inexperienced?" I asked.

"I said Tamara was inexperienced, I definitely was not referring to her," he said.

"I have been waiting all night for this *Tamara*," he said.

"She did not come," he said.

"Oh yes she did," I said.

"Where is she?" he asked.

"Here, Tamara is here. Tamara and Stephanie are one in the same," I said.

"What did you say?" he asked.

"I said Tamara and Stephanie or Stephanie and Tamara are the same person…"

He hesitates as if he does not believe.

"Trust me, she is. For the record Reggie, she is not inexperienced at all. Stephanie has been around the block more than once," I said.

He looks at Xavier, "I thought you said her name was Tamara?"

"See that's what's funny about her, one day she is shy introverted Tamara. The next she is bold and shiesty Stephanie, completely unreliable, definitely not trustworthy. Dad made a mistake hiring her," I said.

"I've had my share of women like that," he said, scouting the room, "who else is in here? How about the one standing next to me?"

"Go find somebody at this party before things get ugly!" he snapped.

"I know she is yours, relax! I not trying to take her away from you," he said.

"You couldn't, even if you tried," he said.

"You're that sure huh?" he asked.

"Yeah I am that sure. You are not her type," he said.

Another inference to Danny, Reggie takes Xavier's advice and leave. I see him mingling with a more sophisticated woman. Stephanie has found someone too. I am puzzled about his comment concerning Tamara, how does he know she is inexperienced? "I didn't know you were familiar with my secretary Xavier."

"I was not familiar with Tamara. The conversation she and I had on Friday afternoon was quite telling, downright creepy. Stephanie looked directly in my face and spoke to me as if she was another woman."

"How did she know we were getting married?"

"I gave her an invitation."

"Why did you do that?"

"I thought I was giving the invitation to Tamara. It was a spur of the moment thing, I felt sorry for her. I thought it would be a good idea for her to meet one of my fraternity brothers."

"Do you know she is calling me her sister?"

"She what?"

"She said she was my sister. She asked if Dad told me about her."

"Are you sisters?"

"No, I don't think so. I had a weird conversation with my mother Friday morning. She said I had siblings."

"Oh wow! Speaking of weird, you know she tried to tell me you were in Florida when I met Kiera."

"I was. All of us, best friends, were there including nuisance Brice."

"You were? I don't remember you."

"Of course not, Kiera was all that mattered to you."

"I don't want to talk about that girl."

"Neither do I, but I do want to talk to Stephanie."

I head toward her, but he tugs my arm, suddenly he smiles, and looks at me. "Babe we will talk about family stuff when we get back to Philly. You haven't told me what you thought of your ring Mrs. Davidson?"

I look at the humongous diamond. It has to be at least three carats. The wedding band has to be at least one carat, both are set in gold. "It's gorgeous! Everything is gorgeous. You made our wedding a dream come true."

"Yes I did, didn't I? Are you glad you chose me? I mean, could the Irishman pull off a fabulous wedding like this on short notice? I know we agreed on a simple wedding, but I couldn't stand the thought of a simple wedding. This is my first wedding too, and I wanted a shindig to remember!"

All of a sudden it seems as if he and I are here alone. I don't know what to say. He knew about me and Danny all this time and never said a word. I don't think I could have kept quiet if I knew he cheated on me.

"I will remember this night forever...I cheated on you and you forgave me, you still wanted to marry me...that tells me a lot about you, you are one of a kind Xavier Davidson and from this day forward I will give you the respect you deserve."

I kiss him, he doesn't kiss me back, in fact he abruptly says, "It's time we thank our guests before they start to leave."

We visited every table to share a group toast and thank the well wishers for their attendance. Many of the people are his childhood friends. Others are his present and former co-workers. My parents aren't the only ones not here. His father Congressman Julius Davidson is not here either. Ms. Gladys and Stephanie must have left early.

"Are you ready to retire Mrs. Davidson?"

"I most certainly am, I am beat."

We express our goodbyes and exit the ballroom. He informs me that he has booked the honeymoon suite. Inside the elevator he pushes the 20th floor, labeled the penthouse. Playfully we make out as the elevator travels upward. When the elevator doors open to the penthouse itself, he scoops me up and carries me across the threshold. I decide to play a fantasy game. "Milord, you are a traditionalist. I am warning you, you better hurry up and put me down before your knees buckle."

He responds in kind, "Milady, you are starting off on the wrong foot. A new wife is supposed to have confidence in her new husband. Do you not have faith in me?"

"Milord, of course I have faith in you."

"Milady I bench press 300 and you weigh nowhere near 300 pounds. However I will put you down, I have been drinking."

He lowers his arms and my feet touch the floor. I walk about the turquoise room, everything in here is turquoise, the loveseats, the drapes and the rugs. Smartly the decorator chose white antique tables and lamps with white shades. Vases and vases of Blush English Roses situated on the tables smell absolutely divine. But it is the balcony that captures my attention. I can see the New York skyline, clear into New Jersey. I would go out and take a look, but we are pretty high up, the wind would chill me to the bone.

A couple of champagne bottles linger inside a bucket sitting on a trolley. A separate trolley holds food, not really food but dessert, the top two layers of our wedding cake. I don't think I can drink or eat another drop. In fact I should sit down, my ankle is really throbbing now, I have ignored the pain all evening, I just can't take it anymore. I plop down on the turquoise loveseat and kick off my heels to rub my feet.

"Are you feet hurting Milady?"

"Not really, Milord, they are tired from my standing on them so long."

He peels off his clothes as he saunters towards me. His jacket lies on the floor as does his shirt and tie. He stands before me incredibly handsome and shirtless. He does the unthinkable, he sits at my feet.

"Let me."

He gently massages my foot, rubbing the soles with his thumbs.

"Milord you were quite handsome tonight."

"As you were Milady, tell me do you approve of our castle?"

"It's perfect Milord, the flowers, the wedding, the reception, all of it."

A red light flashes on the balcony windows, "Wonder what's going on down there?"

I pull my feet from his hands and run to the window. He comes too, unlocking the door. Just as I thought, extremely chilly, he wraps his arms around me, "Must be pretty bad, there has to be at least ten squad cars."

"There's a white car up on the sidewalk, look, there's another car in the opposite lane, can't tell exactly what color it is, it may be a black or a grey. Hope everyone is okay."

"Don't know about that, ambulance just rolled up. If we don't get inside, that ambulance might have to come and get us."

We turn around, still holding onto each other, and go back inside. We walk deep into the apartment, away from the windows, pass the sofa, stopping at the buttress near the front door. His lips travel the contour of my shoulders while his hands ease the zipper. The cool air, still present, causes me to shiver as the dress falls away from my shoulders.

He whispers, "I love you…you are my wife…forever."

I whisper back, "You are my husband…forever."

The dress falls pass my hips. His hands have made their way to my abdomen where he pinches me. He's always playing with my baby fat. They creep upward to cup the fullness of my breasts.

"You are all mine, sacred, to me. I do not want anyone touching you, kissing you, lying next to you."

I meet his desire, pressing my body into him, "From this day forward all or your desires will be met by me…starting now."

News with a twist

We lie next to each other awash in sweat. I close my eyes and think about the day's events. Our day started out with a bit of controversy, but it sure ended with a bang. I am mighty please with the results, just wish I knew the whereabouts of Mom and Dad. Dad will be sad that he didn't get the chance to do the father daughter dance. Mom will be highly upset that she did not have the opportunity to help me pick out my gown. Funny, when I think about it, we did spend quality mother and daughter time at the symposium. Why did I not perceive that it would be the last time I'd see her?

"I want some more cake."

"It was good, how did you know I liked lemon filling?"

"Don't you remember I asked you about our dream wedding cake?"

"No...sort of, what did I say?"

"You said you wanted a wedding cake with lemon filling instead of all that frosting."

"And you wanted a tower of six layers."

"We had to feed all of our guests didn't we?"

"Yes we did."

"I asked the baker who designed the cake to save the top two layers for us."

"Tradition says that the smallest layer is to be frozen until the first wedding anniversary, so make sure you do not cut it."

"How about some real food, did you like those buffalo wings and pigs in a blanket?"

"They were good, how about some of that chicken with those roasted potatoes and peas?"

"The staff left us platters on the trolley," he said, reaching over for the telephone.

I take a trip to the bathroom in search of a bathrobe and find two. I put one on and leave him on the phone with room service. He is placing an order for soft drinks and water. I can't wait for him, I am totally starving. I take the lid off the platters and look at the food, gathering a little of this and little of that. A simple bite into a wing and my stomach feels like it is in heaven. I prepare a platter for him and sit it on the side. He's here, sitting sat next to me, completely famish, he devours his platter in minutes.

"You know you took me by surprise with your dress selection. I thought for sure you were going to pick Rosanna. You kept going on and on about being "very girly" why did you guys lie to me?"

"Your mother felt it was best that you not see me in the dress before the wedding. I happen to agree."

"I am not sure if I like you being pals with my mother. Although she has operated as my godmother, there are habits of hers that I find strange. I don't want you to get too close to her."

"I haven't forgotten what she did to you, I mean she was in your life, but not like she should have been. A godmother is not a substitute for a real mother."

"Room service is here."

He answers the door, it isn't the kitchen staff with the beverages, its the police.

"We were told we could find Ms. Khloe Spencer here."

"Yes she is here. I am her husband, is something wrong?"

"Yes there is, may we come in?"

Xavier steps aside. Two big very intimidating policemen look directly at me. I didn't do anything, what do they want with me? I take a deep breath and stand up to greet them, "I'm Khloe Spencer, how may I help you?"

"I am Detective Michael Skopp and this is my partner Detective Daniel Hobart, we are from the 54th precinct. Ms. Spencer we are sorry to disturb you so early in the morning."

"What can I do for you?"

"We'd like you to answer some questions," said Detective Skopp.

"About what?" I asked.

"Are you the daughter of Gregory and Sharon Spencer?" he asked.

"Yes I am, have you seen them? I have been trying to get a hold of them all weekend, they're not in trouble are they?" I asked.

"There was a car accident downstairs in the wee hours of this morning. Did you know anything about it?" he asked.

"Yes and no, we saw the police activity downstairs from the window, but did not go down to investigate because we are on our honeymoon. Mom and Dad were supposed to attend the wedding, they never came. I have been calling Mom all day, leaving messages. She never returned my calls. I have been worried about them."

"Well we know where they are," he said, "Regrettably I have to inform you, your parents died this morning, from injuries sustained in the car accident that occurred downstairs."

I try to scream, but only air comes out. Xavier wraps his arms around me, nothing he says is coherent, nothing he does helps. I am inconsolable.

He asks them, "Are you sure, are your sure its Gregory and Sharon Spencer?"

"We traced the license plate on the vehicle. It's a rental car from an agency based in Philadelphia. The company confirmed that they rented a 2011 Cadillac CTS to a Mr. Gregory Spencer of Philadelphia."

"Mommy! Daddy! They are dead Xavier, they are dead! I knew something was wrong when she never answered the phone. God please help me, Xavier please help me!"

"I'm here baby, I'm here for you, it's going to be alright."

"We just need official confirmation from a family member," he said.

"Detectives I know her parents, I can ident—

"And you are?" he asked.

"Xavier Davidson, Khloe is my wife."

"I don't want to see them like that. I want to remember them as the beautiful couple they once were."

"Yes he can identify them for you Ms. Spencer," said Det. Skopp.

"Mrs. Davidson," Xavier corrected.

"Mrs. Davidson," said Det. Skopp.

"Can you give us a moment to get dressed?"

"Certainly," said Det. Hobart.

Xavier helps me off the sofa. He leads me to the bedroom, and sits me down on the bed. I feel him forcing my foot in the leg of a pant, my arm in the sleeves of a sweater. I can't help him, I can't help anybody. I can't bear the thought of it. I never got the chance to talk to dad. He wasn't in the office on Friday. "How could this have happened?"

"This just had to happen on our wedding day! I don't know how this all came about Khloe but I promise you, I will find out!"

I sit and wait in the morgue's lobby, my preference. I let him identify their bodies, death does not seem to bother him, but then why should it. They are not his parents, they are mine. This place is most unappealing. I remember when I was a little girl, I decided to be a daredevil and ride my bike down a hill. It wasn't a steep hill. It looked like an ordinary hill. I found out just how steep that hill was. I broke my leg and my bike. I remember the emergency room being a very busy place, with people clamoring in groups talking, nothing like this place. I have been sitting here ten minutes now, and I have yet to see any movement other than the delivery of body bags. The god awful smells around here…I don't think I will be able to erase it from my memory.

"Khloe It's not them! It's not them!"

"Really? Are you sure?"

"It's not them Khloe, I don't know who those two are, but they are not the Greg and Sharon Spencer I know!"

"How can you be so sure Xavier?"

"Khloe your mother is tall and she does not have a beauty mark by her mouth. The lady is short and quite robust."

"But if it's not them, where are they?

"I don't know baby, that lady was not your mother. That lady was not your Mom."

I begin to cry. I should be joyous but I'm not. How can I be when they are missing?

"Babe your Mom is still alive, you hear me? Your Mom is still alive!

"Where is Dad?"

"I don't know, I don't know."

"Well I suppose that is good news. It wasn't them. Where the heck are they Xavier?"

"I wish I knew Khloe, I wish I knew."

"But you said they were staying here at the hotel."

"Yes I did."

"So where are they?"

"Khloe I don't know? You don't think I did something to them do you?"

"I am not saying you did anything. I am reminding you that you told me they were staying at the hotel."

"Okay Khloe okay, I didn't actually see them."

"But you said—

"I made the reservation for them…and then I *talked* to them…on their cell phone."

"When?"

"On Friday morning."

"You didn't see them. You talked to them."

"Yes."

"How did they sound?"

"Your Mom was not happy about our getting married. She thought we were rushing things. I explained to her we had been planning this wed—

"You told her what?"

"I told her we were planning our wedding for months."

"What did you do that for?"

"So she would know that we were not rushing things. That we had thought it out, and decided we were ready."

"That explains the conversation we had at the symposium. Did you talk to my Dad?"

"I never talked with him. The day I talked with your Mom he was not with her."

"Where the heck was he?"

"I don't know."

"I knew something was wrong, I knew it! I should have said no to this whole thing when Mom and Dad did not show up."

"You couldn't back out, the arrangements were already made."

"You made these arrangements Xavier, not me! Do you realize that you may have been the last person to see or talk to them?"

Xavier Davidson

It's my time

"Damn it, go away!"

I'm yelling at a fly that has been buzzing around my ear the last ten minutes or so. Not sure how long I been asleep, the man that was seated next to me is gone. I skim the cabin, only a handful of passengers remain. The plane's interior seem smaller, my hand bangs against the overhead compartments as I signal for the stewardess. She sees me and is making her way to me. She is one gorgeous woman, blonde with brown eyes. I would bang her, but I won't, I am hopelessly in love with Khloe.

"Can I have a Heineken and a double shot of Hennessey?"

"Certainly."

I can't shake the meeting I had with Joseph Coleman. Coleman is a man my father helped land on his feet in Houston. Past favors were being called in and old Joe was reluctant to reciprocate, which made me go further than intended. But that's okay, I made sure to erase any trace of our meeting. No one will be able to identify him. Coleman is now a man who lacks skin and teeth.

"Here you are sir."

I chase the Hennessey with the Heineken and try to exchange the Coleman episode for one with my father. Hmph! My father, the famous savior of the city has a lot of pull and the people love him. Celebrity is a funny thing, a persona all its own, one that has absolutely nothing to do with who the real person. Philadelphia thinks it knows its celebrant. They do not know that he is a man hell bent on me, his son, following

98

in his footsteps. They do not know that my father promised his friend, my lifelong service.

From the moment I was born I was expected to walk the path chosen for me. A path chosen by his friend, granter of all wishes provided that you do all that he asks. I have become a man to be feared. I am known as Julius Davidson's trepidating diplomat. If I come to see you, it's not a good sign. It's best to solve any disagreements you may have had with him before I get there. My presence signifies his final answer. My presence almost always results in favorable conditions, decisions, for him.

I am tired of being that man. Khloe has thrown me a life line and I am taking it. I hope it's not too late for me...God forgive me...forgive me for what happened in Houston...forgive me for all my past sins...from this day forward I promise to walk in all your ways...have mercy heavenly father, have mercy on my soul.

I don't have to wait at the taxi stand, too many cabbies are jockeying for fares. I ask one of them, a short middle-aged man with salt and pepper hair to drive me to the apartment over on 18th Street, the hide out I use to get my head on straight. It's a simple place—one room efficiency with a bathroom and refrigerator. The only window overlooks the sparsely populated avenue. Once inside I carefully inspect the place, inside the closet and under the loveseat. I don't expect to find anyone but one never knows. What I do find is my stash, two small vials of coke. I need a hit.

I feel so much better. I'm ready to face the world, ready to face her. It's seven thirty, she should be awake by now. I'll send her some flowers, roses that are as beautiful as she is.

"Good morning Flora's Flowers."

"Good morning sir, how may we help you?"

"I need ten dozen of roses. I want two red, two yellow, two white, two orange, and two pink. Do you have them in stock?"

"Yes we do," she said.

"Good, I would like them delivered at one o'clock. The address is Spencer Foods, 11006 Roosevelt Boulevard, Philadelphia, PA 19116."

"One o'clock this afternoon?"

"That's right."

"Will you be paying by credit card?"

"I'm charging it to Senator Julius Davidson's account."

"Okay."

"The flowers are for Ms. Khloe Spencer. I have written a poem so it's essential that the cards are in order. Better yet place a note card in a bouquet of each color. Yeah that will work better, a note card in a bouquet of each color."

"Okay."

"For the red roses, it should read—red is for the lover in you...for the yellow roses, it should read—yellow is because you're warm and affectionate...pink is for your elegance and refinement...orange because of my desire...white because of your purity. The very last card should read, There is more to come, beginning at five. Are you sure you are ready to take the next step?"

"Got it!"

"Alright say it back to me."

"Red is for the lover in you, and it goes with the red roses."

"Right."

"Yellow is because we're warm and affectionate—

"That goes with the yellow roses."

"Pink is for your elegance and refinement, it goes with the pink roses. Orange because of my desire goes with the orange roses. White because of your purity goes with the white roses. The last card should read there is more to come beginning at five. Are you sure you are ready to take the next step? That last card—may we stick it in the same envelope as one of the others? I have a better suggestion, how about we put numbers on the card so she will know which ones to read first."

"That sounds good, real good."

"Anything else Mr. Davidson?"

"That's it."

"Okay these are addressed to Ms. Khloe Spencer at Spencer Foods, 11006 Roosevelt Boulevard, Philadelphia, PA 19152."

"Right."

"Thanks for being a repeat customer. We will deliver these exactly as you instructed."

"Thank you and have a good day."

I put the receiver on the base and turn on the television. Good Morning America is still on, it's early yet, ten minutes to eight. The luck of the Irish should be up and running. Daniel McGuiness, owner of the McGuiness Sports Bar, is about to hear the most unsettling news from me. Let me summon Xena, my temptress, to the forefront. She has fooled many people.

"Daniel McGuiness please?"

"This is Danny."

"Sorry to call you so early in the morning. I need to confirm your receipt of our invitation."

"What invitation?"

"The invitation to Khloe Spencer's wedding. Did you get it?"

Dead silence on the other end, "I guess you didn't know."

"No. I didn't get one. I didn't know she was getting married. Who is this?"

"You can expect it this afternoon. The messenger will bring it to the bar's address."

"Who is this?"

"My name is Xena Davidson, her wedding planner. I hope to see you there."

I smile to myself, a good performance in falsetto. I like pulling the sails from someone's wings, especially his wings. After all his dillying and dallying, sneaking and creeping, I am going to give him one last chance to be a man and claim her. If he does, I'll kill him. If she wants him, I'll kill her too. Time to call Dad, I'll probably blow new life into his otherwise dead ass, but then again, he might very well be upset when he learns I am marrying someone he hasn't had the chance to goose.

"Good morning State Senator Julius Davidson office."

It's Kiera, my ex-girlfriend, a woman I underestimated. She's quite a looker, great body, pleasing personality and unscrupulous. She knows what she wants and does not care what she does to get it. We met three years ago, down in Daytona. I was busy playing volleyball with some friends, when she and her friends kept parading back and forth. It was obvious she wanted attention. Stupid me gave it to her, and then came the rumors about her wild antics. People were whispering about her love of men with a certain amount of dollars in their bank account.

At first I didn't care, I thought it was said out of jealousy. But as a precaution I down played my own status by telling everyone my parents were hardworking retailers. She mentioned her mother owned a bakery and barely had money to send. That is when I suggested she apply for the intern position at my local politician's office. I never told her that the politician was my father. My introducing them became the water that doused our flame.

It was a big mistake on my part not to recognize my father as a man. He has faults and desires like everyone else and is not above trampling on anyone to get what he wants. I didn't think his behavior pertained to me. He wanted Kiera from the moment he saw her, even though I made a point of being openly affectionate. He gave her the job as his intern during the day. Somewhere along the way she became his bed warmer at night.

"Hello Kiera, is Julius in yet?"

"Where have you been? I haven't seen or talked to you in months."

"I've been busy, extremely busy."

"I tried calling you, but you never returned any of my calls."

"I have no need to talk to you. Where is Julius, it is very important I talk with him."

"Is something wrong?"

"What makes you ask that?"

"It's eight o'clock in the morning."

"Yes it is, what are you doing there so early?"

"He asked me to come in and help on the amendment."

"Where are the other secretaries?"

"They aren't…I mean they are busy working."

"Working as hard as you, gotcha."

"Xavier I want to talk about us."

"Obviously Julius is not around else we would not be having this conversation. Let me state something. You made the decision to end us. I granted you your wish. Nothing left to say, we are done!"

"No we are not! We are not done Xavier!"

"It is what it is Kiera. You are dreaming if you think things between us can be as they once were. I want to speak to Julius, where is he?"

"He is in the john."

"When he gets out tell him to call me."

"Wait a minute, he's back."

She transfers the call. We broke up when I discovered her at my parent's house. She doesn't want to accept it, but it is what it is. Nothing she says or does will ever change it.

"Hello Xavier."

"Hello Julius."

"How are you?"

"I'm good."

We are waiting for her to hang up, the girl loves to eavesdrop on conversations that have absolutely nothing to do with her. I guess that is how she moves up, by keeping her ear to the ground, dangerous though. One day she could overhear something that could very well be the death of her.

"Kiera, here's $50, go to the Coffee House and pick up some danishes and donuts for the other secretaries."

Smartly Julius sends her out of the office, what I am about to tell him is for his ears only.

He picks up the receiver. "Did the trip go as planned?"

"No it didn't. It ended badly."

"So I can't count on Coleman's support."

"Nope."

"Did you clean up?"

"Yeah,"

"Did you clean thoroughly?"

"Like a slave cleaning masta's house."

"What happened?"

"Coleman was cocky, he forgot who helped him get on his feet."

"How is he?"

"Cold, don't expect to see him anytime soon, enough about him, I have some good news for you."

"What is it?"

"You have to promise not to tell Kiera."

"Okay, I won't tell Kiera. What's the good news?"

"I am engaged."

"To Whom?"

"Her name is Khloe Spencer."

"I see. When did you meet her?"

"Three years ago."

"I thought you were into Kiera?"

"Once upon a time I was, along came a spider and spoiled her goods. I don't want spoiled goods."

"Not a very nice thing to say."

"I want what I want, and she is not it. She is not the one for me."

"Do I know her parents?"

"They are the family that owns Spencer Foods and the Nite-Owl Convenience Store Chain."

"I know of that company, but I don't believe I ever met them. Well when will I meet this Khloe Spencer?"

"Soon I'll bring her to dinner Monday evening."

"I won't be here on Monday. I have to go to Harrisburg, bring her to the house on Sunday."

"Sunday is not good for us, we are going away this weekend."

"I hope you are not eloping. I want to meet her first before you marry her. You guys set a date?"

This weekend, but you won't be there, "Six months from now."

"I'll get Saperstein to draw up a pre-nuptial."

"Don't need one."

"Xavier don't be stupid, let Saperstein draw up a pre-nup."

"I said I don't want one!"

"I'm not letting this woman take you to the cleaners."

"Don't worry about my finances, there will be no divorce. Besides she has her own money."

"Women always want more."

"Only by death will she and I part."

Sweeping her off her feet

It all began three years ago, the year I bought Condo Rosa. That wasn't the original name, but I chose it because of the building's pink brick. I had taken possession of my trust fund, established by my father when I was born. I spent a pretty penny for the place, and it was worth it. I chose the apartment with the most fantastic view overlooking Wissahickon Woods, the part of Fairmount Park just off Wissahickon Avenue. It was remarkable how the city's politicians set aside their differences and concentrated on revitalizing the nation's first capitol. I took advantage of the city's ten year tax abatement and began remodeling. I hired an interior decorator with an eye for attracting upscale clientele. It paid off, Philly was on the move again. The national exposure benefitted me professionally and personally.

And then she moved it. She chose the apartment on the fifth floor in Building D. Some of my windows face the interior courtyard and the entrance to her building. I will never forget the day she moved in. She didn't look glamorous. In fact she was quite dusty and dirty, normal for someone moving, but there was something about her, something magical. I knew she was the one I was waiting for. I introduced myself, as a fellow neighbor. I didn't want her to know my true identity. I wanted her to like me for me, not for my name. Little did she know she had become the new breathtaking view in my life.

I feel better now. Houston is in the past, New York is the future. I'm ready to go home, to Condo Rosa, to get ready. I want to see her. Outside is Pierre, a 1980 Volvo with almost 400,000 miles. It will take me home. It could take me to Texas. I know it can, it took me to Florida last April. I wasn't willing to deal with mass transportation back then. The last time I was on mass transit was about four or five years ago. This young girl with a huge posterior knocked my drink right in my lap. She was cordial, tried to clean up her mess, but I didn't want her help. I wanted her to get away from me and told her in terms that were not cordial.

Pierre is a car that no one would expect me, a successful man-rich man, to drive, which is precisely why I chose it. Precisely why I don't want to be seen, I will sneak into my building using my key and ride up on the service elevator. I will again shower to wash away foreign substances picked up during my travels, substances that may belong to Joseph Coleman. It won't matter, I never ever really feel clean.

My closet is quite cool if I may say so myself. I made use of this awkward wall. Semi-circular in nature and standing mid-way in the middle of the floor, it was too curvy to place furniture against it, so I had the interior decorator utilize it as a partition. She studded it with beams and deepened it about 24 inches. Then she gave it sliding doors with decorative panels. I want to wear that newly platinum suit Mr. Brooks made for me. It's a sharp suit guaranteed to impress her. Where are my Bruno Magli's? Here they are…now all I need is that tie.

"Get ready Khloe cause here I come…first let me make sure you are in the office."

"Spencer Foods."

"Khloe Spencer please."

"She's not in at the moment, care to leave a message?"

"Is this Tamara?"

"Yes it is, who's asking?"

"Her fiancé."

"Did you say fiancé?"

"Yeah Tamara I'm all caught up, can't live without her."

"This is Xavier right?"

"Yes, who else would it be?"

"Just wanted to make sure I was talking to the right person. I didn't know you guys were engaged."

"Yeah we are, actually our wedding is this weekend. Would you like an invitation?"

"Wait, you guys are getting married *this* weekend?"

"Shhh…not so loud! It's supposed to be a secret, but I am including you. Please don't tell anyone I'm bringing you an invitation. When do you expect Khloe?"

"Early afternoon, around one o'clock, Mr. Spencer hasn't said anything about a wedding. He is giving her away isn't he?"

"Yes he is supposed to, Khloe is going to need a maid of honor, care to do me the favor?"

"Of course!"

"Don't tell her I called and don't tell her about our conversation. I want to surprise her."

I close the phone and grab an invitation. Our wedding is supposed to be a secret, our secret. We both said we weren't going to make a big deal, but how could we not make a big deal? It's a life-changing event that should have some mementos. Khloe thinks we are having a small simple wedding, just me and her and a justice of the peace. Our wedding will be anything but small and simple.

I stroll into the lobby of Spencer Foods, right up to the receptionist desk. I shouldn't say receptionist, there is not even a greeter. It's more of a security desk. 9/11 has changed the way many business owners secure their establishments.

"Hello, I'm here for Khloe."

"Mmmm, huuuuny is here. You put my man to shame."

"I do what any man could do, but chooses not to. Enjoying my flowers?"

"Yes I am. She left one here to cheer me up."

"Glad they work for you, but are they working for her?"

"They took her by complete surprise. Heck ten dozen of roses would take any woman by complete surprise."

"Well I want to surprise her again and wait in her office."

"Okay, tell Tamara to let you in."

I walk on around to the executive offices. Tamara is struggling to get into Greg's office. She has too many folders in her arms.

"Here let me give you a hand."

"Hmm, hmm, hmm… you're so damn hot, simply delicious, downright fucking divine."

She is coming on to me, laying it on thick too. Why is she toying with her skirt? She's gathering it up in her hand, coyly she turns to give me a view...she wants me to see her womanly form. I haven't seen a rear that big since that klutzy girl on the train. Whoa she twerks! Her humongous rear shakes like jello. What do I say? I can't say what I am thinking, don't want to crush her gentle spirit. Movement like that suggests she does not have a gentle spirit, she is capable of lust. "Simply delicious, downright divine…"

"Did I embarrass you?"

Sweetie you are embarrassing yourself, "No…yeah…sort of."

"Sorry I never thought you would be embarrassed by something I could say."

I am not a god worthy all of this adulation, "Every now and then someone will catch me off guard, like now."

"It's nice to see a well-tailored brother act like a perfect gentleman."

What does she want from me? "Now you are really embarrassing me, calling me a perfect gentlemen. I am not a perfect man believe me, where shall I put these?"

"They go in here."

She directs me to lay them down on the table. I reach inside my blazer and pull out the white envelope. The expression on her face tells me she is upset. It is better to face rejection head on then to delay reality.

"Here's your invitation. I want you to come. Maybe you can connect with one of my frat brothers. One who does not possess as many flaws."

"Connect with one of our frat brothers? I want to connect with you! I've always wanted to connect with you, ever since we all were in Florida."

"You were there with us in Florida?"

"Yes I was there with Kiera and Khloe. I had a one piece bathing suit while they had on bikinis."

"I don't remember you or Khloe being there."

"We all had our eyes on you. Unfortunately Kiera got to you first."

"Ugh! Kiera."

"Why do you say her name like that?"

"She…I might have been better off with you, then again maybe not. All that is water under the bridge, as you can see Kiera did not win either, Khloe did. Khloe is the right woman for me."

"I can't believe you are about to become legally—

"Tamara you are a beautiful young woman. You deserve happiness, someone who will love and treasure you. That someone is *not* me."

"But it is you. I knew it the moment I laid eyes on you on the beach."

"You would have never been happy with me Tamara. I was a different man back in Florida. I was incapable of being nice or truthful to anyone let alone love them. Who I am today is due to the affect Khloe has had on me. She has shown me that love actually exists, and if I am opened to it, I could experience happiness."

"My happiness lies with you, it is the happiness snatched away by my sisters."

"True happiness is enjoyed by those in love. If you attend our wedding maybe you will find someone who will sweep you off your feet. Like Khloe swept me off my feet."

"I'll let her know you are here."

"Don't! I want to surprise her, let me wait inside her office."

"Okay."

She is hopelessly in love with me! I have known her all this time and she never hinted that she liked me. She has never flirted with me. We never even made eye contact, and now she is saying she has loved me from afar. Something is not right. I should rescind the invitation to the wedding. I cannot imagine her standing there watching me marry someone else.

While I wait I'll call Anne Marie, see how things are progressing along.

"Hello, Anne Marie please."

"Anne Marie here."

"Anne Marie, it's Xavier Davidson, how is the apartment coming along?"

"Everything is in place. I was in touch with Gwyneth Carlson over at the hotel. The room has been booked and they are working on decorations. Everything will be ready for you."

"Thanks."

"Are you nervous?"

"Yeah I am, don't tell anybody."

"It'll be our secret."

"See you around nine."

"I'll be waiting."

I end the call and begin another, this time to check on the limo.

"Jordan Chauffeurs."

"I'm checking on the status of my reservations, Davidson wedding party. I ordered a limousine for me and my fiancée to take us to New York."

"It's here and it will arrive at the address you provided."

"Thank you."

Everything is on track. In 24 hours I will have a wife. I am marrying a young black woman who is vice president of her family's company. I have met plenty of women, none of them were accomplished. I didn't choose them based on this requisite. Rather they were pleasing to gaze upon like the roses I sent. I must say the roses are quite beautiful, chosen to capture her undivided attention that was once solely mine. I shouldn't dwell on the Irishmen but I can't let it go. Not sure what's her fascination with him. It can't be his appearance, the man is thin. Maybe he's a dancer. The best dancers are of small frame. Maybe he's a better lover. Better lover or not I'm not letting her go.

I sit at her desk and survey her office. Very distinguished and on the dark side, executive furniture is always on the dark side. The door opens. It is the sun, bright and beautiful, tasty as honey. What I would give to lie next to you right now, but that's okay the opportunity will be mines tonight. I pull out a pack of cigarettes and light one of them, slowly inhaling.

"It's that good huh?"

I love the sultriness of your voice. "Not as good as you, enjoying the flowers?"

"Yes I did, why so many?"

"Did your mother ever tell you you are supposed to be grateful for the gifts you receive?"

"Yes she did."

I'm going to let this one slide. "Are you ready?"

"Ready for what?"

"What is this? Answering a question with a question, you know what I am talking about--are you ready to take the next step?"

"Sure, let's go, but first I want to touch base with Tamara, make sure she's okay."

"What's wrong with Tamara?"

"She tore out of here like a jet going up in space, something happened."

"I just saw her and everything was fine."

"How long ago was that?"

"A couple of minutes ago, she let me in here."

"How was she?"

"She was fine…how about you worry if I am okay."

Within I was on my feet and standing before her. I went for the kill thrusting my tongue into her mouth, forcing her to open it. I savor the mint flavor within. Damn! This phone always interrupts at the most inopportune times.

"Hello? Oh we'll be right down. That was the limo driver, he is downstairs. We have to get going, you can call Tamara from there."

"Limo! You said limo!"

"Yes I said limo. I want to ride in style. C'mon we gotta get going, get our show on the road. It's only two days, but I promise when we clear our calendars we will sail the world in a month."

"Sail!?"

"Yes sail, okay, fly, whatever method of travel you prefer. We can discuss that in the limo too."

In New York

The drive to New York is anything but quiet. Maroon 5 blares throughout the cabin, we sing along, and I pour glass after glass of champagne. Houston is a blur, my new life with Khloe is coming along, my plan is a quarter completed.

"Drink up sweets! This is the last day you will be known as Khloe Spencer. After tomorrow you will be Khloe Davidson."

There's a million frowns in her face, "What's wrong babe?"

"I hate tunnels."

Protectively I place my arm around her and pull her close, gently kissing her forehead. "Shouldn't be too much longer."

Turns out I was right, the cars begin to move.

"Xavier I want to talk about this weekend."

I glance at her and smile, "I'm not telling you my plan for this weekend. You will experience them one by one."

"Where will we stay?"

"That's definitely a surprise." I refill her glass with champagne, "Drink up my bride to be."

"I really can't drink another drop."

"It's a celebration, the beginning of our life together as Mr. and Mrs. Xavier Davidson."

"That's what I want to ta---

"We're almost there."

"Almost where?"

"Our home away from home."

The limo stops in front of my apartment building. I see Kurt is working this evening. Kurt's a young guy, struggling musician just starting out. I admire him for taking a job that does not have much prestige. He said the job was temporary, needed to pay his bills while his band builds up its street creds. Not too many men in his age group think that way.

"Good evening Kurt."

"Nice to see you again Mr. Davidson, welcome to Monument House, I'll get your things right up to you."

He knocks on the hood of the limo and signals the driver to pop the trunk.

"Kurt I didn't bring anything, what I brought was my lady."

He opens the car door and reaches in. I see Khloe's hand meet his. She scoots to the edge of the seat and graciously she swings her legs outward.

"Welcome to Monument House."

"Thank you," she said.

Kurt jumps ahead of us and holds the door open. I reach into my pocket and give him the usual tip of $50. I escort her into the building.

Her response is "Oh wow!"

The lobby captures her attention in the same manner as it did me when I first came here. The brown marble floors and columns, and metal laminate walls look more corporate office than an apartment lobby. The staff is beyond courteous, one of which is waiting for me at the desks. Anne Marie Palacio, the concierge slash interior decorator, jumps up from her desk and scurries to greet us.

"Xavier, you made it! How was the drive up?" she asked.

"Not bad at all," I said.

"We've made all of the arrangements you requested," she said.

Once upon a time I dated her ever so briefly, but she has not forgotten. I remove her arms from around me. "Thanks Anne Marie, this is my fiancée Khloe. Khloe this is Anne Marie Palacio, the events coordinator."

"So you're the object of this man's desire. I hope you find our arrangements satisfactory," she said.

"Please to meet you, what arrangements?" she asked.

"I already told you, you have to wait and see," I said.

Anne Marie asked, "The curiosity is getting to you isn't it?"

"Yes it is," she said.

"Well I hope it is you ever dreamed of. If you will please excuse me, I have some arrangements to make for another couple," she said.

"Thanks again Anne Marie," he said.

"You are quite welcome," she said.

I glance at Anne Marie as she walks down the hall. She walks with an air of confidence, and rightfully so. I had chosen her because of work she had done on a neighbor's birthday party and some other stuff. I turn my attention to the one standing next to me and guide her to the elevators. The doors opened as we approach. I press number eleven.

"We're on the 11th floor."

"Uh huh."

"They all know you."

"They should, I've had this place a little over two years."

The rental of this apartment was purely accidental. I was in New York meeting with a client, Michael Kokas of Kokas Entertainment. Kokas is a big time executive known for his most famous protégé Miguel, the Latin star with a huge following in Latin America and in the English speaking world. Kokas also owns Digital Vision, known for their outstanding programming in award winning video gaming. I met him at one the gaming conferences where I was representing my company AidlTaim. We were getting much deserved recognition and great publicity for a few notable games we had developed. The union formed between Kokas and myself has been one of business, legal and felonious. Maintaining this apartment has been easy and cost effective, the perfect hideout.

"Did you say you had this place for two years?"

"Yes, why are you asking?"

"When did you get it?"

"About a year after we began seeing each other. I got it for business purposes."

"Oh really, I didn't know you like New York."

"Who doesn't like New York?"

"You...I always thought you hated crowds."

Of all the opinionated..."I never told you that, where did you get that assumption?"

"You have never taken me to any event with a large gathering."

I do hate large gatherings. Crowds can be a huge advantage to me as a criminal. As a businessman I become open prey. I cannot tell her that is the reason. Here is what I will say, "That's because I wanted to focus on you with no outside interference."

"Will you be able to focus on me, solely me, this weekend in this big city?"

"Of course, but the question is will I have your attention?"

"Why wouldn't I give you my undivided attention?"

"Only you can answer that."

"I am baffled, I thought I knew you."

"After three years, if you don't...there's probably a lot I don't know about you. Just like there's a lot you don't know about me," I

119

said, with a little smile, "The beauty of it all is that you will spend your married life discovering me."

The doors open, I make a left turn and begin the trek. My apartment is at the very end of this super long corridor, I pull out my keys in preparation, ready to poke it in the lock. It turns easy and I push the door in, and hitting the light switch.

"Oh wow!"

"Is that you're only response tonight, oh wow?"

She stands in the doorway, astounded. Finally she comes in and heads straight for the double window. Quietly she said, "Oh my god the view is breathtaking."

"Yeah it is. It's what drew me to the place. I could've gotten an apartment on one of the upper floors, but chose to stay close to the ground, 9-11." I closed the door, "Care to see the rest of the place?"

She takes off her jacket and lays it on the sofa along with her purse, "You can begin the tour."

"As you can see the table is here. The galley kitchen is around the corner," she takes a look, "see it's quite small. Just a cooktop, fridge, and sink. All I can do in there is cook and wash dishes."

"Nice."

I move on to the short hall and stop at the first door, "This is a bedroom, not the master bedroom as you can tell by the twin beds."

"Nice."

I am going to get rid of those beds, she doesn't like them, I don't like them either. We don't have children. "Over here are the bathrooms, there are two rooms, one room has a bathtub, the other has a toilet, and here in front of us is the sink."

"Wonderful idea to create three areas for one bathroom."

"I think it's hilarious too, and now on to the final frontier, the room where we will be spending a lot of time, the master bedroom."

"Oh wow!"

"The wow factor again."

"I have no other words to describe it Xavier. I mean this room, it has two gorgeous views. This means we will see the sun rise and set from our bedroom window."

I sneak behind her and nibble on her ear, then pull away, reminding her and myself, "We'll have plenty of time to savor each other. We should go to bed now, tomorrow is a long day."

"What is on our agenda?"

I walk over to the closet and hang up my clothes. "You must wait and see."

"I don't have a change of clothes."

"Well you have to hang those up in the closet."

She climbs into bed wearing only her underwear and snuggles alone under her pillow, the other she adjusts under her head. I am fine with that, I must get to sleep. I need at least a couple of hours of sleep before I leave. I need to be alert for my appointments.

The sleeping pill and the champagne has taken effect. She is completely out of it. It has been hard holding my silence. About two years ago, I had the manager explain to her that the owner, which was me, neglected to have her apartment painted before she moved and would like to do so at this time. She agreed, and I had some surveillance equipment installed. It's not that I do not trust her, I do. It's the business that I do for my father that is most untrustworthy. I would die if something I did came back upon her.

Six months ago those same cameras alerted me about him. At first it looked like a strictly platonic relationship, his coming over for dinner and their comparing and contrasting business ideas. Then one night he kissed her, and she let him. It was she who led him to her bedroom. I kept my cool and told her I was going on a business trip. In reality I had stayed in my condo to watch them, her and her new boyfriend.

She should know I know her secret, and she will. First I want to play a little mind game. Where are those scissors? Oh yeah, they are in the bureau along with the package. I cut the package open and let the articles slide onto the top of the bureau. I stole these articles from her apartment and had them airmailed here. I believe it's the same one she wore one night she decided to entertain that Irish bartender. I cut the straps of her bra and cut at the midriffs. Gently I pull it away from her body and set them aside. Next I cut the panties at the hips and pull them away too. I cut the labels and discarded the rest.

Look at her, my sleeping beauty. I should put these scissors away, the urge to harm is rising to the surface. The blades dig in my hand. I am battling against it, trying to smother the animalistic side of me that takes over and drives me to do the most bizarre. I must remind myself that I am in the lead. She is here with me, not him. She is here because she loves me. I am in the lead. She is here with me, not him. She is here because she loves me. I AM IN THE LEAD. SHE IS HERE WITH ME, NOT HIM. SHE IS HERE BECAUSE SHE LOVES ME.

I have to get away from here. I have to leave right now. If I don't I might do the unthinkable. Can't stick around......I jump off the bed and run to the door, not bothering to lock it.

The fresh air has brought me back to reality. The majority of the time it works wonders, other times I am oblivious to it, like that time in Houston...I have less than ten minutes to arrive at the meeting place of associate number one. He can pretty much defend himself. The place where I am going, the meeting place, is a short distance from my apartment.

While too dark in some spots, I always stand in an area that is somewhat lit. A car drives up on the sidewalk, this might be him. At any rate I will duck behind one of the many buttresses supporting the ramp above. The car doesn't stop until it is under the underpass, a few pillars away from me. Two people get out of the car, I don't know them. They have covered their faces with dark glasses and wide brim hats. They wear dark coats, long coats and dark pants. They have even covered their hands.

"Go open the trunk."

Okay one of them is a man. From the way the second person is struggling with that bag I'd say the second person is a weak man or a woman. Most likely a woman, she is woman. The man has decided to go and help her. Whatever it is, it's still heavy for the both of them.

"Yo, give us a hand!"

"Mother fucker unload your own shit!"

Associate number one is already here. He has more than one transaction scheduled for tonight. I have been watching them struggle with this huge bag for five minutes now. It's too huge to be a duffle bag, besides its glitzy, probably a parachute shaped into a duffle bag. They finally get it out, letting it crash to the ground. The dull sound inadvertently exposes its contents, and it isn't trash. The man tells his partner to wait in the car, he or she does. The man walks forward, dragging the bag with him to the dark alcove. Who is he meeting? I move closer and listen intently, it's another Irishman.

"I was told you were in the market for girls…well I got one for you and she's quite a looker. I expect the going rate."

"I need to inspect the package first…no bruises right? Customer satisfaction is my motto."

"See for yourself…look I need to get going, do you have my money or what?"

The one in the dark hands over an envelope, at this time of the night, an envelope being swapped means one thing--money.

"You've been bringing in quality merchandise. My overseas customers love what we've been exporting."

The man returns to his car where the girl is waiting. He drives to the end of the block and turns the corner. The one in the dark begins to open his bag. Suddenly the glare of headlights appears, a squad car has turned onto the street. I jump into the shadows pressing against the wall, aligning myself perfectly with the buttress. The squad car stays for a few minutes, then leaves.

"Whew!"

Someone else is here. I hear a motor ticking and the crackling of glass. I tilt my head beyond the buttress. The squad car is back, it must have circled the block. This time it sits in the dark and all its headlights are off. Another man, this one with his hands up in the air, is speaking with them. This man is not the same one with the duffle bag, that man was shorter. He is gone and so is the duffle bag. This is not my associate.

The new guy opens the car door and slides into the back seat. Tonight's meeting is cancelled, too much activity. I will meet him another time, if at all. I look up at the sky, it is almost daybreak. The second associate is expecting me. I need to get there fast, don't want to risk Khloe waking up alone.

Marie Colette is not any associate, she is my biological mother. For some reason she walked away from me and Julius, and came back a few years later as my godmother. I have no doubt the godmother story was created by Julius to punish her, but in reality I was the one punished, deprived of natural love. The warmth provided by Gladys was an adequate substitute even though I knew she was not my mother. I am not sure when Gladys entered Julius' life, all I know is that I came home for Christmas break when I was ten and she was living in the house as Julius' new wife.

Living with Julius was very much like the Arctic, cold and distant from the rest of civilization. He sent me away to boarding school as soon as I entered first grade. He felt his boy should not be pampered by a woman, fearing I would become too dependent, too sensitive. Julius needed me, his son to be emotionless, and I was. For a long time I walked thru life doling out my share of heartache and pain, indifferent to karma. During adolescence I battled bullies and became a bully. In my teens I dove into the drug and alcohol scene sampling the latest and oldest drugs to hit the streets. When I graduated high school, I graduated in life. I was a hardcore thug with my own crew.

Despite all the trouble I caused, I was never suspended or expelled from school. School administrators were too afraid of Julius. What they did do was grumble, though not very loudly, about my behavior. Their complaints were addressed by Julius, who in turn excused it, saying I was a boy learning the ropes of life. They didn't dare adhere to their own school policy. Julius was and still is their top fundraiser. He sang their praises and became their top benefactor, making sure they got federal funding and exclusive money from those with excess.

His giving me carte blanche drove me to delve in wilder and wilder binges. I did things a young man should have no knowledge of, and I wasn't alone. Reggie and my boys were there every step of the way. I always had a bevy of young beauties from every culture, leaving a trail of broken hearts, and then came Khloe. Since she came along my emotions have interfered with my thoughts, my actions, and most importantly my job performance. Proof it was time to move into other things, positive things.

I look up at the street sign, two more blocks. I'm walking to clear my mind, reminding myself that the past belongs in the past. I promised not to confront my mother, a promise that is not hard to keep. I'm leaving it up to her. I will let her decide when the time is right. I am on her doorstep, a building not as grand as where I reside but it's suitable. I could grant her a more grandeur lifestyle, except I want to decipher the truth. I enter the stairwell and climb two sets of stairs. I push against the exit door and turn to the right, rapping lightly on the third door. She opens the door. Beautiful Mary mother of God opens the door to me, her son. When will she claim me?

"Hello Xavier, how are you?"

"I'm good."

"Is everything going according to plan?"

"Yes, things are coming along smoothly. I need some women clothing."

"I have some things here. I host private fashion parties, what do you need?"

"Undergarments and outerwear."

I pull out the labels from Khloe's lingerie and give them to her. She takes them with her to the hall closet where I see she has a bevy of suit bags. On the top shelf are shoe boxes and handbags. She searches among the suit bags.

"I have some pantsuits and some dresses. The style of the pantsuit varies—single button, double buttons, double breasted, narrow collar, wide lapels, narrow lapels, no collar, no lapels. What would you like?"

"Something trendy."

She chose a black suit bag and hangs it from the top of the door so she could free its contents.

"As you can see it's a tan suit, single button blazer with a shawl collar. The pant is straight leg, not too straight, a little flared perhaps. The pant also has a flat front, hope she doesn't have a tummy because with this type of pant she will look like she is in early pregnancy."

"She's a little overweight, maybe you can switch them with a more appropriate pant. And I also want something navy blue, it's too late in the season to wear tan, taupe, beige, whatever color you want to call it."

"I do have a navy blue suit, what color blouse would you prefer?"

"I guess white, white sets off navy blue. I also need a dress, I'm taking her out to dinner, oh yeah, lingerie, can't forget the lingerie."

She zips up the sample suit bag and hangs it in the closet with the others. She begins to search again, stopping when she came to a grey bag. She pulls it out and again, hangs it from the top. She checks the pant, takes it from the hanger and searches again. I watch her unzip and rezip every bag until she finds another pair. She takes it and holds it next to the blazer in the hall light, a perfect match. She pushes aside all the colored suit bags and focus on the clear ones.

"What color of dress?"

"What's in fashion?"

"Chocolate, winter white, and of course classic red."

"Any of them will do, she has dark hair. I don't want anything too short nor do I want anything showing too much cleavage. I want something current and classy."

"Okay I have a taupe dress with the one shoulder, it's quite chic. The circles in the dress are sequined."

"Let me see it."

She opens the suit bag and shows it to me, "I like it. Her shoes are black and flat though."

"What size shoe does she wear?"

"I guess about a size 8."

"I have a pair of taupe shoes that match this dress and a little clutch pocket book," she said reaching on the top shelf, "now all we need is the lingerie."

Into her bedroom we go, I have a seat on her bed while she rummages through a cedar chest. She glances at the labels again, comparing them to what she has in the chest. She finally decides on two packages. She hands me the items and I empty the contents onto her bed. One very lacy sexy bra and thong, the other a bustier and matching thong, the last thing I want to see.

"This is not what I had in mind, I want something more conservative, traditional."

"My are you old-fashioned, as a matter of fact I do have something traditional. I had purchased them for myself."

I glimpse the shoes and handbag while she searches. The shoes are quite hot, peep toe stiletto heels. I can see her strutting and swaying her hips, carrying this dainty purse as she enters the restaurant. I will be the envy of every man.

"I take it you will find these more suitable."

I peek the advertisement, "Now this is more like it."

I gave her $500, "Thanks for helping me out."

She took the money, "You are quite welcome. I can't wait to meet the apple of your eye."

"Tomorrow."

Before the latching of the ball and chain

The apartment is quiet, maybe she is still sleeping. She should get up, we have a very busy day.

"Khloe! Khloe are you out of bed yet?"

"Yes I am, I'll be right out!"

"I bought you some things, women's underwear. I think I got the right size."

"Xavier can you bring me a plastic bag? I need to throw something away."

"Sure!"

I find a plastic bag and bring it, barging in the bathroom, "What are you throwing away?"

"It's personal."

"Keeping secrets?"

"No, I'm throwing something personal away. Where have you been?"

"I told you I bought you some things, not sure if I got the right size, but it's the thought that counts."

"Thanks for being so thoughtful. We didn't do anything last night did we?"

I can't help but glare at her, I don't like her question. How could she not remember if we made love or not? I search her soul for truth and sense apprehension. She doesn't trust me. If she doesn't trust me why is she here? Does she love me or does she love him?

"What do you mean?"

"Did we make love?"

"We went to sleep. Don't be in there forever, I'm starting breakfast."

I storm into the galley, preheat the oven, and take ingredients from the refrigerator. Its breakfast time. I crack six eggs over a bowl, add some milk and set them aside. I need a frying pan to cook six strips of bacon. I want them crispy so I will cook them on a high flame. In a manner of minutes they are done, I chop them into bits and add them into the eggs. The whisk whips the mixture to peaks of foam. I pour the batter into four smaller frying pans and place them all in the oven.

"Yo Khloe c'mon!"

"Smells good Xavier, I didn't know you knew how to cook. Who taught you, Ms. Gladys?"

"I learned some things from her, some things from my dad…and some things from you."

"Me?! What did you learn from me?"

I want to say how to be a femme fatale, but I will say, "How to make an awesome omelet.

"So you are paying attention to me."

"I always pay attention to the people in my life. You had no clue I was observing you."

"What else did you learn from me?"

I thought back to our first date and how I instantly opened myself to her, a move that surprised me. I caught myself telling her snippets of my dark secrets. "To be more open with my feelings."

"You used to be so wound up and were never one for words either. Slowly, you began to relax…"

"I'm afraid not enough…for you. I am an introspective person, others see me as brooding. I have to confess, I usually don't let people get too close to me. You are the first in a very long time."

"Why?"

"Because I'm afraid they will disappoint me."

"Have I disappointed you?"

I do not want to answer her just yet so I fit the mitt on my hand and open the oven door. Hot air escapes as I remove the frying pans. I tilt each of them over the platter, they slide out with ease. I answer her with a lie, "No, not yet."

I collect the wheat toast I had in the bread warmer and stack them on a separate plate.

"Here give me one of them."

"I can handle this, you have a seat at the table."

I smile as I juggle the platters I have in my hand and on my forearm on the way to the table.

"The table is beautifully set."

"Yes it is, Anne Marie did a good job of picking out the china."

"She did all of this?"

"Yes she did."

"When?"

"This morning while you were sleeping, it's part of the services she provides."

"Ah yes, *I have to make arrangement for another couple.*"

"Why are you mimicking her?"

She's inspecting the omelets, purposely ignoring me. I guess she's jealous.

"You did a good job on this fluffy omelet. I see you added bits of bacon."

"Take a bite and let me know what you think."

"It's nice and fluffy, mile high, just like mine."

I watch her cut into the omelet and put a piece in her mouth. I love when she eats, the food rolls from cheek to cheek, then she swallows, followed by the sipping of her beverage.

"Tastes fantastic Xavier, will you be cooking me breakfast every morning?"

"Sometimes, we can take turns cooking the meals. Just know you'll be doing the majority of the cooking as part of your wifely duties, and speaking of wifely duties, I expect you to dress respectful at all times."

"I do dress respectful at all times."

"Oh really, you call what you had on respectful? I'm surprised you wear those types of garments to work."

"What types of garments?"

"That hideous green costume you call underwear."

"See that's what I am confused about. I don't wear stuff like that to work."

"What are you trying to say, someone dressed you?"

"Certainly not! I would know if someone was touching me. I don't know what the hell happened."

"I hope you are not insinuating that I put them on you."

"I'm not…"

She is completely duped, she has no clue what happened to her, "Hurry up and get dress. I don't want to be late for our appointment."

"There has to be some explanation for all of this. I did not have on those garments when I went to bed."

"Khloe you did, you did have them on."

"They are not the underwear that I put on yesterday morning."

"Could you please do what I asked of you? This conversation is…okay, fine. I believe you, now please go and get dressed. I bought you fresh clothing, they're in the closet, please put them on."

132

I am glad that you are all hot and bothered by the clothes. Wait till you see what I have planned next. I stand up and slide the chair out from the table. I take it and have a seat right at the hall's entrance. She's back and looks pleased.

"You look nice."

"Thank you, I'm ready. By the way you, how did you know what size to get?"

"I guessed."

I put the chair back at the table and take out my keys. She squeezes pass me and gets a head start to the elevator. I purposely lag behind to check out her frame even though I am well familiar with it. When she is near the elevators I pick up my pace and jog. The elevator doors open and I see her stepping inside. I am there before the doors close.

"Where are we going?"

"You shall see."

"I don't want any more surprises."

The nerve of her! "Neither do I."

"Well we are you taking me?"

"You shall see!"

The elevator's doors sprung wide. Not many people are here in the lobby, just the staff. I give a nod and hastily move along towards a waiting taxi. I am familiar with most of the drivers servicing the area, this one I do not recognize. I enter the cab cautiously though, observing him and his mannerisms.

"We are going to the Meatpacking District," I said.

"Exactly where in the Meatpacking District?" he asked.

"Over on 14th and 9th Street."

"I will take you."

The car pulls away from the curb and merges with the traffic. I survey the inside of the taxi, the guy has a medallion. In my eyes it doesn't mean he's a legitimate driver.

"What is your name?"

"The name is Sayeed."

"What country are you from?"

"Chicago."

"That's an American city, I said what COUNTRY?"

"Egypt."

I search the cabin again. His identification is right in front of me, Sayeed el-Mohammed, that's a nice ethnic name.

"How long have you been here?"

"Several years now, why do you ask?"

"Do you always work my neighborhood?"

"Yes."

"How come I never seen you before?"

"I work here all the time, is there a problem?"

"I know all the cab drivers who service my building."

"I have been working this area for two years now, I never seen you either."

"What's at 14th and 9th?"

Her voice reminds me she is in the cab too, "Clothes, clothes from the hottest new designers."

"Oh good, I've been wanting some new items for a long time now. Can you give me a hint about some of the designers?"

"And spoil the surprise, naw!"

The taxi pulls up to the curb, "Seven dollars."

The driver is waiting, what is he waiting for? Of course to get paid, "Aren't you supposed to let the lady out?"

Sayeed grudgingly gets out. I was going to tip him $50, but he's not worthy. I open my door and give Sayeed $10, not sticking around to see his expression.

"I want to see Avalon's."

"As if you don't already have enough technology."

"I just want to see what it looks like inside."

She leads the way into the white loft style building. It's very open, very machine like, typical electronics store. Laptops are set upon white table with stools and cushioned benches.

"Let's go upstairs."

We walk up the winding acrylic steps only to find more tables and more computers.

"Come on let's leave, they don't have anything different than they do in Philly."

"I tried to tell you."

We turn and leave to venture down 14th Street. We enter Lola's who happens to be right next door. Nothing spectacular about Lola's casual clothing--jeans, tee shirts, skirts, blouses. Khloe finds the place fascinating, buying this and that, and of course she passes the tab to me. I volunteer and pay for it.

Our next stop is a place called The Retreat. Given the circumstances, it is not my type of store. I express my thoughts, not mincing words, basically forbidding her from wearing such articles. I told her I didn't want to see them, not even in my favorite color red. When I picture her in those types of clothing I don't think about the fun I am going to have. I think about the fun she had with him.

We keep moving, silently down the street, pausing and gazing at storefronts. Normally, I would be laughing, talking, but I'm nervous, in a few hours it will all be over. We come across Xapata, a shoe store with some impressive designs. Once again Khloe becomes excited and buys herself ten pairs of shoes and their accompanying handbags. I struggle with five bags, trying to look cool and strong.

"We should take these home."

"We could, but our appointment is right down the street."

"Where are we going now?"

"Butterfly McNeil's, I want you to take a look at her bridal collection."

"Xavier I do want to marry you, but *not* right now."

"What do you mean not right now!"

"Because when I marry you, I want my family and friends to be there, and they are not here. I feel like we are hiding something dirty."

"Khloe the family is here."

"Where?"

"Our family-my parents and your parents, and our friends are all staying at The Gardens. I told them about our plans and asked them not to say anything. I wanted to surprise you."

"My Mom and Dad are here?"

"Yes, Sharon and Greg are here, they are staying at The Gardens."

"I want to see them."

"You will see them, just before the ceremony, your Mom has to help you get dressed and your Dad will give you away."

"Xavier, it is bad luck for the groom to see the bride's dress. Why do you want to help me pick out a dress?"

"I wanted to take you to someone who knows a thing or two about society weddings."

"Xavier we agreed to have a small wedding."

"It is going to be a small wedding."

"But you just mentioned a society wedding, society weddings are anything but small."

"Khloe weddings are not only about the bride, they are about the groom too…I'm not going to look at the dress, I'm just making sure you pick one, the right one."

"Don't you trust me in my choices?"

She's getting cold feet. The groom is the one who gets cold feet, not the bride. I don't like this, she coming up with all kinds of excuses. I just negated all of her excuses and she still insists, what gives Khloe?

"Of course I trust your choices."

"Then you don't need to help me choose."

"Yes I do, you need help choosing the right one."

Our appointment is with Butterfly McNeil, she specializes in wedding apparel. She is the moniker for Madame Marie Colette. Mother has been many things and she tends to excel at all of them, except motherhood. With a flair for creativity, her latest venture is that of fashion designer. She chose to have her boutique built from the ground. It was a wise decision, she attracts hundreds. As soon as we entered the building the store clerks greet us. Geek Amy McCormick in particular forcefully greets me each time she sees me.

"Welcome to Butterfly McNeil's Mr. Davidson, remember me, Amy McCormick?"

"Of course I do, you are a valued employee. I hope they appreciate you around here."

"They do, feel free to look around, and if you need assistance I'll be at the cash register."

"Amy I do need your assistance, could you let Madame Marie Colette know we are here for our appointment."

"Everyone here knows you," said Khloe.

"They should, I spend a pretty penny in this place."

"Who were you shopping for?"

"For me."

"This is a boutique for women's clothing, I don't see any men's clothing in here."

"We have men's clothing upstairs," said Amy.

Amy is still hanging around. Obviously she has heard wild stories about me, why else would she say, *"Feel free to look around,"* I'm not interested. She is not my type, not even in the dead of winter. Uh oh Khloe's jealous, she's ready to scratch Amy eyes out.

Wisely Amy recognizes the look too, "Mr. Davidson she is waiting for you. I'll go get her."

"Thanks Amy."

My mother has arrived. I see her eyeing Khloe from head to toe. Her face is unreadable, I can't tell if she approves.

"I'll take it from here Amy."

"Nice seeing you again Mr. Davidson."

Amy went back to her station.

"I know you are not the father of the bride, you're much too young. Are you her brother?" she asks.

"Actually I am the groom. My fiancée here wants to have a look at your famous bridal collection."

"The groom should not be here."

"I'm here to make sure she gets a gown."

"It is bad luck for the groom to see the dress before the ceremony."

"I don't believe in that old wives tale."

"Well I believe in it! I intend to see you get married so do not jinx it."

"We are not getting married anytime soon. I only came because he made this appointment. I have decided that since we are in the area, I can see some of your designs," said Khloe.

"I suppose there is no harm in his being here. By the way how is the Congressman?"

"Julius' never been better."

Khloe is bewildered by our conversation.

"Please excuse my ignorance; I am talking all *around* you instead of *to* you. My name is Madame Marie Colette and I am Xavier's godmother."

"You guys had me going there for a minute," she said.

"That's our little game we like to play with each other."

A game *she* likes to play, I just happen to play along.

"I see, well my name is Khloe Spencer, and I am his fiancée. Has he ever mentioned me?"

"No, but that is no surprised. Xavier is a bit of a mystery to all of us. I told Julius Xavier would make a wonderful politician, maybe one better than himself."

"I'm not sure if I want to be married to a politician. Those guys…never mind. I would like to see your latest designs in bridal fashion."

"Khloe do you have a particular style in mind?"

"I like several styles. I like the strapless look with the sweetheart neckline. I like gowns with lacy sleeves. I like gowns with rows and rows of pretty frilly ruffles. I like gowns with plenty of vavoom. I like glitz, tastefully done glitz, and that fabric the movie stars are getting, I think it's called tool—

"Tulle?"

"Yes that's it, I like it. It's very feminine, and soft, do you have any gowns with that particular fabric. I want a cathedral train and a veil to match the length of the train."

"So you are the bride of plentiful, no specific style, and willing to try anything new. I hope you are prepared to be here awhile because those styles you mentioned—they are plentiful. Our house beauties will model our floor samples for you to see."

"Thank you."

Mother excuses herself and goes into the back. Look at Khloe! She's all flustered with excitement like most brides. There is no denying, I know she wants to marry me. We follow mother into the wedding salon and walk pass a few mirrors before Khloe notices herself.

"I'm fat!"

"Yes I know."

She packs a powerful punch, but I don't flinch, I stand my ground. We have a seat in the sitting area and wait. I look at her, she is absolutely beautiful, exotic and beautiful.

"Why are you staring at me?"

"Because you are gleaming!"

I pull her into my arms and kiss her on the neck, "Everything is out of place, when I cannot see your face, it'll never be more right than with you by my side. Tonight my dear tonight, you will be my bride."

"Remember we agreed to postpone the wedding."

"I agreed to no such thing! I told you our family is already here, at the hotel. So you cannot use them as an excuse not to marry me this weekend."

Mother has returned, "Fair warning, our gowns begin at $5000 and can run upwards of $25,000. Are you comfortable with this price range?"

"Why ask such a ridiculous question?"

140

"I know you are set for life, the bride's family is giving her away. They are the one who bear the costs, in fact, they should be here instead of you."

How would you know I'm set for life? Is that why you left, because you felt I would be taken care of? "Whether or not she can afford the gown is none of your business!"

"My family can afford the gown of my choosing. In fact, they can afford every gown in here. Now can I see the collection?" she demanded.

"Very well then, I will prepare the models. Oh before I forget, do you plan to wear white or ivory?"

She doesn't like Khloe, I wonder why? She doesn't know her or know of her, how can she dislike her?

"White but if I see a gown I like and it comes in ivory, can I have it made in white?"

"Some of the styles are in ivory because Ms. McNeil felt that particular style looked better in ivory than in white. But if the bride wants white she will make accommodations."

"I always felt ivory was for women who already been married, older brides and single mothers," she smirked.

So you have a sarcastic tongue too.

"Give me a few minutes, to gather the sample dresses and the models."

Mother leaves the room. Khloe is anxious, biting her nails and muttering to herself, "Calm down girl, you're just trying on dresses!"

"Wow, you sitting here all giddy like a school girl, talking to yourself, biting your nails, trying to calm down, and *you just can't*."

"No I can't contain myself, every girl dreams of being a bride, of a handsome Prince Charming from a far distant land, coming to whisk her away to his castle."

"Khloe I am your Prince Charming and I am willing to whisk you away to my magical kingdom, just jump the broom."

The door opens and model number one appears. She is absolutely stunning.

"This is Genevieve. Genevieve is styled in the fashion of an a-line wedding gown. She comes in eggshell white and is strapless, the fabric is silk taffeta. If you look closer at the bodice you will see tiny embroidered butterflies with crystal wings. Organza hovers over a silk taffeta skirt. The organza veil flows from a tiara of crystals and can be as short at your elbows or the same length as the dress. Incidentally, Genevieve has a cathedral train."

"She is very pretty," she said.

"She really looks like Cinderella, who's next?" I asked.

"Next is Rosanna, Rosanna comes in eggshell white and has the sweetheart neckline. The bodice is embroidered with pearls and sequins. The skirt has rows and rows of flowing ruffles made from chiffon leading to a chapel train. The veil is also chiffon and is attached to a tiara of pearls and crystals, and can be any length you want."

"This one is pretty too," she said.

"Who's next?" I asked.

"Next is Kara, Kara comes in white satin and has an invisible bustier, perfect for the sensual bride. This one has plenty of sequins and crystals on the bustier, covering up the bones and important spaces. The skirt has a balloon effect, each layer is held in place by a crystal pendant. In the back a big bow is strategically placed just below the butt."

"Very sexy," she said.

"Too sexy for a wedding, next," I said.

"Next is Marilyn, Marilyn is a slinky halter dress made with white lace. The halter is beaded and has a under slip of tulle. It comes with a short, neck length veil attached to a comb or a tiara."

"Not my style," she said.

"Not very attractive at all, totally inappropriate for a society wedding," I said.

"A small wedding," she corrected me.

"Moving along, next," I said.

"Next is Sophia. Sophia comes in a heavy silk that is ivory in color. Double spaghetti straps and a dropped waist bodice covered in crystals, sets off this elegant yet simple ball gown, perfect for a woman who loves bling!"

"She is very pretty," she said.

"I like her too, how many more do you have to show us?" I asked.

"Just three," she said, "I told you you would be here awhile."

"Yes you did, I want to see what she has next," she said.

"Maria is next. Maria is reminiscent of a flamenco dancer, she is comes in eggshell white and has a thigh high split on the right leg. You can't really see the split because the roses hide it pretty well. Maria is in the mermaid style that is why she is form fitting with roses tumbling at her feet. Oh yeah her back is quite low cut, down to her waist, sweetheart turn around so they can see the back view."

"Too sexy, I like it though," she said.

"My exact thoughts, next," I said.

"Mary is full of grace, quite virginal. The fabric is pure white chiffon. The design is simple, not very decorative except for the lace trimming on the edge of the bodice which smartly covers the woman's bosom. The veil has the same lace trimming and is a chapel train."

"I like it very much, simple but chic," she said.

"It sends a very powerful message, one that I don't want sent out. Next…" I said.

"Lastly—

"We are finally at the end," I quipped.

"Don't pout! You arranged all of this!" she said.

143

"That is why men don't shop with their wives, you all take entirely too long to pick out one outfit," I complained.

"Did I not tell you you were not supposed to be here? Anyway, lastly is Luisa. Luisa is exquisite if I must say so, she is one of our most requested ball gowns. She was made famous by celebrity Maura Hopewell. Luisa is made of white tulle. The strapless bodice has a damask pattern. The skirt has cathedral train with an overlay of embroidered butterflies flying up to the waist. The veil is attached to a crystal tiara and comes in cathedral length."

"Now that is what I call a society wedding dress!" I barked.

"I like it. I want to try on…can you have all the models come back out?" she asked.

"Sure, ladies come back out on the runway please," she said.

All the models returned, independently standing. I must admit they are gorgeous girls. Surprisingly I don't get a rise, not even a little one.

"I want to try on Luisa, Rosanna, Sophia and Genevieve," she said.

"Very well, follow me," she said.

Five is my lucky number and dress number five is the dress I hope to see. Maybe I can channel her to pick number five. Naw that wouldn't work, I don't believe she is in tune with me. If she was, she would realize that I know her secret. Here she comes, oh my god she is beautiful, absolutely beautiful. "You are absolutely breathtaking."

"Do you like the dress?"

"Yes I do, your breasts are about to pop out. I'm sure they can adjust the dress to your measurements."

"This dress has to be adjusted to her cup size. It has a more modest bust line, perfect for the busty woman. By the way, this style of dress is popular year round," she said.

"I like it, but I want to try on Rosanna."

My mother picks up the train and follows Khloe to the dressing room. Which one is Rosanna? Oh yeah, the one with the embroidered sleeves. I don't know about that one, there's not enough time to make adjustments on the sleeves. Here she comes. I didn't think she could get any more beautiful, but she just did. "I like this one too! It's more youthful, maybe a bit too youthful, looks like a prom dress."

"I like it, it's feminine, very girly girly, love the sweetheart neckline and the embroidery on the bodice."

"You are too busty for this, let me see the next one."

They went into the back and returned almost as quickly as they left. Something is up, she does not have on the next gown.

"Did you pick one?"

"Yes as a matter of fact she did."

"Which one?"

"I'm not telling you which one, you'll have to wait until I walk down the aisle."

"I know which one it is, I think, come on, let's go get something to eat."

"I think I should go home and get some sleep."

Suddenly Khloe stumbles, but on what? The floor is spotless.

"Uh oh," said mother.

"It's not what you think mother. We were drinking non-stop on the way here. We went to bed very late and were up at the crack of dawn."

"You called me mother."

"Yes I did…thanks Marie Colette, Mom, for all your help."

A tear rolled down her cheek, "How long have you known?"

I know I promised not to confront her, but I'm tired of secrets. I want to know why. "I've known since I was ten years old, the year Gladys came to live with us. The year you were introduced as my godmother…I was angry with you for a long time. Then I grew up…I saw Dad for the man he is…I'm not angry with you anymore."

She continues, "Your family—

"Don't talk about my family!"

"Very well, Khloe I will call when the dress is ready."

"I am your son! Xavier Charles Davidson, remember giving birth to me?"

"Of course I remember that day."

"Will you call me? For once will you call me! Acknowledge me as your flesh and blood, not your godchild!"

We each look at the other, unable to speak, I just spilled my ugly secret. It was inevitable that I confront her. DAMN! I flip the tables over and storm out. I want to get away, get away from her. I hate how I feel, I feel like I am that needy ten years old boy who came home to a totally different world…I have to go back, I left Khloe alone with her, I have to go back.

Seems I got here in the nick of time. There she is bonding with Khloe, after treating her like dirt. No way! I grab Khloe's bags and walk out of the room, out of the building, to the curb where a cab pulls up. Smartly she joins me.

Confronting worst fears

Back in the apartment we both bypass the kitchen and head straight for the bedroom. I manage to get undress and climb into bed, Khloe snuggles under me. I have been on my feet a very long time. I can't keep my eyes open...

I am cold, so cold. I didn't know it was winter time. I don't have on a coat. Why don't I have on my coat? Every step is a struggle. I am stepping in knee deep slush, freezing slush. I didn't know it was winter time. I didn't know tunnels had snow and ice, tunnels are suppose to be dry, not necessarily warm, but dry. Where is the end? I have been walking and walking and walking, there has to be an end. Wait! I see light emitting from... a door?! That is a door! On the other side is light, maybe it's warm. I have to get there. I will freeze to death if I don't get there. The slush is too deep, my legs are cramping. **Xavier!** *Someone is calling me, who is calling me?* **Xavier! Help us!** *Who needs help?* **Khloe, help Khloe Xavier. Hurry! She wants to hurt Khloe! Please don't leave Khloe with her!**

"UGH! Where am I?"

Oh yeah, at the apartment in New York. Deep breaths man, deep breaths, it was just a nightmare. Someone was in trouble, they were asking me for help. No they were pleading for help, begging me to rescue them. And they mentioned Khloe...help Khloe...who wants to hurt Khloe? I roll over, she is gone. Her side of the bed is lukewarm. She has not been gone very long.

"Khloe!"

I jump up out of bed and poke my head out the door. I don't hear anybody. Maybe she's...I hear the water running, she's in the bathroom. I slowly open the door. She is standing over the sink with her toothbrush in her hand.

"Are you done?"

"Partly, I need to brush my teeth."

"Mind if I get in the shower? We have reservations tonight."

"Go ahead."

I undress and squeeze pass her, stopping right at her backside.

"Remember we decided to wait…"

"And exactly how long will I have to wait?"

"I don't know, a month or two."

"Get the fuck out of here! You must be out of your rabbit ass mind if you think I am going to wait that long!"

"Xavier, you promised."

"I'm not waiting that long!" In a matter of hours we will be husband and wife, and then we can get busy, real busy. "All right, I'm backing up, I'm getting in the shower. See the water is going."

I hear her laughing at me. The door opens and closes, she's gone again. She better be getting ready because surprise number two is on his way. I truly cannot wait to see their reaction. I turn off the water and return to the bedroom. She is sitting at the vanity, styling her hair.

"We have to get going, I don't want to be late they might give our table away. In the closet is a cocktail dress."

"I can't decide what to do with my hair."

"I like it the way it is just brush it."

I think I want to wear brown tonight. It'll go great with the little taupe cocktail dress I picked up from my mother's. I adjust my tie as I turn around to get a glimpse of her. How is it possible that she could be even more beautiful? "Ready? It's time."

The Seafood House's menu is mostly seafood, although there is beef and chicken. I dine on lobsters and oysters. Khloe actually musters up the nerve to try sushi, she doesn't like it and stick with what she knows—swordfish and steak. Afterwards we go dancing at the Red Caravan. As expected its crowded, packed like sardines. We dance over to the bar, someone will get up and we'll grab their seats. My plan works, I see a couple leaving. Khloe pushes ahead of me and is the first to arrive. Another couple reaches for the same seats. He's right on cue. I give my seat to his female companion while we exchange greetings. I bet she's his wife. Judging by Khloe's expression she did not know either.

"What would you like to drink babe?"

"I guess a Long Island Tea."

The bartender comes over and I place my order, "One Long Island Tea and a Heineken with a double shot of rum."

The bartender walks away. Khloe is just sitting here, trying hard to keep a stiff upper lip. "Do you think you'll be okay while I a leak?"

"Of course I'll be okay."

I push my way through the crowd to get to the exit hall. The hall, narrow and long, is a place that not only houses bathroom facilities, but hiding spots where a variety of things take place. I glimpse a man and a woman totally enthralled in passion. Clearly the man wants everybody to see he is enjoying himself. A few men pass by as I enter the bathroom. The last stall closes and I hear someone taking a leak.

"Let me handle my business," they say.

And I'm going to handle mine, I stand over the urinal. I see a dark shadow approaching, too late to react. A lightning bolt hits me on the head. He comes at me again and I duck. I catch hold of his wrist and twist it around his back. I grab a lock of hair and slam his head into the mirror over and over and over, until he is unconscious. I let go of him and he falls to the floor. I rummage thru his pocket and find his wallet. "Rory McGuiness of Philadelphia, so you are from the McGuiness clan, I guess I should get ready for round two."

I wash the blood off my face and hands and spot clean my shirt and suit. I walk back to the bar with a grin on my face and jump into their conversation. "Why are you surprise? Do you know each other?" I asked

"Of course not! I met him the same time you did," squawked Khloe.

This nut is grittin' me, "Problem?!"

Rule number one—*never take your eyes off of your opponent*. Rule number two—*invite him to the floor*. I stepped away from the bar and onto the floor. Patrons in close proximity gave me some room.

"You puffin up at me like you wanna do something, we can do something! Right here, right now!"

"Naw man, I'm just trippin' that's all. Your girl, woman, wife whomever she is to you, we don't know each other. We just met tonight. I met her the same time I met you."

Of all the…this guy is a wuss. You can poke my pussy but you become a pussy rather than duke it out. I dare you to try and knife me.

"Xavier come on, the drinks are here."

It's Khloe, I head back up to the bar and reach for the rum I had left on the corner and look at it. I put the drink back on the counter and motioned for the bartender, "Bartender take these away and bring me a fresh round."

I still have him in my cross hairs, wisely he focuses on his woman. Damn! Now I made her afraid of me. The bartender is back with my drinks. I down both shots in one swallow, followed by several gulps of beer. My anger has subsided, time to break the tension. I pull Khloe close and begin making out with her. "We're here for a special occasion."

"What's the occasion?" she asks.

Now I know you're a pussy. She looks good and all, but what man wants a woman who squeaks instead of talk? I am going to put Khloe on the spot. I want to see if she will tell him. "Our wedding…babe didn't you tell them?"

"No I didn't them. I doubt they would be interested in our lives."

You're wrong babe, look at your boyfriend. His face is all red, as is yours. I guess you love him after all. But that will not stop me from marrying you.

"When is the wedding?" he finally managed to ask.

"Tomorrow," she said.

No she didn't say what I think she said. Let me correct her right now! "Actually we are getting married tonight, at midnight…we should be going. We have to get ready, don't want our guests wondering what happened to the bride and groom."

We leave Danny and Megan behind and head for the stairs. "It feels good to have the last laugh. We must hurry, everyone is waiting for us at the hotel."

"Whoa! Wait! We're not getting married. I just said that to annoy them."

I grab her bicep and fling her into a corner of the stairwell. I don't care who sees us. I don't care if they call the police. What I care about is what she just said. I close in on her face. I want her to see me, really see me and hear me. "Annoy them? Why are you worried about annoying them? You said you didn't know them."

"I don't know them!"

"Lower your voice."

"I'll say what I want and use what tone I want when I say it!"

She is not worth it, too high maintenance! I truly don't have the time or the energy. I let go of her and walk away.

"I guess this is the end," she says, "it should be the end, I don't know you. After all this time, I don't know you, I'll flag down a cab, go back to your place get my stuff and catch the train back home."

No the fuck she didn't! I slap her, and she loses her balance on the stairs. She tumbles in slow motion like a doll falling from someone's hand. I don't care, I walk over and stare at her, fighting the urge to kick her. Instead I scream at her, "ANNOY THEM?! How about you annoying me? You have been jerking me around all day. First you want to get married, then you don't, you claim to love me…but your actions say something else."

"You don't love me either, you just slapped me down the stairs."

"I didn't mean to make you fall. I'm sorry Khloe, I really am sorry."

"Get away from me!"

"Why so you can run to him?"

"I'm not going after him."

"You're right you are not! You are not embarrassing me in front of my family and friends. They are waiting at the hotel for a midnight wedding, and we are going to give them one."

I jerk her up from the ground and began to pull her forward.

"Stop! My ankle, my ankle!"

"What about your ankle?"

"I thurts, it really hurts."

"Khloe look, we have to get going. After the wedding the doctor can have a look at your ankle."

Tears stream down her face, but I ignore them and her pleas.

"I don't have a dress. Marie Colette said the dress will not be ready till next month."

"She brought your dress to the hotel. A hairstylist and makeup artist is also there, as is your mother and father. We need to hurry up."

Outside the building I see a series of taxis drive by. We flag one down and tell him to step on it, explaining we need to be at The Gardens in ten minutes. Once there, I deliver her to the concierge desk.

"Oh Mr. Davidson, you made it. What happened to her face?"

"Gwyneth she fell down the stairs as we were leaving the Red Cavern, make her beautiful for me."

"It's eleven o'clock that gives us less than one hour to take her from average June to Cinderella."

"Do what you can, just get her to the altar on time. I greatly appreciate it, see you in 45 minutes," I said.

I hurry to the bachelor center located on the second floor, the opposite hall from the bridal suite. I glance at my watch, damn I have 45 minutes to get in it gear, my best man Reggie is probably pissed.

"Yo man where have you been? You know how particular you are, you should've been here hours ago!" Reggie barked.

"I know, I know, I know, I'm here," I jump into Mike's barber's chair, "Magic Mike work your magic!"

The clippers buzz around my ears, "You don't have too much back here."

"Yeah I know, but I want to look just as good as she does."

"You getting a shave too?"

"Yeah man I want the works!"

Mike switches the blades on the clippers. He holds them backwards and trims my hairline. The clippers tingle and sting as it cuts. As many years as I have been to the barber I never really liked it, but it's a part of grooming.

"The hair is done. Now let's get that five o'clock shadow off your face."

Mike sprays foam onto his fingertips and spreads it across my face. It's warm and spicy. He lowers the chair and tilts my head back. The straight razor in his hand comes closer and closer. I trust Mike, one of the few people whom I do trust. He wouldn't hurt me. Reggie on the other hand…

"You done man," he said raising the chair, "and you look good. Now hurry up and go get that girl before she wises up and run for the hills."

"Thanks man."

"Yo look, I am supposed to get you to your wedding on time. Let's go man, get to it!"

"What would I ever do without you Reggie?"

"Plenty."

"Excuse me then."

I go into the dressing room and look at the tuxedo on the hanger. It's your traditional tux with the tails and the cummerbund. The shirt hangs alone with the bow dangling inside. The white shirt, plain and crisply starched with the standup collar and bent tips is just the way I like it. I put them all on in less than five minutes. I look at myself in the mirror.

"Damn if I don't look good!"

Knock! Knock! Knock!

Someone is standing at the door. They have been standing there for a full minute and have yet to knock on the door. It's not Reggie, he would barge in, not stand there. I don't have my gun, of all the nights to have another fist fight. Well I'll do what I have to do. The handle turns and the door slowly creaks open. A jump boot, size 13 sticks in the doorway. I know that black and olive boot anywhere, its Reuben. Reuben is an associate of mine. We go back a number of years, when we helped each other do our share of unimaginable dirt.

Reuben scares the beejeebus out of everybody when they first encounter him. I'm not sure what happened when he was born, but something went terribly wrong. His eyes peek out through the narrowest of slits, which makes it all the more peculiar being that they recede in their sockets. To make matter worse they are about to be swallowed by chubby cheeks. All of this on an elongated face. His mother must have laid with a horse. I will greet him, carefully. He was supposed to have met me under the underpass last night, not here, and certainly not now. How did he know I was here at the hotel getting married? Could he have been the one meeting the couple with the duffle bag or the one who slid into the back seat of the mysterious patrol car?

"What kind of work do you do around here?"

"Security."

"I didn't know they hired extra security."

"I was told that a few of the guys would be retiring soon. I'm filling one of the slots. The rest of the time will be divvied up by those already on staff."

"I waited for you last night."

"Can I see your newspaper?"

"Sure."

He grabs the newspaper off my table, "How about them Temple Owls? I'd like to see them win the NCAA Championship before I die."

"I didn't know you followed the Owls."

"Yeah, I do, and the Wildcats."

"Everybody follows the Wildcats…it's doubtful. Temple doesn't have enough talented players. Those kids play their hearts out though. "Why you take this job?"

"I needed an extra job to help pay the bills. Since my wife died I've been struggling with hospital bills so I took this pet project. If it pans out I'm set for life."

"If that is what I saw last night, I hope it works out for you."

"Depends on what you saw."

"A deal go down…cops…"

"What cops?"

"The ones who came, left, and returned. The second time they talked with…"

"Wasn't me."

"I don't know who it was, really did not stick around to figure it out either."

"I gotta a couple of runs to make and you should be getting downstairs. We'll see each other again."

I let him leave first. I know why he came here, he came for me. I don't have time to figure out who sent him, he better not hurt Khloe. I'll wait a few minutes.

Knock! Knock! Reggie barges in, "Yo man who was that weird looking dude?"

"Security."

"Security? They hire anybody these days. What happened to hiring people with some class?"

"I don't know, guess it fell to the way side like everything else."

"You ready man? Scared? Last chance at freedom before you become officially tied to the ball and chain. Sike! She is one woman I would *love* to be tied to."

"You can tie yourself to Tamara?"

"Who's that?"

"I'll show you."

Reggie holds the door open. I continue to talk as we walk, "Since when do you want to be tied to anything?"

"I don't."

We both laugh.

"Xavier man, all the boys are here. I saw your Mom, where's your old man?"

"He's probably dipping in something warm and moist."

"Forever the player, he wasn't at your high school graduation, at the college graduation, now he's not at the wedding? Who needs him?"

"I do."

I hate being needy of my father's attention. Both of my parents are alive and well, here tonight, and yet I feel they are absent from my life. We step into reception room. Red and white rose petals cover the mocha carpet while tea lights light the aisle all the way to the altar. And the altar, it's covered with a silk taupe and tulle canopy. The tables have a crème tablecloth, bouquets of white roses act as centerpieces.

"I must tip Gwyneth. She did a fantastic job on such short notice."

"So we are not the last ones to learn about this wedding."

"Actually we decided to get marry two weeks ago."

"What's the rush? I know you not letting a bun in the oven push you to the altar."

"There's nothing brewing in her oven, better not be!"

"Relax man...chill! Where is the ring?"

Ring? Ring! "Here in my pocket, I forgot to give it to you."

"Oooweeeee! This must be at least three carats!"

"Yeah it is, don't lose it!"

Our walk down the aisle is met with applause and rabble rousing from my fraternity brothers. The boys will always be boys. Ahead I see the Justice of Peace and Gwyneth who is motioning for me to hurry. She places me in my position at the altar. I glimpse into the door way and see her, Khloe is there. The wedding march begins, the audience rises to their feet.

"Stephanie?!"

"Who's Stephanie?"

"Kiera's little sister, who invited her?"

"I don't know, she looks nice though."

"The last thing I need is my ex-girlfriend's family at my wedding."

157

"I would say you are being set up. Does Khloe have a maid of honor?"

"No, this was supposed to be a small event."

"Well now Khloe has one, don't worry about Stephanie. I'll get her if she steps out of line."

"YES!"

"Yes what?"

"She's beautiful."

"I wouldn't go so far as to say she is beautiful, cute is more like it."

"Not her! Khloe, Khloe is beautiful."

"I already know that."

"No, really she is beautiful."

She is the flower that is blooming among the dead in my life and I had the nerve to hit her. She is upset, rightfully so. I never meant to hit you, to make you afraid of me. I see you love me, you are here. Ready and willing to marry me, I will never put my hands on you again, regardless of the circumstances.

"Yeah and she's all yours."

"Who's that walking her down the aisle?"

"Her Dad."

"That's not her Dad."

No wonder she looks upset, a stranger walks beside her. This character is straight out of the fairytale, he is a Captain from the Marine Corps.

"Her father could not be here tonight and has asked me to give her away. I am giving her to you to love and cherish."

"Who are you?"

"My name is Captain Russell, I am a friend of her father."

"I don't believe you, any self respecting father would not let another man stand in for him at his daughter's wedding. I asked who are you?"

"Son, don't ruin your wedding. I will explain everything to the both of you at a later date."

She looks like a lost puppy on the verge of tears. I face Khloe and mouthed, *"I promise to get to the bottom of this."*

The Justice of the Peace begins, "We come together to join this couple in Holy Matrimony. Xavier please repeat after me. With this ring..."

Reggie hands me her rings, "I, Xavier Charles Davidson, take you, Khloe Alyssa Spencer, to be my wife from this day forward. For better or worse, for richer or poorer, in sickness and health, to love and cherish from this day forward until death do we part."

Whew! Almost done!

The Justice of Peace then looks at Khloe, Reggie hands her my ring, "Please repeat after me. With this ring, I Khloe Alyssa Spencer, take you, Xavier Charles Davidson, to be my husband from this day forward. For better or worse, for richer or poorer, in sickness and in health, to love and cherish from this day forward till death do we part."

She said it! She committed to me!!!

"If there be anyone against this marriage, let them speak now or forever hold their peace."

Total silence in the room, nobody better not try to stop this wedding...of course she would, that's why she came. Stephanie is full of it. She's been hacking for a full minute now, pretending to have a cold.

"I'm not trying to stop this wedding, my throat tickles."

You better act like you know.

"I now pronounce you man and wife. You may kiss your bride."

"Khloe bring those luscious lips to me!"

I guess they heard what I said, I hear laughter. I flip her veil and kiss her softly, almost like a peck. The crowd erupts again.

The judge announces, "Introducing Mr and Mrs. Xavier Davidson."

People rush up to us with their cameras, bulbs flashing non-stop as if we were a celebrity couple.

Honeymoon bliss

It's Sunday morning, 2AM and the reception is still going strong. Khloe is happy, very happy. That sick puppy dog look is long gone, for a second I thought she was having second thoughts. But she didn't, she said I do, she is standing right next to me. My plan for Tamara has fallen through, she never came. Reggie has been bending my ear all night long about Stephanie. He likes what he sees, I must warn him.

"Listen Reggie, it's obvious you want to talk to her so go do it," said Khloe.

"I don't know about her. My man here has been saying she is inexperienced—

"How would you know she is inexperienced?" she asked.

"I said Tamara was inexperienced, I definitely was not referring to her."

"I have been waiting all night for this Tamara," he said.

"She did not come," I said.

"Oh yes she did," she said.

"Where is she?" I asked.

"Here, Tamara is here. Tamara and Stephanie are one in the same," she said.

"What did you say?" I asked.

"I said Tamara and Stephanie or Stephanie and Tamara are the same person…"

I ponder what she just said.

"Trust me, she is. For the record Reggie, she is not inexperienced at all, Stephanie has been around the block more than once," she said.

Reggie looks at me, "I thought you said her name was Tamara?"

"See that's what's so funny about her, one day she is shy introverted Tamara. The next she is bold and shiesty Stephanie, completely unreliable, definitely not trustworthy, Dad made a mistake hiring her," she lambasted.

"I've had my share of women like that," he said. I see him scouring the room, "who else is in here? How about the one standing right next to me?"

"Go find somebody at this party before things get ugly here!" I snapped.

"I know she is yours, relax! I not trying to take her away from you," he said.

"You couldn't, even if you tried," I said.

"You're that sure huh?" he asked.

"Yeah I am that sure. You are not her type," I said.

Reggie takes my advice and leaves. I see him mingling with a more sophisticated woman. Stephanie has found someone too.

"I didn't know you were familiar with my secretary Xavier?"

"I was not familiar with Tamara. The conversation she and I had on Friday afternoon is quite telling, downright creepy. Stephanie looked directly in my face and spoke to me as if she was another woman."

"How did she know we were getting married?"

"I gave her an invitation."

"Why did you do that?"

"I thought I was giving the invitation to Tamara. It was a spur of the moment thing, I felt sorry for her. I thought it would be a good idea for her to meet one of my fraternity brothers."

"Do you know she is calling me her sister?"

"She what?"

"She said she was my sister. She asked if Dad told me about her."

"Are you sisters?"

"No, I don't think so. I had a weird conversation with my mother Friday morning. She said I had siblings."

"Oh wow! Speaking of weird, you know she tried to tell me you were in Florida when I met Kiera."

"I was. All of us, best friends, were there including nuisance Brice."

"You were? I don't remember you."

"Of course not, Kiera was all that mattered to you."

"I don't want to talk about that girl."

"Neither do I, but I do want to talk to Stephanie."

"Babe we will talk about family stuff when we get back to Philly. You haven't told me what you thought of your ring Mrs. Davidson?"

She looks at her hand. I knew the ring would have that affect on her. A wedding set like the one I chose for her would affect any woman, she is blushing.

"It's gorgeous! Everything is gorgeous. You made our wedding a dream come true."

"Yes I did, didn't I? Are you glad you chose me? I mean, could the Irishman pull off a fabulous wedding like this on short notice? I know we agreed on a simple wedding, but I couldn't stand the thought of a simple wedding. This is my first wedding too, and I wanted a shindig to remember."

"I will remember this night forever...I cheated on you and you forgave me. You still wanted to marry me...that speaks volumes, you are one of a kind Xavier Davidson and from this day forward I will give you the respect you deserve."

So she admits it. I didn't think she would admit it. She kisses me like I am the last man on earth, but I can't reciprocate, not right now.

"It's time we meet and greet our wedding guests one last time before they start to leave."

Khloe and I visited each table to share a toast, and to thank well wishers for their attendance. Many are childhood friends and former co-workers, past and present. After all the gifts I have given at weddings, baby showers, graduations, and weddings, I better get some pretty nifty things. By the time we made it to the last table we were tired and decided to leave.

"Are you ready to retire Mrs. Davidson?"

"I most certainly am, I am beat."

Thankfully we don't have to travel far, the honeymoon suite upstairs. Inside the elevator we make out as we travel to the 20th floor. The doors open and I scoop her up to carry her across the threshold.

"Milord, you are a traditionalist. I am warning you, you better hurry up and put me down before your knees buckle."

She speaks with an air of Old English, it's kind of sexy. I will respond in kind.

"Milady, you are starting off on the wrong foot. A new wife is supposed to have confidence in her new husband. Do you not have faith in me?"

"Milord, of course I have faith in you."

"Milady I bench press 300 and you weigh nowhere near 300 pounds. However I will put you down, I have been drinking."

I lower my arms and let her feet touch the floor. She walks about the turquoise room, I have impressed her. She wanders the room in awe of the roses, the buffet, and the New York skyline. Finally she sits down on a sofa and takes off her shoes to rub her feet.

"Are you feet hurting Milady?"

"Not really, Milord, they are tired from my standing on them so long."

I let my jacket and shirt fall to the floor as I move toward her. I sit down on the floor and take hold of her foot.

"Let me."

I gently massage it, using my thumbs on the soles.

"Milord you were quite handsome tonight."

"As you were Milady, tell me do you approve of our castle?"

"It's perfect Milord, the flowers, the wedding, the reception, all of it."

A red light flashing on the window captures her attention. She jumps up out of the chair to look, "Wonder what's going on down there?"

I rise to my feet and unlock the patio doors for her. The cool autumn air chills to the bone. I hover behind her and look below. "Must be pretty bad, there has to be at least ten squad cars."

"There's a white car up on the sidewalk. Look, there's another car in the opposite lane. Can't tell what color it is, grey or a black…hope everyone is okay."

"Don't know about that, the ambulance just rolled up. If we don't get inside that ambulance might have to come and get us."

We go back inside, still holding on to each other. I push her away from the windows, pass the sofa, almost to the front door, against a buttress. I kiss her shoulders, soft and silky like rose petals. Her skin is always petal soft. My hands eases the zipper of her dress, it falls away from her body all on its own. I am elated, Milady is where she is supposed to be, here with me. I cannot contain my happiness, I must tell her.

"I love you…you are my wife…forever."

"You are my husband…forever."

My hands make their way to her abdomen and pinch an ounce or two of fat. I love her fat, it's a sign she's healthy. They creep upward to cup the fullness of her breasts.

"You are all mine…sacred…to me. I do not want anyone touching you…kissing you…lying next to you."

She meets my desire, pressing her body into mine.

"From this day forward all or your desires will be met by me…starting now."

We lie next to each other completely exhausted and profusely sweaty. I close my eyes and think about the wedding. It went off without a hitch. The Irishman did not interrupt neither did Reuben. Her parents, I don't know what to say about them.

"I want some more cake."

"It was good, how did you know I liked lemon filling?"

"Don't you remember I asked you about our dream wedding cake?"

"No, sort of, what did I say?"

"You said you wanted a wedding cake with lemon filling in between instead of all that frosting."

"And you wanted a tower of six layers."

"We had to feed all of our guests didn't we?"

"Yes we did."

"I asked the baker who designed the cake to send up the top two layers for us."

"Tradition says that the smallest layer is to be frozen until the first wedding anniversary, so make sure you don't cut it."

"Sure will, how about some real food like some buffalo wings, pigs in a blanket…"

"That'll be good, how about some of that chicken with those roasted potatoes and peas."

"The staff left us platters on the trolley. We need some drinks, I'll call room service."

I reach for the telephone while she leaves the room. We need hydration, plenty of hydration. We need to flush our kidneys, too much alcohol. We have been drinking alcohol non-stop since our arrival.

"Room Service."

"This is the Davidson party in Honeymoon Suite Four. We would like some bottle water and a couple of cokes."

"Will that be all sir?"

"Yes."

"We shall be there shortly."

"Thank you."

I get my bathrobe from the bathroom and join her. Completely starved, I devoured a platter in minutes. I reach for another, taking my time to eat it. It has been awhile since I have been that exhilarated by sex, perhaps because, in a weird way it is new. When she was walking down the aisle she looked like a new creature, her blemishes disappeared and she became flawless.

"You know you took me by surprise with your dress selection. I thought for sure you were going to pick Rosanna. You kept going on and on about being "very girly" why did you guys lie to me?"

"Your mother felt it was best that you not see me in the dress before the wedding. I agreed."

"I am not sure if I like you being pals with my mother. I don't want you to get too close to her."

"I have forgotten what she did to you, I mean she was in your life, but not like she should have been. A godmother is not a substitute for a real mother."

Her words cut like a knife, she means well, but just the same they hurt. Reality always hurts.

"Room service is here."

"I'll get the door, give me a minute."

I rise from the table and hurry to the bedroom to gather my pants. I answer the door, it's not the kitchen staff with a trolley, it's the police. I guess NYPD has demanded that their finest become power lifters.

"We were told we could find Ms. Khloe Spencer here."

"Yes she is here. I am her husband, is something wrong?"

"Yes there is, may we come in?"

I step aside and breathe easy. They do not want me, but what do they want with her?

"I'm Khloe Spencer, how may I help you?"

"I am Detective Michael Skopp and this is my partner Detective Daniel Hobart, we are from the 54th precinct. Ms. Spencer we are sorry to disturb you so early in the morning."

"What can I do for you?"

"We'd like you to answer some questions," said Detective Skopp.

"About what?" Xavier asked.

"Are you the daughter of Gregory and Sharon Spencer?" he asked.

"Yes I am. Have you seen them? I have been trying to get a hold of them all weekend, they're not in trouble are they?" she asks.

"There was a car accident downstairs in the wee hours of this morning. Did you know anything about it?" asked Det. Skopp.

"Yes and no, we saw the police activity downstairs from the balcony but did not go down to investigate because we are on our honeymoon. Mom and Dad were supposed to attend the wedding, they never came. I have been calling Mom all day, leaving messages. She never returned my calls. I have been wondering about their whereabouts."

"Well we know where they are," said Det. Hobart, "Regrettably I have to inform you, your parents died this morning, from injuries sustained in the car accident that occurred downstairs."

Khloe screams, she is screaming at the top of her lungs. I wrap my arms around her and try to quiet her, to comfort her, what I am saying is falling on deaf ears. I turn to the detectives.

"Are you sure, are your sure its Gregory and Sharon Spencer?"

"We traced the license plate on the vehicle. It's a rental car from an agency based in Philadelphia. The company confirmed that they rented a 2011 Cadillac CTS to a Mr. Gregory Spencer of Philadelphia."

"Mommy! Daddy! They are dead Xavier, they are dead! I knew something was wrong when she never answered the phone. God please help me, Xavier please help me!"

"I'm here baby, I'm here for you, it's going to be alright."

"We just need official confirmation from a family member," he said.

"Detectives I know her parents, I can ident—

"And you are?" he asked.

"Xavier Davidson, Khloe is my wife."

"I don't want to see them like that. I want to remember them as the beautiful couple they once were."

"Yes he can identify them for you Ms. Spencer," said Det. Skopp.

"Mrs. Davidson," Xavier corrected.

"Mrs. Davidson," said Det. Skopp.

"Can you give us a moment to get dressed?"

"Certainly," said Det. Hobart.

I help her get up off the sofa and take her to the bedroom where I sit her down on the bed. I squeeze her feet into her shoes and try to ignore her wailing. They slip on her feet, and I get her clothes on. I leave her on the bed and get dress myself. She is completely devastated.

"I can't bear the thought of it. I never got the chance to talk to Dad Xavier, he wasn't in the office on Friday. How could this have happened?"

"This just had to happen on our wedding day! I don't know how this all came about Khloe but I promise you, I will find out!"

Down at the morgue, I go in by myself. I don't know what is going on. Those two detectives show up at our hotel room with a bullshitting story about her dead parents. Greg and Sharon are anything but dead and they did not rent a car. Someone has assumed their identity.

The medical examiner opens a square door, one of many, in a wall. He pulls out the slab that does not extend very far. I look into the face of the deceased woman. She looks peaceful. Her lips are already blue as are her eyelids. I try to envision a smile, probably quite beautifully set off by the beauty mark an inch below the left corner of her mouth.

"It's not her. This is not Sharon Spencer. She is tall and she does not have any beauty marks on her face."

"I wonder who she is," said the medical examiner.

"I don't know, but she is not my mother-in-law. Can I look at the man that was brought in with her?"

"What man? There was no man, she was brought in alone!"

"The detective told us Gregory and Sharon Spencer was killed in a car accident. They said they were in a rental car. That is how they were able to track us down."

"Well this woman was killed in a car accident, but she was alone."

"Did she have any ID, a pocket book?"

The medical examiner looks at his chart, "Come to think of it she did have a pocket book and she had identification. The detectives have it. Since you are saying this is not her, they will definitely be talking to you."

The medical examiner pushes the slab back into the vault. Something is not right. Those two detectives said a man and a woman died in the accident. The coroner said he received the body of a woman, no man was with her. I need to talk with those detectives, find out what happened to the man they said died in the accident. I will ask the medical examiner while he is here, I don't want to upset Khloe any more than I have to.

"Excuse me, the two officers handling this case, Detectives Hobart and Skopp, what precinct are they from?"

"They are not the detectives handling this case. Detectives Cruz and Williams are handling this case. They are from Mid-Town precinct."

"Thank you."

I walk away, replaying everything he just said and what those detectives said to us earlier. If they are not NYPD, who are they? Who sent them? Who is checking me out? I don't like this. They know I have a wife. I don't like this at all. It's time to go back to Philly. I compose myself and act as if I am totally elated. I run out to the waiting area. "Khloe It's not them! It's not them!"

"Really? Are you sure?"

"It's not them Khloe, I don't know who those two are, but they are not the Greg and Sharon Spencer I know!"

"How can you be so sure Xavier?"

"Khloe your mother is tall and she does not have a beauty mark by her mouth. The lady is short and quite robust."

"But if it's not them, where are they?

"I don't know baby, that lady was not your mother. That lady was not your Mom."

Khloe begins crying.

"Babe your Mom is still alive, you hear me? Your Mom is still alive!

"Where is Dad?"

"I don't know, I don't know."

"Well I suppose that is good news. It wasn't them, where the heck are they Xavier?"

"I wish I knew Khloe, I wish I knew."

"But you said they were staying here at the hotel."

"Yes I did."

"So where are they?"

"Khloe I don't know? You don't think I did something to them do you?"

"I am not saying you did anything. I am reminding you that you told me they were staying at the hotel."

"Okay Khloe okay, I didn't actually see them."

"But you said—

"I made the reservation for them…and then I *talked* to them…on their cell phone."

"When?"

"On Friday morning."

"You didn't see them. You talked to them."

"Yes."

"How did they sound?"

"Your Mom was not happy about our getting married. She thought we were rushing things. I explained to her we had been planning this wed—

"You told her what?"

"I told her we were planning our wedding for months."

"What did you do that for?"

"So she would know that we were not rushing things. That we had thought it out, and decided we were ready."

"That explains the conversation we had at the symposium. Did you talk to my Dad?"

"I never talked with him. The day I talked with your Mom he was not with her."

"Where the heck was he?"

"I don't know."

"I knew something was wrong, I knew it! I should have said no to this whole thing when Mom and Dad did not show up."

"You couldn't back out, the arrangements were already made."

"You made these arrangements Xavier, not me! Do you realize that you may have been the last person to see or talk to them?"

Stephanie
Tamara Brown

Envy

I am almost finished. I already put away the laundry, tackled the dishes, threw away molded food out of the fridge, dusted the tables and vacuumed the floor. I know I should have done it this past dateless weekend, but I wasn't in the mood for anything other than cable television and junk food. Besides everybody else was doing their own thing. One of my sisters, Kiera, we have the same mother different fathers, was with Brice. At least I assuming she was with him. They have been together for what seems forever. He is her puppy dog, following her anywhere and everywhere. When she gets bored and starts sniffing at other men, he doesn't care, most of the time he joins them.

He came with us down to Daytona three and half years ago. It was supposed to be just us girls, Khloe, Kiera, and myself. Guess he didn't trust her during Spring Break. I was going for the sole purpose of finding a new man, one that wasn't so enthralled with her. My whole childhood was spent in her shadow. Boys pretended to like me so they could get close to her. It wasn't any different in Daytona. I spotted this brother serving the ball. Sandy-colored dreadlocks pulled back in a ponytail revealed high cheekbones and intense green eyes focused solely on serving the ball. I knew him, he was the man from the train.

About three years prior to Daytona, I was on an Amtrak train going to Washington, D.C., that had a stop in Philadelphia. I boarded the train at the Newark station, North Jersey's major transportation hub. It was my freshman year at the University of Pennsylvania. Mother was too busy to drive me down. She gave me $800 and sent me off with a duffle bag. She wouldn't get me a car. She said there was no extra money left over. All of it would be needed for tuition. She advised me to befriend someone who had a car, that way I could go shopping.

So there I was on the train, struggling with my duffle bag and my cup of soda. I was trying to navigate the tiniest of aisles when I saw an empty seat ahead. I moved as fast as I could, carrying all my junk. I inadvertently bumped this man's arm just as he took a sip of coffee. Our eyes locked for a few seconds. In those few seconds, I felt like I had disturbed a sleeping demon. A nearby passenger handed me some paper towels to sop up the mess I created. His smoldering green eyes said get away, but me, determined to leave a good impression, touched him. He immediately snatched the towels out of my hand and called me a few choice words. I was never so embarrassed or frightened.

You can imagine my surprise when I saw him laughing with his friends on the beach. His muscles glistened in the sun, rippling every time he ran. I brushed aside my fears. I wanted to know everything about him, where did he live, if there was someone special…the opportunity to meet him presented itself. Khloe, Kiera, and I went to a beach party later on that night. All of us had our eyes on him, and vowed to meet him. Oh we pretended like we were mingling with the crowd, feasting on four grills loaded with barbecue and seafood. There were plenty of beverages of all types and some inhalable stuff under the radar.

I sat a few tables away from him, and yet watched him laugh heartily at his friend's stupid jokes. He had a beautiful smile with a perfect set of teeth. Suddenly he got up and walked away. He walked towards the bonfires. We all pursued him, but Kiera whizzed past us like a bee in pursuit of pollen. She snagged him under the arm and walked with him. I couldn't believe what I was seeing, he didn't pull away. Angry, I looked for Brice and told him. He tracked them down, but stood on the side lines.

I threw my hands up in exasperation and kept my cool, waiting for the day I could get revenge. Fortunately, I didn't have to wait very long, revenge found her all on its own. Xavier made the mistake of introducing her to a powerful local politician. Kiera was hired to be his intern, but she became more, all of her own accord. Puppy dog Brice stayed at her side, ignoring the blatant disrespect. Xavier was a whole other story. He dropped her just as quickly as he picked her up on that beach. And then he moved on to my other sister, Khloe.

Khloe and I have the same father different mothers. Khloe does not know we are sisters, our father never introduced us. I am the child he banished from his life. He paid my mother handsomely, $5000 a month for 21 years, to leave him alone. Mother said he was not my father, I don't believe her. I found copies of checks that he signed. I confronted her and boy was she angry. She accused me of snooping in her private papers. I didn't care how angry she was I wanted to know about him. She denied, denied, and denied, citing his name was not on my certificate. Someone named Joe Brown is listed as my father on my birth certificate. I demanded to meet him, he never came to see me. I demanded to see a picture of him, she didn't have one. I asked for an address, the street did not exist.

Then one day, a bird flew by the house. My mother's best friend Alma dropped by. I pretended to leave the house, what I did was hide in the basement and listen. Alma kept asking mother when was money bags coming to town. Mother said he was supposed to come the weekend to bring money for the baby. I took it to mean she was referring to me since I was the youngest in the family. Alma asked mother when was she and moneybags getting married. Mother shrugged it off and tried to change the subject.

Alma wouldn't let it go. She became angry, telling mother he was using her. She demanded to talk with him. Mother said no, and threatened to end their friendship if she didn't stop meddling in her business. Alma, all hot and bothered, left our house. I left out too, running to Alma's house. I asked her who was my father and she told me. His name was not Joe Brown, it was Gregory Spencer, of Philadelphia. She told me if I wanted to see what he looked like, I should follow mother Saturday night.

Saturday night came. Mother was in her room, getting ready. My mother was beautiful that night, all dressed up in her signature black and white. I went outside and sat in the cab I had called earlier. I told him we would be following someone, though not too closely. He said okay. Mother came out and got in her car. When she pulled out from the curb the cab drove behind her. She drove a good ways before stopping at the Grand Hotel downtown. He was waiting for her in the lobby. The only thing I can attribute to him is my complexion and my hair. He is rather fair with black wavy hair. Mother is taller than him, by about five inches. I took some pictures without their knowing. I wouldn't assume they were having an affair. They both had their briefcases opened like they were conducting business. Eventually they went upstairs. I went back home.

I researched Gregory Spencer and boy did I get the shock of my life. The man is the CEO of a company valued at $20 million dollars. I couldn't find anything about his personal life, but I noticed the names of the vice president and the public relations consultant. Both ladies had his last name. With my new college degree I applied for the position of general manager. Dad was impressed with my grades. However, he did not have faith in them because I had no work experience. He recommended I be his executive secretary with the promise of getting the exposure I would need to become general manager.

I agreed, and on the first day of work who did I meet? Khloe Spencer, his daughter and my long time friend. In the four years that I have known her, she never talked about her family. Then he introduced me to his queen bee Sharon, Alma was right. He was using my mother. I kept the job, intent on learning everything about him so I can take my place in the family. One would think he would recognize me, I look just like my mother. He has no clue I am one of his daughters because he never came to see me on my birthday or any holidays. I don't think he has any pictures.

Jezebel is up, that's my nickname for the resident harlot. She'll claim she should have helped. Only I know she had no intentions of helping.

"Hi Stephanie, thanks for cleaning the place. I should have been here to help you. How was your weekend?"

"Not that you care, it was good…considering all things."

"What is that suppose to mean?"

"I guess happiness is not welcomed here today."

"How long have you known you and Khloe were sisters?"

For the record three years, but you don't need to know those details, "Since last year, I found out when I saw my birth certificate. I confronted Mom and she told me."

"He enabled you to go to the University of Pennsylvania while I had to go to Rutgers…I had taken African American history for an easy three credits, that class was emotionally tough. The rawness of the injustices suffered by the African slaves was hard to fathom. How one race forcibly dominated another by any means necessary, and then threw in religion to justify it screams psychopath. Mental illness has been around a lot longer than people think. It is conceivable that it plagued our founding fathers as they too proudly owned and bred slaves, made me think of our family."

"How so?"

"I was forcibly dominated by you. I had to "slave" for things I wanted while everything was handed to you. When I think about all those pretty dresses…"

"When I think about the raw injustice of being made to *share* with a certain someone who thought it was her God given right to call me the most derogatory name…Rutgers is a good school, you shouldn't knock it, be glad I gave you the chance to go to there."

"Stop with the pious act, you are anything but…"

"I am anything but what, a harlot?"

179

"You could be one if you wanted. Perhaps you wouldn't be home alone so much."

"But that would put me on your level."

"I have to go to work."

"Finally the family's green-eyed sociopath exits the room."

"Don't get it twisted! I am not jealous of you or anything you have."

"*When I think of all those pretty dresses…*" I mocked.

"At least I had a date this weekend, where was old Bailey? He wasn't with you was he Donkey?"

"Are you trying to tell me he was with you Jezebel?"

She stormed out, slamming her bedroom door behind her. The clock crashed to the floor. I rushed over to pick it up. It still works, the time said 7:30AM, time for me to leave for work.

What you don't want to hear

Our corporate offices are not very big considering we have 40 stores in three states. We have a CEO, a president and two vice presidents, and one general manager. Our vice presidents don't know their butt hole from a key hole. I could easily do their job…if I was given a chance. Its ten minutes after eight. I don't see Dad's car, Princess is not here either. She'll come in late as always. Oh I forgot she is supposed to be spending mother daughter time. I wonder if they will discuss the copies of support checks and hotel receipts my mother kept. I wonder if they realize that the baby in the photo is me, his secret daughter. I put one of my baby pictures in a yellow manila envelope and address it your Royal Highness-Queen Sharon Spencer. I didn't send a photo of mother and Dad together. I did not want her attacking my mother. To make sure she got it, I stipulated her signature be required.

Inside the building very few people are in the halls, probably gossiping in their cubicles. I can only imagine what they will say about us when they learn the truth. Here comes Phil Little and Malcolm Hayes—Mr. and Mrs… Malcolm would stick around and actually talk but Phil would have a fit.

"Good morning Tamara."

"Good morning gentlemen."

The corridor where the executive offices are located is quiet and I see all the doors closed. I guess I'm the first one in. Dad will probably be in later. I bet he spent all of last night begging and pleading his case.

"Hey Tamala c—

Yikes!!!

"Sorry to startle you Tamala."

Its dipstick Phil Jackson one of our vice presidents. "My name is Tamara Phil, Tamara not Tamala."

"Sorry Tamara, I keep botching your name. Tamara can you let me know when Greg gets in, I need to see him."

"Sure Phil."

"When you get settled I need printouts of this year's quarterly reports. That would be Quarters 1, 2, and 3. I need the same quarters for the year 2011 and 2010. Oh by the way did you schedule our board meeting for November 8th? Make sure you reserve Otto's Catering, they make the best hors d'oeuvres. And please make sure payroll gets all time cards."

"Sure thing."

He finally goes back in his office. I should be telling you, not you telling me. Here he comes again…

"One more thing Tamara, the Regional Managers are meeting with Khloe at what time?"

"Three o'clock."

"Can you make sure she has all the materials and necessary files she will need?"

If you don't go back in your office! …I pull the yearly report from my desk and take it to him. He's on the phone barking orders at someone else. Don't care to hear him degrade the recipient so I leave them. I take the stairs, right outside his door and reserved only for office personnel, to the time clock. They are closest to the employee entrance. I gather the cards and arrange them alphabetically between each finger. Dad is not here, neither is Khloe. Bailey Lawler…where is he? Why didn't he come to work today? Phaedra Mitchell…late yet again, but at least she came.

Finally I get a chance to log into my computer. There are at least 25 unopened emails. I sit at my desk and total the time cards, inserting the hours into our electronic bookkeeping system. The phone rings, the line for general calls blinks. The caller ID says private number, guess it's a grumbling customer. This phone call should not have been routed to me, someone in customer service should have taken the call.

"Good morning, Spencer Foods."

"Is Gregory Spencer in?"

"No he isn't, care to leave a message?"

"No message. I will call back later."

"Okay."

Mysterious! Don't want to leave your name, another girl friend?

The phone rings again. "Good morning Spencer Foods."

"Good morning Tamara, Bill Kessler here," is Khloe in yet?"

"No she isn't Bill."

"What time are you expecting her?"

"After lunch, anything I can help you with?"

"No, I just want to let her know our shipment from Leighton Manufacturing is going to be late by a day or two."

"They are always late Bill."

"I know but this time they have a legitimate excuse the weather out west is horrible."

"You know that's not a good excuse Bill, business must go on regardless."

"Let me know when she gets in."

Never one for small talk, he hangs up before I could say anything else. I don't care if he is an excellent floor manager, he would be the first on my list.

"Morning Tamara, Khloe in yet?"

"Not yet Scott, what can I do for you?"

"Mark Clothier, Liberty Stars…

"I know who he is."

"He just signed on to be our spokesman."

"Wow! He's coming here?"

"Yeah he will eventually, after we come up with the perfect advertising campaign. That's what I want to talk to her about. I've been calling her on her cell phone and she is not answering."

"She probably can't hear it or she turned it off. She's at a mother daughter symposium. I'll let her know as soon as she gets here."

"Thanks Tamara."

"I got a few ideas for that camp—

"I gotta go, call up a few advertising companies, I'll check back here after lunch. Let me know as soon as she gets in."

He's an awfully fast walker, it's like he flew down the hall and around the corner.

The phone rings yet again. "Good morning, Spencer Foods."

"Is Gregory Spencer in?"

"No he isn't, care to leave a message?"

"The name is Moni—never mind, no message. I will call back later."

"Okay."

"Do you have any idea when he'll be in?"

"He's scheduled to be here today?"

"I'll call back later."

"Is there something I can help you with? I am his secretary."

"No, no it's personal."

She hangs up. It sounds like the same woman who called earlier. This time she started to leave her name, she said it was Moni—could that be Monique? Monica? Why didn't she want to leave her name?

The phone rings again, "Spencer Foods."

184

"Khloe Spencer please."

"She's not in at the moment, care to leave a message?"

"Is this Tamara?"

"Yes it is, who's asking?"

"Her fiancé."

She is engaged? She can't be! Haven't seen a ring on her finger, she hasn't expressed any signs of joy, not even a hint of planning a party. Maybe I did not hear correctly, "Did you say fiancé?"

"Yeah Tamara I'm all caught up, can't live without her."

"This is Xavier right?"

"Yes, who else would it be?"

"Just wanted to make sure I was talking to the right person. I didn't know you guys were engaged."

"Yeah we are, actually our wedding is this weekend. Would you like an invitation?"

"Wait, you guys are getting married *this* weekend?"

"Shhh…not so loud! It's supposed to be a secret, but I am including you. Please don't tell anyone I'm bringing you an invitation. When do you expect Khloe?"

"Early afternoon, around one o'clock, Mr. Spencer hasn't said anything about a wedding. He is giving her away isn't he?"

"Yes he is supposed to, Khloe is going to need a maid of honor, care to do me the favor?"

"Of course!"

"Don't tell her I called and don't tell her about our conversation. I want to surprise her."

Surprise her? Honey you just threw me a curve ball, right in the gut. I can't let you get away. I can't let you go to her without letting you know how I feel.

Finally the princess arrives. It must be nice to come to work whenever you feel like it. I open her door and walk in with my pad to give her the morning's brief and to see if her mother told her. "How was the symposium?"

"It was a bit of an eye opener."

That's it? No details? She doesn't seem upset, maybe her mother didn't tell her, "Oh."

"What are your plans for the weekend?"

"I don't know, probably take in a movie or something. How about you, what are your plans?"

"I haven't made any."

I look at her left hand. I don't see a ring on her finger. I don't see a ring on any of her fingers. How dare she not wear his ring? Unless he is lying, what reason would he have to lie? He doesn't know how I feel about him…I think he is telling the truth. Xavier is not the type of man to lie unnecessarily, I don't think…

"How are things around here?"

"Busy as always, Bill Kessler called, he said the coffee shipment would be delayed by two days. Leighton Manufacturing claims their shipment of containers arrived just today."

"The weather out west is horrendous. What affects them affects the rest of the country, anything else?"

"Yeah Philadelphia Liberty Stars' Mark Clothier has agreed to be our spokesman."

"Yayy! I scored my first major contract without Dad. Speaking of Dad have you seen him today?"

"No I haven't seen or heard from him. Someone is trying to get in contact with him. They have been calling him all morning."

"Oh yeah, who?"

"Some lady, she won't leave her name or number. She says it's personal."

"I have an idea who it may be. The next time they call, transfer it to me."

"Sure will. Also Scott Warner wants to speak with you about the advertising campaign involving around Mark Clothier. He's put together a few ideas and wants to get your approval."

"Where's Scott now?"

"He's at lunch."

"When he gets here tell him to see me. Tamara I am starving can you order lunch for me?"

"Sure Khloe."

"I'd like a grill chicken salad with two cups of Thousand Island dressings. I also want garlic bread, two mini loaves, and a large ice tea."

"Any other messages?"

"Remember you have a three o'clock meeting with the Regional Managers."

"You better add a slice of chocolate cake, that'll help me stay awake."

"Sure, that's all that is happening around here unless you need something else."

"No that's more than enough on my plate. Oh wait a minute! I need the folders for all these meetings."

"I had them transported here."

I walk over to the conference table and pull out one of the chairs. That is when I saw them, roses, roses, and more roses, all colors of the rainbow. I reach out and touch them, they are real roses.

"Who's the secret admirer?"

"He's no secret to you, Xavier sent them."

"Oh..."

This bitch gets everything under the sun.

"Is something wrong?"

Something is most definitely wrong and I will tell you when the time is right. "Nothing, I was thinking…wondering that's all."

"Would you like to take a bouquet back to your desk?"

"Nah, they will not have the same affect. They are for you, not me. I should be getting back to work, enjoy your flowers."

"Thank you, I will, could you close the door behind you?"

'Could you please close the door behind you,' obnoxious bitch! What does he find so loveable about her that she deserves ten dozen of roses?

"Tamara are you all right?"

"Will everyone stop asking me if I'm all right!

I turned around to see Malcom and Scott standing there.

"I'm sorry you didn't deserve that. I received some bad news.

"Is there anything we can do to help?"

"Thanks Scott, I will be fine. It will take some time, but I will bounce back, you wait and see. In the meantime Scott, Khloe is expecting you."

He leaves me, and walks into her office. I need some air, some clean fresh air. I hate this building you can't open any of the windows, everything is glass block.

"Hi Tamara, we are here for the regional managers meeting."

"You can have a seat in Conference Room Two, I'll let her know you are here."

Files, files, and more files. I have been carrying files all day. It won't be too much longer. Soon, very soon I will have my own secretary. She or he, whoever, will be carrying *my* files and organizing *my* schedule.

"Here let me give you a hand."

Now is my chance, "Hmm, hmm, hmm… you're so damn hot, simply delicious, downright fucking divine."

There is more to me than this get up, let me give you a sample. I grab hold of my extra wide skirt, gather it in my hand and pull it tight. He's paying attention, yes baby there is a woman under here. Let me show you just how much of a woman. I twerk like I'm a pro, actually I learned from Jezebel, she is the pro. He likes what he sees, he hasn't blinked not once, yes I can show you some other stuff. Kiera is not the only one with talent.

He chuckled nervously and repeated, "…simply delicious, downright divine…"

"Did I embarrass you?"

"No…yeah…sort of."

"Sorry I never thought you would be embarrassed by something I could say."

"Every now and then someone will catch me off guard, like now."

"It's nice to see a well-tailored brother act like a perfect gentleman."

"Now you are really embarrassing me, calling me a perfect gentlemen. I am not a perfect man believe me, where shall I put these?"

"They go in here."

I open Dad's office and direct him to the table. He sits the files down, reach into his blazer and pulls out a white envelope.

"Here's your invitation. I want you to come. Maybe you can connect with one of my frat brothers. One who does not possess as many flaws."

"Connect with one of our frat brothers? I want to connect with you! I've always wanted to connect with you, ever since we all were in Florida."

"You were there with us in Florida?"

"Yes I was there with Kiera and Khloe. I had a one piece bathing suit while they had on bikinis."

"I don't remember you or Khloe being there."

"We all had our eyes on you. Unfortunately Kiera got to you first."

"Ugh! Kiera."

"Why do you say her name like that?"

"She…I might have been better off with you, then again maybe not. All that is water under the bridge, as you can see Kiera did not win either, Khloe did. Khloe is the right woman for me."

"I can't believe you are about to become legally—

"Tamara you are a beautiful young woman. You deserve happiness, someone who will love and treasure you. That someone is *not* me."

"But it is you, I knew it the moment I laid eyes on you on the beach."

"You would have never been happy with me Tamara. I was a different man back in Florida. I was incapable of being nice or truthful to anyone let alone love them. Who I am today is due to the affect Khloe has had on me. She has shown me that love actually exists, and if I am opened to it, I could experience happiness."

"My happiness lies with you, it is the happiness snatched away by my sisters."

"True happiness is enjoyed by those in love. If you attend our wedding maybe you will find someone who will sweep you off your feet. Like Khloe swept me off my feet."

No need to plead my case, he's gone! He's gone and there is nothing I can do.

"I'll let Khloe know you are here."

"Don't! Remember I said I wanted to surprise her? Let me wait inside her office."

I open her office for him and step aside. He make himself at home in her executive chair, propping his feet upon her desk as if it was his. That desk is supposed to be mine, I can't take this. I need to get out of here, drop everything and leave before I hurt someone. I am not even taking my coat or my purse, Bailey can bring them to me later. I am walking out of here. If I can make it to the exit no one will know I am gone. Oh my God, who is coming up the hall? HER! Can I not get a break! Do I really have to look at you at this particular moment? Well I won't look at you, I won't speak to you, I'll look at the floor until I get out of the building…good she has passed me by.

"Hey Tamara, have you seen Dad?"

Damn it! You just had to say something to me! Well I am going to act like I don't hear you. I keep going, the stairwell is in close proximity.

"Has Dad called Tamara?"

She will not leave me alone if I do not give her an answer. I take my time and slowly turn towards her. My eyes, once focused on the floor, now looks squarely in hers. "No he hasn't."

"Has anyone called him?"

"You mean the person I told you about earlier?"

"Yeah."

191

"No they haven't called, neither has your mother."

"Tamara is something wrong?"

Yes there is, something is wrong, and it's you Princess Khloe. You are all that is wrong in my life. "I have a lot on my mind, nothing to do with you."

"For a minute I thought I was making you uncomfortable."

You are! "It's not you. I just received some bad news."

"Can I be of help?"

"There's nothing anybody can do. I just have to wait and let it work itself out!"

"Okay, I won't hold you up."

"You are not holding me up. In case I don't see you again I want you to know you've been a great boss."

"Are you leaving?"

"No, I'm not leaving, I don't want to, but I just might have to take a leave of absence."

"Listen, take the afternoon off. Don't worry about these folders. I will hide them in my file cabinet in my office."

I am going to scream if you say one more thing to me. I got to get out of here, I got to get out of here now. There's the way out of here, the exit is a few feet away.

"Tamara!"

I hear her voice, yet I don't hear it. It's lost in the wind produced by my speed running down the stairwell. I don't want her anywhere near me so I jump off the last two steps of each landing.

"Tamara!"

Oh my god she is following me. She is actually following me…I can't stop her…it's too soon to begin the plan. I burst thru the door and dart across the parking lot to my car. I hit the keyless remote and start the engine. Once inside I press down on the accelerator. The engine revs, I forgot to shift from park to reverse. The tires are scorching the asphalt, smoke clouds the windows. Finally it blows away and I can see clearly. I tear out of the parking lot and down the road. I am free of this place, but where do I go? At this moment I have nowhere to go. I park at the next corner and look in the rearview mirror. Spencer Foods is long behind me. I rest my head on the steering wheel. Today has not been a good day, starting from the moment I arose from bed.

"What's wrong Tamara?"

Someone is at the car's window. I look up, it's Bailey. I hate to say it but Mom was right, you are all wrong for me. I turn away from, and rest my head on the steering wheel.

"Tamara if you don't answer me I am going to bust the window out!"

I lower the window, "Do you always have to act like a mad man!"

"Relax the windshield is not cracked. What's wrong?"

"Everybody here dotes on Khloe!"

"Everybody like who, our coworkers?"

"Yes!"

"She's our boss, what would you like us to do, act like she doesn't exist?"

"That would be a good start."

"You need to cut this baby shit out and grow up! They dote on Khloe because she is Spencer's daughter. If you want to keep your job, you better start doting on her too."

"She's not the only one I am griping about. Back home everybody dotes on Kiera. Nobody takes a second look at me. I can't believe I'm crying over someone who knows I exist but does not desire me. You

193

don't desire me either, I am just someone you want to play with…it's my fault. I had my own group of friends and I let you push them all away."

"That's what this commotion is all about, because you didn't see me this weekend? You need to get over yourself. I told you I was spending time with the boys."

"The boys…hmmm….don't you mean Kim, Keisha, and Kadijah?"

"Here you go again, that is old news. I told you I called them in front of you to see your reaction."

"Why couldn't you extend me common courtesy Bailey? Anybody with an ounce of respect would not have been talking to other women in my presence. You talked to them like I was not even in the room. You didn't care about my feelings…"

"I don't care about your feelings!"

"You…"

"I what? Don't clam up now, finish what you were going to say."

"What's done is done."

"Sure is, there is no taking it back."

"Bailey what are you doing here?"

"I got a job."

"You already have a job."

"This one pays more, way more. It pays $10,000 but I need some help, someone I can trust. I need you…you're the only person here that knows my business."

"I don't know Bailey. I have a lot on my mind."

"C'mon there's no danger involved. It'll be a piece of cake."

"I have a job to do too, and it's not going to be pretty. What do you want me to do?"

"I have to escort someone somewhere. All I need you to do is drive."

"Who is it?"

He raises his eyebrows as if I had asked about a covert operation. "Why are you looking at me like that? It's a simple question anyone would ask. Why don't you want me to know who it is?"

"You want to make an impression on him? Here's your chance."

"When do you want me to drive the car?"

"Now."

"Now?"

"The person I am supposed to be escorting is waiting for me in the car."

"Where is the car?"

"I'm parked in front of Spencer Foods. I came to get you."

"Oh."

"We will take your car home. I'm going to follow you. You will park your car and then you will get in mine and drive us."

"Oh, where are we going?"

"To park your car at your place."

"That's not what I meant. Where am I driving you?"

"To your house to park your car."

"You don't want to tell me."

"You getting the picture."

"I'm not helping you. I have my own agenda."

"He is your agenda."

"Who is?"

"Gregory Spencer."

"What about Greg Spencer?"

"He wants us to escort him somewhere. He's willing to pay."

"You are right, he is my agenda. Follow me."

Can I do it?

He asked me to be the maid of honor, and that I will be. I will show him I can rise above difficult situations. My gripe isn't really with Khloe. It's with Dad and his ignorance. I'll stand for her to let her know that I am here to support her in any way needed. What kind of dress does a bridesmaid wear? I should have asked him if the wedding was formal or informal. I think I want to go with a formal gown. I don't want to outshine her, I will pick blue. A strapless column blue gown with a little train and some flowers in my hair, it will definitely get Dad's attention. Maybe when he sees me without my glasses he will realize that he is looking at his long lost love, Carolyn Brown.

In New York

I give my invitation to the concierge. It's a good thing I chose a formal gown, the setting is absolutely gorgeous. Candlelit tables with gorgeous floral arrangements are set on both sides of the aisle. And speaking of the aisle, it is in no means short, rather it is long and elegant as if it were inside a cathedral. For extra effect, white and red rose petals sprinkle its entire length, at the end is a canopy the place they will say their vows. I hope she realizes how lucky she is. I hope she appreciates him. If she doesn't I will be there to pick up his pieces.

Here she comes down the hall. I will wait till she gets here and then I will tell her. She is standing right next to me and has no clue it's me her secretary. Finally she looks at me.

"Hi Khloe, I heard you didn't have a maid of honor so I'm here to take the position."

"How did you know I was getting married?"

"Xavier gave me an invitation."

"I want my dad, he should be here. My mom and dad should be here."

"Dad couldn't be here, but he's here in spirit."

She wants to leave, she can't, actor Mark Cunningham is here. I am getting my money's worth, his costume is very impressive. The medals really do look like military medals. She can't get away. He's got her under the arm. Poor Khloe, right now, I am the only familiar person.

"Tamara you should take your glasses off."

She is being courteous, probably because of Mark. I suppose now is as good as any time. She needs to see me as I really am.

"You are beautiful Tamara, did you know…what a minute, Stephanie!"

"So are you sis."

"Sis? Stephanie, what…who…why?"

"Yes, we are sisters. Didn't Dad tell you about me?"

The music plays, my cue to walk down the aisle. Up ahead is Xavier, looking quite dapper in his tuxedo. I stand opposite of him and I guess his best man. I try not to focus on him, but I can't help it, he is gorgeous. The wedding march begins and everyone rises to their feet. They turn and face the aisle to watch Khloe begin her walk. The tiara makes her really look like a princess. Xavier is completely mesmerized by her, he was right. He is not the one for me. Tears well in my eyes, this is way I want my husband to look at me. She finally arrives.

"Her father could not be here tonight and has asked me to give her away. I am giving her to you to love and cherish," said Mark.

Xavier looks quite ferocious. He's forgotten where he is. "Who are you?"

"My name is Captain Russell. I am a friend of her father."

Mark handles himself very well. He does not engage Xavier with his own dominating personality.

"I don't believe you, any self respecting father would not let another man stand in for him at his daughter's wedding. I asked who are you?"

"Son don't ruin your wedding, I will explain everything to the both of you at a later date."

Mark steps away from the altar and has a seat.

The minister speaking reminds everyone why we are here.

"We come together this evening to join this couple in Holy Matrimony. Xavier repeat after me, With this ring I Xavier Charles Davidson...

Look at that magnificent diamond he's putting on her finger. Why could it not have been me?

"...take Khloe Alyssa Spencer to be my wife from this day forward, for better or worse, for richer or poorer, in sickness and in health, to love and cherish from this day forward until death do we part."

"Khloe repeat after me, With this ring I, Khloe Alyssa Spencer, take you, Xavier Charles Davidson, to be my husband from this day forward, for better or worse, for richer or poorer, in sickness and in health, to love and cherish from this day forward until death do we part."

"If there is anyone is against this marriage, let them speak now or forever hold their peace."

My throat itches, it's the pollen in the room. I better say something before they jump to the wrong conclusion, "I got a tickle in my throat. I am not trying to stop this wedding."

Everyone sighs.

"I now pronounce you man and wife. You may kiss your bride," said the Judge.

"Khloe bring those luscious lips to me!"

Xavier flips her veil and gives her a peck on the lips, very appropriate for a room full of people. The crowd erupts into cheers.

The judge announces, "Introducing Mr. and Mrs. Xavier Davidson."

People rush forward with their cameras, bulbs flashing non-stop. Wait till I tell Kiera her beloved married her best friend. She is going to be blown away.

Kiera Smith

More than I bargained for

The phone rings, I know who it is. I don't feel like working today. I am tired and drained from all the drama. I spent the weekend with Brice in Jersey City visiting family and old friends. Two couples we went to high school with gave us wedding invitations. Another couple, Lisa and Robert, became parents again for the fifth time in five years. Byron Gray, the boy everyone said was destined to be in NBA, was found dead in Lincoln Park. The stories we heard about him all pointed to gang initiation. It left everyone puzzled as to why he was targeted. My next door neighbor Mrs. Walker also died. Her death was not so surprising. She was old, 87 years old to be exact.

Our friend Jason supplies Brice with a couple of bundles every other month. This time he introduced him to his new friends, highly recommended for the potency of their product. It was explained that a tiny tablet was all that was needed. Brice wasn't interested in establishing new relationships. He is not keen on new people. He has always said that "new friends" could be your downfall. He told them he was content with things as they were. The new guys pressed on, offering more, way more than a couple of bundles. They threw in the added bonus of keeping half of the profits. A hunch told me not to trust them. I know Brice feels the same way.

Brice told them their offer was enticing, but he had to pass. He explained that now was not the time to offer a new product to his customers. Many of them were unemployed and he did not want to draw unnecessary attention to himself. I could tell they weren't use to things not going their way, they became relentless. Both sides went back and forth, both stuck to their guns. Then a big guy walked in, he had to be least seven feet of pure muscles. He stood in front of the entrance. That doorway was the only way out. It was clear negotiations were over. It was time to comply or else we weren't leaving alive.

Brice didn't like being intimidated and refused to back down. They subtly reminded him, by giving me a quick glance, that his decision would not affect just him. Wisely he took their offer, except he renegotiated the terms to his favor. They handed us what looked like a thousand silica gel packets in a box. They told us there were three tablets inside each packet. All we had to do was find a way to distribute the packets. On the way home I reminded Brice that silica packets are usually placed in shoe boxes and leather handbags. He decided that would be the way he would get rid of it, especially since he is set to open his shoe store next week. The phone won't stop ringing, might as well answer it. "Hello."

"Are you up?"

Oh good, it's not who I thought it was.

"Yeah."

"I need your help."

"Look Brice, I can't help with that. I can't take the risk."

"You suppose to be my woman, at my side."

"And you suppose to be looking out for me. You should not want me in the middle of your business."

"I don't need help with that! I need help organizing my party."

"Oh, what do you want me to do?"

"I want to have my party at Revolution."

"You're going to jeopardize Revolution for them?"

"I'm going to get rid of those packets. You said they are usually in shoe boxes, so I am having an exclusive party where I will sell some shoes."

"I don't know Brice."

"It'll be easy. I will invite my customers only. When they buy something I'll throw in 2 or 3 packets. I should be able to rid of them in one night."

"Then what?"

"I'll give them the money, all of the money, and then step off. I am stepping off from Jason too."

"Will they let you?"

"I am the Captain of my fate, not them!"

"Anything else Captain?"

"That's it for now, bye!"

Donkey is up. I hear her stirring around in the living room. I know I shouldn't call her donkey, her real name is Stephanie. Mom punished all of us every time we called her that, it didn't stop us. Every time we saw her down in the bakery with a slice of cake, pie or a couple of cookies in her hand, we called her donkey. Her rear is quite huge, as if everything she ate settled there. Our teasing did not stop her from eating. She ate whatever she wanted when she wanted.

Last Thursday, she told me her little secret. It wasn't a small secret per se, it was mind blowing. Mother is somewhat highly educated. She did not attend college, instead she went to a cooking school. She can prepare any kind of dish you want, but her specialty is cakes. Ownership of the bakery came about when she interned at Carolyn's Cakes. Carolyn O'Casey loved my mother so much that when she was ready to retire, she thought my mother would be the best person to continue her work. She made the right choice, mother not only kept the old customers happy, she gained new ones. I just wish she was lucky in the men department.

With four children, she has never married. All of our fathers walked away and never looked back or so I thought. Now I learned Donkey's dad is quite loaded and she is related to Khloe. Everyone that is important in my life is connected to Khloe. First there was Brice and now there's my little sister Stephanie. I cannot believe they are sisters. For as long as I have known Khloe she never mentioned having siblings.

My stomach cries out for food, maybe Steph cooked breakfast. I opened the bedroom door, shock at what I see. The place is clean, everything put away. The place looks like an apartment and not a college dormitory. She has a sad look on her face. I thought her news would have her on cloud nine, after all she is an heiress. I wonder if she spent the weekend with Bailey.

"Hi Steph, thanks for cleaning the place, I should have been here to help you. How was your weekend?"

"Not that you care…it was good, considering all things."

"What is that supposed to mean?"

"I guess happiness is not welcomed here today."

She wants to gloat about her and Khloe. Well she can, I have known Khloe a lot longer than she.

"How long have you known that you and Khloe were sisters?"

"Since last year, I found out when I saw my birth certificate. I confronted Mom and she told me."

"He enabled you to go to University of Pennsylvania while I had to go to Rutgers...I had taken African American history for an easy three credits at Rutgers. The class was emotionally tough. The rawness of the injustices suffered by the African slaves was hard to fathom. How one race forcibly dominated another by any means necessary, and then threw in religion to justify it screams psychopath. Mental illness has been around a lot longer than people think. It is conceivable that it plagued our founding fathers as they too proudly owned and bred slaves, made me think of our family."

"How so?"

"I was forcibly dominated by you. I had to "slave" for things I wanted while everything was handed to you. When I think about all those pretty dresses…"

"When I think about the raw injustice of being made to *share* with a certain someone who thought it was her God given right to call me the most derogatory name…Rutgers is a good school, you shouldn't knock it, be glad I gave you the chance to go to there."

"Stop with the pious act, you are anything but…"

"I am anything but what, a harlot?"

"You could be one if you wanted, perhaps you wouldn't be home alone so much."

"But that would put me on your level."

"I have to go to work."

"Finally the family's green-eyed sociopath exits the room."

"Don't get it twisted! I am not jealous of you or anything you have."

"*When I think of all those pretty dresses…*"

"At least I had a date this weekend, where was old Bailey? He wasn't with you was he Donkey?"

"Are you trying to tell me he was with you Jezebel?"

I slammed my bedroom door. I guess she threw something after me, I don't care. Oh is she assertive, I guess I can attribute that to Bailey. I would have never guessed Donkey would find herself a man, but she did. I just wish he wasn't so sleazy and old, he is 15 years older than she. Why she didn't go for someone with a bit more class, someone like Xavier, is beyond me. I know she likes him. She would check him out when he came to pick me up. I didn't have to worry, he paid her no attention whatsoever. The one I did worry about was Khloe, everybody liked her, including Brice.

Khloe and I met in graduate school four years ago. She was sitting in the auditorium with a few other young women, chuckling at something one of the others had said. I was sitting a couple of seats over from them and gradually became a part of their group by adding comments here and there. I quickly discovered we liked a lot of the same things and had some things in common, most notably overbearing mothers. We also liked the same type of guys, well-developed triceps, eight packs, light colored eyes and a little on the wild side.

One guy that I know she did not really like was Brice. He had followed me from Jersey City, supposedly to keep me from other boys. That was short-lived. I ended up trying to stop him from being with other girls. We would argue, fall out of love, fall in love, argue some more, then start the process all over again. Khloe groaned whenever she found herself our referee. Being that she was from Philadelphia and Brice and I were from Jersey City, she gave us a grand tour of the city. He immediately noticed the tall slender women on and off campus. He also noticed her. I would catch him glancing at her, and she at him. My gut told me there was someone else, someone like my best friend Khloe. I confronted them both and they *both* denied it. I didn't believe them although I falsely apologized for being insecure. When I was home I did not have to fight to garner attention. I was the girl who had the boys eating out of the palm of my hand.

Spring Break was more in my favor. Khloe, Stephanie and I went to Florida. Of course Brice followed behind us, ditching us almost as soon as we checked into the hotel. I took advantage of the freedom, coming to the realization that he did not own me nor did I own him. We were not married, talk of marriage never even occurred to us. Therefore we could do whatever we wanted with whomever we wanted. And since he was hell bent on seeing other people, I was going to let him.

We girls broke out in our new bikinis, parading up and down the beach in front of large groups of men. They were all gorgeous, and superficial, something I already have. I stopped to check out a volleyball game. The men playing were superbly fit, but one of them stood out. He was of a beautiful brown shade with copper hair. His slim physique showed solid muscles whenever he darted about after the ball. He was a natural man, simply breathtaking with playful green eyes that complimented a small face. His smile showed a perfect set of 32 pearly whites. Stephanie and Khloe saw what I saw. We cackled about him that whole day, speculating how each of us would capture his undivided attention. He was our new found trinket.

He knew I was looking at him. He met my gaze on more than one occasion. Even when Stephanie and Khloe ventured off on their own to mingle with others, I would catch him staring at me. Later on that night I learned his name, Xavier, a name I would have never guessed. I also learned a few more things about him, under the pier, which led me to call him Tiger. According to the Senator, Xavier is still single and does not have a significant other.

This damn phone just will not stop! "What do you want?!"

"Where are you? You were supposed to be here an hour ago?"

Damn! It's the call I have been dreading. "Senator I can't come today. I have an excruciating headache."

"Come to work, let me make it all better. I'll see you in half an hour."

"Senator I'm telling you I can't, I just can't do it this morning. I just laid my head on the pillow."

"So you are saying *no* to me?"

"Yes."

"No you are not. Now you do what you have to do to get here. I expect to see you in a half an hour."

The great senator has summoned me. He does not ask, he demands your presence. People come running when he calls. People stop talking to listen to his voice. He is highly respected. How he and Xavier became good friends is a mystery to me. Their friendship is more than constituent and representative, which is why Agents Skopp and Hobart approached me. They wanted to know about the two of them, but were mum when I asked why. So I told them no, I know which side my bread is buttered on.

I have this job because of Xavier. He knew I was a political science major in need of employment. He knew the Senator was hiring interns for his office. Unfortunately my taking the job ended our relationship. One thing led to another and the next thing I knew I was the Senator's new Barbie. All I had to do was bend over for ten minutes or so, three times a week and collect a $1000 tax-free paycheck. How could I, a middle class college student from New Jersey responsible for the payment of a $100,000 in loans say no?

I pull into the empty parking space in front of the office. Most of Philadelphia's congressional representatives have an office in the heart of the district they represent, which usually means a commercial strip. The drawback to that is you have to find a parking space, and then you have to feed the meter every two hours or you find yourself with a nice $50 ticket. I find one a few cars down. Dawn and Kathleen, the other secretaries, are not in yet. Not that I am surprised, the Senator likes to role play. Sex at the office gets him all gushy like a little school boy. It would be easier and more respectable if we met like two consenting adults. One thing prevents that, his old hag of a girlfriend Gladys.

I open the door to find him sitting at my desk with his infamous scowl. I never met anybody so impatient, so needy, and yet so cold. He claims to love Xavier as a son, yet he went after me, knowing we were seeing each other. The truth of the matter is I still love him and if I could go back in time, I would not have taken this job.

"What took you so long?"

I can't tell him the truth. I can't tell him that I was with Brice and barely escaped with my life trying to broker a drug deal. He doesn't even know about Brice. He thinks he has me all to his lonesome.

"Where were you this weekend?"

His voice startles me back to reality, he is standing behind me. I don't even remember him leaving the chair. As usual he toys with my hair. Think! Think of a plausible lie. "I spent the weekend cleaning up the place, how about you?"

I sense he is composing a lie too.

"Attending a fundraiser up in Allentown, I would have brought you along...its election year and all, why start the tongues wagging."

"Yeah, why start the tongues wagging..."

"I miss you Kie..."

His breath is hot on my neck. I push him away and tell him. "I am not in the mood."

No is never in his vocabulary, he grips my arm and my hair.

"What's the matter with you?!"

"Oww, Julius let go of me!"

"Not until you tell me who were you with?"

"I wasn't where I was supposed to be was I? You should have asked me to come along. It's not like you have a wife...why won't you take me? Am I only good enough to bed and not be seen?"

I guess the truth hurts, he release me. I walk away, far away from him.

"Where are you going?"

"I am going back home."

Defensively he moves to block the door, "Baby girl we discussed this already. My constituents might not take too kind to me dating a woman young enough to be my daughter."

"All you think about it your precious political career."

"Does it not pay your bills?"

I did the only thing I can do, go to my desk and start working. Once again he stands behind me and begins kissing my neck. I push him away.

"Come here…"

He reaches for me again, and I do a quick side-step, giggling at his stumble. He regains his balance, and slaps me across the face. I know why he hit. He doesn't like it when I laugh at him. Sometimes I can't help but laugh at him. He's a big shot with an infantile penis.

"I know you been with someone, who was it?"

I run from him, back into one of the offices. I try to close the door, but he barges in, knocking me back against the desk. I scour the room for cover, there is nowhere to go. I cower in the corner, my hands cradling my head and face. He pounds me over and over, demanding to know what I did the weekend. I have to get him off of me.

"Okay stop hitting me. Stop hitting me! STOP HITTING ME NOW!

He heard what I said and stopped.

"WHAT IS WRONG WITH YOU?"

I can't believe what is happening. He hit me. He never hit me before. No man has ever hit me. He is still standing there, prepared to hit me again. He is not aware of what he has done. He has given me the upper hand.

"Julius I went home to visit my family, okay, I went home to be with my family."

"Why?"

"Why? What do you mean why? People visit their family all the time. Am I not allowed to see them?"

"Of course you can. I'm sorry I lost my temper like that, I didn't mean… get up, get up off the floor. I don't like talking to people's backs."

He helped me up off the floor and turned me towards him. He looked at my face, relieved it didn't have any marks.

"Are you okay Kiera?"

"No I am not okay Julius, you beat me, and for what, because I was not sitting around moping?"

"I said I am sorry."

"I need money Julius, a lot of money."

"How much money are you talking about?"

"Ten thousand dollars."

"Why do you need that much money?"

I move away from him. Actually stepping out into the hall, closer to the entrance, he is not going to like what I have to say.

"I want ten thousand dollars, two thousand dollars for every lick you heaped onto my head."

"Oh really, you think you can blackmail me into giving you money."

"This is not blackmail, this is assault. I don't think your constituents would want you as their representative when they hear of you beating me. A state official assaulting his young intern, imagine the media coverage."

"Fine."

He goes to his office. I hear him shuffling things, probably looking in his drawers. I don't know who he thinks he is kidding, he never keeps anything in the drawer except a few pads and pens. I know he has already turned off the security system, but what *he* doesn't know is that I have my own camera system in place, logged into my internet account. I will have videotapes for as long as I need money. I scream out, "It's in the wall safe."

"You know where everything is don't you?!"

"Of course, that's why you hired me!"

He has the checkbook and pen in hand.

"Julius I don't want a check, you think I am stupid? Before I get to the bank you can put a stop on it, give me cash. I want ten thousand dollars in cash."

"That would draw attention."

"A check would draw a whole lot of attention, and quicker than cash will. Just withdraw so much every day until you hit the magic number."

He scrambles to his office and returns just as quickly.

"Here's two thousand, that is all I have at the moment. I am sorry I should never have put my hands on you. Come here…"

A girl gotta do what she has to do…ten thousand this time, $100, 000 the next. He knocks everything off the desk and sits me upon it. His hand worms its way up my skirt and yanks my panties. I must admit I find him exciting. Brice never does anything exciting. I guess it's because he's busy bedding every woman that'll open her legs. He doesn't feel the need to impress me.

At least he has the much needed length, Julius' daddy short-changed him. Nevertheless I close my eyes and swap faces. Brice's for Julius, Xavier's for Brice's, I imagine nibbling on Xavier's ear while Julius humps away, moaning and groaning. He'll be finished in 30 seconds or so, and I'll smile coyly. He actually believes he pleases me, if only he knew. No one pleases me the way Xavier does.

"First call of the day, what time is it?"

"It's 6AM. Get the phones Baby Girl, we can continue this later on."

He adjusts his pants while I composed myself. "Good morning, State Senator Julius Davidson—

"Hello Kiera, is Julius in yet?"

It's the one I let get away. "Where have you been? I haven't seen or talked to you in months."

"I've been busy, extremely busy."

"I tried calling you, but you never returned any of my calls."

"I have no need to talk to you. Where is Julius, it is very important I talk with him."

"Is something wrong?"

"What makes you ask that?"

"It's six o'clock in the morning."

"Yes it is, what are you doing there so early?"

"He asked me to come in and help on the amendment."

"Where are the other secretaries?"

"They aren't…I mean they are busy working."

"Working as hard as you, gotcha!"

"Xavier I want to talk about us."

"Obviously Julius is not around else we would not be having this conversation. Let me state something. You made the decision to end us. I granted you your wish. Nothing left to say, we are done!"

"No we are not! We are not done Xavier!"

"It is what it is Kiera. You are dreaming if you think things between us can be as they once were. I want to speak to Julius, where is he?"

"He is in the john."

"When he gets out, tell him to call me."

"Wait a minute, he's back."

I transfer the call. I needed to hear the words from his lips, and boy did I ever. He is as cold as Julius. Why is he calling him so early in the morning, to gloat about his new life? Agents Hobart and Skopp might be on to something, but what could they be looking for? Julius has never done anything imperfect except sleep with me. He's never done a political favor or compromised his office for anyone to invoke the suspicion of the FBI. I ease the handset off the base and listen in. From what I can tell, nothing unusual has happened.

"Kiera."

He knows I'm listening. I ease the receiver back onto the base and clack on the keyboard.

"Kiera!"

I look up, and find him in the doorway.

"Kiera, here's $50, go to the Coffee House and pick up some danishes and donuts for the other secretaries, you know what they like."

He walks me to the reception area and gets my coat out of the closet. He walks me to the car and watches me leave the parking lot. I see him in the rearview mirror waving goodbye. I guess Agents Skopp and Hobart are on to something.

Back in Philadelphia

An unintentional slight

I must thank God for my husband. Maybe it was meant for Xavier to be here at this time in my life. I don't know what I would have done if he wasn't here. I am on the verge of falling apart. Mom and Dad are missing and no one has a clue to their whereabouts. The suspense is killing me. However, life must go on, I have to continue running things, making the decisions I was groomed to make. I can't let it fall apart. There has always been a business in the family, beginning with my great grandfather Charles Spencer.

The elder Charles died of a heart attack when my grandfather was 12. He left his wife and son a small store and a little money. Luckily his son Charles Junior—my grandfather, had worked side-by-side with him. He was knowledgeable in keeping the store functional. Much to the chagrin of would be swindlers and racists who fumed that a "colored" man knew just as much as they did. The store was located on a corner bristling with traffic and people. Through the years the business grew, thanks to the creation of a bus stop. The family moved to a bigger house within walking distance, enabling grandfather to walk to work every day.

Grandfather befriended Ed Fairfax, a man with many connections. Fairfax told grandfather about a business for sale, one that had gas pumps. Its location was on a main street that had a large amount of traffic. Grandfather took a look at the lot and bought it on the spot. He realized that vehicles would need gas and drivers would want refreshments. It was grandfather's idea to put a second store on the lot with the gas pumps. Dad came along and expanded. First he put a store in each neighborhood, oftentimes buying lots equipped with gas pumps. He partnered with Penn Cruise, a new oil company looking for distributors of its gasoline. Then Dad decided to extend hours of operation to 24 hours. The finishing touch was the name change, from Spencer Grocer to Nite-Owl Convenience Stores.

The next year Dad delved into the manufacturing of our own product line. He began scouring land sales, looking specifically for dairy farms. A farmer out in Clarion was selling his family farm. Dad convinced him to become our partner, giving him an outlet for his dairy products. The dairy line became known as Spencer Dairies and included ice cream. The working class of the suburbs became his focus when he developed Spencer Foods, our line of quality take-out food at affordable prices. Finally, he expanded our coffee line. Rather than sell our basic run-of-the-mill regular coffee, Dad looked for a coffee grower. He subcontracted with Mauna Kea Coffee Company out in Hawaii, with the agreement that we would have our own line of coffee. Spencer Café was born soon after.

Grandfather was extremely proud of Dad. He never dreamed his father's simple corner store would turn into a multi-million dollar business. I was expected to continue the family legacy so when I turned twelve I spent my summers at the company. I learned first-hand each department and what role it played in the company's success. Dad was hard on me because he knew they would be. He was right. With my proven work experience and my college degree I was able to silence my critics, namely the board members who questioned the wisdom of Dad's decision.

Since taking my rightful place at the helm, my employees have been nitpicking about their assigned tasks. They stubbornly leave out important facts in quarterly reports in the hopes of undermining me. There's not a day go by that I do not hear whispering in the cubicles. Resentful employees gripe about my age and others analyze my ability to make financial decisions. Vice President Philip Jackson openly voiced his professional opinion the day Dad presented me to the board. They listened to his concerns, but recognized that I had *earned* the title of vice president. From then on I triple checked all and any recommendation from anyone, especially when they came from

Jackson. He is still angered by my appointment. I look at my life partner, all the drama that occurred in New York is something of a blur. I am thankful I have someone to lean on. "Thank you Xavier."

"For what?"

"For being here."

"I will always be here for you Khloe. What are you going to do?"

"Go to the police and file a missing persons report."

"Yes you should. You should file one with both departments."

"Why both?"

"Because they originated from here, Philadelphia, I know I talked with your mother on Friday morning, but who is to say that she ever left Philadelphia."

"Yeah I was thinking of that, I also was thinking of the lady in the morgue. She was found in a rental car supposedly rented with Dad's credit card. Who is to say that she did not have anything to do with what happened to them?"

"Its plausible baby, anything is plausible."

The limousine pulls up to my apartment building. He peeks out the window.

"We we have to decide where we are going to live. My place or here, at your place, I prefer we start off with something new."

"I think that is a good idea, a place with none of our previous history."

He tells the chauffeur, "Thanks for the outstanding service. I will definitely use you guys again and highly recommend your company."

"Thank you."

The chauffeur unloads our luggage and sits them on the sidewalk. Xavier grabs them and carries them inside to the lobby. I push the stop button and the elevator's doors remain open until he finishes loading. I advise a few of my neighbors to take the other elevator for we will be awhile. They flash a fake smile and board the next one. He brings the last of our things and puts the elevator in motion. The doors open to my floor and I hear him. I hear Regis whimpering at my door. "He knows I'm here."

"How can he know? You are nowhere near the door."

"He knows."

Regis, my golden retriever, claws at the door and barks incessantly as I approach. As I move closer I can hear the excitement mounting, his barking increases in tone as does his pacing. As soon as I open the door he charges me, causing me to stumble backwards. I compose myself, kneeling on my knees. He ferociously licks my face, runs down the hall, circles back, and runs to me again, all the while barking insanely.

"Good God, I never knew he'd get so excited."

"Of course he does, he's a baby."

"A baby!"

"Yes a baby, haven't you ever own a pet?'

"No I was away at school."

I pull Regis by his collar and lead him inside the house. Home sweet rink of a home, he has definitely been here alone. I open the windows. Cool air wafts in and pet dander floats. He frets at my feet.

"Definitely time for your monthly shampoo, are you hungry?"

"I paid the concierge to care for him."

"They didn't do a good job, the place stinks! I'm gonna have to get new furniture and carpet."

Regis whines and follows me in the kitchen. I open a can of dog food and scoop it into his bowl. He immediately gobbles it down. Feeling guilty, I gave him a little more and pour a glass of water in another bowl. He finishes both in five minutes.

"We have to get a new place," he says, fanning his nose.

"You look for the place, I'll take him outside," I whistle, "C'mon boy let's go outside."

Regis runs to the living room and waits at the door with his leash in his mouth.

"I'll walk with you. I have to meet with a client. I should be home around six, what are we having for dinner?"

"Dinner? I hadn't thought that far ahead, maybe we can dine out."

I attach the leash to the collar and move out into the hallway. Regis is in a hurry, he is pulling me fast. Xavier lags behind to close the door. He runs to catch up to us. We continue talking on the elevator.

"Here, you forgot your umbrella. I doubt I will want to go out, you can order take-out. Whatever you choose will be fine with me."

"Chinese, Soul food, Gianni's or Sushi?"

"I want some food for the soul."

The doors opened into the lobby. Regis drags me along, but I do manage to wave at my neighbors.

"Khloe, let him go before he drags you across the street!"

"He might get hit by a car."

"That dog will be just fine, you would be the one to get killed!"

I ignore Xavier's pleas and hold the leash till we cross the street. Only at the outskirts of Clover Park do I take off the leash. Regis runs as if it's his first taste of freedom. Saki, my godmother, and Sasha, her white Samoyed, are here as usual.

"Good morning Saki."

"Good morning Khloe, it's a beautiful day isn't it?"

"Saki you are the only person I know who thinks a rainy day is a beautiful day. Have you seen or heard from my Mom and Dad?"

"No I haven't. It's been awhile since I've talked with either of them."

"They were supposed to be at my wedding. They never made it."

"You got married?"

"Yes."

"You got married and did not invite me? The mother who loves you, gave you money to buy things when your father told me not to, how could you forget about me?"

I feel like I'm six years old again, being scolded for not being respectful to my elders. In a lot of ways she's more of a mother to me than my own. People always thought Saki and I were mother and daughter because we strongly resemble each other.

"It's my fault. I forgot to extend a personal invitation to you. Please accept my apology."

"No I will not accept your apology. Who are you?"

"My name is Xavier Davidson and I am her husband."

"Why am I just meeting you?"

"I don't know, judging by your reaction, I should have met you a long time ago. Please do not think I intentionally slighted you by excluding you from our guests list. Had I known about you, I would have made sure you were seated close to the altar.

"You had a church wedding?!" she blurted.

"No, actually we were married at a hotel," I said.

"What hotel?" she asks.

"The Gardens in New York City," he said.

"You had a fancy wedding in New York…" she asks.

"Yes we did, actually it was a surprise wedding. I made all the arrangements," he said.

"That was our family's responsibility, not yours!" she said.

"I know…Khloe and I have been dating three years and we felt it was time to go to the next level. Ladies I have to go to work, can't keep my clients waiting. We must get together real soon," he said.

"No you cannot leave now. Not until you explain to me, we Japanese have an engagement period of at least eight months.I feel like I failed you. I promised to keep an eye on you."

"Again, I am at fault. I thought I had contacted all of the relatives," he said.

"Oh my god! Are you with child?" she asked.

"No Saki, I am not pregnant," I said.

"Then why you two run away to get married?" she asked.

"We didn't run away," I said.

"We just did not want to wait to get married," he said.

Saki sobs. I broke her heart with my selfish plans.

"I am your mother Khloe. I should have been there. A mother should see her daughter's wedding."

"Saki, you have been like a mother to me, but you are *not* my mother."

She walks away, jerking Sasha's chain and shouting at her in Japanese.

"Xavier if anybody would have approved of our wedding it would definitely had been Saki. She's so understanding, and easy to talk to. I can talk to her about anything. I can't talk to my mother about anything. Mom is so judgmental, she's like the doomsday prophets with all kinds of warnings—don't do this, don't do that…"

"How come you never told me about Saki?"

"I don't know."

"From her reaction, it's obvious you are very important to her."

"I had no idea. I have to make amends, but how?"

"Go to her, go to her now and talk."

"Okay, you go to work. I will be fine. C'mon Regis we have to go."

Silence is Broken

I knock on the door of Saki's apartment. She answers with eyes almost swollen shut. She has been crying, nonetheless she invites me in. We sit on the balcony, atop wicker chairs with overstuffed pillows. Quietly we gaze at Fairmount Park. I am not surprise we are out here. It is the place she always retreats to when she is upset. I see she has anticipated my visit. On the small chest is a teapot and two cups.

"My parents—your grandparents said hello."

"You saw them recently?"

"I flew to LA this weekend, George and I showed them pictures of you, of us. The pictures we took at Shofuso."

She takes out the photo, a 4x5 taken last year. There is another photo, older and bigger, an 8x11. Saki looks to be 17 or so, she resembles me so much, I am her clone. The only difference, I am a shade darker.

"My parents find it remarkable that you look so much like me. They have no idea you are my daughter."

"Saki you are not my mother."

"But I a—

"NO YOU ARE NOT!"

"I HAVE PROOF!"

"I want to see it. I want to see it now!"

She leaves her chair and head for the Schefflera in the corner. She pulls the tree slightly forward and reaches behind it. She's pulling out a suitcase. Brown and pretty weather beaten, she hands it to me. Why is she giving me an old suitcase?

"Open it."

I do as she says and click the locks on the ends. Inside are photos and papers. Where do I begin?

"I was saving these for a very long time. I was waiting for the right moment. Start with the birth certificates."

There are two birth certificates. Baby number one was a girl born on September 1, 1988. Her parents are Sharon Scott Spencer and Gregory Maurice Spencer. That would be me, but wait…my birthday is the fifth, not the first.

"Keep reading."

Baby number two was also a girl born on September 5th, 1988. Her parents are Saki Nakamura and Gregory Maurice Spencer.

"You had a baby girl, where is she? What happened to her?"

"I gave her away."

"Why?"

"Her father refused to claim her."

"What do you mean he refused to claim her?"

"Her father had two loves. He claimed to love us both, but he could only marry one. It was important to him to marry a girl with stature. I was not of his stature."

"So who was the other girl?"

"Sharon Scott."

"My mother was the other girl?"

"Yes."

I can picture her holding onto him for dear life regardless of the circumstances. It is something she tried to instill in me, but it is a weakness that I will not own. "Saki you miss her, your daughter, don't you?"

"I did, still do. I was able to see you just about every day."

"If I am your baby, what happened to the baby Sharon Scott had?"

"It died."

"No it didn't, I'm here, I'm Sharon Scott's baby. My birthday is Septermber 5th...

"Her baby died."

"How?"

"She was stillborn. There is a death certificate in there."

I looked at all the papers and found the death certificate. Baby number one died September 1, 1988.

"I don't understand. How did I come to live with Sharon and Greg Spencer?"

"Sharon was in a bad car accident. She was knocked unconscious and had to be rushed to the hospital. Her baby was delivered during emergency surgery. It still died..."

"I didn't die, I am still here!"

"Yes you are."

"So why do you keep saying I died?"

"You didn't die Khloe, you are alive and well. Sharon's baby died."

"I'm confused. What the hell is this all about?"

"It's about you learning who your mother really is."

"Yes and my mother's name is Sharon Spencer."

Saki shakes her head, not wanting to accept what I said.

"She is not your mother, I am."

"Explain to me, how you came to be my mother."

"I've already told you your father had two loves, Sharon and myself, now I will tell you the rest of the story. It's not pretty, when I think about it I am amazed at your father's love for me."

"Are you saying he was in love with you?"

"Hmph! I wouldn't call it love. Your father loved Sharon and only Sharon. When their baby died, I found out just how much he loved me."

"What do you mean?"

"He did not want Sharon to know that her baby died."

"Why not? They could have had another baby later on."

"Yes they could have, but Greg did not want to wait. He was insistent in keeping his baby's death a secret…suddenly he wanted you."

"What do you mean he wanted me?"

"He suggested that he and Sharon raise you as their own."

"He didn't want you, he wanted me."

"Yes."

"Wow!"

"There he was, breaking *my* heart to keep *hers* whole."

"How did that make you feel?"

"Used. I was so devastated that I went into premature labor. You were not supposed to be come until November."

"So you are saying that he wanted to raise me as his child with Sharon."

"Yes."

"If I am your daughter, why would you agree to such terms?"

"I did it because I had to, I could not take you home. I could not tell my parents I had a child by a man I did not marry. I did what was

227

best for you…besides, your father promised to let me see you whenever I wanted."

"You became my godmother."

"Yes."

"As far as I am concerned, you let him manipulate you."

"In hindsight I agree. Your father had told me he loved me for months on end, and I believed him. Then one day I saw him with her.

"With who?"

"Sharon Scott."

"What happened?"

"It was too late to end the relationship, you had already formed. When I told him he was furious."

"Why?"

"Sharon was pregnant too."

"Two women, two babies…what a sleaze ball!"

"Your father is not a sleaze ball. Playboy, yes! Sleaze ball, no!"

"Just who is my father?"

"Your father is Gregory Spencer."

"So my Dad is really my Dad."

"Yes."

"You may not know it, but there were times when you were more of a mother to me than *she* was, remember my prom dress? The burgundy one with the halter top?"

"Oh yeah, the dress that would have gotten you pregnant. I took it to the tailor and had the slits sewn up and a bib inserted. You called me a party pooper."

"I did, and I'm sorry."

"And I told you *you* were forgiven."

"Mom, I mean Sharon, she didn't care, but you did, now I know why."

"Sharon is not the domestic type."

"But I don't look anything like Sharon!"

"No you don't. You look like me."

"Didn't she ever put two and two together?"

"Eventually she did, and she thanked me."

"She thanked you!"

"Yes she did. She acknowledged the hurt and pain I felt and thought it best you get to know me."

"Mom, I mean Sharon, is sweet like that."

We sip on the tea is silence. I meditate on the unbelievable revelation. I too have a mother masquerading as my godmother. I thought I knew my family, in reality I don't. I don't know them at all and I am not sure I can handle learning about them. I look at my watch.

"I should be going, I have to prepare dinner."

"So now you are a wife. I see why you ran away with him. He is quite handsome and extremely considerate. Not many men take the initiative of *wanting* to get married. If I was in your shoes, I am not sure if I could resist the urge either. Do you love him?"

"Yes I do, I don't know what I would have done if he hadn't been with me these last 24 hours. I really don't."

"What's wrong?"

"Detectives from New York came up to our hotel room. They said my mother and father were dead in a car accident."

"Oh my God, Greg! Sharon! They can't be!"

"They're not! Xavier identified the bodies because I could not bear it. He came back and told me it wasn't her."

"Why did the police think it was them?"

"Because the people that died was in Dad's rental car."

"Have you called them?"

"I've been calling them both and they are not answering their phones."

"Where could they be?"

"I have no idea."

"You need to go to the police."

"The police in New York are already investigating."

"You need to contact the police here, who is to say they made it to New York."

"That's what Xavier said, I am scared though."

"It's okay to be frightened, but try not to be. This could all be one big misunderstanding."

The last laugh

"Does my girl know how to throw a party or does my girl know how to throw a party!"

"I really outdid myself this time didn't!?"

"Yes you did, the place looks nice, very nice, love the stage and the mini runway. Is the band here yet?"

"Yes, Abolition is here."

"I hope they are some good."

"Word is they are the hottest band around, on the verge of a recording contract."

"They better be smokin'! How about the models?"

"They are here, along with the wardrobe."

"What wardrobe?"

"I found some clothes that would really look great with your shoes... I went a little over budget."

"How much over the budget?"

"About five grand."

"Yo Kie I am not money bags! Why you spend so much?"

"First impressions go a long way Brice."

"Yeah, I should be able to sell plenty of shoes in this atmosphere. Oh by the way, everybody in here had their invitation in their hand right?"

"Yes they did."

"Good. I only invited my special clients so things could run smoothly."

"Let's have a good time tonight and forget *our problem*."

"I can't do that! The purpose for this party is to sell shoes…if they discover a surprise in their box I don't know anything about it. I don't know how it got there. You understand?"

"Yes I do."

"Let's do this."

Brice takes to the stage and the crowd cheers, giving him much respect.

"Thanks for coming to the grand opening of Revolutions, where my shoes that will be the centerpiece of ground breaking accessories. Won't you give my girl a round of applause as she makes her way to the stage. Kiera Brown is the one who put together this fabulous grand opening."

I had no idea he was going to call me. At least I will get some public recognition from one of the men in my life. "Good evening to our guests, I hope you are in the mood to spend some green because this fashion show is guaranteed to capture your attention. Tonight's items are a must have in your closet."

"I hope you have something for an old fart like me."

Oh my god it's Julius, what….Brice snatches the microphone from me.

"Who would you be?"

"I am State Senator Julius Davidson. I decided to pop in, unannounced and uninvited, my intern neglected to inform me of your grand opening. If she had told me I could have channeled some funds your way. There is a wealth of money available to first time business owners," he said.

I didn't know his district included Northern Liberties. Is there a place not within his reach? I look at Brice, he is calm and cool, but underneath I know he is upset. The presence of a local politician throws a wrench into his plan. This was supposed to be a private party not a media event. If Julius becomes involved it will be a media event escalating into a collaboration with a legal eagle of the highest kind. Brice does not need this.

"I have forgiven you Senator for crashing my party, and I will permit you to stay, provided that you take a seat and spend half of your congressional paycheck."

The audience chuckles along with Brice completely unaware of the strange circumstances. My boss and lover show up at a party hosted by my boyfriend. What does he want?

"I guess I can contribute to your success. I must say this place has plenty of snazzle. I can't wait to see the fashion show."

"Well you won't have to wait, let the fashion show begin."

I watch as the people take their seats along the runway. I give security instructions for our seats, the two in the back near the beginning of the runway, to be reserved for us. With everyone in their seats and the lights dim, we take to our seats. Not long after we sit, Julius came, demanding to sit next to the new businessman. Brice is unwilling to sit next to him and request that I swap seats. I grant him his wish and sit in between them. I am going to sit here and not say anything to either of them.

Julius has over ideas. He purposely rests his arm on the back of my chair to nudge me in the back. I squirm a little and immediately Brice notices, wondering out loud why I'm so antsy. I want to scream *'Julius stop tickling me'* but if I do, it would cause more questions, not only with Brice, but with this audience. And then I would lose the leverage I have over him. No, I will sit here quietly and ignore Julius, let Brice bash in the limelight. Look at how he beams from ear to ear. People not only focus on the shoes, but on the whole ensemble. I should consider expanding into apparel. A few more dollars from Julius will make it all possible.

Without warning, the music stops and the lights come on. Security steps aside as two men in black suits push their way towards us. It's

Agents Skopp and Hobart. Hobart takes the microphone from the emcee and storms the stage.

"I am Inspector Hobart and this is my partner Skopp, we are from Licenses and Inspections."

What a ruse! Two months ago, they said they were federal agents, now they're saying they are city inspectors. Just who are these characters and what do they want? Are they after Julius or are they after me and Brice?

Julius intervened, "Inspector this is a private party is something wrong?"

"Yes sir, sorry to interrupt your par—

"It's quite alright, state your reason for being here," said Julius.

"Well sir an anonymous tip told us there was counterfeit merchandise being sold here," said Hobart.

"Officer as I stated this is a private party, no goods are being sold tonight," said Julius.

"Sir I have a search warrant to search the premises," said Hobart.

Brice barked back, "I don't care what that paper says, you are not searching my place! I don't have any counterfeit merchandise in here. Whoever your anonymous tipster is, they're lying!"

"I see you will not cooperate with the authorities, Skopp cuff him."

Agent Skopp glances at me then looks away, choosing to remain silent. He is letting his partner do all the talking.

"Wait a minute, I mean *he*, does not have anything to hide. Brice let them look so they can get out of here," I said.

"No I will not let them look! This is a set up, a black man starts a business without the help of a bank and the police want to come in and sabotage?!" he screamed.

Hobart spoke, "Officer cuff him and read him his rights."

The young and burly officer approached Brice, "You have the right to remain silent. Anything you say can and will be used against you in a court of law. You have the right to an attorney. If you cannot afford an attorney one will be provided for you, do you understand these rights?"

"No I don't understand anything, I am illiterate!" Brice snapped.

"Take him down to the police station," said Hobart, "Sorry folks the party is over."

"Are we free to leave?" asked a guest.

"Afraid not," said Hobart.

"Why not?" asked the guest.

"As of now, I can charge you with criminal intent. You are here to knowingly buy counterfeit goods," he said.

"Bullshit! I am getting a lawyer, you cannot hold us here while you decide what the charges will be," said a guest.

"I can hold you for 48 hours on the charge of suspicion," said Hobart.

I cannot believe it! This chaos is because of Julius. I have to stop him. "Wait a minute! Revolutions has a contract with the fashion houses to sell their goods. I have copies of those contracts signed with the representatives of the fashion houses if you care to see them."

"Yes I will take a look at them," he said.

"Where is Brice?" I asked.

"For now he is sitting in the van, if you want me to release him, let me take a look at those contracts," he said.

Agent Hobart follows me into the office. He closes the door behind him, and whispers.

"Listen closely, we are here today because your boss, Julius Davidson, told us to come here. He said you and your boyfriend Brice were selling drugs out of this store."

"He's lying!" I shouted.

"Shh!…We have to look like we are doing our job. Now do you see why it is important that you help us?! You either help us nail him or he is going to nail you!"

I tried to post bail for him, but they say it was not an option. Brice has to stay there until his trial date. They would not let him have visitors, not even a phone call. I had to do something, I couldn't leave him in jail, he has never been incarcerated. The best I could do is hire a criminal lawyer. The best in town is Covington and Covington. Cecil Covington said the charges were serious, 200 silica packets were found. They were taken to the lab to be analyze, confirming police suspicions. The tablets were ecstasy. The police charged Brice with intent to distribute. Prosecutors recommend Brice be given the maximum jail time.

I went home to get some sleep. I can't keep worrying about him being locked away with all those murderous convicts. I have to keep my eye on Julius, he's the cause of last night's trouble. He came there to see what I do and who I am with when he is not around. Since he wants to know what I do, I will show him plenty, and he will not like me at, especially when he finds himself behind bars.

Donkey stirs yet again, I hear her in the living room. Although she is a pain in the rear, I need to bend her ear. Better that it be hers than Khloe's, seems like she's waiting for me.

"Look at what the cat or in your case the dog, dragged in."

"Stephanie, where were you this weekend, I needed you!"

"In New York, at my sister's wedding."

"Michele's wedding is two months away."

"Not our sister, *my* sister."

"Khloe tied the knot?"

"Yes she did and the wedding was a dream come true."

"Who did she marry?"

"Xavier."

"Xavier who?"

"Your Xavier."

Bad news in this family always occurs in a series of three's. First there were Julius, then Brice and now Xavier. Donkey sits there and gloats, sipping on coffee as if it was the finest coffee in the world.

"Right now that has to take a back seat to what has happened."

"Why are you so upset?"

"Brice was arrested!"

"What did you do this time?"

"What do you mean *what did I do*? I didn't do anything!"

"That is always your defense isn't it Kiera! Everyone around you gets in deep shit and you always come out as the innocent one smelling like a rose."

She is right, this time she is right. Brice would not be where he is if it were not for me. I can't hold it in any longer, the stress is getting to me, tears fall from my eyes.

"Why weren't you there?"

"Why wasn't I where?"

"At Khloe and Xavier's wedding?"

"Stephanie what are you talking about? Khloe is dating Danny the bartender."

"Geez you are late. Danny is old news, two years old to be exact."

"What the hell are you saying Stephanie?"

"I'm saying you can't say 'my Xavier' anymore. He's gone."

"What do you mean he's gone, where did he go?"

"With her."

"With who?"

"Khloe, he officially became Khloe's."

"What do she has to do with this?"

"Plenty! Shame you are the last to know, but that is always the case. Aren't you her best friend?"

"Enough with the cryptic talk, exactly where Stephanie did Xavier invite you?"

"To his wedding."

A sink hole opens under my feet. I am going under, I have no air, the air has escaped the room. I can barely talk.

"Are you saying that Xavier got married?"

"Yes I am! He and Khloe were married this past weekend. Funny, you are Khloe's best friend and yet you are the last to know. Guess you're not in her inner circle like you thought."

"I don't believe you."

"I knew you were going to say that, I have a little souvenir from their wedding. I made you a copy so you can keep this one."

I open the paper.

Mr. and Mrs. Gregory Spencer

invite you

to observe the midnight nuptials of their daughter

"He couldn't have, he couldn't have gotten married! It was supposed to be me! He was supposed to marry me!"

"Seems like I'm not the only one who wasn't with her man."

"That's just like you to be sarcastic instead of sisterly."

"The black cat looks for sympathy."

"Donkey don't you have somewhere to go?"

"As a matter of fact I do, time for me to leave for work. You should go see someone and talk out your feelings, wouldn't want you to commit suicide or something."

"Bye bitch!"

"Ooh she's mad. She is stuck on the hot tin roof all by her lonesome…Xavier is gone, Brice is in jail, guess that leaves old money bags Julius."

I hurl a book at her just as she close the door behind her. I should be hitting myself with that book, right over the head for being stupid. When did they get engaged? I didn't know they were seeing each other. Why wouldn't she tell me about Xavier? I made the biggest mistake of my life. I made Brice, my high school sweetheart, second in my heart, and for what? For two selfish people incapable of caring about anyone else! It is time I went to work too, and when I get there my disposition will still be the same. Sweet, innocent Kiera on the hunt for information that can send Julius and his friend Xavier to that hell called jail. First I'll call Julius, "Julius it's me Kiera. Did you know Xavier was getting married? "

"Uh… no…he told me he was engaged. When was this wedding supposed to have taken place?"

"This weekend."

"No he didn't."

"Yes he did."

"He would not do that without the family being there."

"Well he did, my sister Stephanie was there."

"Why would he invite her and not invite his father?"

"Upset because he did not invite you?!"

"Damn right I am upset! He is my only child. I should have been there for my boy."

The phone falls away from my hand, my knees buckle, he called Xavier his son. Neither of them ever referred to each other as father and son…they both…I slept with them both. How could I have been…how could he willingly let me sleep with his father?!

"I am going to call him right now."

You can call him, but I am going to see him in person. I have to have confirmation, they cannot be father and son, they just can't.

240

The past is not the past until it is cleared

My drive into Center City is not going as planned. Vine Street is congested as always, it's the thoroughfare almost everyone uses to reach or leave downtown. Thankfully my building is not too far away. It's an old building that I bought dirt cheap and rehabbed. The only thing now is the entrance. Seven white marble stairs, fancy for a hat manufacturer, lead into the building. The interior decorator, the same one I used for Condo Rosa, was thrilled to have a blank slate and I was thrilled to have her, things are definitely not the same.

The smell of coffee infiltrates my nose as I trot up the marble steps. Betty, my secretary, is at the desk, totally engrossed in a book. She loves to read, an attractive attribute and a detractor to her beauty. Normally I see her reading non-fiction, today I'm not sure what that is, the cover is black and plain. "Good Morning Betty, what are you reading?"

"Dante's Inferno, and boy is it good."

I am quite familiar with the book, and with Murphy's Law. "I didn't think you were a fan of fiction."

"Oh this isn't fiction, this is a true story written by—

"I know who Dante Alighieri is, not buying into his revelations of hell."

"You may have a point. I don't know anyone who has had such revelations. Speaking of revelations, I heard you, mister die-hard loner, got married."

"Yes I did."

"Congratulations. Which one did you pick?"

"Khloe."

"Glad to hear you didn't choose hoochie mama."

"That girl was not going to be the kiss of death to me. Anything interesting in the mail?"

"The usual, bills and junk, I gave it to Jeffrey."

"Let me know when Aurelius Kokas gets here."

"Sure, do you need me to pull files?"

"No, everything I need is in my office."

I continue on to my office. Jeffrey Singletary and Billy Feit, my partners should be in. I could have chosen a couple of my frat brothers but I chose to go outside the loop. Strangers always work better for me, they are free of the assumptions that come with familiarity. I stop to take a quick glance into the conference room. Jeffrey and Billy are working.

"Hey Xavier, wasn't expecting you to be in today. I thought you would be on your honeymoon."

"I promised her we would go on a honeymoon at a later date Jeffrey."

"Man the ceremony was beautiful, the food was good, and the women—bon apetite."

"Billy what women?"

"The chicks that were there. You didn't notice because you were focused on your bride, and rightfully so, she was the most beautiful woman there."

"I am glad you enjoyed yourself. You guys need anything I'll be in my office."

"We're good."

My office is across from them. I throw my things on the leather sofa and look at the pile of messages awaiting me. All of them are from my father, might as well get it over with. I picked up the handset. "Julius."

"Xavier what is this I hear about you getting married?"

"I did."

"You said you were coming to dinner."

"We are."

"Before the wedding, you were supposed to come to dinner *before* the wedding, not after."

"I didn't want to wait."

"Why not, what was the hurry? Am I becoming a grandfather?"

"We are not having a baby."

"Kiera is devastated. She has been crying non-stop."

"Lend her your shoulder."

"That's cold Xavier."

"No colder than you spoiling my goods."

"What's that suppose to mean?"

"You can keep her, she's all yours."

"Son what are you talking about?"

"I'm talking about you sleeping with Kiera."

He is silent though I hear him breathing, "You thought I didn't know didn't you?"

"Xavier I never touched her. I never touched Kiera."

"The way you never touched Gladys?"

"Don't talk about your mo—

"She's not my mother. I mean she's not my biological mother."

"She is your mo—

"No she is not! I've seen my birth certificate, the one you kept hidden from me. I asked Gladys, and she confirmed it."

More silence, more breathing except this time it's heavier.

"Xavier, Marie is not…" he paused again, "son she is not what you think."

"And what is that? What am I thinking?"

"You think she is sweet as pie…she is like a diamond, beautiful, shiny, and hard."

"Being married to you made her hard, just like you made me hard…only a madman would send a six year old to a boarding school on the other side of the world."

"I was trying to prepare you—

"For what? To take over?"

"No, to prepare you for the world! Son life is about the survival of the fittest, and I want you to be a survivor. A survivor of anything life throws at you, including a woman who is beautiful and hard like Marie Colette Amou-Landes."

"Marie is not as hard as you make her out to be."

"Oh really! Well why didn't she stop me from sending you to that school huh?"

"I don't know."

"She could have, she knew you were going there. Did she ever come and see you?"

"No."

"Thought not, son she knew the name and address of every school you attended. She's seen all your report cards. It was her idea to pretend to be you godmother."

"Her idea!"

"Yes, her idea. Marie's a woman who prefers pants to dresses."

I always thought I had the father from hell. In reality my mother is there too, standing right by his side. Two lumps of coal, porous to anything corruptible and abominable.

"Dad I have to go."

I hang up, not wanting to hear another word, another lie from the great humanitarian whom I let pull me into his bed. The humanitarian turned out to be lion, stealthily seeking the best of the best. Now there is a lioness in my mist, extension 22 is lit.

"Yeah Betty."

"Xavier I guess I don't have to worry about you too much anymore. I'm calling to ask is you would like to order lunch with us?"

Feed a cold, starve a fever or in my case feed my temperament. A nice diversion for my thoughts, "I'll have the usual."

I focus on my work, gathering the materials I was using before I went to New York. It's not finished but it's a general frame of my ideas. Kokas should be pleased with the promotional package. Its industry standard, guaranteed to garner the attention of hard core gamers. The main character Matthew Peters is an undercover cop. He walks the tightrope of life, fighting criminal urges. Matthew must commit certain crimes to maintain his street cover and advance to the next board. He must do so without getting a single scratch anywhere on his person. He sees a lot of unsavory characters making transactions of all sorts. To earn quick money Matthew engages in shooting craps, attending a card game to someone's house, meet a contact in a speakeasy, sample drugs, and act as guardian angel to the public he's sworn to protect. Jeffrey and Billy, the programmers make the action happen. Both are computer geeks with criminal urges all of their own.

I storm into his building, waltzing past Betty. I dare her to stop me. I dare her to utter a single word.

"Kiera may I help you?"

"No you may not! This is between me and him, and no, I don't need your help finding him, I know exactly where he is!"

I hear Betty telling him an ex with an axe to grind is in the building. If he takes her cue, he'll realize it's me, his fiancée. I don't care, I have something to say and he's going to listen. I march on toward his office. I hear the door opening as I get closer. By the time I get there the door is wide open. I stand in the entrance.

"What's up girl?"

"I've been calling you all weekend. Where have you been?"

"Getting married."

My heart skips several beats while nausea replaces my nerves of steel. I've already heard the news, but hearing it from his mouth is leaving me reeling, "To whom?"

"To Khloe."

He admits it with glee. I struggle to get the words out, "I didn't know you were seeing her? How could you marry her when you promised to marry me?"

"I made no such promise. We were friends...at one time lovers, brief lovers...and then you did—

"What? I did what?"

"You did the unthinkable Kiera, you slept with my Dad!"

"Xavier I never slept with your Dad"

"But you did. You want to know how I know? My Mom heard you and called me. I saw you leaving their house. Another time, when you went over there, I went over there too, and I heard you. I heard you freaking my old man."

Tears are rolling down my cheeks. He acknowledges their relationship, they are father and son. All this time they have been playing a game with me. I have to deny his accusations. I cannot confirm them, no matter what. "I did not sleep with your Dad. I don't

246

care about what you think you heard. I would never sleep with a dirty old man."

"Are you calling me a liar?"

"Those are your words not mine. Look, I was at the house because Julius asked me to come over and help him with his work."

"At two o'clock in the morning? You could have said no. You should have said no."

"I couldn't."

"Why not? Why couldn't you tell him no?"

"Because…" I didn't finish my sentence.

"I thought so."

"I needed the money Xav, that is why you got me the job remember? If you thought I was sleeping with your father, why didn't you say something?"

"Don't question me!"

He is lost for words, guess he never thought I would question him, well I am, "Why not? Why can't I question you?"

"Because we are over, you are my past."

Just like that he buries me. He sits at his desk, eyes concentrating on the laptop.

"I am the past because you want me in the past. When I think about it Xavier, you were always looking at someone else. I did not satisfy you."

The pen fell from his fingers onto the desk. A few clicks and the laptop close. The papers spread out over his desk, he collects one by one and pile them upon one another, accumulating into a small mountain. The mountain is preserved in an expandable folder, held by a string he wraps around its perimeter twice before a final lap around a clasp. He places the folder behind him and on top of the printer. The laptop is moved too, onto the bottom shelf of the printer table. The desk is clear, his eyes focus on me.

"It is not all your fault Kiera, it was me too."

Did my ears hear what they think they heard? Did he confess fault in the demise of our relationship? He steps out from behind his desk and come to the front. We stand face to face, eye to eye, is he about to kiss me?

"I wanted a fresh outlook on life, someone with a different approach."

"Different how?"

"My girl went to work for my dad and became a $1000 a week, tax-free intern."

My hand makes contact with his face. From the expression on his face he's never been hit by a woman. He responds in kind, blood oozes from my nose. I back away from him, just a little. He doesn't react to my movement, his stance is firm and stoic. He really believes I chose Julius over him.

"Xavier your father asked me to come over and help him with his work."

"Kie, Julius always wants help. He knew you were seeing me. He was testing you. He tests everyone around him. He wants to see how much you will lap up, how far will you go to please him."

"Xavier you were always lapping after him."

"No. no, that was your job and from what I heard and saw, you are pretty good at it."

"You are no different from me—you sneak and marry my best friend."

"Stop with the victim act! You and I were over long before Khloe happened on the scene."

"We both met you at the same Spring Break function. You chose me, you had me, and then you went after her."

"She's a respectable girl!" he yells, "When I dated Khloe out in the open nobody had anything to say about her. I couldn't say that about you."

"If you were out in the open how come Julius never met her?"

"Because of what he did with you, he'll never met her. Not until *I* am ready."

"Your Khloe is not as pristine as you think. She's seeing that sports bar owner."

"I know all about them."

"And you trust her?"

"Yes."

"Well then you know about these."

His eyes narrowed as they pour over 8x10" glossies of his beloved and her lover. One has them intertwined in the heat of the Moment. Another show her on top, and the last shows them nestled in each other's arms. The color has left Xavier's face. Oh no, is he? Nah…he can't, is he on the verge of tears. I can't believe what I am seeing. Big bad Xavier is crying, uh oh he is angry, very angry. He jumped up from his chair and flipped his desk over. I backed away, out into the hall. I turned to run, something yanks me back.

"Get back here you dirty ho, everybody needs to know about you!"

He stood behind me, his arms encircle me like a tire. I can't break his grip, his hands cup my face.

"Hey Jeffrey and Billy come over here, come meet my ex-girlfriend."

His friends stand in the doorway, "What's up, what's going on Xav?"

"Want to know why she's my ex? She sleeps with my dad."

They shake their head in disgust, "So that's what happened."

"That's right, you heard correct, she sleeps with my dad. Don't you think that's a good reason to break up with someone? I mean how can you trust a girl who sleeps with your dad?"

"You can't Xav, you made the right decision," said Billy.

"C'mon man let her go man, you've moved on. You picked a woman of worth and you married her," said Jeffrey.

"I already let her go, see she is free," he said, releasing me.

I backed away, far away, out of his reach.

He continued, "I'm done with you. I don't care how many pictures you bring to me, I will not leave my wife, do you hear me! I will never leave her. Stay away from her. Stay away from me. You are no longer welcomed in her house."

"You don't get to tell me to stay away from my best friend!" I shouted back.

He lunges at me, but Jeff and Billy intervene telling me to leave while I still can. Xavier grumbles at them, mumbling every expletive known as he tries to break their grip. I scramble down the hall, out the main door to the street. I keep moving despite the blaring horns pressed by pissed off drivers because I sprint in front of them. I can slow down now, I'm safe, I guess they were successful in holding him back.

"You think your free of me because you married her. Wrong assumption, if I can't have you…"

Here is my car, safe and sound, right where I left her. I must call Danny. "Hello Danny, I just found our next candidate. Wait something just fell on the roof of my car. What the hel—

"You trick!"

Oh shit! It's Xavier, he's on the roof of my car. He's pounding the windshield with his fist.

"You cheap trick! You should be standing on the corner, and when I get my hands on you that's exactly where you will be going, on the corner, with all the other tricks!"

He continues pounding, the windshield cracks. Blood fills the cracks, the windshield resembles a mosaic. Shards of glass fly in my lap. He's made a gaping hole, his bloody hand reaches for me, I slide down in my seat. I have to move the seat back. It's the only way to escape his grasp. Bad move, he's caught hold of my clothes. He pulls me towards the hole, snarling like a mad dog.

"Let me give you something you won't forget. When I am finish, no one will want you."

I wrestle to free myself from his grip, nicking my hands on the glass. A piercing pain sears above my eyes and around my nose. Warm liquid runs down my face as the pain intensifies. Suddenly I fall backwards. I am free.

"Are you okay? Can you open the door so I can make sure you are okay?"

"No! No! Go away! Stop! Please leave me alone!"

"Kiera, it's me Jeff. I'm just trying to help. I called for an ambulance, they should be here shortly."

I opened the door.

"Kie are you alright? Of course not, that was a silly question to ask."

I reach for my face.

"No, no, don't do that, you don't want to infect it."

I scream in horror, "He's ruined my face! He's ruined my face!"

"Miss you are lucky, a few inches more and the glass would have cut into your eye. Who did this to you?"

Should I or shouldn't I? Should I report this? Should I tell the police what he did to me? I never imagined Xavier hurting me, hurting

251

anyone. Who would have thought he was capable of being a madman. I am not going to let this slide. He will not get away with this. Both of them will pay for what they did to me.

"My boyfriend…in a fit of anger."

"This is a case of domestic violence. The police will be in to take your statement."

"Thank you. Do you have a mirror? I want to see your work."

"Miss I don't think it's a good idea to…"

"You said I had a few nicks."

"Yeah, they are nicks, and scars. They are deep…the stitches will hopefully aid in the regeneration of cell growth. If not, you should invest in a good plastic surgeon."

The female police arrive, "I am Officer Williams. I was told you want to file a complaint."

"Yes I do. I want the bastard who did this arrested."

"You know who he is?"

"His name is Xavier Charles Davidson and this happened at his Center City address."

"What prompted the attack?"

"He accused me of…never mind. I don't want to file charges. I want to forget the whole thing."

"Are you sure this is what you want?"

"Yes I am sure."

"Are you afraid? Afraid of what he might do if you file this complaint?"

"As a matter of fact I am."

"Don't be, there are plenty of places that house victims of domestic violence. He will never be able to find you."

"I change my mind, I don't want to file a complaint."

"A minute ago you were determined to get the man who did this, and now you have changed your mind."

"I am going to a place where he will never find me."

"That's good, I am glad to hear it. If he attacked you once, he will attack you again."

"He will never get the opportunity to put his hands on me again."

"By the way, what is your name?'

"Kiera."

"Kiera?"

"Just Kiera."

"Okay Kiera, I am not going to file this complaint because you declined."

"Thanks Officer Williams."

She close her tablet and put her pen away. She's going to report this, I just know it. Why can't I think before opening my mouth?

"Officer Williams, can I have that piece of paper?"

"What paper?"

"The one you wrote my complaint on."

"I'm sorry I can't. Whatever I write in my tablet has to stay in my tablet."

"But I told you I don't want to file a complaint."

"And I am not going to. You said you didn't want to file a complaint and I am going to honor your request."

Lieutennace Greenberg from the precinct in my parent's neighborhood, says he has all the information he needs to begin the investigation. Mom and Dad are not dead. I believe I would know if they were dead, my gut would tell me, but something has happened. I want to go to their house and check. Maybe something is there, some clue. Their cars are in the driveway, I touch the hoods. They are cold, very cold. Dad's briefcase lies on the front seat in open view. Since when do you leave your briefcase in the car? Nothing is out of place in mother's car. She didn't leave anything behind, not even her eyeglasses, she always left a pair in the car.

Xavier and Saki could be onto something, maybe Mother and Dad never left the city. The rental car does not make sense. Mother and Dad like to make a statement. Whenever they take a trip out of town they always hire a chauffeur. For them exercising clout among their peers and gaining recognition in the press is extremely important. I am glad I kept my old keys I can inside and look around, but I am afraid to go any further. It is quiet, eerily quiet. The home alarm system should have been triggered by now. Upon entering the home you have ten seconds to key in the code. It's over a minute and the alarm is still silent. "Mom? Dad? Anybody home?"

They don't answer. I'm still waiting for the alarm system to kick on, maybe it's broken. There is a way to find out, the alarm box is hidden in a panel in the back of the stairs. I flip open the panel, no wonder it did not go off, it's not on. They did not set it. If they were intent on traveling to New York, they would have set the alarm system. "Mother? Dad?"

I don't know why I bother calling them again. There is no one here but me. The house looks like it usually does everything in its place. This room is immaculate. The arrangement of the furniture is just the way mother likes it. The open floor plan was not suited to her liking, but after looking at 18 plus houses, Dad forced her to choose one. So she chose the house resembling a Mediterranean villa. She took the furniture and created her own walls. Certain rooms of this house were for certain people. The living room was a very formal area, reserved strictly for guests. The family room located off the kitchen was reserved for intimate friends and extended family members. Neither area resembles life lived in the last couple of days. Could that be the story upstairs? Only way to find out is if I go up there. Back to the foyer and up the stairs. "Mother? Dad?"

I know no one is in the house, but I thought I holler out anyway, just in case someone who shouldn't be *is* up there. At the top, I stop and look, all the doors are open. They should not be open, mother always keeps them shut. She always said that the best way to foil a burglar was to make them believe someone was home. I want to check their room first. I want to see if any clothes and suitcases are missing.

Their room is double the size of mine. The last time I was in here, the room was dark. Mother chose dramatic black wallpaper, its saving grace was the gold shells. Each one was inside a diamond separated from the others by a thin gold border. The paprika bedding gave the room added drama. I see she commissioned Venus again, she has outdone herself this time. Love the color scheme, sky blue, gold, turquoise, cream, and what I would call creamsicle. It's so peaceful here. Their room was always a source of peace for me, probably because we spent a lot of time at the vanity.

I sit on the vanilla bench with baroque cloth. My eyes are immediately drawn to the roses swirling along the mirror edges. I remember coming home from school and finding this vanity table in her room. Vanilla in color and high gloss, I used to look down at the table and see myself. I would open the drawers from the top and peer inside. Hundreds of lipsticks and eye shadows neatly lined one behind another.

I remember the day I was sent to my room. It had rained heavily that entire day and I was antsy, sassy. Mother sent me upstairs as punishment. In anger I made a detour to her room. Defiantly I took a cherry lipstick and smeared some on my lips. I found red nail polish and painted my nails. Mother walked in just as I was screwing the top back on. I knew I was in trouble, and braced myself for a spanking. She didn't hit me nor did she punish me. Instead she said one day I would have a turn and she would be there to help me get ready for a party. "Mom you missed the opportunity to help me get ready, you both did."

I am Saki's daughter. I favor her so much. I have her almond shaped eyes, slender nose, and her long jet black hair. Her hair is poker straight while mine is full or ringlets. Dad gave me his pouty lips. Luscious lips are what Xavier calls them. He also gave me his big forehead, which I conceal with my curls. What I did not get from Saki is her super smooth porcelain skin. Saki has an unusual beauty regimen that she shared with me. Every morning we applied a skin crème called Uguisu no fun, fancy word for bird poop to our face and neck. The thought was quite disgusting, but the results were amazing. It removed all the impurities in my face. My face and hands are always soft and smooth. Danny used to be in awe of my skin, he said it was flawless. I bet he doesn't say that now. I should go see him and apologize. I know I shouldn't but I need to explain.

I peer into another drawer and find a box, a brown flat rate box, six inches thick and quite long. It is addressed to her and was delivered last Wednesday. No name on the return address, just a post office box number. I unfold the flaps to look inside and find paper, stuffed to the very top. I take the box over to her bed and disburse the contents on the bed. The papers turn out to be receipts, hundreds of receipts. They are receipts from a hotel in East Rutherford, New Jersey dated April of 1989 all the way to January 1990. Daddy paid for a single hotel room, he must have been there on a business trip. I didn't know we had business contacts in Bergen County New Jersey.

I forage thru the rest of the papers and run across a picture of a baby. She's a happy baby. All dressed in pink and laughing hysterically. Her name is probably on the back, oh no she didn't …she is lying! She has to be lying!

To my advantage

"Did you put Greg Spencer in a safe place?"

"Yes I did. He's in a place where no one would think to look."

"Good. I need you to stay there with him, make sure he's secure."

"Okay, but that will be another ten grand."

"Fine. Don't harm him…I just need him to be out of the way for awhile."

"What about her? What do we do with her?"

"I haven't decided what I'm going to do with her. Right now she's in the perfect position."

Nothing out of the ordinary is going on at work. Dad is not in yet neither is Khloe. I guess Khloe is still on her honeymoon. I'll check in with butt head Phil Jackson for details on today's agenda.

"Morning Tamara, Khloe in yet?"

Southern drawl, yuk! There's only one person with a southern drawl and that is Bob Cummings, the transport from Oklahoma. I hate a man with small eyes, he's not bad looking though. "Not sure Bob, I just got here myself. Let me check with Phil."

Bob chose to sit on the sofa a few feet away from my desk. This man sure loves his western wear. Every time he comes here and it is not often, he is always dressed in western wear. He's been in the city long enough to be citified. Somebody should give this man a fashion makeover. I put my things on the desk and walk over to Phil's door. I hear someone crying, sounds like a small child bawling. I know he didn't bring his kids to work. "Phil? Is everything okay in there?"

Why isn't he answering me, I know he heard my big mouth. I want to know what's going on. I poke my head in and look at the back of his chair, it faces the door. "Phil?!"

Well there is no child in here, oh snap, he's watching a movie. He should have done that last night when he was home, not on company time. Talk about abuse of power! I'm going to remind him that there is work to be done. "Phil?"

He is moaning so loud he doesn't hear me, the chair trembles—oh he has it on massage.

"Damn it girl don't you know how to knock!"

"Well well well, Mr. Pain in the ass is caught with his dick in his hand, jerking off to…what is that…kiddie porn???"

"Shut up! Shut your mouth right now!"

"You should be shutting up your pants, not telling me to shut my mouth!"

"Get your black ass out of her right now!"

"I will…and your white ass is going to be leaving too!"

"You're just a secretary. You can't get rid of me, you don't have any power to get rid of me."

"She might not, but I do! I saw the whole thing, totally inappropriate, totally unprofessional. Lord have mercy, a vice president looking at porn eight o'clock in the morning on the company computer…sad, real sad."

"That laptop is mine. Okay, my personal property and you better not touch it."

"C'mon Tamara leave this jerk in his fantasy."

Bob closes Phil's door, "Is Greg in yet?"

"No."

"I'll sit and wait for Khloe. She needs to know about him, damn pervert!"

"I will give her a call."

I use the phone at my desk, "Hi Khloe, it's Tamara. Bob Cummings is here. He would like to speak to you and your Dad. Your Dad is not in—"

"Tamara it's imperative that you tell no one that Dad is not in yet. I will be in this afternoon. I have a very important appointment I have to keep."

"What do you want me to tell Bob Cummings?"

"Tell Bob I will be in this afternoon. If he wants to hang around or come back he can."

"Okay, I think I should tell you there was an incident around here."

"Let Phil Jackson handle it."

"It involves Phil Jackson. I am a witness to it as is Bob."

"Is it serious?"

"Extremely serious."

"What happened?"

"I don't think I should tell you over the phone."

"Doesn't sound good, does it involve theft of funds?"

"No, more of a sexual nature."

"Please don't say sexual assault."

"Not out and out sexual assault, nevertheless it is a federal crime, not to mention breaking the company's code of conduct."

"Has he broken the company's laws regarding moral conduct?"

"Absolutely, it's grounds for dismissal."

"I won't go that far, there has to be an investigation first."

"It happened here, in his office less than 15 minutes ago."

"Oh boy, never figured Phil to be stupid."

"Neither did I."

"It'll have to keep until I get there. Just carry on with your daily duties and don't make any waves with him."

"Okay,"

I put the phone on the base and whisper to Bob Khloe's instructions. I excuse myself and go into the bathroom. I take out my cell phone and stand next to the bathroom window, I get a signal. This is my chance to move up and move him out of the way. "Hello I want to report a crime…"

I return to my desk and wait for the fireworks. Here comes Bob, "Coffee smells good."

"I'm staying to wait for Khloe so I made a fresh pot. I need a cup."

"Good idea, cups should be in the cupboard. Can I help you with anything?"

"Yeah, I need a work area. I want to double check my work before she gets here. I'm sure the figures are fine, but I need to keep myself occupied."

"How are the café's progressing along?"

"Tamara in my area they are quite popular, profits are up. People are opting for the more healthful lunch and early supper."

"So you met your profit margin by how much?"

"We projected our profits to increase by seven percent. Intentionally low balled it, surprisingly we exceeded those projections by ten percent."

"So your profits increased by 17 percent."

"Yes."

"Not bad. How many café's are in your region?"

"Right now I have five. We put them in areas where there are none or very few dining facilities in or near industrial parks. We hired chefs…the public is very pleased, Khloe will definitely be impressed.

"How many café's are slated to be constructed?"

"I'm looking to put three more in my region."

"Your region could use it. Strategically you are in better position to have excellent profits since you are catering to the business sector. Describe the décor for the cafés."

"We are keeping it simple but classy. Square tables with four chairs, white tablecloths, white china, and stainless silverware, not too simplistic."

"How many people can be seated?"

"Initially we decided to keep it small so we seated 50 people. Now we have to expand to seat 75, employers thought it wise to give their entire workforce the same lunch period."

"Wow!"

"Yeah, exactly, I met with company executives and set aside a specific hour for each company."

"How many companies are you servicing?"

"Ten."

"That's a good size crowd for a test market. I would like to visit one of your cafes."

"You're more than welcomed. I'll ask Khloe after we tell her the news. I'm sure she'll give you the aft…who called them?"

"I don't know."

Philly's finest are here, right on time. I dare you to tell me to shut up now.

"Excuse me, we are looking for Mr. Philip Jackson."

"His office is right there."

I wonder if he straightened himself up? Being the smart ass he is I'm sure he did. I can't hear all that they are saying, but I do hear them ask to see his laptop. He asks them why, and they give him no explanation. He tells them no because there is nothing on there that will interest them. He asks them why they are here, and they tell him Rachael called. Rachael, meaning me, and not his wife. He rants and raves, calling her every name imaginable and then denies the accusations. The officers leave his office and come out and stand next to my desk.

"As of now operations will cease, all computers will be seized…

Phil storms out of his office and shouts at them, "On what grounds, you have no probable cause!"

"Someone called us and said an executive officer from Spencer Foods Incorporated was looking at child pornography on a laptop at corporate headquarters. As you know the owning and/or viewing of child pornography is a federal crime."

"The only executive officer in the building at this moment is Phil," I said.

"Wait a minute!" Phil yelled, "You just said my wife called you, now you are saying "someone" called you. Who really called you with this story?"

"It was anonymous," said the officer.

"There you go right there, the person is lying. Why else would he or she hide their identity?" asked Phil.

"He's afraid of you, afraid of losing his job," said the officer.

"He, you said he," Phil reminded them.

The police did not confirm or deny the identity of the tipster. Instead they ask, "Where is the company president?"

"He's supposed to be in later," I said.

"Well you should call him because Spencer Foods will not be allowed to conduct business until our investigation is complete."

"What type of time frame are you talking about?" asked Bob.

"Until we find what we are looking for," said the officer.

"Tamara you better give Khloe a call."

I pull out my phone and give her a call, her voicemail picks up. I leave a message and mark it urgent. She calls back, when I relay the events, she said she would be here in 15 minutes.

There she is, Miss Stephanie Tamara Brown, working as our secretary. What is she up to? What does she want, money? Dad pays her the going wage for an executive secretary. That is the key isn't it— Dad. Dad is the one who hired her. Did he hire her because he wanted to, because of her skills or was it because he was forced to? "Tamara can I see you in my office?"

"Sure."

I carry Mom's box and sit it on the table. I search for the photo I left on top of the pile. I find it, scrutinizing every facet of the chubby little face. Here she comes, casually strolling in with Tamara's signature look and attitude—very docile. It is a look I cannot recall her ever straying from. She is not that much different at Spring Break, except for the clothes and the glasses, the attitude is the same. I don't think it's an act. Rather it's a state of being. She's not after money, she wants something else. She wants acceptance. Unfortunately her acceptance hinges on the physical comparison to Dad. I don't see his unforgettable forehead or his nose.

"The police was here for Phil Jackson."

"What did they want with him?"

"They wanted to search our computers."

"Search *our* computers, for what? What were they looking for?"

"They got a report about Phil viewing child pornography on a company computer."

"Are you kidding me? Of all the…where is Phil?"

"He is meeting with Kessler."

"Oh he is?! Stephanie we will have to continue our conversation later. Never mind, you know what? I am going to handle this right now!" I pull out the photo, "Do you know who she is?"

Stephanie smiles, "It's me, where did you get it?"

"I found it with these papers, this box as at my parent's house. Do you know anything about this?"

"Yes, you are my sister."

"No we are not sisters! Who told you that?"

"We have the same Dad."

"What do you mean we have the same Dad?"

"Your Dad was having an affair with my mother. Those receipts prove it."

"All those receipts prove is that he spent a lot of time in East Rutherford and he gave Carolyn Brown way too much money. For what, only God knows!"

"He gave it to her for me."

"Let me see your birth certificate."

Stephanie has her own envelope with her, which means she anticipated meeting me. No wonder Mother was so upset. With all these secrets coming to light I can only imagine the anguish she must have felt. The love of her life has three separate families. She pours everything on my desk. I see her birth certificate, its red and white typed with a black font.

"Baby girl child Stephanie Tamara Brown was born on November 10, 1987, 12:20AM to Carolyn Andrea Brown and Gregory Maurice Jones. I knew it! Dad's name is not on your birth certificate."

"I know it's not. It's not there because he demanded that it not be listed."

"Because he is not your Dad, now is he?"

"Yes he is, Gregory Spencer is my Dad. Why would a man pay child support if he didn't have to?"

"What child support?'

Stephanie hands me the same receipts I already had and some new ones. They have the same dates, years, and most importantly the same signature as the hotel receipts. There is no question, Dad gave her mother money. He paid her mother five thousand dollars every month for 21 years.

"Now you tell me, why would Dad pay that much money every month if I were not his child?"

"Stop calling him Dad! He's not your Dad!"

She has a point, why pay 1.2 million dollars if you don't have to? If he was the father wouldn't he want proof? Wouldn't he demand to know for certain is she was his? "I know why he paid all that money, your mother threatened him. She threatened to tell my mother."

"No she didn't! If she wanted your mother to know, she would have told her a long time ago."

"No she wouldn't have. My Dad was giving her plenty, why rock the boat…this is about you. What do you want Stephanie?"

"I want him to admit he's my father."

"What happens if he doesn't?"

"He will."

"You sound certain."

"He will tell you I am his daughter."

"Don't be so sure Stephanie. It seems like he went to extreme measures to keep you a secret.

"I know he did. I can't wait to hear why."

"Maybe he did it because he *really* felt you weren't his."

"But why would he pay all that money? Why support a child that is not yours?"

"Listen Stephanie, I just found out something about my Dad that is quite unsettling. Something that, if you had tried to tell me before today, I probably would have slapped you."

"What's that?"

"He is not as nice as he appears to be."

"This I do know."

"This also means that you and I are in the same boat, neither of us knows who Gregory Maurice Spencer really is. Our questions for him will have to wait until he gets back. Now let's talk about Phil Jackson, tell me from the beginning what happened."

Stephanie cleared her throat, "This morning I went into his office to tell him Bob Cunningham was here and I saw him."

"What was he doing?"

"He was looking at naked pictures of children."

Unbelievable! Everything hits the fan as soon as Mom and Dad disappear. Astonished by her statement, I asked her, "What did you say Phil was doing?"

"I said he was jacking o—

"No, that's not what you said. Start over, from the beginning."

"I went in to Phil's office to let him know Bob Cunningham was here to see him."

"Why didn't you call him on the phone?"

"I did, he never answered."

"How could you be certain he was in there?"

"Because I had brought him a folder he had requested earlier. He never left the office."

"You said Bob Cunningham is here to see Phil. Where is he now?"

"In Conference Room 2."

"Back to your story, you went into Phil's office because he never answered the phone. You were going to tell him Bob was here to see him, then what happened?"

"The back of his chair was facing me. I noticed it was shaking, almost in a rocking motion. I heard him moaning and groaning, and I heard humming. That is when I realized the chair was massaging his back, so I walked up to him and…"

"And what?"

"That is when I saw him."

She is embarrassed, her face is flushed with color, "Stephanie what did you see?"

"Phil's hand was wrapped around his erect penis."

"What?!"

"He was jacking off to a movie. A young girl was being raped. He turned the volume down so no one could hear, but I saw her face. She was screaming for help, and there he was, enjoying every minute of that poor girl's pain!"

"I don't…"

I had to sit down. Her words, I know what she said, I heard her loud and clear, but what she said can't be right. I cannot picture him doing what she is accusing him of, it's totally out of character. Phil is very professional. He takes pride in his work. He loves the adulation and prestige that comes with being a vice president of a well known company. He is married and the father of two girls. There is no way he could have a serious character flaw such as pedophilia. I must consider the source. Stephanie and I have been friends for a number of years, in which she has been masquerading as a secretary to a man she thinks is her father. Kooky is definitely calling her.

"Something has to be done."

"Yes I know, that's why I called the police."

"You what?!"

"I called the police. The way he yelled at me, I felt threatened."

"You felt threatened."

"Yes I did, besides they were already on the way."

"Says who?"

"The police said his wife Rachael called them to complain about him and his viewing child pornography on his laptop."

"I doubt she would report him to the authorities. To do so would cast them *both* in a negative light, she would lose everything. Speaking of losing everything, do you think it was wise of you to call the police?"

"Yes! We have to take a stand."

"We?!"

"Spencer Foods has to let its customer base know that its employees are a visual representation of the company. Only employees with a stable psyche and morals similar to the company values are considered for employment. Therefore, those that hired are obligated to adhere to the contractual agreement they signed on their hiring date. It is unfortunate that Vice President Phil Jackson did not comply with the company's bylaws. Regrettably, Spencer Foods has to terminate his employment."

"Whoa! Wait a minute! You cannot terminate Phil Jackson without an investigation and you need Dad's approval."

"I'm not going to fire Phil Jackson, you are!"

"I just told you that I cannot do that, there has to be an investigation. He is the senior officer so he will be given the benefit of the doubt, besides there is no one to take his place."

"Yes there is."

"I suppose you are talking about yourself."

"I have the qualifications, but that is not my focus."

"What is your focus?"

"Making sure Phil's mess does not muddle our reputation."

"If it is muddled it will be because of you. Lesson number one, think before you call the authorities. If you have a problem with the personnel, handle it in-house. Where is Phil?"

"Are you suggesting that if someone around here commits a crime and I know it, I shouldn't call the police?"

"That's not what I am saying. I am saying you have to think of the repercussions. You have to have a plan in place--a prepared statement condemning such action and a community response. In this case, Spencer Foods would have to align itself with an organization devoted to the prevention and/or dissemination of pornographic material. Where did you say Phil was?"

"He said he was meeting with Bill Kessler."

I walk over to my desk to use the phone. I need to talk with all of them to get their side of the story beginning with Bob Cunningham. She is still standing here, waiting for instructions. From that little speech she gave moments ago, it sounded like she has memorized her own instructions, for us. "By the way let's keep your claim amongst ourselves until Dad comes back… hey Bill, Khloe here, can I see you and Phil in my office in about 20 minutes or so, thanks."

I called the conference room where Bob was located and told him to come to my office. I also called Chris, our chief information officer.

"Are they all coming?"

"Yes they are."

"What about Greg?"

"Dad is indisposed at the moment."

"You don't know where he is do you?"

"No I don't, and no one around here can know that. Who is the lead detective?"

"He didn't give his name."

"Stephanie how can you be so sure of their identity?"

"They are with Phaedra, I can let her know you are here."

"Not yet. I need to talk with the senior officers."

"Well you had better hurry, the FBI will probably be here too."

"The FBI?!"

"It is against the law to possess child pornography."

"I know it is!"

Country Bob has arrived, I ask Stephanie to leave us alone. I want to hear what he has to say without any input from her.

"Hi Bob, I understand you were here this morning. Can you tell me what happened?"

"I'll tell you what I saw and heard. I heard Phil Jackson screaming at Tamara. He was telling her to get her black ass out of his office. I jumped up and ran in there to see what was going on, and that is when I saw him."

"Exactly what did you see?"

"He was adjusting his tie."

"Did you see anything on the computer?"

"No, it was closed."

"Tamara said she saw him watching child pornography on the computer."

"I didn't see anything like that. The police came in and said they got a report. Someone called and told them he was looking at child pornography on the company computers. They said they were shutting us down."

"She told me. Did they?"

"No they didn't, they said they would be back though."

"They have no reason to come back, we have no such filth floating around on our network," he said.

It's Chris Muncie, he is responsible for keeping our computer system safe and secure, and also for reporting any inappropriate employee activity. Chris is nearing retirement, but he knows his stuff. If Phil was watching that junk on our computers, he would have rung the alarm immediately.

"I am not sure where the accusation came from but I assure you no one in any of our facilities is looking at kiddie porn or any other kind of porn. It has to be on his personal computer."

"Thanks for the reassurance, Bob I need to have a private conversation with Chris. In the mean time can you prepare a written statement as soon as possible. I need all the details, the time, what you saw, Phil's responses…can you tell Tamara to write one too, thanks."

Bob closed the door as he exited. Chris looks at me with his famous furrowed brow, "What's going on?"

"Do you know anything about the incident between Phil and Tamara this morning?"

"What incident?"

"I will tell you the specifics at a later date. What I can tell you is that right now I have two people hurling accusations against Phil for inappropriate conduct, which can be misconstrued as sexual harassment or racial discrimination if I do not handle this carefully."

"What kind of inappropriate conduct?"

"One employee says he was masturbating, the other is saying that he screamed a racial epitaph."

"Oh geez is that why the police are here. She freaked out cause she saw him playing with himself!"

"If what she is saying is true would that be on videotape?"

"Yes it would unfortunately."

"I need to see that tape."

"I'll get right on it."

Tall and wafer thin, Chris is gone. Damn! I just thought of something else, "Chris!"

He returns just as quickly, "Yes?"

"I don't want the police to see it before me."

"Gotcha!"

He leaves once more, nearly bumping into chief suspect. I hear Phil, talking in his usual air of superiority, totally appropriate for executive leadership, unappealing to subordinates.

"Okay little miss muffet, are you comfy sitting on your tuffet?" he asked.

"Actually I am quite comfy, how about yourself?" she spewed back.

"Well the spider is here to chase you away permanently," he said.

I had better get out there before he makes matters worse. He sounds like he's about to go on the war path.

"Get your things and vacate these premises immediately! Your services are no longer needed. Phaedra will be here shortly to escort you out."

"You can't fire me Phil, you don't have the authority!" she snaps back.

"I'm still your boss! Either you leave quietly or I will pick you up and throw you out myself!" he yells.

Stephanie stands defiantly behind her desk. Phil inches toward her, circling her desk. He is ready to pounce, unaware that she has picked up the desk lamp. I have to stop this right now.

"Phil can I see you please."

Surprisingly he stops where he is and follows me. He even closes the door behind us. He is pretty angry, but I think he realizes what could've happened had I not intervened.

"I don't know who the hell she think she is, but she is barking up the wrong tree. Telling the police I was looking at child pornography…I got kids of my own, why would I look at such filth?"

"Phil if you weren't looking at child rape, what were you looking at?"

"I was watching a movie. Yes it was quite graphic, but there were no children involved. I showed the police my laptop, and they left."

"They are gone?"

"Yes, they are gone. There is no crime looking at sexually graphic material."

"Nevertheless Phil you broke the company's bylaws."

"Says who, that four-eyed wannabe Caucasian?!"

"There is no need to spew racism Phil."

"Yes there is, does she have any idea of the damage she has done to this company?"

"No she doesn't, not yet, but getting back to you. I have grounds to have you removed from the premises."

"The hell you do!"

"Yes the hell I do Phil, what you did this morning can be construed as sexual harassment, racial discrimination at best. And just now, what were you going to do to her Phil?"

"I wouldn't sexually harass that sick puppy if it was the last live thing on this earth! Khloe, we have to get rid of her. She called the police, not my wife. They came here because of her! Before I knew it the police were accusing me of possessing kiddie porn."

"That's what I was told Phil, and I was also told that this all started because Rachael filed a complaint."

"Khloe, Rachael did not call the police. She did not file a complaint, Tamara did. If you don't believe me, call her and she will tell you. Rachael she would never jeopardize my career and our lifestyle with an outrageous lie such as this."

He picked up the handset and dials.

"Here talk to Rachael yourself."

I take the handset and return it to the base. He sounds sincere. Other than Bob backing up his story, I am not so sure he's telling the truth. I have to find the truth.

"What about Bob what saw? Is he lying too?"

"Yes he is, I would never walk around with my dick hanging out of my pants."

"Phil…that is not what Bob told me. You just told on yourself, which means what Tamara said is true."

"That bitch is lying!"

"Phil I have made a decision. To retain your employment would be detrimental to the company and erode employee morale."

"I didn't do anything wrong!"

"You have broken Section 2-Article 2 of this company's bylaws, in which you swore to upheld. You have engaged in conduct unbecoming of an executive officer, thus made this company liable to lawsuits."

"Is she saying I sexually harassed her?"

"No she did not, at least not yet. In the event she decides to…"

"I didn't sexually harass her!"

"It's your word against hers. If I did not know you, I would think you were coming on to her."

"I would ne—she's not even my type!"

"Phil I am terminating your employment effective immediately. You have to turn in your laptop. All paperwork is property of Spencer Foods and Nite-Owl Conveniences, Inc."

"You can't have it! My work is on it."

"Phil I will take over the deals you were working on, the laptop stays here."

"You spoiled little bitch, did you hear me? I said you cannot have it."

"Listen dickhead, you are fired. I am firing you for breaking the moral clause of your contract."

"You little bitch, I am the senior officer. You cannot fire me without the board's okay."

"Spencer Foods does not have a board."

"Yes it does, I created one."

"Spencer Foods is an organization privately owned, solely owned by the Spencer family."

"You are not privately owned anymore. Spencer Foods is on the verge of going public."

"You cannot put a company on the open market without the CEO's signature, without my mother's signature, without my signature."

"Khloe your Dad put the company on open market. He said he was going to tell you after the wedding."

"I don't believe you."

"I'll let him tell you."

"Great!" Another subject matter for Dad to clear up, "The chain of command specifically says that the senior officer should be notified of all problems. Phil you are the senior officer, but you are also the event

275

causing the problem. Therefore, I am next in line, Bruce and Phaedra will escort you out of the building."

"No need to muck up this company's reputation, I will leave on my own. Don't gloat about your new found power! I want you to know you are not in charge. When all of this is said and done, you will be the one leaving."

He storms out of my office and enters the common area. He heads toward Stephanie, who is oblivious to his presence. He is going to hit her.

"Stephanie move!"

She glances up at him and pushes her chair away.

"Don't worry I'm not going to hit you. I will tell the both of you since you're here, I am locking my office. Everything had better still be in its place when I get back. I am using seven of my vacation days. Maybe by the time I get back Greg will have told you the news."

He departs quickly. Both of us breathe a sigh of relief, but he yells out a decree. "Phaedra I don't need to be escorted anywhere. I am still the VP of this company!"

Phaedra appears at my door, "Are you okay?"

"Yeah I am fine."

"I see he is on a roll, hasn't been this peeved in quite some time. I suppose he's embarrassed, everybody's talking."

"Phaedra you should remind them all he is still our vice president."

"Damn! I told them he would still be walking around here. If you have any more outbursts call us immediately."

"Will do, Tamara can I see you in my office?"

She follows and sits confidently in a chair. She is not going to like what I have to say either.

"Stephanie I am sure you are traumatized by this morning's events so I am suggesting you utilize some of your vacation days too."

"You are blaming me. He was caught doing something wrong, and I am the one sent away."

"I am not sending you away. I am just suggesting that you take a couple of days off to regroup, and you should take them. He is taking his."

She has a serious frown on her face, she doesn't like my suggestion.

"You need help investigating his claim."

"Stephanie he's lying! He can't take this company public without mine or my mother's signature."

"Are you sure?"

"Yes I am sure."

"Okay, I will do it. I will take some days off *and* I will ask about Phil's claims."

"Who are you going to ask?"

"Someone who would know if Phil is telling the truth or not."

I want to go far away, not be in ear shot of anyone who can come to me or call me. I need a good stiff drink, totally exhausted from this morning battles and all its revelations. I have two mothers, a secret sister, and a philandering Dad. Silence is broken. The silent ones are talking with devastating results. I don't think I can stand to hear any more news, good or bad. I think I will go into town, that's pretty far enough. Oh yeah, Edibles is nearby. Edibles, with its black and white flooring and small tables, is the bistro that gave me the idea to start our own.

I leave my car keys with the parking attendant of a nearby parking garage. I better hurry, I remember the long lines. We all had to wait to be seated the last time I was here. Oh good, it's not standing room. Today the maitre d' recommends the table next to the window. It is perfect. I don't want to talk to anyone. I don't want to hear another human voice. I want to look out this window and imagine the lives of the strangers walking by. I order a glass of white zinfandel and toy with the dinner napkin while I wait for its arrival. Outside, I see the many people walking the streets. Some are casually dressed and some are in business attire.

A couple strolls by my window, romantically holding hands. They stop in front of my window to pose for pictures. The man removes the camera from his neck and snaps a photo of his female companion. The woman takes the camera and snaps his. They stop a passerby, hand him the camera and pose. The man pulls her close and gazes lovingly into her eyes. The amateur photographer wisely captures the shot and the next, photographing the couple begin making out. It is clear they are tourists enjoying the sites and each other. I wonder if they are really happy or swept up in the excitement of exploring a strange place. The man flashes a dazzling smile, a smile that reminds me of Danny. I need to talk to him, make amends for what happened in New York. I shouldn't, I know I shouldn't, but I need to explain. Come to think of it McGuiness' is not very far from here. I can walk it.

The sports bar is the only one in a ten block radius. One thing I have learned is that no matter what time of day or what's happening in the world, people gravitate towards them. I put on my sunglasses and enter the premises. I want to sit quietly and observe before speaking to him. I want that table in the corner. It's away from the patrons, if he decides to scream and shout it won't be in plain sight. Sean the bellboy brings a bin load of freshly washed beer mugs, shot glasses and wine goblets. He stacks them on the counters below the serving area and on the shelves behind him.

Danny walks in, he's as handsome as ever.

"Would you mind bringing me a bag or two of those peanuts and...never mind, I'll go get them."

I watch him disappear into the kitchen area and just as quickly as reappear with the bags and a stack of bowls. Seems like he's moved on with his life.

"Danny is the corn beef ready?"

"Yeah Sean it is, we are waiting for it to cool off before slicing it."

Danny pushes back a lock of wavy black hair, the same lock that is always dangling in his face. He takes his fingers and wipes the sweat off the bridge of his nose. Rory comes out of the kitchen carrying a cutting board. He sits at the end of the bar. Danny finished filling the condiment dishes and joined him. He pulls the cutting board away from Rory and places it in front of him. He also takes the fork and knife out of Rory's hands. He slices a piece and tastes it. "Rory this is your best yet!"

Danny gets a beer mug and filled it with draft beer. He takes a couple of swallows.

"Thank you. Think your girl's back home now."

"No she isn't. I've been there already. No one is there but that damn mutt of a dog. She's not answering her cell phone either."

"Don't be so sure, look behind me."

Danny gazes at my table and glance at Rory. He gives me another look. I can see his furrowed brow. He takes the fork and jabs it into the meat, slicing another piece cut. He pokes it into his mouth.

Rory whispers, but not low enough, I can still hear him. He glances at me while he is whispering in Danny's ear. He wants me to hear everything he is saying.

"Stop making a fool of yourself over her! Albeit she's a looker, you will never be able to bring her home. Look, our bank is low. We can get money, lots of money not just dutch gold. Her husband won't want her after her face turns up all over the internet.

"What are you talking about?"

"I'm talking about pictures. Pictures from those hidden cameras installed in her apartment. I must admit that vixen got a nice fanny--we will become instant millionaires."

"What cameras? Are you saying you have photos of us?"

"Oh were you havin a good time."

"Of all the despicable things you have done."

"As if you are an altar boy!"

"Mind yourself Rory!"

"There are plenty of our kind, what about Siobhan? She's a nice girl with fewer complications."

"Rory go greet the liquor deliveryman and this time, make sure the whole shipment is here."

"I'll do that, only if you stop grieving like some mutt."

Rory leaves Danny sitting at the table, staring into space. He's probably digesting Rory's comments as am I. Rory mentioned pictures…I hope…they couldn't have, Rory has pictures of us, Danny and myself. Our affair is not a secret, never was, they intend to make money. He can't…I can't allow them to do that. I can't let Xavier...

"Ya bloody home! Where have you been all weekend?"

Less than a second ago he was sitting at that table. When—

"Khloe! When ya leave New York?"

He's reverted back to his native tongue. His pronunciation of words would make you think he just got off the boat.

"This morning, Danny, I…"

"Oh we are here to get married," he mocked, "Things didn't look rocky between the two of ya!"

"Danny how did you know where to find me?"

"I tell ya in New York, ya mind anything I said to you that night?"

"A—

"Of course not, you were busy rubbing my nose in your glee. Anyways, he led me to you. He sent me an invitation to this bar, told me where I could find you and invited me to watch you marry him."

"He—

"You effin idiot! He wanted me to see that you were all his and you know what? You are, but we will see for how long…the divil is always pokin' what belongs to the son. The son's a good son, he'd *anything* for de old man…be careful that you are not next, and even if you are, you cannot come to me. You are my past, and the past will stay in the past."

He jostles the table as he stands up. It is done, officially over between us. I downed the whiskey sour in front of me.

"Contrary to what you may think Danny, my husband and his family are not devils."

I left $10 on the table to cover my tab and take excess napkins from the holder to wipe my eyes. I have been here long enough, its best I go home and continue my drinking spree there, after I take Regis out.

Home is not always the answer

I'm going home. I can't believe I let my anger get the best of me again. I almost killed her in broad daylight. I should've kept my cool. What she showed me is no different than what I have already seen. Perhaps she got under my skin because those photos remind me of her and Julius. There was a time when I really really liked her. Kiera was the party girl, the one who kept everyone laughing. I met her at a time when I needed humorous laughter. I made the mistake of helping her. Who would have thought a simple employment opportunity with my dad would mean the end of our relationship.

I am sure she will run and tell Julius. Not that I care, if he was there I probably would have attacked him too. I need a hit. I need to dull the pain in my hands, probably bits of glass embedded in them. I beat the heck out of her windshield. She is lucky it wasn't her face. I tried to pull her through the hole, Jeffrey and Billy intervened in the nick of time. When I think about it, maybe I did accomplish something in losing my temper. She now knows she should move on with her life. "Hello hideout, did you miss me? I missed you. Don't know what I would do without you."

I parked in front of the door, and scurried inside. Didn't want to pull attention to myself, I am covered with blood. Even though it's my own blood people would think the worse. If I went to the hospital they would ask questions. I don't feel like answering questions. I don't feel like talking. I need time, time to think about my life with my new wife. I had told Khloe we were going to start anew. Our past and the people in the past were pushed back into the past. Then Kiera comes and clobbers me over the head with those pictures.

I hold my hands under the cold running water of the kitchen sink. The water heightens the pain. I search the cabinets for hydrogen peroxide and pour it on my hands. Looking at the foam brings a flash of Joseph Coleman's contorted face. I shouldn't have gone down there. I shouldn't have touched him. It's too late, what is done is done. I rinsed off the foam and patted my hands. I skim over the surface with my fingers, I don't feel anything. I slathered on antibiotic cream and wrapped them in gauze. I need to think about something else, let's see what's on television, the afternoon news should be on, wonder if I made the news? Father God I need to curb my anger, one homicidal rage per day is one too many.

"Good afternoon I am Stuart Fullerton with today's top stories. The focus has been on two disturbing domestic violence cases in our viewing area. Beginning with case number one, murder is the scene in the Kensington this afternoon. A man has been arrested for strangling his wife. Police say 32 year old Vincent Santiago beat and strangled his wife, Maritza Santiago, 28, early this morning. Police say the motive was jealousy. The victim's family is saying Vincent's behavior was influenced by his use of "wet," also known as PCP. Santiago is being held for trial."

"Damn maniac killed his wife, somebody is going to strangle him…as soon as the gate is closed."

"Our second tale of domestic violence involves fugitive Felix Castro. Castro was captured in Puerto Rico this morning. He was wanted in connection with last year's murder of *his* wife Carmen. Police was called to the gruesome scene by the couple's ten year old daughter Nelly. Little Nelly told police her father came home early from work and became enraged because there was a man in the house. Carmen who was stabbed over a hundred times died at the scene."

"Not judging this guy."

"BREAKING NEWS…this just in…a videotape has just arrived at our studios…it involves State Senator Julius Davidson and a young lady."

"I made the news after all, damn!"

"What we are about to show you is shocking to say the least. It involves State Senator Julius Davidson beating a young woman in his office."

Wait! They said State Senator Julius Davidson, that's Dad! They are talking about Dad and a young lady, what young lady? There can only be one young lady they are talking about and that is Kiera. Oh shit! Dad beat a woman?

"The video takes place in the Senator's office, we can't tell which office nevertheless it is quite shocking. If you look in the left corner of your screen you will see a young lady cowering in the corner. Senator Davidson is standing over her, pummeling her with his fists."

"Oh my god he is really beating her! Look at him, he is going completely ballistic!"

"There is more…apparently the lawyer representing the Senator's wife, Gladys Davidson, is filing for divorce. Mrs. Davidson's press secretary Julie Gelb just confirmed that the divorce petition is on its way to family court. She also says Mrs. Davidson has moved out of the family home to an undisclosed location."

"That bit of news is not surprising. She should have left years ago."

"Has anyone been in contact with the Senator's office? Ladies and gentlemen we have official confirmation from the Senator's office. His press secretary Susan Richter is confirming the end of the senator's marriage, citing irreconcilable differences. As far as the video is concerned, she is denying the presence of the Senator in the videotape. She says she has no idea who that young lady could be, but sources tell us that the young lady being beaten in the video is the Senator's intern Kiera Smith. We will be preempting our regular scheduled programming throughout the evening as this news story evolves. I am Stuart Fullerton, good day."

"Damn!"

I hurl the cigar box across the room. Its contents, crushed marijuana leaves, litter the floor along with the Top papers. They are not divorcing over irreconcilable differences, it's because of Kiera! I have to call Mom, Gladys, and tell her not to go through with the divorce. It is inconceivable for Kiera to take her place.

"Hello boy."

I stoop to greet Regis. He bows his head and meets my hand, whining and licking it. I rise to my feet to keep my hands away from his mouth. The television plays, barely above a whisper, I guess she was watching it. She's fast asleep. The air is stagnant, smells like dog, not food. I guess she was too tired to prepare dinner. That's okay, what's important is that she is here, home, with me.

"Regis," I whisper, "Are you hungry?"

He replies with a lowly growl.

"I guess she didn't feed you either. I'll order the all-American cheeseburger and fries for the wife and myself from the commissary and then I'll go in and feed you."

He yelps in excitement, hearing me order the food. This post nasal drip is quite annoying. Now I know why the headmaster refused to let a dog in the school, allergies. I grab a couple of napkins from a stack on the desk to wipe my nose. The small green and black beer mug in the center of the napkin caught my eye. They are from the sports bar.

"Khloe!"

Wisely Regis leaves the room. She only stirs and goes back to sleep.

"The hell if you will sleep I want an answer and I want one now, Khloe get up!"

I yank her by the ankle, and watch her eyes flash a bewildered look as her hands grasp the sofa. I let go of her and she scoots back into the chair. She begins to smooth her hair off her face, and rub her eyes.

"What's up?"

"These!"

I threw the bar napkins in her face, "They are napkins from the bar. What were you doing at his bar?"

"I was downtown this afternoon so I stopped in for a drink."

"For a drink!"

"Yes, only for a drink."

"Was your boyfriend there?"

"Yes he was. I felt like I owed him an apology."

"For what?"

"For stringing him along."

"Boy are you *so* concerned about his feelings. Tell me how did it go?"

"Not well."

"Of course it wouldn't, did you think it would?"

"To be honest, I don't know what I thought would happen."

"We promised to forgive and forget Khloe, in New York, remember?"

"Yes we—

"Well why did you go see him? Do you think he misses you?"

I threw the photos at her and wait for a reaction. She picks them up one by one, gazing at them.

"Where did you get these?"

"You really want to know?"

"Yes."

"Your best friend Kiera."

"What...where...how! How did she get these?"

"I don't know, she brought them to my office today."

She is still staring at them, trembling like one ill-prepared for the cold. Her expression tells me she had no idea they were taken, no idea of their existence. Someone has set her up and I know who.

"These must be the photos they were talking about."

"What did you say?"

"I overheard Danny and his cousin talking about these photos. He was telling Danny they were going to be rich, but Danny didn't want to hear it."

"I figured that was the plan. Listen to me 'cause this is the last time I am going to say this. From here on out, I want you to stay away from him."

"You don't have to worry its ov—

"I know it's over. It was over before it started, but you did not know that."

"What do you mean?"

"I need you to stay away from them. Stay away from that bar, don't call him. If you see him, leave, walk away, act like you don't know him. Do you understand?"

"Yes."

"I am going to get them for doing this to you."

"Xavier let's go to the police."

"If you call the police, it will be in the news and we don't need that."

"I don't want you to get into trouble because of me."

"I am not the one in trouble, they are. They should have thought of that when they took those pictures. Will you do what I asked of you?"

"Yes."

"Thank you."

My cell phone vibrates on my hip. I take it out, it's Julius. "Khloe I have to go out for a while."

"Where are you going?"

"To see Julius."

"Who's Julius?"

"My Dad."

"Oh, was he at the wedding? I don't remember seeing him."

"No he wasn't."

"When will I meet him?"

"Not sure, listen I have to go, I'll ask him for a date."

"Okay."

I close the door behind me and lock it. I want to make sure she is safe. It's my job to take care of her. I am not going to his house, I'm going to my condo to talk. Being there will enable me to keep an eye on Khloe. I know what he wants. He wants to talk about today's events, which is just as well because I want to talk about the news I heard this afternoon. Carefully I exit her building, looking around for police and local journalists. Only god knows what else Kiera has said and to whom.

The lobby inside my building is scarcely populated, easy for me to race to an elevator without the interruption of small talk. I walk into my apartment with the lights off. I want them off, I don't want anyone to know I am home, again, no interruptions, besides the phone gives plenty of light. I flop on the sofa and dial Julius' number. Surprisingly he answers promptly.

"Have you lost your mind boy?"

"Have you lost yours?"

"Sort of."

"Damn right you did. You always told me that only a coward would hit a girl. I turned on the news and what did I see, you beating the crap out of Kiera, what was all that about?"

"It's not as bad as it seems. I paid that girl an exorbitant amount to close her mouth."

"Apparently it wasn't enough, shame that girl got two beatings in one day."

"Did I not teach you boys are not supposed to beat on girls?"

"Like father like son, where's Mom?"

"She left the house."

"So it's true, you guys are splitting up."

"Yes we are."

"I don't want to hear this!"

I hang up the phone and look at my watch, counting the minutes. He will call back, he hates when I am angry at him. Right on time, my phone vibrates again.

"Hello."

"It's not a good thing to hang up on me."

"It's not a good thing to threaten me."

"Boy you are supposed to respect your elders."

"And a father is supposed to respect his son and not slumber with what is his."

"So that's what you are mad about. You are mad because I took her away from you. Son if another man comes and takes a woman away from you, she was never yours."

"See that's why you are in the predicament you are in. All your hard work of carefully cultivating a squeaky clean image just went down the drain. And it was all because you took what was mine."

"All is not lost."

"Oh yes it is, my services are off the table. After what she did today at my office, threatening me and what is mine...you need to sit her down and school her or else."

"Else what?"

"Else she get the same treatment as Joseph Coleman."

He doesn't have a comeback line.

"I guess this phone call is making it official."

"What is official?"

"You and her?"

"I love her, son."

I hang up the phone again. His words bother me. I have a new life with my new wife, yet his words, *I love her son,* bothers me. What the hell is that? The phone rings yet again.

"Hello."

"Hello Xavier, how are you? How's the bride?"

It's my mother, my real mother. I guess she heard the news.

"I'm good mother, and my bride has never been better. When she's happy, I'm happy."

"Glad to hear it. I heard about Julius, is it true? Did he really attack his intern?"

"No, it's probably a vicious rumor."

"They said the video came from his office."

"I know I saw it too. If he did, he can kiss it all good bye."

"I wonder who gave that television station the tape?"

"I have an idea."

"The intern."

"You got it, she is angry with Julius and with me."

"Why would she be angry with you?"

"She used to by my girl."

"Oh really, what happened?"

"She aligned herself with him."

"Slut."

"Precisely."

"Thank goodness you found someone with some class."

"As soon as I saw her I knew she was the one."

"So I gave you my gift of perception."

"Maybe you did, but I know for a fact Julius ingrained it in me. Sorry, I don't mean to push your contributions to my life aside."

"Yes you did Xavier, yes you did. Your Dad has always been your hero, no matter how much he abused you and pushed you away. You always idolized him."

"I think idolized is too strong of a word."

"No, I don't. You look up to him as if he is God."

"If you felt Julius was abusing me why didn't you step in?"

"I tried. Every time I tried he would threaten me."

"Threaten you with what?"

"To tell about the crime I committed a long time ago."

"You… the Madame of Amou Landes commit a crime, impossible."

"Nothing is impossible. Everyone is capable of committing a crime Xavier."

"What exactly did you do?"

"When I was a child I was always fighting, even after I graduated from high school."

"That's my story too, what else?"

"I threw acid in the face of a rival."

"So I did inherit something from you after all."

"How did Julius come to know about it?"

"He was there, it happened because of him."

"I swear that man is always in the middle of everything."

Beginning of the End

A phone inside his suitcase has been ringing non-stop for ten minutes now. With everything that has been going on, we haven't had the time to unpack. I never knew he had two phones. Nothing wrong with the concept, most businessmen have more than one cell phone, but why is his tucked away in his suitcase? Who is so persistent? Maybe it's him trying to locate his phone. Maybe it's someone else, someone who could tell me a little more about my husband. Our trip to New York was an eye opener. Xavier is a man with many secrets. He told me early in the relationship he hated large crowds. The time we dated reflected that, often visiting places on the off-beaten path. They were interesting choices, showing a softer and subdued side of him. Now, he has shown me his apartment in New York City, the most crowded city in our country. He never did tell me how long he had that apartment, could there be others?

A more alarming facet about him is his ability *to* keep a secret. I often think about the oddity of our wedding day and our wedding night, his insistence on marriage. It was smart of him to hire a wedding planner. Anne Marie and Gwyneth did a fabulous job. They made my wedding a dream wedding for any bride. Nevertheless I can't ignore the dark undertones, to purposely invite your rival to your wedding…was he looking for a reaction? Was he trying to force me to choose? Well I did choose, I chose him, was it a wise decision, I'm not sure. He waited to our wedding night to proclaim his familiarity of my affair with Danny along with a vague threat. The threat of harm should he find me in a situation he deems inappropriate with anyone other than himself. His phone is still ringing…who is calling him? "Hello."

"Who is this?"

I recognize this voice, it sounds like my former best friend Kiera. Why would she be calling him? "To whom am I speaking?"

"Kiera Smith."

It *is* her! "Why are you calling him?"

"What do you mean? What are *you* doing answering his phone?"

"I am his wife, I can do that?"

"You're his what?"

"You heard me, I said I am his wife and I can do that!"

"Since when?"

"Since early Sunday morning."

"Did not know you were seeing each other, didn't know you were engaged. There are things friends share with each other, clearly I am not a friend."

"No you are not my friend. You ruined our friendship when you kept insinuating Brice and I were creeping behind your back!"

"Brice confessed to me."

"Brice lied! I wouldn't sleep with him! Why would you think I slept with him?"

"What reason would he have to lie about the two of you?"

"To make you jealous stupid!"

"Don't call me stupid okay! I'm not the one getting played here."

"Played?! Who's playing me?"

"Xavier."

"You know you got a problem. You couldn't handle Brice and I being platonic friends…look Xavier chose me over you, which brings me to my next question, why are you calling him? If you have Brice you should not be calling Xavier."

"Now I am about to tell you something you can't handle…I'm calling him because we are still seeing each other."

"Bullshit! You two were over before we even left Florida."

"Says who?"

"Says he."

"He lies!"

"You are the one who lies. I've been with him since our return from Spring Break, a whole three years. He hasn't had time for you."

"Oh really?"

"Really…anything else you want to tell me?"

"Enjoy yourself now 'cause hell is around the corner."

"Concentrate on the one who stands beside you before he leaves you too."

I'm not waiting for a response. I'm holding the power button until the phone shuts down. Three years! Three whole years and she is still carrying a torch for him. She is weird. The girl is attractive and she knows it, she flaunts before any man, even those who are not remotely interested. Eventually they all reciprocate, and then *she* ruins it by going on the hunt for bigger fish with more prestigious pockets. And she will still hold onto Brice, and he onto her. I can't figure those two out.

Regis licks my face before I could turn away, yuk! Love the dog, hate his breath, his golden floppy ears are so soft. I love how they hang alongside his regal face. His eyes squint, enjoying the attention. "Boy you want to go outside don't ya? Get some fresh air, take care of business, get a good brush down…I could use some fresh air too, and a coffee cake from Sunil's. While I'm there I will most definitely get you a snack, how about some dog biscuits?"

He barks with excitement and does his little dance, a mad dash. He waits at the door, watching me put on my trench coat. I know it's chilly, after sundown the night air is always chilly, I should wear a scarf. November is fast approaching, every morning I gaze at the spectacular foliage and see the acorns dangling from limbs high up in the trees. I can see them because the trees are thinning out. We step outside the lobby, good thing I have on a coat, it is quite nippy. The ground is still littered with acorns. I know the grounds crew swept them. They sweep them up every day.

Regis leads the way, gently pulling me along our street. I can picture the area being overrun with foxes, and the Colonials hot on their trail with their hunting dogs and rifles. The developers of Fox Run did a fantastic job of carving out a residential area while maintaining the look and feel of the woods. Up ahead is School House Lane and Clover Park. We won't go to the park, we'll keeping walking down School House till we hit Lincoln Drive.

Sunil's is far, not too far to walk, but far enough, its good exercise. The sky over us is filled with stratus clouds. It will rain tonight, sooner rather than later, I smell the moisture in the air. Hopefully we will be back home before it starts. I glance around, it's dark and lonely. No one except us is out here. I had forgotten the first rule of defense class— never isolate yourself. It was stupid of me to come out here alone. Regis is still pretty much a pup, not strong enough to defend me. We will be okay, I'm certain there will be other people, besides there's plenty of traffic."

I stand corrected, Regis and I are the only things walking about. There are plenty of cars, some of them slowing their pace so their occupants can spew derogatory comments. I ignore them and continue to focus on getting to the store. This was a bad idea I should be home, safe in my house where my husband left me. I can't call for help. I left my phone in the house. We better get out of here, we pick up our pace and jog, Sunil's is not that much farther. More and more cars are slowing down, asking me if I want a lift. Regis barks at them,

296

unknowingly giving away his age. They smile and call him young buck, and then offer to purchase him. I tell them he is not for sale. They get angry, call me a few choice words and leave.

Realizing the danger, we run faster and faster up Lincoln Drive till Sunil's marquee bring light to the area. Regis stays put while I shop inside. This time I will not casually stroll up each and every aisle. I'll get what I came for and leave. We cross the street and sit on the park bench, I am a bit winded. I give him a few of the dog biscuits and pour some water in his mouth. "You are such a good boy, so amiable, always helpful, and never angry. What would I do without you, huh?"

"Evening, gorgeous pup you have there, what is his name?"

I look up. It's Mystery man who sits in Clover Park. As always he appears out of nowhere. I am not sure about this. He waits till I am alone to talk to me. I look at the marquee again and relax, I am not totally alone. If I scream loud enough someone across the street will hear me. Someone sitting in their car or pumping gas in their car will see me. I am safe right here where I stand. "Regis."

"Odd name for a dog."

"He's named after the talk show host. Are you familiar with the morning show Regis and Kelly?"

"No. I rarely have time to watch television, and when I do it's the evening news."

"Oh."

"I have been admiring you for some time and I wanted—

"You call it admiring, I call it stalking. A fine looking man like yourself should have a black book at least two inches thick."

"I don't take kind to being insulted. I know I am ugly, there's no need to rub my nose in it."

"Sorry, I shouldn't have said that."

"Incidentally, I do have a book…what you Americans refer to as a black book…however it does not mean I have it easy with women."

"Why not?"

"I'm picky, I prefer women that are not very-well known if you know what I mean."

"Does that include me?"

"You are a first-class lady. I'm curious about your male friend."

"Don't be."

"Oh but I am. A mutual friend of ours was quite ticked off at you earlier today. We thought you were a good judge of character…you picked a rather capricious man for a mate."

"What do you mean?"

"You do not know him do you? I mean *really* know him."

"Why don't you say what you came here to say."

"Your new husband is a very precarious individual. He has a lot of connections—political and street—a dangerous combination."

"How do you know these things?"

"I know because I am assigned to work with him."

"Well that makes you dangerous too doesn't it? Perhaps I should run for my life."

"You can't leave just yet…the things I have seen, a girl like you should not be with a man like that."

"What do you mean you are assigned to him?"

"I have a duo position. I work with him and I was asked to look after him."

"What kind of work?"

"I am not at liberty to say."

"Who assigned you to look after him?"

"They prefer to remain anonymous."

"Why are you so worried about him?"

"Xavier has the expertise to get rid of things, anything that is a hindrance to him. Do you know what I mean?"

"No I don't know what you mean! You presume to tell me about somebody that I have known a lot longer than I've known you!"

"Yes I do."

"Well I don't want to hear—

"Yes you will hear me. You will hear everything I have to say. Have a seat, your dog will be fine, it's quite a story, one you should be aware of."

I sat down on the edge of the bench, leaving plenty of space in between us, "I'm listening."

"You and he were in New York this past weekend."

"How do you know?"

"I followed him. I followed him the entire time you guys were in New York. I followed him one night to an underpass. A man and a woman got out of their car and dumped a huge sack. A man stepped out from the shadows and gave the couple an envelope, the couple leaves. Shortly thereafter the police arrive, quickly surveying the area, they leave. Five minutes after them comes another squad car. The man in the shadows steps out and joins them, getting in their car. They leave and never returned.

"What was Xavier doing?"

"He didn't do anything, but watch."

"Well what is the point of the story?"

"He was there to meet the guy from the shadows. Want to know what was in the bag?"

"Not really."

"I'm sure you don't, I will tell you. It was a young lady. She was alive, but unconscious. I opened the bag so she could get air, and then I called the police."

"Are you saying that he was involved in a kidnapping?"

"Yes, among other things."

"I don't believe you. How do I know you are not trying to set him up?"

"It was him! He uses his connections to escape jail. He's never been arrested because the witnesses are too afraid to report what they know. Most of the time there are no witnesses."

"Yet another facet of him, albeit it darker."

"Children of the affluent can be just as evil as children with no means, sometimes more so."

Regis has returned to my side. I quickly attach his leach.

"Are you going in now?"

"Yes I am, I got to get away from here, away from you! A maniac whose been stalking me and is now setting my husband up to be a criminal."

"You are in danger!"

"Yes, the danger is you!"

"The danger is him, not me!"

"Goodnight."

"Heed what I said, be careful of him."

He left of his own accord, quickly crossing the street. As he climbs Rittenhouse Street I hear his slew feet shuffle against the pavement, echoing in the stillness. Finally he disappears over the ridge, far away from me. I reach out for Regis and he moves in, allowing me to rub the top of his head. We both feel at ease, me with his silk fur sliding between my fingers and him enjoying the strokes. The conversation with stalker replays in my mind. His intention was to tell me something he thought I needed to know. What he said is somewhat similar to Marie Colette's story. Strangely, they both claim to know Xavier a lot longer than I, and yet they seem to want to help me, not him. They paint him as someone who is morally corrupt with a preference to walk on the dark side. I am not sure if he alone is in the dark. The dark is descending upon me fast brought in the guise of help. "C'mon Regis, it's time to go in."

We jog home, taking the same route. The cool breeze is now a cold wind blowing pretty hard. The trees whip high above us, blowing dirt from the curbside towards us. It's impossible to jog with my eyes fully open. I am worried, I know I saw stalker disappear over the ridge, but I can't forget how he showed up at the park. He came out of nowhere. Will he reappear, out of nowhere? School House Lane is just ahead. "C'mon Regis we're almost at the home stretch."

The wind pushes us down School House Lane, making it almost impossible to stand. We finally arrive at our street. "We can slow down now, Whew! You're panting just like I am, that was a good workout wasn't it?"

I can't help but feel uneasy, am I being followed? Is he lurking somewhere close by? I look over my shoulder, I don't see him, I don't see anyone, what I do see is home sweet home. A few more yards and I will be able to rest in my warm comfortable bed. Rain pelts the road and me, the wind blows my hood off my head. "C'mon Regis, you can drink water when we get home."

I yank the leash pretty hard, but he keeps quenching his thirst by licking the rain off the grass. I wrap the leash around my fist several times before tugging harder.

"C'mon Regis! We don't have time to chase cats."

He doesn't budge. He stands defensively with his ears alert, facing the far off bushes.

"C'mon Regis, nothing is there."

He still doesn't budge. He is growling under his breath. The fur on the nape of his neck is erect. Something has caught his eye, I am standing right next to him and I don't see a thing.

"Regis we are getting wet, it's time to go in."

He grits his teeth and begins to snarl and growl. He's pulling me forward. "Okay, so you're turning into a strong young man, sorry bud you are not going over there."

He continues snarling and growling at the hedges. "Oh shit!"

I finally see what is fascinating, it's not good. It's a Rottweiler, big, and black as night. He runs toward us. I try to pick up Regis and run away, but he jumps out of my arms. The Rottweiler pounces on Regis, covering him completely. I don't see him, but I hear him, a god-awful cry for help. I release the leash and focus on the collar of the Rottweiler. I pull and pull on what seems like a ton of weight. I kick the big black dog in the ribs, in the hopes he will feel pain and let go of Regis. The dog doesn't flinch. I am losing this tug of war, I am losing Regis. I can't let him kill my dog. I punch and punch and punch him in his ribs, in his head, and in his face. Suddenly he let go and backs away. Regis tries to rise to his feet, but fall's back down. His golden coat is drenched in blood.

"Come here boy, c'mon let me look…Ow! Regis! Hey! Stop, take it off of my head. I can't see, stop, eww! What is that smell? I can't breathe, help! Help!"

Collision of the wildest sorts

I could have turned here at the light and then made a quick left. That entrance is closest and rather informal. I consider it to be an exit, the entrance is farther down. Its grandeur, masonry brick walls on both sides makes me feel like I am going somewhere distinguished, to see someone important. He is important, to me. I am going to talk to my father in a place where we cannot be interrupted.

Lincoln Drive, a drive forged through the woods of Fairmount Park, is reminiscent of a raceway. In fact, many of Philadelphia's most important thoroughfares are quite scenic and serene. They all contain hidden challenges that must be anticipated, forcing drivers to heed caution signs. The sudden turns and hairpin curves require a decrease in speed, something many people neglect to do, resulting in people being hurt, maimed or killed.

I never knew this place existed. How Bailey stumbled upon it is a mystery, Bailey's specialty is thievery and swindling, not history. Never in a million years will I believe he found this place on his own. Whoever is paying him knew of this place quaint little Rittenhouse, America's first paper mill has become our perfect secluded holding cell.

"C'mon will ya! You've been stuck on red longer than three minutes now!"

Maybe the light is broken…will you look at this! Those damn people zoom around the corner so fast that the wheels left the roadway. Good thing no one was in their way, they would have been smacked. "Finally!"

The light is green. If I stay in my lane everything should be okay. I glance to my left and to my right. The coast is clear, even in my rearview mirror. I drive thru the intersection, the driveway is just a little ways down.

"Whoa! This must be your friends…will you look where you are going? Don't come over here, stay in your own lane! Stop! Stop! Stop!"

Thank god I have on a seat belt. I would have sailed thru the windshield. They clipped my left rear, shoving me into the guardrail. Problem is the guard rail did not slow me down, it broke in half and I slid downhill. The emergency brakes are the only thing that kept me from sliding into the creek.

"Are you okay?"

"No Speed Demon, I am not okay, I just been hit with an airbag traveling as fast as you were!"

"Sorry about that, what is your name?"

"Stephanie Brown, why are you driving so fast and in the middle of the road?"

"I can't hear you. Let me deflate the airbag."

He pokes it with something and presses on it, the air expels. My head comes to rest on the steering wheel.

"I didn't hear what you said before."

"I said why are you driving so fast and in the middle of the road?"

"I was trying to merge and you wouldn't let me."

"This is a residential area, not the Grand Prix!"

"I don't see any houses."

"If you had thought it through you could've stayed in the opposite lane, it was wide open, but no, you had to collide with me!"

"Instead of ranting and raving you should've been paying attention."

"First you wreck my jeep and now you are calling me crazy. I'm not the one fleeing the police."

"Who says I'm fleeing the police, I don't hear any sirens."

"Speed Demon you were going way too fast to be leisurely driving."

"Indeed I was, and for that I apologize."

He's quite attractive, thick black hair and a bit of an accent. He appears to be nice, but nice people do not do what he just did to me.

"Did they not teach you driver's etiquette when you took the exam?"

"Of course they did, as did my mother."

"If you were in a hurry and wanted to jump ahead of me, all you had to do was blow your horn."

"If you knew that was my intention all you had to do was hang back."

"Damn! If there's damage to my new jeep because you brazenly have no regard for life…look at the damage you caused!"

He offers to help me out, but I push him aside and walk to the front of my vehicle on my own. Glass lies in the blades of grass, it's from my headlight. The headlight is completely smashed in, wires dangle from the socket. The bunched up hood sits up in the air. The front and side fender is a goner, the tire seems to be unaffected.

"I wonder if she works."

"Let me pull you back onto the road, it will be easier to start the engine."

"How are we going to get the jeep back up the road?"

"I have some rope in my van."

He runs up to his van. I hear the door slide open and close. He is back with thick cable rope. He lays on the ground and scoots partially underneath.

"I am going to tie this rope to the mainframe, it's the only place secure."

"Okay."

He carries the loose end of the rope with him, up to his van. I hear his van start, then I see my jeep jerk uphill.

"Keep going!"

I follow the jeep as it moves uphill, till the wheels rest on the road. He jumps out of his van and unties the ropes.

"Get in and start her up!"

I hop behind the wheel and turn the key in the ignition. She starts up right away, "Thank god I bought that grill guard or you would have to purchase me a new jeep."

"Miss I don't have a new jeep to give you."

"You have insurance don't you?"

"Of course I do."

"Go get your insurance card while I look for my cell phone, we need a police report."

"We don't need the police for a simple fender bender. Besides you are fine, you have been talking non-stop since I met you. We can settle this between ourselves."

"In this country fender benders are supposed to be reported to the police. Police reports are required to accompany insurance claims, didn't you know that?"

"No I didn't."

"You're not afraid are you?"

"Afraid of what? It was a simple accident."

306

"You broadsided me and I almost ended up in the creek. The police most definitely need to know what happened here."

"I *said* we can handle this ourselves."

"I am not scared of you. They need to come and see the damage you caused. Your gate is so messed up you won't be able to open it. It's a shame, you have a nice van, love the color—champagne gold. The black trimming sets it off, tinted windows are not necessary."

"Stop talking about my tinted windows."

"In these times tinted windows are almost synonymous with drug dealers or the rich and famous. You don't look like you are rich or famous."

"You keep insinuating I am a criminal when you know nothing of me."

"Speed Demon I don't know you nor do I know *of* you. I do know that people who drive at excessive speeds are either intoxicated or they are running away from something."

"You keep insulting me. I don't like being insulted."

"You are offended because I think you are a criminal. Maybe you should not act like one."

He reaches into his back pocket and pulls out his wallet. The wallet is pretty thick. I watch as his thumb separate the bills and his lips count silently. He stops and hands me more than a few.

"Here take this, it should cover your expenses."

"Brand new vehicle, no insurance, but plenty of cash. I guess I should be grateful for small favors."

He turns and walks away from me. He is going to his van. He slides the door open and reach inside. I hear him rummaging through what sounds like a toolbox. Something on the seat moves, it partially hangs off the seat. My eyes zoom in to see what is white between the folds of a black blanket. The blanket fell away, exposing more. The white has a navy blue boomerang in the center. He closes the door and walks towards me, carrying a tire iron. Not sure why he needs that, I don't have any flat tires. Stoically he stands within inches of me, giving me the opportunity to gaze into his eyes. He stares back, unexpressive and eerily quiet. From the corner of my eye I see the tire iron rise into the air. I feel it graze my throat.

"The money will cover your expenses, right Stephanie Brown?"

Instinctively I nod in agreement, not willing to learn what would happen next. He reaches around me, and places his hand on the door handle. I move aside and the door opens. His hand rests on my shoulder and very gently pushes me into the cabin. I swing my wobbly legs under the steering wheel, peripherally looking for the accelerator and still keeping eye contact. My hand shakes with fear though it manages to shift from park to drive. He steps back and closes my door.

"Goodnight Stephanie Brown, do we need to meet again?"

"No, I think once is more than enough."

"I thought you would see it my way."

My foot eases up off the brake pedal and I drive away. A glance in the rearview mirror tells me he is still there in the same stance, staring me down as if I was the criminal who caused him harm.

"Wait a minute, now I have the power! I should turn around and run you off the road, shove you straight into the woods! You think giving me money is going to solve your problems, well it isn't! You are not getting away with what you have done to me, we shall meet again Mr.....damn, I didn't get your name or your license plate!"

My temper simmers down by the time I approach the driveway. The parking spot I used before, under the oak tree, is available. The oak is probably as old as this settlement. Its limbs extend far out, the perfect canopy to cloak my presence. I came tonight to see if Dad was still alive. Bailey said that he was not going to hurt him. He said he was told to keep him here for a little while. I don't believe him. This is something I would never have imagined Bailey to be capable of doing. Stupid me, eager for revenge assisted Bailey in what I thought was a trip to New York. Dad hired Bailey to drive him and Queen Sharon to New York, instead there was a detour. Someone hired Bailey to make sure they never arrived in New York. That day Bailey held them at gun point and marched them into the cabin by the creek. Bailey made Queen Sharon tie Dad up. He then turned the gun on her and marched her to another location. I don't know where, I didn't follow them. I went on to New York and stood as my sister's maid of honor.

I came here before, to talk to him. I never saw him, too embarrassed. Now I am ready for answers, I want to see Dad and ask why he never came to see me, why he never called me. He came to see my mother quite often. On Friday she would get all dolled up and tell us she was going to meet Mr. Greg. She would come back Sunday morning and say he sent *me* his love and some money. I was expected to give my sisters some and save the rest for college. He always *sent* his love. He himself, never uttered a single word.

I better hover a few feet away from the road. I don't want Bailey's people to know I am here. I know he has help, there's no way he could do this alone. Up ahead are several houses dotting the hilly landscape, each house sits higher than the next. Each is painted with evergreen trimming along its windows, doors and roofs. The bridge is in view, the house by the creek is only accessible by the bridge. Every step I take causes the bridge to gently sway and creak. I stop and drop to my knees to wait for things to settle down. The water swiftly rides over the rocks lying on the creek bed. It is dark and murky, swirling as it meanders along the flood walls.

When I see him, where will I begin? Do I start off with a bang and ask directly why has he abandoned me or do I play 20 questions and have him guess my real identity? Either way I have to prepare myself. Gregory Spencer is a complex man, this I know is fact. As his secretary, I have been privy to his dealings, both business and personal, he is not always fair. His business comes before everything and everyone, including Queen Sharon who I have heard him described as second-best. He did not elaborate on what was meant. I took it to mean that she was not his first choice.

I knock on the door. No one answers, but I hear someone mumbling. I peered into the smallest of windows, what have I done! Dad sits there alone and in the dark, completely covered in rope.

"Dad! Dad! I'm sorry Dad! I'll help you, hold on Dad! I'll be right there!"

I can't get in, the door is locked! I'll never fit thru this tiny window either. Bailey opened the door.

"You finally ready for some answers?"

I push him aside and barge in. "Oh my Lord, Daddy I am so sorry I never meant…Bailey do you always have to go to extremes?"

I inspect his body, all that I can see, the only exposed parts of his body are his head and his feet, everything else is covered in hemp rope. Bailey even went so far as to connect his hands and feet. I peel the tape from his mouth. Dad breathes in rapidly.

"He needs air!"

I run to open the door, but Bailey shoved me aside.

"No, he's fine, he will be better if he slowed down and stop breathing so fast."

"My secretary set me up!" he shouted before gasping for air. He took in a few more puffs, "How stupid could I have been to believe that she, a mousy looking young woman would be incapable of participating in such a plan."

My disguise was a little too perfect. He has no idea that I and Tamara are one in the same. I put my glasses on.

"What do you want? Why am I here?" he asked.

"Think of all the dirt deeds you have committed, that should give you a clue!" said Bailey.

"Daddy I don't want to hurt you I just want to talk to you."

"Tamara, why are you calling me Daddy?"

"You are my Dad. Do you prefer I call you by your first name like I've been all along?"

"Tamara you know I have one daughter, and her name is Khloe. I do not have any more children."

"What about your other girl?"

"What other girl?"

"Stephanie."

"Tamara I just told you, I don't have any other children."

Oh you do have other children Greg. I am not sure why you don't want to own up to it. "Do you know a woman named Carolyn Brown?"

He does, he gave me the dirtiest of looks. "How do you know about her?"

"She's my mother Greg."

"Oh I see…Carolyn does have daughters, as a matter of fact she has three, and not one of them is named Tamara. So you see, you cannot fool me, you are not one of her daughters. Her daughters are bright and intelligent, too intelligent to be in the company of gangsta boy here. Come to think of it Tamara you can do a whole lot better than this character."

"My name is not Tamara, I just told you that so I could get the job."

"Who are you then, what is your name?"

"My name is Stephanie Tamara Brown-Smith."

He is silent, quietly staring at me. He knows my mother and he knows the names of her children. He knows she has a daughter named Stephanie. He is uncomfortable. His eyes shift from me to the floor and back again. He is my father, I know it, and I think he knows it too. We both share the same pug nose, the same smile, and the same attitude.

"What is this all about? What do you want from me?"

"I want you to acknowledge me as your daughter."

"Who told you I was your father? I am not your father. My name is not on your birth certificate."

"Of course it isn't, you paid my mother over a million dollars to keep your name off of it."

"I would never deny my own child and I would never pay anybody that much money to keep a secret, especially a baby."

"Yes you did, you paid Carolyn, my mother."

"Look Tamara, Stephanie, I am not your father. Your mother is lying to you, she knows who your real father is."

"Yes, and it's you."

"What proof do you have that says I am your father?"

"The proof is in all those checks that my mother brought back after spending the entire weekend with you, along with your very words, "*I send my love.*" You sent five thousand dollars every month for 21 years."

"I gave Carolyn that money for herself, not because of you. How she chose to spend it was her business."

His words pierce my soul, they echo much like mothers the day she told me the truth. The day when she said Gregory Spencer was not my father. I refused to believe her then and I refuse to believe him now.

"Why do you keep denying me?"

"Because I am not your father."

"She said you always asked about me, specifically me, by name, and sent *me* money. Why would you give all that money if you were not paying child support?"

"Because Carolyn need money."

"I don't believe you! You always asked about me, no man would give a woman that much money unless it was for child support."

"I asked about you specifically out of concern, not because you are my child. Your father deeply wounded your mother, look call your mother, I want to talk with her now!"

"Here you can use my phone," Bailey offered.

"Thanks, but I have my own phone."

I dialed home, she picks up after the second ring. "Mom I am here with Gregory Spencer."

"Stephanie what are you doing with Greg?" she asked.

"I wanted to meet my father," I said.

"He is not your father, Stephanie, I have told you that numerous times," she said.

"Why are you always lying to me Mom?" I asked.

"Who are you talking to like that girl?! You better watch your mouth, I am not one of our friends!" she snapped.

Unfazed by her command of respect, I continued. "You are right, you are not one of my friends, you are barely my mother. What kind of mother would deprive her child the company of her own flesh and blood?"

"A mother who knows the father of her children, and Gregory Spencer is not yours!" she said.

"Only because you do not want him to be," I said.

"Only because I am not, now may I speak with her please?"

I pressed the phone to his ear, "Hello, this young lady claims that you Carolyn Brown is her mother, is this correct?"

"Yes it is."

"How do I know if you are the same Carolyn Brown that I know?"

"Your birth date is April 16th, 1956. Your family is originally from South Carolina. The company you run was started by your grandfather. Your first wife name is Saki Nak—

"Okay you are the Carolyn I know. Look, this young lady has been masquerading a whole year as my secretary. She claims to be your daughter Stephanie, is she?"

"She's your secretary?"

"Yes!"

"How did she get to be your secretary?"

313

"She applied for a job as a manager, using the name Tamara Brown. I was impressed with her skills, and decided to give her a job as *my* secretary. She never said her name was Stephanie Brown. She never said you were her mother."

"Stephanie is a troubled young woman and that boyfriend of hers, that no-good old head is making matters worse," she said.

"Yes he is, he has taken your daughter to a new level of criminality. They are holding me hostage as we speak," he said.

"What! Stephanie what have you done! Stephanie!"

She squawks loudly like always, she is always squawking, and right now I don't want to hear her. I close the phone and put it in my pocket.

"What do you want from me?" he asked.

"I want you to acknowledge me. Acknowledge me like you acknowledge Khloe."

"You want to be recognized as my daughter."

"Yes."

"But you are not."

"Yes I am."

"No, you are not. You will never be because I am not your father."

"If you want to walk out of here alive, I advise you to be a man and admit she is your daughter."

"I will never admit to something that is not so, I don't care if you kill me. You are not my daughter. You were never my daughter. You will never *be* my daughter!"

Vomit spewed from my mouth. Specks of it dot his face and his body, much of it landed on our feet. My nose burns, my head throbs, his words, *You are not my daughter. You were never my daughter. You will never be a daughter* repeat themselves.

"Shut up, shut up, SHUT UP!"

"Tamara! Shh…come here Tamara."

Bailey is calling me. I don't want him, I don't want him near me, but he is. He pulls me to him and wipes my face with his hands.

"Shhh…it's over, it's all over, everything is out in the open. You got your answers."

"Yes I did, now you can do what you were paid to do."

"It is up to anonymous to decide what is to happen next."

I leave them alone in the cabin and head home. I cross the bridge, not caring about the noise. I only want to get away, far away, from him. I run up the driveway, out into the open, not caring if anyone sees me. Gunshots ring out. I turn around, a women dressed in red stands on the bridge. Bailey runs out after her.

"You are mad, looney tunes mad!" he shouted, "When someone like you have a gun, everybody should head for the hills."

"Where is she going?" she asked.

"I don't know, let her go, okay! Let her go, your husband did her real dirty," he said.

Sharon is the one who hired Bailey?! But that day Bailey and I picked them up, she acted totally surprised! The woman deserves an award.

"Greg does everyone he comes into contact with dirty. By the way where is he?" she asked.

"Still in his chair, waiting on us to make a decision," he said.

"Well he won't have to wait too much longer," she said.

Someone is coming. I hear the raggediest of engines chugging down the drive. I better get off the road, they are driving without their headlights. I ran to the back of the nearest house and peek around the corner. It can't be, it just can't be, it's the van. The same van that almost shoved me into the creek!

The driver gets out and greets the woman. It is him, Speed Demon, the man with the thick curly black hair. I can't hear his voice, but I am sure it is him. Headlights shine upon them, so much so that she hides her face. Another truck arrives, pulling up alongside the van, the area is black again. Speed demon goes to his van and pulls out a duffle bag. He gives it to the new driver who then loads it into his truck. I wonder what's in the duffle bag, it looks awfully heavy. Sharon sits in the front seat of the new driver's truck and waits. He shakes hands with Speed Demon, climbs into his truck and pulls off. Speed Demon gets into his van and leaves.

I want to go home. I want to get there as soon as possible. I venture out, running toward the road.

"Forget everything you saw tonight Tamara!"

I turn around to talk to Bailey. "What is going on, is Dad in that truck?"

"After the way he talked to you, you still call him Dad?"

"He is my Dad and I am going to prove it."

"He is no longer a concern of yours, you understand me?"

"No I don't understand, Bailey what have you gotten yourself into?"

"Oh shit! Greg is loose, she didn't shoot him, she set him free."

"That's good."

"No it isn't, she left me holding the bag. I am the one who held him against his will. Kid you and I can go to jail for a very long time."

"I am his daughter. He would never send me to jail."

"He doesn't consider you to be his daughter Tamara. We can't let him walk out of here alive."

"Yes we can."

316

"No we can't, stay here."

"What are you going to do? Bailey? Bailey come back!"

He ignores me and keeps going, easing his way to the front.

"Dad! Dad! Look out Dad! Bailey's coming to hurt you!"

Dad turns around a second too late. Bailey leaps on him, knocking him to the ground. He sits on Dad's chest and begins to choke him. Dad reaches for Bailey's face and grabs it. He lets go and tries to remove Bailey's hands from around his throat. He is powerless, his arms falls to his side.

"Bailey stop! Let go of him, you are killing him!"

He doesn't hear me. I have to stop him. I grab a loose brick near the steps and hit him. I hit him as hard as I can in the back of the head. Bailey let's go of Dad and cradles his head. Dad gasps for air.

"Get up Dad, hurry, we have to go, hurry!"

He rises to his feet, but stumbles backwards. He is weak, he leans on me and we run, up the driveway. I turn around to see if Bailey is following us, he is gone.

"C'mon Dad, hurry! We have to hurry before Bailey comes back."

We make it to the street. I flag a police car and tell them what happened. They rush Dad to the hospital and ask me to stick around to answer some questions. I am not afraid, whatever will be will be, I am just glad my father is still alive.

All the business at hand has been handled and I can go home. It's pouring, the wind is howling, hurricane season is still in effect. I never did look at the weather forecast. Kiera has been the focus of my entire afternoon, seems like she is poised to be my stepmother. Hmph, Dad loves her. Well he can love her all he wants, I am done with Kiera. I wish I could say the same for him. Unfortunately he will be in my life till one of us dies. What I will do is curtail my activities involving him. I have a new lease on life and I will follow it into a totally new direction. Sister Alice taught me about God when I was boarding school. She said he was the one to call on whenever I need guidance or help. I promised him I would change my ways, but then I graduated, went home and became swept up in Dad's agenda.

I must admit Dad leads a pretty exciting life. Wheeling and dealing with the who's who of Pennsylvania, meeting the up and coming in Washington. Those guys are no different than the average man on the street, they just know how to present their case better. I hope God can forgive me for the momentary lapse of judgment this afternoon and all the other stuff. I need his help. If I am going to be with Khloe I will most definitely need his help. I just heard a clap of thunder, sounds like a thunderstorm has rolled in. I hope Khloe isn't going to try to take Regis out for a walk. I better go home before she attempts it. I run to Khloe's building, Saki and her dog are in the lobby. They must have just come in from an evening walk. They are drenched with rain. She has blood all over her.

"Hello, what happened to you?"

"Have you seen her?

"Seen who?"

"My daughter."

"I'm sorry, what is your daughter's name?"

"Khloe, Khloe is my daughter."

"She said you were her godm…never mind, anyway Khloe is upstairs."

"No she isn't."

"What do you mean she isn't?"

"She has to be out there, somewhere, she wouldn't leave Regis outside by himself."

"What do you mean Regis was outside by himself?"

"He is hurt, badly hurt."

"How? Where is Khloe?"

"That is what I am asking you. No one has seen her, she is not answering her phone. One of her friends came by not too long ago, I told her I would tell Khloe she stopped by."

"Where is Regis?"

"I took him to the vet, they had to do emergency surgery."

"Why did he need surgery?"

"He was bitten pretty badly, but the vet says the animal's teeth did not puncture any arteries. He expects Regis to live."

"Where did you find him?"

"Over in the parking lot, along with one of Khloe's sneakers. I'm scared, something bad has happened. What if they hurt her, what if—

I didn't wait for her to finish her sentence. I leave her standing there in the lobby alone. I know what I told her Khloe, I told her to stay home, and she agreed. She is supposed to be upstairs, she had better be upstairs. As soon as I got off the elevator I knew something was wrong, the door to the apartment is opened, wide opened. I went inside, everything is the same as it was when I left.

"Khloe? Khloe?

She doesn't answer. I go into the bedroom and check the closets. I check the bathroom, the kitchen, no sign of her.

"It's just like you to be hard-headed! Wait, Saki said your sneaker was in the parking lot."

I jump on the elevator and ride to the lobby, thankfully Saki was still there. I ask her about the sneaker and she hands it to me. It is Khloe's sneaker, blood seeped into the crevices in and around the sickle on the sole. A piece of paper falls to the floor, it came out of her shoe.

"Saki, did you put this in here?"

319

"No, what is it?"

"It's a note."

I hand her the sneaker and kneel down to pick the note from off the ground. It is folded into a simple square, on the flip side is my name. The note is addressed to me:

> Dear Xavier,
>
> You said I was the best thing to happen to you. On our wedding night you claimed to love me. Well if I am so loved by you and the best thing to ever happen to you, how could you sleep with my best friend? That's right I know about the two of you. Your girlfriend called today and told me all about it. Are you going to say that it is all in my head? Are you going to deny having a girlfriend? I gave you one more chance, forgiving your past indiscretions and it seems to be a mistake. I have had enough of you and your lies. My life has been nothing but pain since I met you. As of today that pain will cease. I am gone forever so don't bother to look for me. You are free to see whomever you wish.
>
> Khloe
>
> PS: You will be hearing from my divorce attorney.

"Nice touch Kiera, I see you've been practicing her handwriting. Unfortunately you just broke the perimeters that I have set for you, now you will suffer the consequences. Khloe is not the one leaving, it is you. You will be leaving my life once and for all."

"Who is Kiera?"

"Someone I wish I never met."

Algon, the title of her street, is most fitting cause soon she will be *all gone*. She better be there. For her sake she had better be there. Somebody in this house better have some answers. She knows where Khloe is, I know she does. She wrote that note, which tells me she probably helped them take her.

Brazenly I park directly in front of her door. This is the first time I will actually go inside. I try to casually walk up the pavement, my anger eats me. I don't care who sees me, I don't care who hears her. I arrive at her door and banged, screaming her name.

"Kiera!"

The lock clicks. The door slowly eases open a quarter of the way and then stops. I am able to see pretty much the whole room, no one is in there. However, a door does not open by itself. Someone opened it, but who? I gently push the door, my eyes dart about the house, now it all makes sense. The place is appalling, Tamara and Kiera make more than enough money to furnish and brighten this place, why haven't they done it? I venture inside, stepping bit by bit. If anyone is in here I want to be the one with the element of surprise. I hug the wall and turn the corner. A figure steps out from the kitchen. Brice looks into my eyes with a finger pressed against his lips, he whispers, "They are in there."

"Who's they?"

He comes and stands close to me. "Kiera and her new man are in the second bedroom, across from the bath. She doesn't know I am here. She doesn't know I opened the door, do whatever you got to do."

"Wait a minute, are you throwing her under the bus?"

"I'm tired of her and her games. Her games is what got me locked up. Thanks to her and that old man, I am looking at serious jail time so do what you got to do. I just did what I had to do for me."

He leaves me in the doorway.

"Hey Brice, do you know where Khloe is?"

"No, not exactly, that stupid bitch helped that Irishman. They're both in the back room talking about what they did."

He walks out of the house. I never thought I would see the day when he would tire of her. His reference to the old man could only be Julius. I hear her husky voice at the end of a narrow hall.

"Look at that handbag, it's Prada! I bet she paid a thousand for it. Maybe she's carrying a couple of thousand, at least a couple of hundred. I never thought of Khloe as dumb. How smart can you be when you lose your pocketbook? Can you believe this? She lost her driver's license, credit cards—she has nine credit cards, nine! What does one person need with nine credit cards?"

"Plenty Kiera, plenty."

I knew it, that's how she got those pictures, Danny is her source! This girl is really getting around, from Brice to me to Dad and now to him.

"She is still carrying her college ID, we graduated four years ago. Here's her social security card, an address book, three checkbooks…three! I had no idea she walked around with all of this.

"Me neither, I could have robbed the bank long ago, *just* like I robbed the others."

That's your plan isn't it, to rob her. After you rob her then what?

"Can you picture her going to her favorite store, the exclusive Neiman Marcus? Not that she needs new clothes, but because she got it like that. Anyway she gets to the cashier, so sure of herself, and they scan her card. Guess what? It's rejected!"

"Impossible!"

"That's what she is going to say. She'll whip out another, they will scan that one, and it too will be rejected.

"No way!"

"Those will be her exact words *no way*! I wish I could be a fly on the wall when she stands at the counter speechless."

"Why?"

"To see the expression on her face, that cashier will look at her like she's a wannabe. Khloe will be dumbfounded—

"And crying…don't forget crying…'cause they will look at her like she is a commoner who does not know how to manage her money."

"Yeah crying cause she's embarrassed and humiliated. Do you think she will remember how she embarrassed and humiliated us?

"No, people like her only think about their wants and desires. Does she have any cash in there?"

"There's 1,2,3,4, ten 20 bills."

"Only $200, that's it!"

"I finally got revenge on her."

"This is not a joyous occasion."

"Ha ha ha! Don't tell me you are falling for her again."

"Don't laugh at me, don't you dare laugh at me!"

"Danny, calm down, I am not laughing at you."

"They could kill her and it will be our fault because we took her to them, she doesn't deserve this,"

Took her where? Where the hell have you taken her? Who is they? What the hell is going on? I gotta calm myself, got to stay calm if I expect to get her back alive.

"You do love her."

"Love is too strong of a word."

"No, it's the right word for you. Why does everyone fall for Princess Khloe?"

"We need to stop this before it goes any further."

"How will we do that without implicating ourselves?"

"I can leave an envelope giving her location at the police station."

"I don't believe this, we go through the trouble to get her and now you want to let her go?"

"Yes!"

"Wait til M—

"You know you always get on my fuckin nerves!"

What was that? Did he hit her over the head with something?

"Hello…"

Who is he calling?

"I want to report a crime. I came home from work and found an intruder inside my home."

Whoa! He called the police on himself?

"Yes I came home…she attacked me with a butcher knife, I had to shoot her. I believe she is dead. I think her name is Khloe Spencer, at least that what her identification says."

Wow! He has completely flipped the script. He's making Khloe the perpetrator.

"I live at 7312 Algon Avenue, my name is Rory McGuiness."

And he's implicating his own family, this guy…

He hangs up the phone. I hear drawers and doors opening and closing, you can't leave! I kick the door in and dive right on top of him. We both land on the bed, splintering it. I punch him in the face as hard as I can, but he isn't fazed, throwing his own punches. My teeth shudder in their sockets. We tussle, rolling off the bed and onto the hardwood floor, eventually rolling into open space. We break loose from each other and rise to our feet, panting for air. After a few more breaths I manage to hurl an accusation. "We didn't fight in New York, but we made up for it today. I hope you're ready to die 'cause you will."

"One of us will definitely die today, but it won't be me."

"Didn't think you were the type to hurt someone," I said, looking at Kiera laying against a wall, "where is she?"

"Right there in front of your face."

"Not her, where is Khloe. What the hell have you done with Khloe?"

"I didn't do anything, except what I was paid to do."

"Which was?"

"Bring her to New York."

"New York? Why New York?"

"I don't know, and to be honest with you we didn't ask."

"Who's we?"

"Me and the girl propped up against the wall."

"So you are saying someone asked you to bring her to New York?"

"Yes."

"Exactly where in New York?"

"Not too far from Times Square."

Could they be, no I would have remembered them, but it was dark that night. All I remember…

"Did you take her in a duffle bag?"

"Yes we did."

"Why a duffle bag? Why not just carry her there?"

"Because we were instructed to bring them in duffle bags."

"Them?"

"I meant her."

"No, you meant exactly what you said them. Who is them?"

"I will only answer your questions Khloe. Anything else is none of your business."

One of the knives strapped on my forearm is loose. I feel it at my wrist, perfect timing. I flick it directly at him and it lands, right in his upper chest. He falls to his knees and holler out in pain. Traumatized and weak, he reaches for the knife to pull it out. I rush over to stop him, if he pulls it he will bleed out.

"Listen, you will tell me everything I want to know. So if I ask you about your business you will give me an answer right?"

He panted, "No…no I won't."

"Guess you need an incentive." I push on the handle of the knife, just a little. Blood gush onto his shirt, I am a confident that it is in his flesh and not in or near any main arteries. "Tell me again, who is them?"

"Girls."

"You are putting girls in duffle bags. What the fuck are you doing with them?"

"I don't know what they are doing with them, I am only doing what I was told."

"Who is paying you to do this?"

"Can't say, we meet them in New York, under the underpass, they give us the money, we give them the bag and then we go home."

That night in New York, I was supposed to meet Reuben below the underpass. Instead these two showed up, and then those cops…somehow he found me at the hotel...Reuben you never cease to amaze me, I take that back. The one you least expect is always the one to betray you.

"Irishman I want the name of the person who told you to kidnap Khloe."

"I already told you I don't know their name."

I shove the knife deeper into his flesh, ignoring his cries of pain. I have exactly one minute to get what I need.

"Old Danny boy, I need the name, the name of the person...ahhhh!"

"How do you like that?"

Once again assumption stabs me in the back. Kiera is alive, well, and awake.

"I thought he killed you."

"No, I am still around," she said.

"Not for long, while you were unconscious, he called the police and said you were an intruder that he had to kill. He told them your name was Khloe Spencer."

"Liar! Liar! He would never do that!"

"Care to stick around and explain to the police how you got Khloe's handbag with all her identification?"

She pulls the knife from my back and thrusts it in his heart. She then turns and steps on my hand that is holding the knife in his upper chest. He is most definitely dead. This girl is more than your simple whore, she can kill. She lunges at me a second time with another knife in her hand.

"This is for messing up my face."

I scramble to my feet and jump back just as the blade comes at my midsection. I strike her from behind, knocking her forward. The knife flies out of her hand. We both dash for the knife, but I get it first. I grab her, twist her arm behind her back and point the knife at her throat.

"Now unless you want to join him, you better tell me where the hell is Khloe."

"Khloe is in New York, ready to be exported."

"Exported where?"

"I don't know where. I suppose to one of those countries with a preference for women like her."

I bop her in the throat with the butt of the knife. She goes limp in my arms. I let her fall to the floor before picking her up to carry her to my car, skirting by the looming crowd of neighbors.

"I'm taking her to the hospital, can't wait for the ambulance. Tell them we are at the hospital."

"Okay."

I act like the concern boyfriend and gingerly sit her in the back seat. I attach the seat belt, guaranteed to hold her. They are not your ordinary seat belts. They are belts without a release button. I drive away from her block, looking for a secluded area. Tookany Creek Parkway is perfect, a stretch of road with very few houses and traffic lights. I put on my four-way blinkers and pull over to the side of the road, pretend like I'm having car trouble. I slide my hand under my seat and feel around for the secret compartment. I always keep a couple of syringes just in case of a situation like this one. I take one them and stick her in the ankle. It will make her sleep for more than a couple of hours. When she awakes the exchange will have already occurred and she will find herself in a bag going to a country that prefers women like her.

Old friends meet again

The blood on the back of my shirt is dry. The pressure from leaning against the car seat probably helped stemmed its flow, nevertheless it is painful. I've return to the apartment to clean up. Kurt said he will keep an eye on the car. I don't have to explain anything. Five hundred bucks compels him to understand that she is in a deep sleep after a night of drinking. He asks if I need any assistance, and I take him up on the offer telling him I need a parachute. He said he could have one sent over in as little as fifteen minutes. He offers to help, but I told him I could manage.

Reuben should arrive in the next hour or so and when he gets there I will be ready. I called him as soon as I hit the city and asked for a meet. He will stand around and look for me, and I will text him to come down the manhole. At first he will gawk, and then he will laugh. He knows how much of a devil I can be. His guard will be down and I will sting him. Little ole me, the one he is assigned to protect and watch over, has the potential to pull the wool over his eyes. He will be scared, but he will give me what I want.

I prop Kiera against a pipe, she's still sleeping. I gave her another shot after I arrived here. It's a sedative, I want her to sleep not die, dying would be too easy. I want her to suffer the same fate she had in mind for my Khloe. Someone just stepped on the manhole cover. It's Reuben, I know it's him because he always shuffle his feet. I send him a text message and he steps away from the manhole. He slides it over and maneuvers himself down the stairs. He does not call my name. He realizes that someone, namely the police, will be patrolling the area. Instead he shuffles along the tunnel, knocking on the walls.

"Reuben, I am over here."

He turns around and shuffles towards me.

"What's in the bag?"

"The usual, this one is smoking hot, she knows how to work it. She will enjoy your clientele and they will most definitely enjoy her."

"Can I see her face?"

"No…not until I get Khloe back."

"Khloe? Oh yeah the girl you married, I thought you knew how to hold onto your women."

"I do Reuben, I do."

"Well then why are you asking me about her?"

"Because she is missing Reuben! I was told by the one over there in that bag that she was brought here. Would you know anything about that?"

He sighs, he does know about this. "Did you take her Reuben?"

"She is here, in New York, but I did not take her Xavier."

"I thought you were looking out for me Reuben!"

"I was, I still am…the powers that be, they are opposed to your new bride."

"What do you mean opposed?"

"They feel she is not suitable for you, therefore, they demanded that she be removed from your life."

"Who is *they* Reuben?"

"Xavier I believe you already know the answer to that question."

"They can be any number of people."

"Think blood."

"Blood? I am already bleeding like a pig…you mean a blood relative, which one?"

"Who has been so opposed to you from the very beginning?"

"Lots of people! Dad, her parents, Tamara, Danny, the one over there in the bag…"

"Think closer…"

"Marie Colette! She's not close to me! I stand corrected, she is, she is my mother. But she doesn't' know anything about Khloe."

"She knows plenty."

"I bet she does thanks to that one over there in that bag. Take her, send to a place where she will be most lucrative. A place where it will be next to impossible for her to return."

"Are you sure you want me to do that?"

"Yes I am sure, I have never been surer of anything in my life. Where is my mother keeping Khloe?"

"On the boat, you had better hurry, the boat is about to set sail."

"Where is she going?"

"To the Far East, and once she get there you will not be able to find her."

"What slip is she in?"

"She's not docked in New York. She is docked in Jersey City.

"Where in Jersey City?"

"On Port Jersey Boulevard, almost into Bayonne."

"It will take us forever to get back into New Jersey!"

"Us!?"

"Yes, you are driving."

Reuben infuriates me. He is driving at his leisure. To pass the time I ask him a question, one that I always wanted to know the answer to.

"Hey Reuben, how did you come up with this disguise?"

"What disguise?"

"One green eye and one blue eye, and the shuffling of your feet like you are an old man."

"Oh that's easy, they are not a disguise. My eyes really are green and blue, some shit called Heterochromia iridum."

"Sorry to offend you, I just thought it was a brilliant disguise to throw people off."

"Some people are downright afraid. By the way the shuffling of my feet is hereditary. Your mother did not care."

"My mother hired you!"

"Yes she did, who did you think I worked for?"

"My Dad."

He chuckles, "Your Dad would not hire somebody like me because he cannot afford me, it was cheaper to train you."

He pulls the car into the spot next to the slip, "Let me go inside and distract them, then you can sneak on board."

"You are leaving something."

"No I am not, Madame will be upset if I bring her on the boat."

"She won't be if I bring her."

Reuben trudges inside the boat alone. He leaves the door slightly ajar, my cue to come. I crouch down and scoot inside, dragging a sleeping Kiera with me. The coast remains clear. I inch further and further, checking inside a cabin on my route. It is filled with boxes, nothing out of the ordinary. The next two cabins yield the same results. She has to be somewhere on this boat. Uh oh, someone is coming. I turn around and go back to the cabin with the boxes. I lay Kiera against the back of the wall and push the boxes in front of her, leaving space for myself. I sit next to her just in time, they have entered the room.

"How is she?"

"She is fine Marie. She is already on the boat."

This is what my dream was trying to tell me. *They* are trying to hurt her. Two women, both claim to want the best for us. Both try to hurt us, are they psycho or what?

"Those two did the job better than expected. I didn't think they could pull it off."

"They were close to her, as close as one could get. That is what made it easy."

"Saki what are your plans for her?"

"To take her back to Japan and introduce her to my culture. What are your plans for him?"

"To hand my business over to him."

Khloe is not going anywhere but home with me, and I am done with illegal activity. When will we you and Julius do your own dirty work?

"You know they could both rebel against us."

"It wouldn't surprise me, are we not rebellious?"

"Yes we are. We both went against our parent's wishes and look where it got us…"

"We both had to leave our children behind."

"We did what was best."

"And at that time it was best to let their fathers raise them."

"They didn't do too bad of a job, Greg raised my daughter to become the vice president of his company."

"Yes, and Julius raised my son to be a charismatic persuader, the perfect person to take the helm from me."

333

Oh my god! The two of them are friends, old friends! They purposely left us behind are and now they want to come back into our lives. Well I'll be damn if I let them!

"You mean he raised a killer. A killer with no conscious."

"Don't insult my son. Your daughter is not as precious as gold nor is she as pure as the driven snow. Your daughter married my son because she wanted to, not because he forced her."

They are not going to get away with what they have done. I stand up. Saki loses the blood in her face. Mother nervously stands there with a smile as if she was expecting me. "Quite judgmental Saki, considering you do not know me."

"I know your parents very well, and I am confident that the apple did not fall from the tree," she said.

"I think I understand why Khloe did not tell you. She sensed that something was not right within you." I looked at my mother, "Just as I always sensed that something was not right within you. It isn't fair of you, two against one. Why? Why did you do this to us?"

"I had your best interests at heart. She cheated on you once and you married her anyway."

"What do you mean she broke my heart once?"

"I've seen those filthy pictures. She seemed to be enjoying herself immensely with that man."

"You want to know who broke my heart, the woman who showed you those pictures. I loved her first, but she preferred Dad. Khloe made a mistake. It is the woman who seeks to embarrass me that causes me the most hurt, not my wife."

"She was most unsuitable for you."

"But you used her to abduct my wife. This situation says a lot about you…and you Saki, what's your stake in this?"

"My stake is to make sure my daughter is safe, and that means sending her away from you. You are not the right person for my daughter. If I had known she was seeing you, things would never had progressed this far."

"That's the trade-off you bargained for when you opted to let someone else raise your child. Incidentally, how do you two know each other?"

"We met in college," said mother, "right after the disastrous relationships we were in ended. We shared our secret and helped each other through the pain, enabling us to enjoy life. It was Saki's idea to become a part of your lives by demanding to be your godmothers."

"Hmph! Godmothers are expected to care for the children after the death of the parents…did it occur to either one of you that the easiest thing to do was to be the mother you were supposed to be?"

"We did what was best," she said.

"Saki you thought letting our fathers raise us was best! I hate to see what kind of response real love would provoke from you. Where is she?" I asked.

"Where is who?" she asked.

"Khloe! Your daughter, I know she is here with you, don't bother denying it. Just tell me where she is," I said.

The both look at each other, unsure of what to say next.

"You cannot have Khloe, she said, "You are too dangerous. Your lifestyle is too dangerous. Someone will kill her to hurt you."

"She is right Xavier. Khloe will just be a liability in our family. She does not know how to think on her feet within seconds, seconds that could very well be a matter of life and death. Are you willing to put her in jeopardy?"

"You are no better than Dad!" I screamed, "You are satisfied with seeing me unhappy, with no one to share my life. You want to keep me in your square peg because you are as miserable as he is. Fortunately this apple has strayed FAR from your tree, I am willing to claim what I love and I am not ashamed to show it. I have a second chance at life and I am taking it. I will have my own family with Khloe. My children

335

will know that I am their father and will not be sent away to live with someone ELSE!"

"I did it for your own good. I love you Xavier. I loved you enough to keep you out of my life," she said.

I countered, "You were unwilling to bond with the new family you had created. Unwilling to be on the inside of the core because you preferred to be outside the core. You are stupid do you know that! You sacrificed me to stay with them, tell me was it worth it?!"

"What do you know about them?" she asks.

"Enough to be thankful for the small favor you did for me."

"I am afraid you will have to find yourself another wife because I will not allow my daughter to stay with you," she said.

"How do you propose to keep a grown woman at home with you?" I asked.

"I have a variety of ways, in which you will never lay eyes on her again," she said.

"My god, two souls blacker than black have paired up to turn my universe on its ear," I gripe.

"If saving my daughter's life means turning your universe on its ears, than yes my soul is blacker than black, and if you stand in my way your heart will cease beating," she said.

"Do you think I cannot provide for Khloe?" I asked.

"Yes!" she said.

"I have plenty of money," I said.

"I know you do, the money is not an issue. It is your other activities that are of grave concern," she said.

"Exactly what are you referring to?" I asked.

"Look Xavier, I know what you are and I know what you do. I know some of the people that you do those things for. Those people now know you have gotten married. What they do not know is that your wife is my daughter. You have to let her go."

They know because of the wedding. Khloe said she wanted a small wedding, just the two of us. But me, I wanted to share my joy with everyone. I knew the risks and threw them in the wind. "And you? Are you willing to see me, you son that you profess to love, unhappy?"

"I am not willing to see you get hurt. I can find a more suitable wife for you. Someone who can withstand all our illicit affairs, lend a helping hand and possibly serve as backup," she said.

"Saki believe me I will do anything to keep Khloe safe, anything," I said.

"Anything like holding her parents captive?" she asked.

"I don't know anything about that," I said.

"Sure you do, I know it was you who arranged for Greg and Sharon to be held at that little historic settlement your father has pledged x-amount of monetary funding."

"You know where they are?"

"As do you."

"Know I don't. You cannot and will not put this on me."

"I got to give to you, it's a place hardly anyone knows of except maybe history buffs. I know what drives desperation. Your mother and I have both been there. Desperation can lead you to do things you never knew you were capable of. Do you remember the college prank perpetrated by your friend Reggie, selling dots laced with PCP on the street? How about that little girl called Jane up in Pittsburgh? Remember how she was lured into the woods by a man and left to die because her father would not play ball with a certain businessman. Think back…to the time someone was beaten senseless because they were bold enough to confront you. A person had acid poured on them because they refused to do your father a favor. And I just can't forget about your mother's business—fashion designer, drug smuggler,

337

human trafficking, etcetera etcetera etcetera. By the way, where is Julius' former assistant Joseph Coleman?"

"Speak of things you know to be fact," I said.

"These are facts. As I have said, I know some of the people you do things for," she said, "Those same people kidnapped my daughter. Khloe was safe and sound until you came along. If someone had not told me she was taken, neither one of us would know of her whereabouts! You should be thanking me."

"Where is she?" I asked.

"She is gone, well on her way, far away. I have the means to protect her just as your mother has the means to protect you, provided that you listen to her."

"Khloe is not going with you!"

"Xavier she is already gone, and there is nothing you can do about it."

"There is something that I can do about it, I can erase your existence."

"Xavier stop, please! You are frightening me!"

Oh my god, its Khloe, she came from the room behind mother. The look on her face says she has been listening. "Khloe are you alright?"

"Please stay where you are? Please don't come near me."

"Don't be afraid of me, I would never hurt you."

"You are right, you will never hurt me. You have to let me go, Xavier I do not belong in your world."

"There are some things I have to tell you."

"I think I heard more than enough. I don't like what I heard Xavier, they make you out to be a monster."

"I was…once upon a time I was not a nice person. I was someone you would *not* want to know unless you traveled in the same circles."

338

She is shivering with fright. I have to make her feel at ease, comfort her the way a husband is supposed to comfort his wife. I moved towards her.

"Stay right where you are Xavier! Do not come near me."

Surprise, she has her own gun. "Okay, I will stay here. I need you to listen Khloe. I want to expl—

"Explain what? Why you hurt and kill people?"

"I don't hurt people Khloe, I never hurt anyone."

"Xavier I just heard everything my mother accused you of. You didn't deny it. If it was not true why didn't you deny it?"

"I didn't deny it because your mother does not know what she is talking about. My mother is right here, ask her yourself."

Mother came to the forefront.

"Khloe your mother is quite an exaggerator. I am a fashion designer, my business is fashion design, not criminal activity. If anybody here is a criminal it is her. Khloe you are here because your mother paid someone to bring you here."

"Liar! Like always trying to get the mess off of you and onto someone else, Khloe your husband is responsible for your parents being missing," she said.

"I did not harm Greg and Sharon. You did, and you know where they are," I said.

Khloe cries profusely, "How could you, how could you stop my parents from coming to my wedding?"

She believes Saki's lies. I have to set the record straight. "I didn't stop them from coming. I don't know what happened to them, honestly Khloe, I did not have anything to do with what happened to them. The only thing I know is that they did not want you to marry me. I thought they would come to the wedding and try to stop it, but they never showed up."

"Where are they Xavier, what have you done with my parents? Are they dead?"

"I don't know where they are Khloe, I really don't know where they are."

"I don't believe you Xavier, you killed them so now I must kill you."

She aims the gun at me. I duck, and then I see her fall to the ground.

"What happened? Who touched her?"

Khloe mumbled, holding her wrist. I tried to help her to her feet, but she angrily pulls away.

"I did," said mother, "I was not going to let her kill you. She is fine, I just hit her on the hand with the lamp. Now I tell you both the truth! Ms. Sayonara here knows what happened to Greg and Sharon and yet she was willing to let her daughter kill someone while she stands there in silence."

Saki does not utter a single word in her defense. Mother is telling the truth.

"Khloe your Dad is in the hospital in Philadelphia. His secretary, Tamara Brown has been charged with kidnapping," she said.

"What?!" she gasps.

"Yes it is most unfortunate, Tamara walked into the web of your mothers," she said.

"What do you mean mothers?" I ask.

Mother explained, "Mother number one—Sharon—stumbled onto the truth about Tamara and became very angry. So she and mother number two—Sayonara here—conspired to kidnap your father with the help of Bailey. Problem is Tamara has been left holding the bag."

"Where is Sharon?" Khloe asks.

"Nobody knows," said Saki.

"I know," Mother said, "Sharon is hiding in her childhood home with Bailey."

"I don't believe it," Khloe said.

"Saki call her," she said.

Saki reluctantly reaches into her pocket and pulls out the phone. She dials the number and someone answers immediately. She hands the phone to Khloe who listens. The phone falls from her hand. I hear the other person, it is Sharon. Sharon is alive. Khloe runs to me and bursts into tears.

The truth speaks

I sit impatiently beside the window that faces Broad Street, waiting for Dad. Albert Einstein was where he was taken. Normally he would have been taken to Chestnut Hill Hospital where his doctor is on staff. Somehow he wound up here, surprisingly he is quite content. I can only assume it is because he views it as an opportunity to donate money. He wasn't really hurt, just rope burns, dehydration, fatigue, and a mild case of hypothermia. What *was* hurt was his ego. He always prided himself on being a good judge of character. He never saw Tamara, I should say Stephanie-her name is Stephanie, coming. I did not either, and I have known her a lot longer. Her disguise had me completely fooled.

I was told by the police that she accompanied him to the hospital and filled in all the details. Dad dismissed her sincerity and demanded she be arrested for her role in his kidnapping. He said she was present the day he and mother were taken. He also said she did not try to stop it, which null and voided her story as an innocent bystander. When asked what her motive was, he said she was blackmailing him with the preposterous claim of being his daughter. Stephanie was immediately taken into custody. Soon thereafter, Bailey was captured. He pleaded guilty and offered to tell the whole story, provided that he receives a lighter sentence. The district attorney agreed to the terms. Unfortunately Bailey did not live up to his end of the bargain. He has skipped town and has not been seen or heard from. I gather from his disappearance that he intends to let Stephanie take the fall.

Dad should be back by now, where is he? The people at the nurse's station should have some idea of his whereabouts. Jackie, the Asian nurse who was here when I arrived is still on duty, she should know where Dad is.

"Jackie I'm looking for Gregory Spencer, I was told he went for MRI testing early this morning."

"Let me check and see if he is still downstairs."

She picks up the phone and taps a few numbers. The nurse on the other end speaks quite loudly. Jackie does not have to repeat what her co-worker is saying. I can hear everything.

"He is still down there. There's a backlog of patients."

"He hasn't been seen yet?"

"No he hasn't."

"Can I go down there and wait with him? I need to talk to him about some stuff."

"Sure he is on the lower level, look for the signs on the walls. They will take you directly to the MRI Center."

"Thanks."

I ride the elevator to the basement. The signs are just as she said well written and clear, I see him in the MRI Center, sitting in his wheelchair by the reception area watching television. I am sure they aren't looking at MSNBC, his favorite show. The only good thing about this whole ordeal is that he was forced to take a much needed vacation. He's complained of pain for months, never taking the opportunity to get checked out. Hopefully the source of his pain has been caused by the weight of carrying secrets and not disease. I walk up behind him and give him a hug.

"Ahh! Don't touch me!"

"It's me Daddy, it's me."

"Whew! I'm sorry, I shouldn't have reacted that way."

"I take it you are still traumatized, are you happy to see me?"

"Of course, for awhile I thought I would never see you again."

343

"During that ordeal I bet you didn't."

"I *am* happy to see you. How are you?"

I nod, can't risk speaking. I would only end up bawling. "I'm fine, happy to find you alive. I had the most wonderful wedding. It would have been better had the two of you been there."

"You married him?"

"Yes, I married him."

"You can get an annulment. What made you run away and get married without us being there?"

"I was in love with him."

"I understand that part, I am referring to your willingness to exclude us from the ceremony."

"I wasn't trying to exclude you from the ceremony. Xavier kept saying you and Mom were already in New York. He said that I would see you later on that night. I kept calling mother and she never answered her phone."

"That's because we were being held against our will, any news on your mother's whereabouts?"

"The police are still looking for her. They are also looking for Bailey."

"What do they want with him?"

"He and his anonymous partner organized the whole thing."

"What whole thing?"

"I heard he was paid to make sure you did not arrive in New York. How do you feel about that?"

"Angry, hurt, a little sad…"

"Why sad?"

"Because I loved her."

"Daddy, whom do you love, Bailey or Mother?"

"I am going to admit something that I never admitted before."

"What's that Dad?"

"I am a despicable human being who sometimes does vile things in enormous proportions. You may well view me as a nightmare."

"What did you do?"

"Push me up to the desk."

I turn him around so he can face the nurse.

"Do you have somewhere me and my daughter can talk privately?" he asked.

"Yes we do, there is a room directly behind me," she said.

"I intend to take my test, I just need to tell her some things, you know family matters," he said.

She pushes him, and I follow, to the room on the opposite side of the wall.

"I will come and get you when they call your name," she said.

"Thanks," we both said.

Dad added, "Please close the door behind you."

The door is closed. Fluorescent lights reflect on the mauve walls. It and the simplistic paintings give the room a aesthetic feel, a perfect pick me up for patients. I don't mind the room being bright. I sit down in one of the high back chairs and wait for him to speak. He doesn't. Whatever he was going to tell me he shoved back into his memory. I will start the conversation. I want to know what he started to tell me.

I asked him again, "What did you do?"

"For starters, Sharon is not your mother."

"I know that."

"Who told you?"

"My real mother, Saki."

"Yes she is your mother."

345

"I suppose I always knew deep down inside she was my mother, she is so rigid…everything has to be just so…and I look a *lot* like her, nothing like Sharon…why did she have to pretend to be my godmother?"

"Saki did not have to pretend, she wanted to. Did she tell you she *had* to be your godmother instead of your mother?"

"Yes, are you saying she is lying?"

"Damn straight I am!"

Then he paused. He just stared into space. I waved my hand in front of his eyes and he does not blink.

"Dad! Dad!" I called, shaking him, he still did not answer me, "Something is wrong, we need the nurse!"

"No we do not! I am fine, I was just thinking of how I am going to explain to you what I have done."

"Well you always said the best way to tell something is to just come out and say it. Say whatever's on your mind Dad."

He looks at me square in the eyes.

"Okay…here it goes. I did something a long time ago, 24 years ago. It is something I am not proud of, and when you hear this story you are not going to be proud of me. There is a chance you might actually hate me. That will not matter, what will matter is that you know the truth."

"What truth?"

"Saki is your mother. I dated her and Sharon at the same time."

"You…a philander?"

"Yeah, me, you probably will be calling me a whole bunch of other names when I am done…anyway both women conceived at the same time"

"Slimy! Absolutely slimy!"

"Yeah I was back then, all I thought about was what I wanted. I demanded to have my needs met by any woman who peaked my interests. I actually thought I had the right to pick a new woman whenever the old one got on my nerves."

"You were that immature and selfish?"

"I am not proud of the way I behaved back then."

"You shouldn't be, by the way who captured your attention first, Saki or Sharon?"

"Saki, your mother. She was exquisite back then—

"She still is."

"Yes she is quite beautiful, soft porcelain skin, the blackest of hair…very refined, with complications."

"What kind of complications?"

"Her family…race relations were just beginning to break free from restrictions. Saki's family is very, very traditional, entirely different from ours. Our family holds tight to its value, but does not close the door on strangers invited into the family. Your mother's family is different. They will not extend a welcoming hand to anyone who is different. They will even go so far as to disown their flesh and blood rather than being dishonored. Their place in their society is more important. Do you understand Khloe?"

"Yes I do understand, more than you will ever know…why did you not marry her?"

"I did not want a woman who valued her parent's opinion more than her own. It was clear how they felt about me and how they would feel about you. Saki was okay with that."

"What did the two of you do?"

"Saki went away, into hiding. I took care of her financially while she carried you."

"How did you meet mother?"

"I met Sharon, at my friend Ernie's. He was having a party because his folks were away. Sharon was on the dance floor...she could really move..."

"Earth to Greg."

"I am still here in the earthly realm. All the guys liked your mother. She was the life of the party, made everyone laugh. She wasn't—

"Complicated."

"Exactly."

"I loved them both, and wanted to keep both of them."

"No way!"

"I did keep them both for a little while, then fate intervened and forced me to chose."

"What happened?"

"One night Sharon and I was out having dinner, she was eight months pregnant then—

"How far along was mother with me?"

"Sharon was seven months along, Saki was nine months. Anyway back to Sharon, we were on the way home that night, September 5th, 19—

"That's my birthday!"

"Yes it is...a car, driving extraordinarily fast, slammed into us. He hit the passenger side, where Sharon was sitting."

"What about the baby?"

"The ambulance rushed her to the hospital, straight into emergency surgery. They tried to save both lives, but could save only one."

"That baby has the same birth date as me?"

"Yes, your sister would have been 24 years old too."

"How is that possible?"

"I'm trying to tell you how."

He hung his head low, looking into the magazine he was reading before I came.

"I was devastated that the baby died. I knew Sharon would be also, so I made sure she never knew the baby died."

"How could you hide that?"

"It was easy to hide from her, Sharon was in a coma for almost a month. I told the doctors I did not want her to have any visitors. I did not want anyone to tell her the baby was gone."

"Why not? It's not like you could substitute...oh my god!'

In the pit of my stomach is the sensation of nausea, my blood pounds through the veins in my temple. I am not sure I want to know what he has done. I have the urge to run, but if I run I may never know the truth. "What did you do?"

"I went to see your mother. Saki was hiding at a friend's house, too afraid to let her parents know you were on the way. I wanted you, even though you were inside of her. You were not willing to come into the world yet, stubborn back then...I wasn't willing to wait. I made Saki go into labor."

"How?"

"I gave her something. I poured it into her drink when she was not looking. I watched her drink it. She started screaming in pain that something was wrong and I should take her to the hospital."

I ease out of the chair as he comes closer to me. I back up, unable to take my eyes off of him. This hideous monster, who hides behind the best designer suits and runs a multimillion dollar company, is capable of committing murder of the worst kind. He is still coming toward me.

"It all worked out, you finally came into the world. Saki went back home to her parents as if nothing ever happened, and you, you lived with me."

He touches me. His cold, clammy hands have the nerve to touch me. "I could have died! You could have killed me! You could have killed her!"

"But you didn't, the doctors said you were unaffected, they said you would have a normal life."

"You just took her baby."

"No I did not just take her baby, you were a child she did not want! I wanted you, okay, and I made sure you had everything you were supposed to have."

"I can't wait to hear your story about Stephanie."

"What about her?"

"Is she your daughter?"

"How many times do I have to tell you, no she is not my child!"

"Don't you find it strange that she went to the extreme, working as your secretary for two years just to get to know you?"

"It's downright weird."

"Dad if she wanted to hurt, she could have at any time."

"So what are you saying?"

"I don't believe she helped Bailey kidnap you and Mom."

"Oh for god sakes, don't be so naïve."

"I am not being naïve. I think you should do DNA to make sure she is not your daughter."

"If I do that, it will give credence to her story and I will not do that."

"Dad did you have an affair with her mother?"

"Yes I did."

"Did you pay her mother $5,000 a month?"

"Yes I did."

"Why?"

"I don't care to discuss that with you…I am not that girl's father. That young lady is a criminal and she is where she belongs, in a jail cell."

"Funny, you should be sitting right beside her. I wonder if what you did to me and my mother is a crime. I am going to have someone look into it. I will be back with an answer."

I have to thank her for sticking around. She could have easily fled the scene, not accompany him to the hospital and certainly not fill in the details. I will make sure her court appointed attorney knows the whole truth and I know exactly how to pull it off. Seems like I got here in the nick of time, in 30 minutes visiting hours will be over. The guards scan and prod all over me, I feel like I am being molested. They guide me to the visitor's room and tell me where to sit. Stephanie comes thru the door shackled like a slave. Instantaneously I am hugged. I tell her to take the seat sits next to me.

"How did you find me?"

"Your story is all over the news. They're asking for the public's help. How is it being in here? Is anyone bothering you, do you need anything?"

"I am in solitary confinement. They put me in there for my own safety. Have you talked with Kiera?"

"Not since all of this happened."

"She hasn't come to see me."

"I'll let her know you want to see her. How about your mother, would you like me to contact her?"

"Yes I would like that very much. Her number is in a phone book at the apartment. The lawyer has the keys.

"Okay."

"Have you had a bail hearing yet?"

"Not yet, my lawyer is working on it. He says he thinks the bail is going to be high because of Dad position in society."

"Exactly what happened Stephanie?"

"What happened is I confronted Dad. I confronted him with the truth, and he denied me. He denies being my father."

"I know he does, I just left him. Be glad is not your Dad."

"Why should I be glad? You had him to yourself the last 23 years and you don't want to share him with me!"

"I never said I did not believe your story. I just said be glad he denies being your father."

"I don't understand, why do you keep saying that."

"He's a horrible man. Someone who should've died instead of a baby."

"You sound hurt, what's happened?"

"I just left him. He told me some of the horrible things he did when he was younger. The horrible thing he did to my mother while she was pregnant with me."

"What?!"

"Yes, he used and abused my mother just like he used and abused yours. By the way, I asked him about you and he flat out denied it. We don't necessarily need him to prove your story. We have everything we need right here right now."

She looks around.

"Are you seeing something that I don't?"

"Yes I do, blood, our blood. Blood tests will prove whether or not we are sisters, subsequently proving paternity. For your sake Stephanie I hope he is, cause if he is not…you will be stuck in here for a very long time."

Happiness at last

It is so peaceful here that the birds chirping high up in the Hemlocks have awakened me. I suppose they are busy putting the finishing touch on their nests. Something we will be doing this afternoon. It was a smart decision to come here. We are away from the press, the police and bad memories. We have chosen a home in an area that neither one of us has any connection with.

I love this house. We acquired this house two days ago, bought it as is, making the homeowner extremely happy. He told us he had the house on the market for months. We didn't bother to ask if the home had any problems. We didn't care. All we wanted was to get away from everything and everybody, from the lies. When the keys were placed in our hands we realized that we did not have any furniture. So we stopped in a local furniture store and bought the essentials—a bedroom set, a suede sectional, and a dinette set. A little further down the street was an appliance store. In there we bought a slick stainless steel refrigerator with matching stove, and a washer and dryer. Across the street was another store specializing in home décor. From them we bought bed linen, towels, china, cookery, utensils and glasses.

The house is as spacious as the condo and the best part is I don't have to get dress to take Regis out. All I have to do is open the patio doors and he goes out by himself. Poor Regis limps as he walks. The veterinarian explained that several cartilages were completely severed during the attack. He said he was successful in reattaching them, but Regis has not regained the full use of his leg. Xavier and I both wonder if he ever really will.

This is a welcome change to a horrifying week. I sincerely hope that nothing else rises to the surface. The secrets are out. There cannot be anymore lurking in the closets of my past. My life unraveled and then just as collectively came together. I must say I am stronger than before. Not afraid to say no, not afraid to ask questions, not easily baited, not afraid to voice my opinions and desires. I finally realize that nothing is ever as plain as black and white. The people in my life have muted shades of gray injected into their well being, especially the one lying next to me.

These last two days have been nothing but bliss. We have reconnected on a much deeper level, telling each other about our childhoods, our fears. When I told him the story of Stephanie, Dad and myself, he wondered aloud if the Julius and Gregory were related. And then he warned me. He didn't like the way Stephanie inched her way into the company and suggested that there was more to her tale than wanting recognition. Likewise, I asked him why he kept me on the outside for so long. He said it was to protect me from what or whom he never did explain. I did not let his sudden silence stop me from probing. I kept at him, till he finally told me. He was afraid that I would prefer Julius to him. Why on earth would he think I would fall for his father? Because of Kiera, he tried to reassure me that I was his first choice but I remember Spring Break. She was the first to get an evening alone with him, guess she rocked his world. "What shall I wear today?"

I push the covers aside and sit upright in bed. He reaches out and finds my waist. He tries to pull me backwards.

"I am not done loving you."

"You are for now. I have to go to work. See how things are doing, make sure they are running smoothly."

He lets go of me and lies back down in the bed.

"We are supposed to finish shopping for our home today. When is your Dad going back?"

"He is supposed to be back today. After work we can do some more shopping, I promise."

He sighed, exhaling stale air disdainfully.

"Have you decided what you are going to do about Stephanie?"

I rise off the bed and head for the bureau.

"When I get the results from our DNA I will make a decision, they are due back today."

"Are you ready to accept the consequences?"

"What do you mean?"

"Are you willing to accept her as your sister?"

"I don't know, I am not sure if I could consider her a sister."

"Personally I don't think she is. If your Dad says he is not his father, I would listen to him. There could be a reason, a very good reason why he is so adamant."

"You know I asked you a question before and you never gave me an answer."

"An answer to what question?"

"I asked you why would Dad pay a woman over a million dollars for a child that is not his."

He sat upright on his side of the bed with his back towards me.

"At that time I wasn't sure if you could handle what I had to s—

"Which is?"

He hesitates again, pivoting in the bed. I can see his face in the mirror. He wears a thousand frowns.

"Xavier, would you please speak your mind!"

He got up off the bed and walked over to me. He looks in my face, "Alright I will tell you what I think. I think your father is on the DL!"

"What is the DL?"

"Creeping with men the way a man creeps with a woman."

I slap him. I don't know why I hit him, I asked him a question and he gave me an answer. An answer he knew I would not like. He stares at me. It's as if he is contemplating his next move.

"I'm sorry I should not have slapped you, I had no right."

"No you don't have the right, but I suppose I deserve it. How about this, how about we both keep our hands to ourselves."

"I think that is a very good idea."

He walks thru the master closet and into the master bath. I hear the shower running, he is bathing. What if he is right? The only person who would really know the answer to this question is Sharon, and I know exactly where she is.

The street looks the same, exactly the same as it did when I came here 20 years ago. I came with Sharon to see her childhood home, a three story Spanish hacienda, huge for a couple with only one child. Mother said she had plenty of friends on the block and they would often travel from house to house having all sorts of fun. I wonder if she is having fun now.

I don't think mother is here. The front lawn has a layer of leaves at least a foot deep, the shutters look quite battered and faded. A section of gutter has detached from the roof and more than a few shingles have fallen off. Mother is not here, if she was the place would be in the beginning stages of repair. I travel to the side of the house, to the patio, if mother is here the patio furniture will be out. There is no patio furniture, but the patio doors are opened, I enter the house. Someone is living here, there is a humongous wide screen television back against the wall.

"Hello there."

I almost jump out of my shoes. It is Bailey, looking very relaxed and well fed.

"What are you doing here Bailey?"

"Living here with Sharon."

"Living here? Where is my mother?"

He hollers out, "Sharon, get down here and handle your business!"

"Business?! I am business huh?"

"Yeah, hers."

"What about Tamara? Do you care at all about Tamara?"

"No, as a matter of fact I don't. Why should I care for small fry when I got the biggest catch of the day?"

"I guess I can see your point of view."

Mother made it down the stairs. She is anything but a scared kidnapped victim. I have never seen her look so beautiful. I wonder if she knows what has happened.

"Hello Khloe."

"No good morning kiss on the cheek?"

"You are a grown married woman why do you have need of me?"

"We, Dad need you! He thinks you are dead!"

"Your father knows I am not dead. He knows I am not going anywhere anytime soon. Well I stand corrected I am going on boating trip real soon. You and Xavier should come, your father will be there."

"Dad's going to be there, on the boat with you. Is he coming too?"

"Of course Bailey is coming, your father invited him."

"What kind of game is being played here?"

"One that your father started and I am going to finish. Bailey will you excuse us please, I would like a little mother daughter time."

Bailey leaves the room. I am not sure what part of the house he disappeared into mother's touching my hand startled me. "I frightened you!"

"Yes you did, do, I am easily frightened these days."

"I tried to warn you at the symposium. You didn't heed anything I said did you?"

Oh my god, I had forgotten everything she had said to me. I was so sure that she was trying to keep me from my friends. "Hmph! You were trying to warn me about Kiera and Stephanie weren't you?"

"Yes I was."

"Why didn't you just come right out and say that they were not who I thought they were?"

"I was trying to break you out of that tunnel vision of yours. Khloe you are successful in business but a bit of a daft when it comes to relationships."

"I guess I am, I did not have a very good teacher now did I?"

"Young lady, I will not be disrespected!"

"You already were. I guess that's why you are here, in this house with the cleaning boy. What's the matter Mom couldn't do any better?"

"Your father is not a good husband. He's a good father, but not a good husband. All he thought about was you and your mother Saki."

"So you knew she was my real mother."

"Of course I did, your father loved her first."

"Well if he loved her, and you knew he loved her, why did you marry him?"

"Because I wanted him too."

"Where does Stephanie's mother fit into all of this?"

"She was right there with us, only thing is she was smart enough to not get pregnant."

"Who do you think is Tamara's father?"

"How the hell should I know Khloe! You should ask your father."

"I did already, he says he is not the father."

"Well why did he pay that woman all that money, it can't be because of her frock tail."

"See that's what Xavier said, he also said something else, which is why I came to see you."

"What did he say?"

"He suggested that maybe Dad is a little fruity."

"Rubbish your father is a sex fiend! Maybe, just maybe, he has progressed onto other things and she knows about it."

"We took a DNA test, Tamara and I, the results should be in today."

"Well if she is, she is welcomed on the boat with us."

I enter the offices, everyone is crying and packing up. Something is wrong, something has happened. Even Phaedra is sitting as her post crying.

"Phaedra, why is everybody crying and cleaning out their desks?"

"We are under new management."

"New management?"

"Yes your father said he was cleaning house from top to bottom. He has hired new people and expects us to train them."

"He what? Where is he?"

"In his office with that snake Phil Jackson."

Oh I had forgotten all about Phil and his threat of taking the company public, could he have done it? I ran to Dad's office and found him behind his desk. That's a good sign, he would never give up his desk if he were not in control.

"Hello Dad."

"You are late! I have been calling you all morning don't you answer your phone anymore?"

"Yes D—

"Well why didn't you take the call?"

"Are we in some kind of a crisis?"

"Damn right we are in a crisis, I told you you are not supposed to let the public know when something is wr—

"I didn't let anyone—

"It was all over the news! You were supposed to handle it in-house!"

"Phil, Stephanie, look damnit1 I handled it as best as I could. Stephanie accused Phil of looking at child pornography."

"So I heard, I also heard that she was the one who called the police."

"I am not sure who called them. I got a report saying that Rachael called the police."

"A total fabrication, Rachael would never jeopardize his career. No, Stephanie called the police all on her own, which is exactly why I intend to see that she spend a number of years in jail."

"Dad, did you take the company public?"

"Yes I did."

"Why?"

"To make us some money, Khloe things cannot stay the same no matter how much we want them to. It is time we branch out into other venues."

"You are taking a tremendous risk, a board could vote you out of your own company."

"They wouldn't dare…

"That's one of the threats Phil hurled at me while you were gone."

"We will be having our first board meeting real soon. I will make sure you are there."

"Thank you. Are you going on the yacht with mother?"

"Yes I am, we haven't been boating since the Bahamas. Time to get some fresh air, new perspective."

"So you are at peace with her?"

"I love your mother. I will always love Sharon no matter what."

"Will you love me, no matter what?"

"Of course I will, why wouldn't I?"

"I have something to tell you. Stephanie and I took a DNA test."

"You what?! What the hell is wrong with you, did you not hear me say that that rodent was not my daughter? Get it through your head Khloe, you do not have a sister!"

A matronly woman pokes her head in the door. Dad invites her in, "Delores Macintyre this is one of the our vice presidents, Khloe Davidson."

Interesting, he called me by married name. "Please to meet you."

"I take you have something interesting for me," he said.

"I have a certified letter—

"You could have opened that at your desk!"

"Sir it is not for you. It is for Ms. Davidson."

I extend my hand out to her, "I'll take it Ms. Macintyre."

"Okay you delivered your letter, I am sure you have other things to do."

Delores hurries out of the office.

"Dad why are you so rude to her?"

"I'm not getting comfortable with another secretary, ever."

"Dad Stephanie was an once in a lifetime event."

"You damn right she was. What's so damn important that she could not wait to give you that letter?"

"It's the lab results."

"You really did it, you really did take a DNA. Well open the envelope, get your hopes and dreams all crushed."

I ripped open the envelope, "The results are in, Dad we are—sisters. Stephanie is your daughter DAD!"

"Let me see that damn letter!"

I threw it at him and storm out of his office. He is right I am not ready for this.

Stephanie arrived at the docks in advance of everyone. I can imagine the conversation she had with Bailey. I told her I did not think she should come, but she insisted. She wants to spend time with dad. The girl is glutton for punishment. Ever since the confirmation letter she has been hanging around the office. The threat of a phone call to the police does not frighten her in the least. She knows it's a veil threat, it would embarrass the company and us. I wanted to forgo this trip, but Xavier wasn't hearing it. He said that I was the one who opened the can of worms so it was my duty to fan the flies.

The yacht is pretty big. It can hold up to 20 people. It's six of us and we have four crew members. Hurricane season is in full effect, the weather man does not expect any storms our way, but warn of rip currents. John Cusard, the boat's captain is taking us down stream to Virginia Beach. He is an excellent captain and is quite pleasant. All we have to do is listen to his command and have fun.

"Hey John everybody is aboard, so we are free to leave the port whenever you are ready," said Dad.

"Will do sir, but first I need to go over the rules with your guests," he said.

"I will round everyone up and we'll meet you at the bar," he said.

Xavier and I follow Dad down into the cabin. The others are already there, sipping on pina coladas and mojitos. We have a seat at the very end of the bar and wait for John.

"Hello everyone, my name is John Cusard and I am the ship's captain. I just want to go over some basic rules to ensure everyone arrives in Virginia Beach safely. The first rule I want to state is that no one is allowed on deck at night by themselves. The second rule is a life jacket is required whenever you are on deck. The third rule is that I would like very much if everyone can curtail their drinking. Too much drinking usually leads to fist fights and my men are not security guards. Can everyone agree to adhere to my rules?"

We all grumbled in unison.

"Yes."

"Very well then, we are ready to embark on your journey," he said and went upstairs.

Xavier and I retire to our cabin and take a bit of a nap, we aren't really tired but that is the excuse we give. Xavier suddenly wishes we were not here. He said he feels like something is going to go wrong. I remind him he is the reason we are stuck on this boat. He laughs and says he could kick himself. I told him to go ahead.

We return topside to find everyone a bit tipsy. Stephanie and Bailey and Mother are quite snippy with each other. Dad is sitting there, obviously enjoying the show. Seeing that Stephanie is becoming increasingly stressed, Xavier volunteers to take her up for a bit of fresh air. I don't mind, seeing mother and Bailey together was more than she or I can bear. Bailey abruptly leaves mother and follows them. I follow him. I run after him. My climb up the stairs is interrupted, Bailey is blocking the entrance.

"Bailey—

He bolts. I race up the steps and find him standing port side, deeply inhaling and exhaling. He is looking at Xavier and Stephanie. She sits on the bow, near the lines that hoist the sails. They are talking quietly, Bailey doesn't like it. I am going to stop him before he gets out of hand.

"You know Bailey mother is waiting for you downstairs," I said.

"Fuck her!"

"What do you mean? Are you jealous of Stephanie?"

He advances towards them. Xavier sees him and rises to his feet.

"Is something wrong Bailey?"

"Stephanie get over here!" he shouted.

"Wait, wait a minute, who are you talking to like that?" he asked.

I added, "Yeah why are you talking to her like that? I thought you had snagged a bigger catch?"

"Mind your fucking business Khloe!"

"Hey look, don't talk to her like that!"

I better move before he turns around and hits me. I creep over to starboard side. Stephanie is sitting there like a scared mouse afraid of the big bad cat. I reach out to her. "Stephanie come with me."

Our hands meet and she steps off the bow. She hugs me and leans on me for support though she is taking the lead, clearly she wants to go to the cabins. Suddenly she is wrenched away from me. I look for her, she is in the grasp of an incensed Bailey.

"Let me go! You are going to make me fall!" she screamed.

"Yeah let her go Bailey, you can't have them both!" I screamed.

"I thought I told you to mind your business!" he shouts at me.

"And I thought I told you not to talk to her like that!" Xavier snapped, shoving him.

Bailey shoves Xavier back. He places an arm around Xavier's neck and the other arm between his legs. He lifts him up, his feet is a couple of inches off the ground. Oh no, he is trying to body slam him. Xavier must sense what is going to happen and foils the plot. His sudden surge of strength picks Bailey clearly off the ground. Oh no, "You can't, Xavier stop! Stop before you kill him."

Xavier releases Bailey. He falls backward, right into us. I bump my head and elbows on the deck. Groggily I pull myself up, but Stephanie is still down. I hear her moaning. "Stephanie, Stephanie are you alright?"

"Yeah, my side hit the lever," she said.

I looked at the lever. It controls one of the sails. A little rope has unraveled itself. It is on the floor next to her feet.

"C'mon Stephanie sop being a big baby, get up!" Bailey demands, actually helps her up.

"What's all the commotion up here?"

"Mom, Dad, Stephanie fell. The rope is wrapped around her ankle. Wait Bailey her foot is caught in the rope."

"Here let me help," said Xavier.

The more they try the tighter the noose, Stephanie screams out in pain. The crew hears her and come to help too. They struggle to get her foot a loose, it seems impossible, the line is turning red. The line is cutting into her leg. All of a sudden Stephanie rises in the air. Her head dangles downward as she rises higher and higher. The northeasterly winds toss her around like a rag doll. Her blood curdling screams is giving me the chills. Everyone race to get her down. One of the crew members checks the switches that manage the lines.

"The pulley for that line is stuck!" he yells.

"We will have to lower her manually. Each of us will have to help hold the line steady so that she will not bang into the pole," said Captain Cusard.

Bailey offers, "Let me go up the pole, I can help steady the rope as she is lowered."

"You will not go anywhere near her!" said John.

Some of the crew members go on the port side to focus on the pulley manning that line. The others hold firmly onto the rope. A crew member begins his ascension up the mast, grabbing hold of the line when it came close to him.

I hear him say to her, "Don't worry miss, we will have you down as soon as possible."

The crew on the ground is working as fast as they can, lowering her inch by inch. She is now arms length above the deck, but is swinging side to side. The crew member who had been assisting her had to let go of the line so that he could regain his own balance. She holds out her hand to Dad, he is closest to her. Dad lifts his arm and barely grazes the palm of her hand. Bailey stands near the edge of the deck, ready to grab her when she comes his way. Stephanie swings close to Dad again. This time he reaches out and grabs her hand, but he pushes her, hard. Stephanie's body slams into Bailey, knocking him overboard. The line on her leg snaps and she plummets head first into the ocean.

"Man overboard," screams the crew.

Already donning their life jackets, they jump into the ocean. I look over the deck. All I see is the line that was holding her floating on the water.

Xavier pulls me away. "Come with me, I want to show you something."

"Show me what?"

He shifts his eyes to his left side. "Do you see what I see?"

I glance over his left shoulder. Dad is standing there, next to Sharon. They smile at each shamelessly, undaunted by the fact that two of our friends just drowned at sea.

"Tell me, what do you see?"

"They don't care about them. You think he pushed her on purpose?"

"Of course, she was reaching out to him and he did not want to help her. Your father wanted her dead, he wanted them both dead."

"Maybe they aren't."

"Yes they are, if they weren't they would have been thrashing about in the water screaming for help. Do you hear them?"

"No."

"He has always said he did not have another daughter, and now he doesn't. If I was in his shoes I probably would have done the same thing."

I take a step back and look in his face. He means what he is saying, but why is he saying it? "What do you mean?"

"There is nothing worse than having people you intensely dislike in your life. When they refuse to leave, you have to remove them."

I don't like what he just said. It brings to mind the confrontation on his mother's boat. Saki spoke of his irreprehensible acts, and he denied them, calmly and coolly, not like someone who hates being called a liar. Most people get hot under the collar when you make false accusations against them.

"Come here," he said, hugging me, "I know you are scared—

"I am scared," I said, laying my head on his shoulder.

I lay my head on his shoulder to hide my face. I don't want him to know that I am afraid of him. Danny was right, Xavier is the devil. The devil in my life, and I must get rid of him. I decide to look him in the face. "Have you ever gotten rid of someone you thought to be a nuisance?"

"Yes I have." he said.

"How did you do it?"

"Well Khloe, if someone refuses to leave you alone, how would you get rid of them?"

I pause, not lost for words, thinking. *How will I rid myself of you? How will I get rid of you before he you get rid of me?*

www.ingramcontent.com/pod-product-compliance
Lightning Source LLC
Chambersburg PA
CBHW081149170626
46813CB00009B/3123